A MATTER

OF

GREAT IMPORTANCE

IN TWO PARTS

BY

IVAN A PEARTREE

Order this book online at www.trafford.com/07-2599
or email orders@trafford.com

Most Trafford titles are also available at major online book retailers.

© Copyright 2008 Ivan A Peartree.

All rights reserved. No part of this publication may be reproduced, stored in a retrieval system, or transmitted, in any form or by any means, electronic, mechanical, photocopying, recording, or otherwise, without the written prior permission of the author.

Note for Librarians: A cataloguing record for this book is available from Library and Archives Canada at www.collectionscanada.ca/amicus/index-e.html

Printed in Victoria, BC, Canada.

ISBN: 978-1-4251-5772-2

We at Trafford believe that it is the responsibility of us all, as both individuals and corporations, to make choices that are environmentally and socially sound. You, in turn, are supporting this responsible conduct each time you purchase a Trafford book, or make use of our publishing services. To find out how you are helping, please visit www.trafford.com/responsiblepublishing.html

Our mission is to efficiently provide the world's finest, most comprehensive book publishing service, enabling every author to experience success. To find out how to publish your book, your way, and have it available worldwide, visit us online at www.trafford.com/10510

Trafford
PUBLISHING

www.trafford.com

North America & international
toll-free: 1 888 232 4444 (USA & Canada)
phone: 250 383 6864 ♦ fax: 250 383 6804
email: info@trafford.com

The United Kingdom & Europe
phone: +44 (0)1865 722 113 ♦ local rate: 0845 230 9601
facsimile: +44 (0)1865 722 868 ♦ email: info.uk@trafford.com

10 9 8 7 6 5 4

For Charlie and Thomas

PART ONE

— CHAPTER ONE —

Lady Barbara was a fake. A likeable fake? Very much so, but a fake for all that. She had not been born into the aristocracy nor was her status acquired by marriage but ever since her early childhood she had held high aspirations to becoming a lady—and so a lady was what she was.

The people of East Bergholt, the village where the lady presently resided, and those who were closely acquainted with her, knew her to be an impostor of course, but they were always tactfully discreet about the matter, never wishing to give offence; after all, one does not go around implying to a lady that her designation in life is somewhat dubious, no matter how well founded the accusation might be and especially when the lady in question happens to be the Lady Barbara Fisher-Jones.

Her ladyship was a very wealthy lady, very wealthy indeed, although she never ostentatiously displayed the fact but rather went about her life modestly with a philanthropic attitude. She was also tall, elegant and exceedingly beautiful with slightly rippled mahogany hair, which was always held immaculately in place by a deep velvet band. Many of the eligible gentry in the locality, unsurprisingly, clamoured for her favours, as did the not so eligible but all of these irritants were instantly dismissed with a curt smile and the raising of a neatly pencilled eyebrow. In short, the lady had no time at all for the frivolous flirtations of over zealous layabouts.

Lady Barbara lived in a spacious and most prestigious home, much more like 'The Mansion', which it was named, than the four terraced block of houses it actually was. Ten years earlier Lady B. had wormed her way onto the local council's housing committee and with the gifts the good Lord had bestowed upon her, she acquired the block of nicely isolated terraced houses, together with a comprehensive conversion programme. In actual fact the block had been condemned for human habitation some six months prior to its resurrection but no one saw fit to make this a point of obstruction and so the sale went hastily ahead for an undisclosed sum to the very nice lady.

In no time at all Lady Barbara had set up home in the now impressive looking mansion overlooking the rippling River Stour, as it meandered gently through its renowned valley, in the midst of acres of lush green meadowland where horses and cattle grazed to their hearts content. All in all, the carefree environment in which she lived delighted the lady immensely promoting a feeling of complete wellbeing and assured inviolability. Not surprisingly, the very nice lady was indeed very happy with her lot.

Lady B's daughter, Felicity, however, who lived with her mother at The Mansion, was not quite so happy–at least not on this particular bright summer's morning when all should have been tickety-boo. The nineteen year old, at this particular point in time, was looking decidedly peaky as she sat in the kitchen mulling over a problem that had infested her mind for months.

Unlike her mother, Felicity Fisher was not a fake in any way shape or form in fact quite the opposite. Her natural beauty in body and soul was there for all to admire and to applaud; even Mother Nature with all her creative skills and cunning stratagem must have found it difficult to come up with such perfection. She possessed a countenance of rare beauty with her long hair hanging down her back even to her hips with a lustrous ebony sheen. And the firm roundness of her lithe body was a picture of unadulterated loveliness causing excruciating heartache to the male population in and for miles around the village of Bergholt.

As afore mentioned, Felicity Fisher was not a fake, not in the accepted sense of the word anyway. She had always been unpretentious in every way, and ever since her early childhood she had exhibited modesty when others might have avoided the commodity plus a real sense of kindness and consideration for all about her. Yes, she was indeed the genuine article all right as anyone who knew her would willingly attest.

Felicity and her mother's propinquity was satisfactory enough and the only flaw in the relationship, but such a minor one, was that Felicity opposed most vehemently her mothers irrational pomposity even to the point of refusing to use the double barrelled surname she found so pretentious. Felicity Fisher was who she was and Felicity Fisher was how she'd stay— for a while anyway.

After an hour or so of deeply moving and private broodings and the concentrated mulling of her dire dilemma, Felicity at last decided to approach her mother head on, hoping to avoid the guilty speculations that were racing through her pretty head and to secure a more sagacious solution to her current predicament thereby ending months of extreme and torturous anxiety. However, to engage her mother in a lengthy conversation was always a tedious business and one she had always tried to avoid whenever she possibly could, but to confess to having missed seven or eight months, (her reckoning had gone adrift after five), without even a spec of the red stuff being apparent would be tedium personified, not to say a trifle frightening. But that is what Felicity now planned to do, she felt she had employed delaying tactics for quite long enough, now was the time to face facts no matter how chilling she considered the task ahead to be.

The opening of the kitchen door interrupted Felicity's thoughts with alarming instantaneousness and the swirling butterflies fluttering inside her pent-up stomach made her feel uneasy. She gathered her wits about her and decided the confrontation with her mother was to begin at once.

Lady B. immaculately dressed as always, the golden rule being to always give the impression of being at the pinnacle of ones demeanour no matter what the occasion, walked into the kitchen with all the grace of a prima ballerina casually carrying a trug of carrots and roses on the crook of her arm as if part of her ensemble.

"You *are up* then Felicity," said Lady B., with the merest hint of sarcasm in her voice.

"No mama I'm still in bed," answered Felicity with equal acerbity. "Of course I'm up; after all it has turned nine you know."

"Yes dear, I'm well aware of the time," said Lady B., ending the acrimonious banter.

"Mama, I think that I need to talk to you of a matter of some delicacy if you could spare me a moment or two," said Felicity, hesitantly and with a reddening countenance.

"Yes of course darling, what seems to be the problem?" replied Lady B., smiling; and abandoning the trug in the kitchen sinks, she followed her daughter into the drawing room.

"Well," started the daughter straightening herself upon the dark brown leather-covered chaise longue and facing her now seated mother. "It appears that I have got myself pregnant." She winced inwardly.

"No dear that is something you just cannot do on your own how ever fertile you may consider yourself to be. How many months have you missed?" asked Lady B., still smiling.

"Oh, just the one, --- but," Felicity's sheepish lying was interrupted by her mother instantly.

"Oh come dear! Missing just the one month can be caused by almost anything: anxiety, stress, ---" Lady B. was in her turn interrupted by Felicity before she was able to set out her list.

"No mama I'm not at all anxious, or anything else for that matter, you see I have missed a month simply because I am pregnant," she replied, her reddening deepened as she pondered the telling of the episode and commenced the chewing of the bottom lip dubiously.

"You see, mama, a couple of young men and myself went for a walk past the woods up on Touchy Hill a few weeks ago. Someone had brought along a couple of bottles of champers so we all sat down, had a few drinks and—chattered,—well suggestive chat really—and then one thing sort of led to another, if you know what I mean."

"Sounds to me that you have been a bit of a trollop my dear," said Lady B. who by this time had ceased to smile.

"Me, a trollop?" Felicity immediately went on the attack, knowing it to be the best form of defence. "You're a fine one to talk about trollop-ing mama! Exactly how do you think I got here?" said Felicity, seemingly seething.

"Now Felicity, you know very well all about your father, I have told you many times before," replied Lady B., slightly taken aback.

"That 'your father'," aped Felicity, still flying high, 'was an important senior Attaché at the American Embassy who was killed when his plane ditched in the Atlantic.' Yes I know mama I've heard it all a million times before. You've been peddling that old cart for far too long; it's about time it visited the breaker yard if you ask me. Anyway your dear brother Jack put me straight about my father years ago. You spent a sensual afternoon, to put it politely, with a matelot who was on leave in Brixham. You met him on the harbour and had a mad passionate affair with the man. I ask you mama, a matelot, you know, a jolly jack tar with a wife in every port. That's how I came about. Oh don't worry, I'm not ashamed of it at all, rather proud in fact, at least it shows you were human just once in your life.

"Dear mama, you have to face reality," continued Felicity, just a tad more soberly, "both you and I are no better than all the other Fisher women, why, even your mother, God rest her, had four husbands, and they are just the ones she admitted to. It's in the genes mama, that's where it is,—it's in the genes!"

It was quite some time before the ashen faced Lady Barbara could bring herself to summon up some sort of defence and then with only a feeble attempt at best.

"Jack Payne had no right to disclose my private and confidential matters to you. No right at all," she said as assertively as she was able, which only seemed to fuel the proverbial fire.

"It seems to me you are saying that I had no right to know who my father was. Now that's not on mama, and you know it. You had no right at all in keeping this from me," retorted Felicity taking up the verbal onslaught once again trying desperately to steer the conversation away from her own predicament thereby hoping to lessen the impact as her mother inclined her head.

"Anyway, I had better telephone Randolph straight away to see if he if he is able to see you this afternoon no sense in hanging around," said Lady B. totally ignoring her daughter's outburst and once again regaining a look of dominance.

"Mama, do we have to involve that senile candidate for the loony bin? He is pretentious beyond belief," said Felicity, adopting an obdurate attitude.

Lady Barbara seemed rather concerned at Felicity's response to her proposal and tried to gain her confidence.

"But Randolph is a wonderful specialist darling, and he has been a friend of mine for over ten years, you know that."

"Specialist my aunt fanny," retorted Felicity, assertively. "Specialising in warts, in-growing toenails and questionable back aches? Mama, a specialist is one who devotes his career to just one or two aspects of medicine. You simply cannot have an across the board specialist mama. The man is a bigger fake than you."

"That is quite enough of that thank you," said Lady B., abashed but not wishing to prolong the embarrassment by making a further scene. "I shall speak to him right away."

She walked over to the telephone table, lifted the black receiver and dialled the number of the local cottage hospital.

"Cattawade Cottage Hospital," this was the curt voice of the defending dragon that always seemed to be on duty.

"Put me through to Mr Richard, I need to speak to him straight away," said Lady B. sardonically, carefully omitting any nicety.

"Mr Richard is busy this morning and will not be taking any calls at all," returned the receptionist, which caused Lady Barbara's hackles to rise immediately.

"I shall rephrase my request. This is the Lady Barbara Fisher-Jones speaking and I require to be put through to Mr Richard at once," said Lady B. with the utmost of fervour; the fire from the dragon was doused at once.

"Oh Lady Barbara, of course," offered the dragon, all sweetness and light. "I really ought to have recognised your voice straight away, how very remiss of me; I shall put you through to Mr Richard this very minute.

After a short intermission a cheery male voice took over from the dragon.

"Mr Richard as in Cliff speaking, ha, ha," his guffaw was fatiguing to the extreme.

This had always been his telephone intro ever since he arrived at Catterwade. Everyone knew this, was thoroughly bored by it, but entered into the spirit of the thing with some alacrity, there seemed little alternative.

"Now how may I help you my dear Lady Barbara? Not feeling a teensy bit under the weather I hope?" The specialist was in a frivolous mood apparently, which the lady found to be most welcome.

"No Randy, I'm fine," said the elegant lady still feeling slightly touchy by the receptionist's response. "It's my daughter Felicity—I want you to see her straight away—a matter of some delicacy you understand."

"Ah yes, indeed," replied Mr Richard, a slight pause ensued. "I could fit her in tomorrow afternoon; that would be the earliest that I can ---" his sentence was shortened unexpectedly by Lady B.

"You don't appear to have grasped the situation Randy. I want you to see her now—this very afternoon," said Lady B. and prevailing upon his better judgement added: "hospital equipment does not grow on pear trees or any other type of tree for that matter you know." The very nice lady's attempt at blackmail she felt would work, she knowing precisely how much cash she had raised for the hospital in the past twelve months.

"No indeed not—quite so, let me see now, would three thirty suit you both?" asked the specialist accommodatingly.

"Perfectly," said the lady with no hint of appreciation whatsoever. "I'll see you then."

As the refined lady replaced the black receiver she noticed the broad figure of a man slowly passing the drawing room window. With haste she called out to her 'on loan' gardener.

"Mr George—oh Mr George," she cried out. Then again less formally, "Walter—could you spare me a moment of your time please?" as she hurriedly lifted the latch to the heavy oaken front door.

Lord Gilson, one of the lady's closest friends, employed Walter George as head gardener together with his wife May Maydie, who performed miracles in the kitchen, at the Orvis Croft Estate where he resided. He and Lady Barbara arrived in the village within a few months of one another and had been firm friends ever since. The benevolent lord loaned both gardener and cook to Lady B. as and when the demand was issued and without any expense to herself and in return for this favour the very nice lady helped his lordship with various and important charitable works; or so she said.

"My dear Walter how *are* you?" she asked, stepping out onto the cobbled pathway.

"I'm passably fine ma'am thank you," replied Mr George, quizzically. "Was there something I can do for your ladyship?"

Her ladyship could gush with the best when the need arose and now was the very time.

"Yes Walter, I did need a small favour. I was wondering if you would be good enough to pass a message to the lovely May Maydie for me. I have rather an important guest for dinner this evening and I rather hoped your dear wife would oblige in performing one of her usual sensations. Please tell her that I am indeed sorry for the very short notice and I shall be pleased to leave the menu entirely in her most capable hands. She really does prepare the most delicious food and it is rather important to me for the evening to be a total success. May Maydie has never let me down in the past and I am sure the meal will surpass all expectations as usual."

"I'm sure that will be quite alright ma'am," said the gardener. "Do you think that a little cheese on toast will be up to the mark?" he amusingly added.

Walter's dry humour was never wasted on Lady B. in fact she liked the man, liked him a lot.

They both laughed most heartily together before Walter finally excused himself. "Well I shall be off home now m'lady and I shan't forget to pass on your message to May. She'll be tickled pink, I'm sure." With that he was gone chuckling to himself as he went.

Lady Barbara re-entered the house to find a somewhat agitated Felicity waiting for her and standing with her hands on her hips as if looking forward to a further set-to.

"You have got some nerve mama; you push that lovely Lord Gilson's generosity to the limits. How he tolerates you taking advantage of him like that I shall never know. Why can't we do our own cooking anyway, after all we are not entertaining anyone of importance, or are we?

"Anyway why on earth do you call Walter's wife May Maydie?" she asked, now offering a reluctant smile. "Surely they are variants of the same name aren't they?"

"Yes indeed they are. Walter told me, when I asked him the very same question, that when she was a baby she was christened simply May Dale, but close members of the family affectionately called her Maydie. When she started school, however, she discovered to her horror that the rest of the children in the class possessed two Christian names. So one day, when the headmaster asked her what her name was, she replied, 'May Maydie sir' and so it has stuck with her ever since."

Felicity at last allowed the hovering smile to break through. "Not yet another fake," she exclaimed.

— CHAPTER TWO —

Not wanting the whole village gossiping about her business, Lady Barbara decided to drive the clean and shiny twenty horse power black Bentley to the cottage hospital herself that afternoon, thinking that she would no longer need the services of her chauffer any more, him being the biggest village gossip anyway.

The lady's principles would never allow her to be early or even on time for an appointment, she could on no occasion bring herself to be seen waiting for anyone. And so it was precisely ten minutes past the half-hour when the big black Bentley arrived in the car-park of the cottage hospital and a further five minutes saw them into the empty waiting room. Empty that is, but for a rather plump lady sitting behind an ancient looking mahogany desk squeezed tightly in a badly lit alcove. The defending dragon shuffled her feet then rose from her seat as the two ladies entered the room.

"Oh Lady Barbara," she said, withholding a smile as she spoke. "How nice to see you once again." Her words were glib and not in tune with her manner. "I'll just inform Mr Richard that you have arrived and then I shall show you through to his consultation room," she continued her edict disingenuously.

"No need, I know the way," said Lady B. brusquely as she walked through the door to the passageway, almost without opening it, and followed along the short passage to the only office door marked Consulting Room and entered the voluminous room without knocking.

A square faced, bald headed man, dressed in a smart grey suit, which was partly covered by a brilliant white coat, sat behind a large and exceptionally tidy desk smoking an unlikely cigarette held in his mouth by a stumpy holder. He rose from his cushioned chair, placing his cigarette and its holder carefully into a shining glass ashtray, and flitted across the room with dainty steps to greet the two ladies, carrying his hands above waist level in a most peculiar and feminine posture.

"Oh Lady Barbara, how nice to see you once again," he said, copying his receptionist's greeting to the letter although unlike her he expressed his welcome with a sincere and friendly air. "And Felicity too, this is indeed a pleasure."

"Randolph!" The curt, begrudged acknowledgement from the lady was cutting and the specialist openly cringed as it was uttered.

"And how are you my dear lady?" asked Randolph, trying to regain his equilibrium from the impolite and almost abrupt rejection.

"Fuming!" answered Lady B. staring deeply into the eyes of the neatly dressed little specialist. In actual fact she wasn't fuming in the slightest; she merely considered the resolute facade to be an advantage as it usually meant having a would-be-adversary on the defensive.

"Now what seems to be the problem?" asked Mr Richard, trying to act the concerned professional.

"It's Felicity, she's missed a month," replied Lady B, maintaining her ungracious attitude.

"Now what month would that be?" asked the specialist, trying to inject a little breeziness into the proceedings and looking downcast because he hadn't.

"Now what month do you suppose it to be?—Last month of course." A genuine expression of annoyance had caused the lady's face to flush and then it was gone in a trice as if she had pressed her control switch.

"I see," said Mr Richard, now showing a moment of concern. He then turned his attention to Felicity who failed to conceal her boredom by providing a cavernous yawn.

"Exactly when was your last normal month Felicity?" he asked.

"Five weeks ago," Felicity lied with no compunction whatsoever.

"Good, good—that's fine." The specialist's left eye twitched, involuntarily.

"Perhaps you would like to undress and lie on the couch behind that screen."

Felicity laughed and Lady B. coughed.

The specialist looked from one lady to the other in quick succession and his face, changing to a deep crimson colour, exaggerated the faux pas he had made together with his complete ignominy.

"Oh err—yes so sorry. What I really meant was would you go behind the screen, remove your clothes and lay on the couch; you'll find a suitable gown hanging behind the screen perhaps you would put it on."

After an adequately professional examination Mr Richard washed his hands, dried them and then dithered as he eventually made his way to his desk to make some hasty notes.

"Yes–err–hmm -" he spluttered once again. "Felicity, I shall need various samples from you before you leave so that we can eliminate any less obvious problems. One has to be extremely careful in ones diagnosis these days you know, as all sorts of underlying problems may be present."

Both Felicity and her mother looked puzzled at this disclosure but after Felicity had succumbed to the various fluids being routinely taken from her body for testing, she became somewhat agitated, and anxious to move things along she looked over to her mother.

"If that's all mama, perhaps we might go now, I'm feeling a trifle bored."

"Yes of course dear," said the very nice lady, and feeling in complete sympathy with her daughter's lack of enthusiasm she turned to the specialist.

"Perhaps you will have some idea of what is going on by the time you dine with us this evening Randy?"

The invitation was all too obvious to the excitable Randy who dithered and fidgeted again in an alarming way.

"Ah yes, thank you, yes, so kind; we will certainly do our best. Err, would you like me to dress for dinner?"

"You will do fine as you are," said Lady Barbara, and with the words left hovering in the air they departed.

Mr Richard went back to his seat, placed another cigarette in the stubby holder and sat there looking quite stunned and extremely thoughtful.

Absolutely nothing was left to chance as far as the Lady's strategy was concerned; everything now being meticulously orchestrated to produce maximum effect; even the morning fresh vase of roses was carefully replaced and May George was encouraged to flit round with the duster and unnecessarily tidy both the dining room and drawing room. Lady B. even offered a helping hand to the tiny lady which was instantly refused.

And so it was a re-fashioned Lady Barbara Fisher-Jones who greeted her guest that evening with a much higher degree of benevolence in her approach than was displayed earlier that day. As instructed, Mr Richard's attire was as it had been during the afternoon appointment; even his shirt and tie had not been changed and it was obvious that the specialist had arrived straight from the cottage hospital. But something in the man's manner had altered however. *'He now wears a more concentrated look, verging on the edge of perplexity,'* thought Lady B. as she chattered to her guest. And what was more he carried this dire expression of mystification throughout the duration of the meal. Even May Maydie's superb cauliflower cheese, which was his very best favourite of all time, of which Lady B. was fully aware, failed to lighten his sombre mood. Of course, he heaped unfettered praises on the tiny May as she flittered from place to place, but he was obviously a very pensive Randy, very pensive indeed.

After dinner had been thoroughly scoffed and the time for brandy and coffee had arrived and after Lady B. had been totally bewildered by her guest's continuous grave and dour mood, the very nice lady suggested some fresh air. *'A stroll around the gardens perhaps might dislodge whatever it is that worries this obtuse man,'* she thought. They picked up their drinks and sauntered out onto the freshly mown lawns, minus Felicity, and Lady Barbara, taking the specialist's arm, broke the deafening silence that existed between them.

"What on earth is the matter with you Randy?" she said unsympathetically. "You have displayed a mood of total preoccupation for all of the evening. It is so unlike you to behave like this, perhaps you will be good enough to unburden yourself. Was the meal not to your liking or the wine perhaps?" asked the lady with some vigour hoping to shake her guest from his appalling mood.

"No—no, indeed not, splendid meal—splendid, as always." A small pause, "its young Felicity you know—a bit concerned about her that's all—yes that's it—just a little concerned," said Randolph, attempting a reassuring smile.

There then followed a longer pause, eventually being broken this time by the hostess.

"Well you jolly well can't leave it like that you know. Exactly what is wrong with my daughter? Are you saying that she is not pregnant after all? Contacted some sort of bug has she? Come on Randy I need to know, surely you must see that," said an exasperated Lady Barbara.

Randy thought for a while gesticulating with his hands and fingers, as he ruminated, as if he had been struck dumb.

"Yes of course dear lady --- yes certainly --- of course. That is --- perhaps we should include your daughter in our discussion --- yes that's it --- we must include Felicity." The little man's disjointed statement did nothing to alleviate Lady Barbara's fears and so she hastily directed him toward the house once more.

Lady Barbara and Randolph Richard had found Felicity curled up on the chaise longue in the drawing room munching on a green apple and looking cock-a-hoop.

"Hello you two," she said cheerily as they entered the room, "that was a jolly short walk, not started to rain has it?"

"No darling it isn't raining, Randy needs to have a chat with the two of us," said Lady B. "So perhaps you will be good enough to stow that apple away for the moment."

They each found a seat and sat in a semicircle.

"Over to you then Randy. What appears to be the problem," said Lady B. "Is my daughter with child or isn't she."

"Oh yes," started the specialist cautiously, "most definitely she is—er, pregnant that is—but not by one month, more like eight."

"What," exclaimed both ladies together? Lady B. continued the sentence, "but she's not even showing a ping pong ball under her dress, so that can't be right."

"Yes indeed—I do see your point—err—quite a puzzle isn't it? But I can assure you both that the examination and tests I personally carried out this afternoon do confirm precisely what I have just said." He paused briefly before continuing. "Now, either some one is telling porkies or we have a phenomenon on our hands." The specialist fiddled with his fingers once again and then decided to bring the end of his kipper tie into the exercise fiddling with that as well.

Felicity was unmoved. "The latter then," she exclaimed, turning very slightly red in the face as she spoke. "I do not ever lie and especially not over a matter of this gravity."

"Hmm, yes, quite so—I do see your point—I do indeed," replied Mr Richard soberly, stroking his chin and staring at the floor and the ceiling alternately. "But not showing in the slightest and missing just the one month—yes—most extraordinary—most extraordinary indeed." The bewildered little specialist continued in this vein for quite a while longer. Eventually he stood and wandered around the room as if seeking some sort of inspiration then retook his seat with a bowed head.

"Anyway Felicity," he said at last, "I have booked you in for further tests tomorrow at ten in the morning and I have also arranged for you to have a scan at Colchester Hospital in the afternoon—all of this if it meets with your approval and convenience—of course dear ladies."

For all of this time Lady Barbara was looking unsettled and staring into space as if she was mulling over an unsolvable problem in her mind, which of course she was. She looked askance at her daughter needing to know why she had laid this complicated problem at her door.

"Randolph," she said hesitantly, "is there nothing you can do to put things right, as it were? After all, the problems these situations can cause are immense." The look on the very nice lady's face was a worried one and her words failed to hide what she was feeling inside. "Can't you?" She began again. "Couldn't we somehow…."

Randolph's unsure attitude changed in a flash and he interrupted his hostess with an unnerving look. "No, Lady Barbara," he said forcefully. "Certainly not—quite out of the question—far too late. Besides, totally illegal, surely you must know that."

The evening finished abruptly.

— CHAPTER THREE —

The following day should have started on a fairly good note, at least the birds were singing chirpily in tune and everything seemed hunky-dory with the rest of the world. But all was not good with Felicity. The young popsy was feeling a trifle peaky this sunny morning when she should have been in fine fettle, even though she had not slept that well throughout the longish night. However, she was up and dressed long before her mother had even stirred; contrary to the norm. She had tried desperately to sleep longer this morning but it was a hopeless battle to keep her eyes closed with so much plaguing her mind. She sauntered around the house aimlessly, trying to concentrate her attention on the situation in hand and all the while dreading the forthcoming morning meeting with wishy-washy Randy.

For the whole of the night she had been remonstrating with mama, in her muddled mind, about the previous evening's dinner charade and was now feeling the effects of night starvation to the uttermost and was altogether in an abominable mood.

She calmed herself slowly by the process of consuming copious amounts of coffee and decided to approach her mother yet again. Perhaps while mama was still in bed would be best she thought, when, hopefully, she might still be feeling a little drowsy. Having arrived at this conclusion she would now throw off the shackles of sleepiness and proceed bucked up and readily squared for battle—then—upon further reflection she modified the ruse, thinking perhaps a more subtle approach was called for.

After she had carefully loaded the breakfast tray with coffee, cornflakes, milk and sugar, four slices of neatly cut toast, butter and helpings of her mama's favourite preserves, Felicity climbed the stairs to her mother's bedroom, tapped gently on the door and walked boldly in.

"Good morning mummy," she said, with a welcoming smile. She had never in her whole life ever used the term 'mummy' before, well perhaps once or twice when she was very little and then only because she had heard other children of her age address their mothers in that way; far too common, far too intimate.

Lady B. failed to answer.

Changing tack, Felicity greeted her mother more formally as usual, with a silvery smile playing on her lips.

"Good morning mama," she said, maintaining the silvery smile.

Lady B. stirred herself and looked up.

"Oh sorry darling, I was miles away—yes—good morning dear, are you alright?—Sleep well?" she answered sleepily. "What's the weather doing this morning?" Then noticing the unexpected breakfast tray Felicity was carrying she added with a pleasant smile. "Oh thank you dear, how lovely."

After Lady B. had finished most of her breakfast Felicity sat her bottom on the edge of the bed and rudely stared at her mother squarely in the face. Then, when she was satisfied she had gained her mother's full attention, she commenced very calmly with what had bothered her for much of the night.

. "So," she said. "That was why you invited that quivering quack to dine with us last night, plying him with brandy and false benevolence." The silvery smile drifted slowly from Felicity's lips. "You hoped he would get rid of my baby for me didn't you?—Mama, you are despicable. Did it not occur to your dishevelled mind to consider I might have something to say on the matter? Did it not occur to your better judgement that I might just want to keep my baby? You were and are as you have always been, just thinking of yourself and what other people might think and say about us. You consider my having a child shameful don't you?—An abomination is it mama? Well let me tell you this—I intend to keep my baby and to bring him up with all the love he needs and more besides—and if it is without you mama—then so be it."

Lady B. was yet again taken aback by her daughter's controlled verbal onslaught, dumbfounded even. Her mettle, she felt, had ostensibly deserted her and her mind was swimming with the vein attempt in regaining some semblance of control. Only slowly did she manage to give the outward appearance of self composure. Only slowly did she manage to exercise her self-possession.

"No darling you have it all wrong," she was pained to observe. "Of course you must keep your child --just as I kept you."

Unfortunately, it was almost inevitable for the very nice lady to add a proviso—and she did.

"But—perhaps a quiet holiday in Brixham with Uncle Jack might be just the thing; after all having a baby can be very taxing—very taxing indeed."

"NO MAMA," Felicity's reply was loud and resolute. "I will NOT be cast aside like some disgraced dog. We are in this together mama or I'm on my own—it's up to you.

Mother and daughter drove in strained silence to the Catterwade Cottage Hospital that sunny morning. Even the twittering birds seemed to loose it as they entered the big black Bentley and to Lady B. everything seemed upside down and higgledy-piggledy. Nevertheless, she cast her anxiety temporarily to one side and concentrated on the job in hand, namely driving, and for the first time in her life Lady Barbara was early for an appointment; by a whole five minutes in fact.

The now sombre looking specialist was in the waiting room giving certain instructions to the defending dragon when the two ladies arrived, and he ushered them into his consulting room with hardly a word of greeting which did not sit well with her ladyship.

"What's the matter Randolph?" she said, unsmiling. "Not got a bout of indigestion after yesterday's evening dinner I hope"

"No, dear lady—no. Just some unexpected business reps. plaguing the life out of me, that's all. Don't worry; we shall not be disturbed by them I can assure you of that."

He skipped over to his desk and gathering a handful of typed notes he began to study them closely. Suddenly he looked up from the papers and turned to Felicity.

"Tell me, did I ask you yesterday Felicity if you have experienced any movement—movement in your tummy I mean—of course."

"Oh yes. Within a couple of days I felt a sort --of fluttering. And then a few days later he began to stretch himself. Now it happens all the time. But it's not an unpleasant sensation—more like—well—more like he knows exactly what he is doing and moves very gently so as not to cause me any discomfort—if you know what I mean. It's all rather beautiful really," said Felicity, breaking the tension that existed.

"Well I cannot pretend to have the answer to this phenomenon or to understand how it could possibly have come about." Then catching himself he added. "Oh I perfectly understand how you became pregnant in the first place Felicity, I didn't mean to imply to you I didn't. But thereafter, that's the puzzling bit, yes most extraordinary. I have researched all of the text books and discussed your case with many of my colleagues and all to no avail. All I can come up with is either a most unusual tadpole has fertilised a most unusual cell—or, one unusual cell has been fertilised simultaneously by six most normal tadpoles and the cell has failed to subdivide as one would have expected. This, I suppose, could possibly account for the unusual acceleration of the pregnancy—yes most interesting most interesting indeed. You see, as far as I can make out, your pregnancy has been sped up six fold, if, as you say you are just over the month—say one and a half months—so the dominating factor is six."

The pensive man rose from his chair and commenced to promenade around the sizeable consulting room scratching his head most vigorously as he did so. Then after alternately examining the ceiling and the patterned carpet once more, (it was very clear that the little specialist did his thinking, for the most part, upon his feet), he resumed his place behind his desk.

Then with much finger counting he continued to expound his theory.

"Then all things being equal, as it were, and if the dominant factor is indeed six, as I suspect, then your baby will reach maturity, at say, between three and three and a half years of age and he will be empowered with the strength of six men, if he's a boy."

"Which he most definitely is," interrupted Felicity.

"Err yes, quite so," returned the specialist. "As I was saying, he will stand between thirty and thirty six feet in height, again at maturity and have the I.Q. or mental capacity of six intelligent adults. Phew, that is quite a man."

The two ladies glanced at each other then raised their eyes to the ceiling outwardly grinning.

Just at that moment the telephone rang. Mr Richard answered the contraption in his usual tedious manner then excusing himself to the ladies he hurried from the room.

As soon as the specialist had left, Lady B. turned to her daughter saying: "how many young men did you say you had walked with darling—you know—on that day some six weeks ago?"

"I didn't mama, but since you have asked there were six," answered Felicity, hesitantly.

"In love with them all—are you dear?" asked Lady B., searching.

"I'm quite fond of all of them mama, some more than others maybe, but that's to be expected surely. But they are all desperately in love with me it seems," answered Felicity, her face alight with self amusement.

"So it would appear darling," rejoined Lady B. "Cannot make up your mind which one to choose as a partner, maybe. Needed to assess which of them was the more virile, maybe," said Lady B.

"Something like that I suppose," answered Felicity looking down at the floor. "But it wasn't a bit sordid mama, really," she hastily added.

"No, no of course not darling, it never is. But I have the answer to the debateable question about which you seem to have certain reservations—the winners are in reverse order so to speak—think about it darling," said the very nice lady.

Just at that very moment the door opened and in burst the lively little specialist dancing with glee and beaming all over his square face.

"That was an eminent colleague of mine from Harley Street don't you know. He is one of the close acquaintances who I approached to obtain a professional opinion. It seems he was in the area this morning and decided to pop in to have a word with me. It is most gratifying to learn he supports my theory one hundred percent. He seems very interested—yes very interested indeed and wants to be kept abreast of matters as they develop. Gratifying, most gratifying indeed.

As he spoke a small pool of water appeared around Felicity's feet and she coughed in order to obtain attention.

"Er, excuse me," she said, grinning from ear to ear, "but I think that something is happening—Jonathon, I assume, is now on his way."

All eyes went smartly to the floor and then to each other. Suddenly Mr Richard leapt into the air clicking his heals together as he did so. Lady Barbara smiled fondly at her daughter.

"Don't worry darling, I'm sure that everything will be alright."

"Alright mama!" laughed Felicity. "It's more than alright it's MEGA MARVELOUS."

The little specialist, Mr Richard, having regained some of his composure and displaying a much more earnest expression opened the door that led to the passageway that in turn led to the reception, calling for the midwife Sister Armstrong at the top of his voice. And he was still summoning the sister as he hastily walked into the reception area but nobody seemed to be paying much attention, at least no reply was heard. The receptionist was sat reading a magazine in her usual alcove looking slightly twitchy as she stowed it quickly away.

"Ah, Mrs Drago," he said, his voice now being excited and intoxicated with a boyish enthusiasm. "Have you seen our midwife? Any idea where she might be? Would you page her for me?"

The defending dragon raised her large antiquated horn rimmed spectacles to the top of her head before she answered.

"She popped out about ten minutes ago Mr Richard she shouldn't be long now," said Mrs Drago, protectively.

Mr Richard turned as if to retrace his steps to his consulting room abandoning his look of excitement for one of deep concern and annoyance, when the outside door flew open as if a gale had suddenly exercised its wrath and a short plump red faced woman entered looking rather more than a little panic-stricken. She was dressed in her starched sister's uniform but minus her white head garb.

"Ah Sister Armstrong—there you are. Look I do wish you people would carry out your personal errands in your own time, we have a crisis on our hands at the moment. A young lady, Felicity Fisher to be precise, has gone into labour quite unexpectedly and we must afford her the smoothest delivery possible. Might I suggest the filling of the new delivery pool; don't think we could be more genteel and natural than that, do you?" said Mr Richard regaining much of his buoyancy.

The disconcerted look on the midwife's physiognomy gave way to an expression of immense relief and with a grin which stretched the full width of her face she said:

"The pool is already filled Mr Richard—sir. If you recall Mrs Lloyd was expected in this morning—yet another false alarm I'm afraid—most unfortunate—er for Mrs Lloyd that is—fortunate for us though—or rather for Miss Fisher.

"Oh and Mr Richard, I do apologise most sincerely for popping out like that, I only went across to ...."

"Yes, yes sister, enough of that let's get the show moving shall we? Do we have a porter available? A trolley might be useful don't you think?" said Mr Richard, as he hastened away to his consulting room.

Lady Barbara and Felicity were sitting chatting away quite nonchalantly when Mr Richard breezed in.

"Well ladies you will be pleased to know everything is organised. Mrs Armstrong is a most capable midwife and it is she who will be assisting me with the delivery, so you can rest assured you will be in very good hands. Now, how about some refreshment while we wait—a refreshing cup of tea perhaps? Oh and by the by—I have decided to use our brand new delivery pool—if you are in complete agreement of course. It is quite large as birthing pools go more like a small swimming pool really and quite the latest thing I can assure you. Most natural way of giving birth available—or so the experts tell us," said the little specialist proudly and getting excited once again. "Now Felicity I expect you are just a little apprehensive," he continued. "Well, I can assure you that you are in safe hands my dear, so please don't be afraid."

Felicity smiled serenely at the specialist. "Relax Mr Richard; it's me that is having the baby you know, not you. But really I'm fine, no pain or discomfort at all—just completely—what's the word? Yes—euphoric—that's it, completely euphoric and I just cannot wait to meet my darling Jonathon, so please don't be anxious or concerned in any way; I'm not."

The mother-to-be was not only perfectly composed but positively overflowing with an abundance of ecstasy and altogether glowing with rapturous joy; the sort of feelings that only mothers-to-be can experience at the onset of a perfect delivery.

"So sorry ladies;" said Mr Richard. "It is so easy for us men to get just a little apprehensive and excited about the prospect of new life while the more gentle sex exude all the calmness taking things wholly in their stride; how different the two sexes are, remarkable. And you Felicity, not only predicting the child's gender but settled on the little chap's name as well—my, my, what extraordinary people you are, truly extraordinary.

"Well, young Felicity when you feel the time is right just tip us the wink and we'll have you in the jolly old pool before you can say 'Jack Robinson', but there is still time for refreshment if you so desire."

"Perhaps we might pass on the refreshment thank you Mr Richard and maybe go to the pool right away. I know that my darling Jonathon is just waiting for me, he's so considerate," said Felicity beaming.

"Yes—yes of course—right ho. I'll just summon the porter to bring up the trolley then we can wheel you down there in next to no time at all," said the specialist in a state of jovial satisfaction.

"No need for that," said Lady B cheerfully. "I'd have thought you'd got the message by now Randy. Felicity will walk down—in fact—run down I shouldn't wonder. Come on let's go!"

And so they skipped down to the delivery room, where Sister Armstrong would be waiting for them, laughing and chatting as they went.

The spotless aseptic pool in the humid delivery room was pretty well filled to overflowing with a warmth slightly above that of body temperature and looked more like an infants paddling pool than a piece of surgical equipment. However, the water looked extremely inviting and so Felicity, without direction, abandoned her clothes, together with her inhibitions, and jumped into the water removing the final piece of her lacy underwear as she did so. She splashed about before backing herself to the pool's edge where Sister Armstrong was nervously waiting for her. Almost as soon as the midwife managed to manoeuvre Felicity into an appropriate position, the not so tiny baby arrived eluding the fat fingers of Mrs Armstrong and proceeded to flounder in the water until he had gained his confidence then proceeded to swim around the pool in a manner not unlike that of a dolphin, much to the delight of his mother and to the amazement of the onlookers. On and on he swam, round and round he went, up and down as though he had been swimming for all of his life.

At last his mother's enraptured joy could be contained no longer and she gently gathered up her baby in her arms with complete adulation.

"Welcome my darling Jonathon," cried the mother as her tears of joy mingled with the droplets of water upon her face, "welcome to this wonderful world."

Post script

The narrative up to and including the birth of Jonathon Fisher may seem to many of my readers to be contrived in such a way as to be somewhat implausible at best and wholly fictitious at worst, differing wildly from what many may consider to be the true story. The only explanation on offer is that all enlightenment was derived from a ecstatic mother who would never consider that giving birth to a son of Jonathon's obvious talents to be other than worthy of being elaborated to a greater extent.

Now read on.

— CHAPTER FOUR —

And so it was that the famous Jonathon Fisher was born into this troubled but wonderful world. Famous? Well for a short time anyhow. The calculating specialist, Randolph Richard, not appreciating the family's need for privacy, had contacted the press at the earliest opportunity in order to attain his own acclaim. However, self and importance, being the two key words in the little man's vocabulary, were not complied with in the slightest.

"The Lancet must surely expect a thesis from me at the very least," he was heard to say four days later and just as the trio was making it's way to the big black Bentley from the maternity ward. But it didn't happen for the hapless specialist, his hopes were dashed in an instant, for his so called friend and colleague from Harley Street, well aware of the specialist's fatuous nature, had humoured him beyond belief, and so all of the media's attention was focused on the son, the mother and the grandmama, much to his own annoyance and consternation.

T.V. cameras, reporters and the paparazzi all gathered together at The Mansion hoping for a glimpse of the new phenomenon which had just arrived but were courteously rebuffed and dismissed with a kindly word by the Lady Barbara Fisher-Jones.

"Wherever did you get such nonsense?" she asked with a gracious smile upon her lips. "Surely you didn't believe in miracles of that nature did you? The virgin birth only happened the once you know and that a very long time ago. What has occurred to this family has not been in the least unusual and certainly not miraculous, not in the way that you seem to have in mind anyway; quite mundane in fact, just the usual everyday occurrence that comes out of any old maternity ward for most days of the week and from every hospital throughout the land for that matter; you know, nothing special."

The poignant flippancy of the lady's words was wasted on the reporter's shallow minds and had little or no lasting effect. And so they packed their gear into their various cars and vans and looking decidedly dispirited at their lack of success, they moved out.

All the outrageous predictions about the thirty foot giant that was made by the not so eminent specialist did not come to fruition of course. Nevertheless, Jonathon did grow to be an extremely bright and handsome young man with locks of white blonde, wavy hair and a demeanour akin to that of his mother. He stood almost six foot one and a half inches at the age of sixteen and was still growing, with a truly magnificent physique and abnormal physical strength.

When Jonathon was in his nineteenth year and with his grandmother's considerable encouragement and his own motivation, he finally obtained a coveted position at Cambridge University where he obtained a first class honours degree in biology and a further year of intense reading saw him with his master's degree. And although Jonathon was an intelligent young man no one career had attracted him thus far. He was continuous in debating the various ideas with his mother and grandmother about the possibilities in teaching, but heading a class of motley students, be it at grammar school or university level, just failed to inspire the twenty three year old, leaving him coolly frigid in spirit. And so Jonathon decided on taking a year out in order to ponder the rest of his life's plans, after all there seemed to be no rush, no rush at all—time enough to enjoy some of life's real pleasures yet to be discovered.

One pleasure that Jonathon cherished above all else, except that is, the uncommon pleasure he derived from the society of his doting mother and fond grandmother, was the exhilaration he obtained from swimming. Swimming to him, at this period of his life, was fundamental, almost a basic need. Anywhere really, the sea, the pool, the river; ah, yes the river. His resplendent body would cut through the water at astonishing speeds and he was able to stay beneath the water's surface for minutes on end exploring and admiring all the wild life in his beloved River Stour. Every morning, long before most people's days began; he would leap the fence opposite his home and hare across the mead that separated The Mansion from the river and plunge into the depths of The Stour, swimming to the neighbouring village of Dedham and back again in time for breakfast. These indeed were halcyon days for the young Adonis, especially the late spring days, the summer and the early autumn days, when the sunshine gilded the earth and caused the reflected light to play transcendental patterns on the water's surface and brought cheerfulness to the sons of man.

But not all of spring's mornings were so inspired; the sun hid itself at times for hours even days causing many people to experience a kind of moroseness which shouldn't have been manifested. And although the weather patterns did and do appear to play a role in mans bearing, its dissidence is largely tolerated and murky days are lived with, alongside the days of the sun.

One particular cloudy May morning, Jonathon had entered the river at his usual spot and was swimming silently in the direction of the tiny neighbouring village of Dedham, leisurely admiring the ever watchful coppiced willows which lined the riverbank with their shimmering, dew moist, pliant branches drooping into the Stour's dark forbidding waters, when a moorhen, some one hundred yards ahead was disturbed by an intrusion. The bird took off splashing noisily as it left its hiding place amid the dark green reeded muddy bank with a lively high pitched 'kik-kik-kik' voice endlessly reverberating over the water's surface; its legs trailing lifelessly behind.

Jonathon increased his stroke until he reached the spot where the moorhen had been and looked searchingly into an adjoining tributary known locally as the Dead River. Venturing up the tributary a short distance and elevating himself above the surface of the water he could clearly see a rusty bicycle lying on the far bank close to the rickety bridge that spanned the murky waters, its rear wheel rotating slowly as it lay on its side. Jonathon turned his head to the centre of the river; his attention was drawn to an object floating on the surface of the water close to the central support of the decaying bridge. With six powerful strokes Jonathon reached the floating chequered cloth cap, the top of which was still dry, and picking it out of the water, he threw the cap onto the river's bank close to the still rotating wheel of the bicycle as it squeaked tediously with each gyration. Almost with the same movement he dived to the reeded muddy bottom of the Dead River to search its depths for an explanation.

For three long minutes, and without a single breath of renewed air, Jonathon scoured the turbid waters, at times becoming entangled in the long, grey, slimy reeds and scarcely able to see an inch in front of his face; even his once shiny face mask was now almost rendered useless by the dense deposits of muck and sludge. Back and forth the big man swam, slowly, desperately, reaching, feeling, his hands constantly oscillating before him and all the time probing, probing.

All at once, a hand, like unto the hand of a man, seemed to latch onto Jonathon's right ankle, the sheer weight of it dragging him further down to the lifeless bottom of the muddy river. Rapidly Jonathon turned, his own fingers fastened onto the black greasy hand then onto the lifeless arm of the man, a big heavy man, whose body was being tightly locked by the rangy reeds to his quietus.

The young Adonis, employing all of his considerable strength, and after resurfacing several times to replenish the life sustaining air, at last managed to free the corpse from the reed's vice like grip, then slowly raising it to the water's surface he pulled it gently to the muddy shore close to the rusty cycle that still lay there waiting to be wheeled away; the once rotating movement had now been stilled.

Jonathon repositioned the stranger face down on the grassy verge and lifted the centre of the weighty body upwards arching him slightly at the waist so that the filthy water might drain from his huge chest cavity. He then turned the lifeless man onto his back, struck the sternum area of his wide chest with a clenched fist solidly and commenced breathing clean air into his lungs with their mouths firmly juxtaposed and alternately pressing down hard on his sternum with his strong right hand. It was a desperate attempt and it was a hopeless one–Jonathon knew it to be hopeless but he continued the resuscitation attempt for twenty minutes until common sense eventually prevailed.

He stood up sadly and stared down at the forlorn figure lying on the rich green grass and slowly wiped a speck of mud from his eye. The catastrophe had to be reported, he knew that, and reported quickly, before all else. He considered the options open to him; he could swim back up the river the way he had come or he could run to the village via the lane. He gave a thought to the bicycle lying nearby and examined its condition. Useless, the front tyre was completely flat and ripped and the wheel buckled beyond repair. He decided upon the latter of the two alternatives.

The ascending lane, which led to the village from the rickety bridge, was steep and stony with deep ruts that had obviously been made by the continuous use of heavy farm vehicles over the years. The lane being so narrow that the same ruts had had to be used each time a tractor ventured that way thus deepening the troughs with every trip. As Jonathon made his way up the hill carefully picking his way in his bare feet, he considered in his mind, how fast an out of control bicycle would be able to travel down this impossible track until it collided with some obscure boulder at the bottom and thereby tossing it's rider over its handlebars and into the muddy river. He stopped a while and re-examined the lane's surface. It was certainly dry enough, so the grip on its surface should have been sure. There was some sand and gravel but nothing deep enough to cause a problem; the heavy vehicles had seen to that. And the stones that lie at the bottom of each rut, (there were two) had also been dealt with by tractor power. *'Not a disastrous surface for cycling on, all things considered,'* thought Jonathon to himself. *'Even so, the bike couldn't have been going that fast, or the rider would have been in danger of coming a cropper long before he had reached the bridge. Anyone with a modicum of sense would have gotten off his bike at the top of the lane and walked the blessed thing down. I don't see it happening at all, must have been deliberate,'* he concluded.

Within five minutes, Jonathon had reached the top of the lane and walked a short distance along an actual 'B'road that led into the East Bergholt village to where, he remembered, stood a bright red telephone box. He entered the kiosk lifted the black receiver, dialled 999 and waited.

"Police please," he answered the operators question calmly and quietly. It was no time at all before he heard the fairly familiar voice of the local bobby, Sergeant Pedley, and explained to the said gentleman with the drowsy voice at the other end of the line, exactly what had happened that fateful morning.

"Oh dear dear me," he said. "What a thing to have to wake up to. You're sure about this then Jonathon are you? Not sendin' me on some wild goose chase I don't s'pose,"

"No sergeant I'm afraid that the matter is real enough, I don't think anyone would be up to playing tricks on you, not at this time in the morning."

"Well you better get back to the bridge where the body is Jonathon an' I shall be with you directly."

Jonathon replaced the receiver and made his way slowly back to the dismal little bridge and to the lifeless body that would be lying beside it.

Everything was much the same as when he had left the place not more than fifteen minutes ago. The bridge was still there and the river had not dried up. The rusty cycle and the chequered cloth cap both lay on the bank as before, but the body of the big man was nowhere to be seen.

Jonathon searched the whole of the local area diligently but found no trace of anything at all that was relevant to the incident. He returned to the rusty cycle to assure himself that it had not in fact been moved or tampered with; it most certainly had not.

At that precise moment he heard the sound of a car's engine as it cautiously manoeuvred its way down the stony lane. And then he noticed it, a word carelessly imprinted in the surface of the muddy bank beside where the body should have been. Just the one word 'BY'.

— CHAPTER FIVE —

Sergeant Pedley exited his Morris Minor estate motor car, quietly closing the door after him and walked slowly and deliberately up to Jonathon, surveying the morbid scene at the same time.

Jonathon's story of the body that he had dragged out of the muddy river but which was now, very much, missing didn't appear to surprise the tall policeman in the slightest.

"That'll be old Herbie Watts," he said, "I'd know that bike o' his anywhere. Still not got that rear light fixed like what I told him to, I see. Still, it won't matter any more, not now. Bin a drinkin' to the early hours I shouldn't wonder, like the slop he was. Still we mustn't speak ill o' the dead I 'spose. All 'as said he'd do it one day though, take 'is own life I mean—daft ol' bugger. He'll be in the river ag'in Jonathon, you know that don't you. I 'spect he made 'is mind up t' do it a'ter he'd had quite a few last night. Needed t' do it I 'spose an' no one was gonna stop 'im not even a man as big as yerself. Well he's at rest now, at least I hope 'e is.

"This is a favourite spot for suicides, no tides in this bit o' the river see; it's a dead end an' all. I 'spose tha's why they call this bit the Dead River. Don't worry yerself none Jonathon we'll soon 'ave 'im out o' there—in the meantime 'haps you wouldn't mind just poppin' in t'the police station a little later on this mornin' t'make a statement, you know just t'keep things tidy like and keep me records straight."

An extremely pensive and sorrowful Jonathon swam slowly back up the river to the spot where he had entered it two hours earlier and dressed. The big world didn't seem so bright and cheerful now, even though the sun had managed to break through. The trees had lost their lustre; as if anyone gave a damn. The birds, they were still singing, but how were they to know any different, noisy, mindless bunch. He wasn't quite so fast at crossing the meadow that bordered the road opposite his home as usual, and the small herd of black and white Friesian cattle turned to stare at him as he passed, their long eyelashes occasionally blinking away the annoying flies that feasted on their mattered eyes. The cattle half expected the customary greeting from the young Adonis, but none came, so they resumed the business of chewing the cud. He tried to steady his mind by forcing it on happier times, times when the river meant everything to him. Now he wondered if it would ever be the same again. He used the five bared gate that led out onto the roadway that passed directly by his house, instead of leaping the fence as he usually did. And with head and heart bowed low he entered The Mansion gate.

Jonathon had intended entering his home by the rear entrance which led directly through the kitchen, hoping to reach the seclusion and privacy of his own bedroom before he could be interrogated by either of the ladies. There, he might rest awhile and try to rationalise his thoughts before having to face the mothers; not that that would be a dire experience in itself; the mothers would always be caring and sympathetic he knew that, but he felt the need for time by himself just now; a few moments to reflect would be good.

These private quiet moments would have to be put on hold for the unwelcome voice of Walter George called out to him from the side garden compelling him to at least pass the time of day.

"Hello Jonathon, you alright then? Been for a swim I shouldn't wonder," said the beaming gardener.

That was the second 'I shouldn't wonder' he'd heard in the past hour from as many people. Jonathon forced a sort of smile, but it didn't come easily or convincingly.

"That's right Walter," said Jonathon, desperately trying to maintain an air of cheerfulness. "How are you keeping these days? Still suffering from that huge hernia are you? It's about time they repaired it for you I should have thought. Tell you what—why don't you have a word with my grandmother? I'm sure she will be pleased to pull a few strings on your behalf; have that Mr Richard down at the Cattawade Cottage Hospital running around in all directions, you may be sure off that."

Just then a worried looking Felicity came out through the front door her anxiety showing to the uttermost.

"Jonathon, wherever have you been? You should have been home over an hour ago, I have been out of my mind with worry," she said, anxiously biting her bottom lip.

"Now you know there is no need to worry about me, I'm a big lad now mother. Look, do you mind having a word with grandmama? Poor Walter here has a hernia as big as a coconut and nobody appears to be the slightest bit interested, something should be done," said Jonathon, most thankful for a change in the conversational direction.

"Yes Walter of course how awful for you, I really didn't know you were suffering. I'm sure that my mother will be pleased to have a word for you.

"And now Jonathon if you are up to it, please take your bath because breakfast is ready and will spoil if you're not quick."

The big man failed to get as much time to himself as he would have liked but he did linger in the bathroom much longer than usual by showering, bathing then showering again. (Actually this was Jonathon's regular bathroom ritual when coming in from a swim in the river ever since his grandmother had complained of the rank smell about his person after his swimming in the river some years earlier.)

And so he finally made himself presentable then sauntered down to the breakfast room where his mother was patiently waiting for him; Lady B. was the last to be seated as was her unalterable right.

During breakfast the ladies both asked Jonathon why he had been so late in returning from his early morning swim and the disturbed facial expression he had worn since his return did not go unnoticed. Jonathon was naturally horrified by every aspect of what he had experienced that morning, nothing could have shocked his nervous system more, but even so, he did not wish to give the subject an airing until he had come to terms with the incident himself. However the ladies didn't seem to want to give up their quizzing, probably thinking he had met with some female who he was wishing to keep a secret and so it was with some relish that they continued the good natured banter. Finally Jonathon succumbed to their relentless curiosity and detailed his dolefully unhappy experience which was received with the utter dismay expected.

"Whatever makes someone feel like taking their own lives like that I wonder? Their minds must be in such a turmoil and in a state of wretched unhappiness that it really doesn't bare thinking about," said Felicity, reflecting her words with complete sadness on her beautiful face.

Her mother reached out to touch her daughters arm desiring to quell all unpleasant thoughts.

"Darling," she said compassionately, "these terrible instalments in life happen comparatively infrequently or so we are led to believe, but when they do they seem to issue shock waves that devastate. But the root cause? Well there are probably a multitude of reasons and one can only use supposition, unless all of the facts are truly known. My guess would be that the most common cause is gross unhappiness brought about by money, or the lack of it, and love, or the lack of that. Everything seems to be hinged on these two impostors these days. But we must face the fact that the biggest part of the human race, down the ages, has managed to get by without either one of those two commodities being available. Modern living, however, paints a totally different picture; one seems to be at deaths door if one is down to one's last three thousand in the bank or been spurned by some adventurous lover. And lack of love also promotes loneliness which, superficially, is a state of existence where no love is present at all, either giving or indeed receiving. You see, darling, most people have quite deserted their standards these days and they seem not to have their religion to fall back on any more as was the norm not so very long ago. It's a sad thing to lose one's faith, sad indeed."

Felicity appeared to perk up a little after her mother's assertion and was nodding her agreement.

"Thank you mama, that philosophical pronouncement was very aptly put and I couldn't agree with you more but it doesn't lesson the pain that exist on these unhappy occasions although it might heighten the opportunity for rediscovery of faith, who knows?" said Felicity brightening up some more, "anyway there won't be any such terrible occurrences in this family if what you say is true."

"I certainly hope not indeed," said Lady B., after which a long silence ensued. "Let us get the unsavoury taste of this unfortunate business out of our mouths," she continued smiling. "How do you both feel about paying a brief visit to Devon? We can book in at the Northcliff Hotel in Brixham for a couple of weeks and visit the dowdy relatives there. You haven't seen Uncle Jack for over a year have you Jonathon? He and Eileen will certainly see changes in you and I am sure they will both be pleased to see us even though they will probably bore us all stupid. Anyway the change of air will do us all good apart from anything else. So what do you both say? Are we agreed?"

Mother and son looked at each other, smiled reluctantly then slowly nodded their heads in bemused agreement.

"But why Brixham? I can think of pleasanter places to spend a few days," said Jonathon looking more than a little disappointed.

"Because we have to keep in touch, much as the idea seems slightly disagreeable. And besides, that's about the only place we are sure of in accommodation comfort at very short notice. You see, I think we should go tomorrow."

"Yes it's a splendid idea mama," rejoined Felicity, all smiling and winking at Jonathon. "Now how should we travel down? Charabanc, train or do you intend to take our ancient motor car—if it's up to the journey."

The thought amused Lady B. who gave out a derisory chuckle.

"That is priceless dear. The thought of me travelling down to Brixham by charabanc or even by train for that matter simply horrifies me. What ever possessed you to think of that? Yes of course we shall take the Bentley. It was only serviced a couple of weeks ago and the man at the garage was very kind in commenting upon the car's wonderful condition despite its age. He even went as far as to say that he would love to own it should I eventually decide to sell. So yes, of course the Bentley is up to par for the journey and the run out will probably do it good, well the battery anyway. Jonathon, you can drive if you feel you are up to it and we know that the driver's seat adjusts back far enough to accommodate those wonderfully long legs of yours so we shall all be very comfortable I'm sure. Perhaps I should telephone Jack to expect us tomorrow evening; hopefully he will volunteer to arrange our accommodation for us at the Northcliff as before.

So we had better spend the rest of the day sorting ourselves out and packing our cases ready for the off."

"Look grandmama, I know it's a bore, but I have to visit the cop shop later this morning. The sergeant was adamant that he needs a statement from me, so I shall do my packing when I return. I don't need to take much anyway."

And so taking his leave of the ladies he wandered off to his room in search of a little solitude; a few minutes of quiet in which to ponder the early morning events he felt would be helpful.

He lay back on his covered bed casting his eyes to the ceiling for a while then closing them to relive the moment when he took to the water and swam to where the moorhen had taken to the air. He saw the cycle once again on it's side with it's wheel slowly rotating ghoulishly and the cloth cap floating near the bridge's central pillar; a pocket of air inside keeping it afloat. *'So it was the pitiful victim entering the water that disturbed the bird and nothing else otherwise the rotating wheel would have stopped long before I reached the scene. So he could only have been in the water for a couple of minutes at most,'* he judged reflectively. *'So how come he was so tangled up in the weeds and how come he was even at the bottom of the river in so short a time? It doesn't make sense.'* His pondering was interrupted by his mother as she ventured to her own room presumably to pack.

He allowed a moment to empty his bemused brain before he drifted back to the river and to resume his search for some clarification, some explanation to the confusion in his mind. *'Perhaps the body and the cycle were not connected with each other; perhaps the cycle didn't belong to the body in the river. Just a minute Sergeant Pedley recognised the cycle as belonging to Mr Watts so they had to be connected. But the body hasn't been recovered yet so we don't know for sure that it was he who I pulled out. What's the use in continuing in this vein when I am not yet fully acquainted with all of the facts?'*

"Jonathon, are you alright darling?" His mother's voice seemed a little uneasy. "Don't drift off to sleep, or you might miss your appointment with the police this morning. We don't want them to think that you don't care now do we."

"Mother, stop you're worrying; I'm on to it, OK."

— CHAPTER SIX —

The local police station, which had been the home of Sergeant Pedley for the past five years, was barely a mile away from The Mansion and so Jonathon decided to walk the short distance; after all the weather was now pleasant enough and he thought that the fresh air would clear away some of the cobwebs from his clouded mind. And taking his time over the stroll he reached his destination in fifteen minutes flat.

The door bell was answered by a very pleasant looking middle aged lady with greying hair who Jonathon knew to be Mrs Pedley, the sergeant's wife.

"Hello Jonathon," she said, in a quiet voice, "my husband told me to expect you but unfortunately he's out at the moment; gone down the street for a haircut. Won't you come in and wait for him? I've just this minute made a fresh pot of tea if you would care for one; I'm sure my husband won't be long."

"No thank you Mrs Pedley I've only just eaten breakfast but I should like to wait for the sergeant if it would be convenient," said Jonathon.

The loud slamming of a car door was heard from the outside and caused the lady to turn smiling toward the doorway.

"Ah, I believe that's him now," she said.

The tall, slim, slightly balding police sergeant entered the room looking neat about the head.

"Jonathon, there you are. Mornin' to you agin'. Please come into me office then you can make your statement, It won't take us long," said the sergeant, smiling broadly.

The two men entered the tiny office and sat down on chairs placed either side of a polished desk which ran along side the widest wall on which hung a copy of a modern portrait of the queen smiling down. The sergeant reached for a form from the stationery draw of his desk and commenced to fill it in with precise correctness.

"A bad business this is Jonathon—a bad business an' no mistake. Only just heard over the car radio that they've recovered the body took 'em nigh on an hour t' get 'im out of the water; everythin's bein' handled by the boys in blue from Colchester. There'll 'ave t'be a formal identification of the body o' course. Don't ask me how, but they reckon it's 'im alright, poor ol' sod. That aint no way for anyone to go, now is it Jonathon? Takin' yer own life like that, it aint natural that it aint. Still tha's the way some people deal with their problems, but it's not for us eh Jonathon? No, not for us.

"Anyway, tha's enough o'that, we got some writin' t'do. Now what I want from you, is for you t'tell me in yer own words exactly what it was that you was doing down by the river so early in the mornin'. Oh, I know how you like yer early mornin' swim; the whole village knows that I shouldn't wonder. But you just tell me as if you don't really know me at all. Now you just take yer time 'cause I shall be tryin' t'write it down as you tell it me, OK?"

Jonathon accurately related to the sergeant all that had taken place since five thirty that morning adhering closely to the facts and being careful not to include any of his own opinions or views. When he had completed his statement he was asked to read the transcript carefully and to sign the foot of the page as confirmation to the accuracy of its content. This done he handed it back to the friendly policeman.

"Now, there's bound t'be a post-mortem and then an inquest which you will be asked to attend so don't you go leaving the village for a while 'case we need t'contact you," said the sergeant.

"Well to be perfectly honest with you sergeant, we are planning to spend a few days down in Devon, in fact we are arranging to motor down to Brixham tomorrow morning."

"Now who's the 'we' bit?" asked the sergeant, slightly taken aback and bending one of his eyebrows quizzically.

"Oh sorry, maybe I should have mentioned that I shall be accompanying my mother, Felicity Fisher and my grandmother Lady Barbara; the three of us were hoping for a fortnights break," said Jonathon hopefully.

"Of course, the Lady Barbara Fisher-Jones aint it—well now tha's quite different—you be goin' with the lady an' all. Tha's altogether different that is. Yeah, that'll be alright Jonathon s'long as you can leave me with an address so as we can contact you if and when we need to—yeah that'll be alright," repeated the sergeant.

The two men then stood up and shook hands, the sergeant expressing his gratitude for Jonathon's time before they said their farewells and parted.

Peculiar thoughts crowded Jonathon's mind as he walked away from the police station that morning, the same repetitious thoughts that had bothered him as he lay on his bed an hour earlier. *'Why hadn't that wretched wheel stopped turning by the time I reached the bridge? Why didn't I hear the splash as he entered the water or even a shout? Who disturbed the moorhen, him or me? How could Mr Watts have recovered sufficiently enough to walk back into the river once again? The eyes in the cyanosed face were oddly open—not a flicker. I checked his heart beat—no pulse. No breathing either—completely lifeless, yet he was able, not only to get back into the water but to write a farewell gesture in the muddy bank before taking his very last walk, odd, most odd. Of course the message could have been inscribed earlier, a day or so earlier maybe, by some youngsters and I didn't notice it. So much was happening to confuse my mind, so perhaps it was there all the time and I just wasn't aware of it, who knows?'*

So agitated indeed had his mind become that as he continued his walk, his eyes were watching his feet rather than being focused on all around him. Suddenly, a voice intruded upon his thoughts. Timothy Travers, his boyhood friend and the son of Colonel and Mrs Travers, called out to him from across the road, bringing his mind once more back to reality, and walked over to greet him.

"Hi Jonathon, how are you feeling? After the experience you had this morning pretty shook up I should imagine," said Tim, with a serious look upon the face that was usually all smiles and jolly."

"Oh hi there Tim, my mind was miles away, sorry," said Jonathon trying to perk himself up for his friend. "Me? Oh I'm fine thanks, how about you? I hear that you are leaving us pretty soon, off to Canada or so I hear. Parents beginning to suss out your hanging around the place too much?"

"Come on Jonathon stop trying to dodge the issue, I could see that you were more than a little thoughtful this morning but surely you can discuss the whole thing with me, after all we've known each other for long enough haven't we? Out swimming in the river weren't you—when it happened?" Tim's interminable inquisitive nature would not be wholly satisfied until he was aware of the finer details of the saga, *'but not from me–not yet'* thought Jonathon.

"That's right, but how come you know so much. Seems to me you know as much as I do—wonder how that got around so quickly—where did you get the information Tim?" asked Jonathon, puzzled.

"I went down the street for a haircut earlier," said Tim, enthusiastically. "Our esteemed bobby was there having a trim—need I say more? Well you know how he likes gossiping don't you? Not a bigger gossipmonger upon Gods earth. He couldn't wait to tell the whole shop all the gory details, and the place was pretty full at that. You know, I am quite sure he's not supposed to talk the way he does; someone will have a go at him one of these days or report him. Anyway I expect the whole of the village is buzzing by this time you know how quickly bad news travels. So what happens now? Have they discovered who the body belonged to? Pedley said it was a Mr Watts whoever he may be, must say I've never heard of the fellow."

"Yep, apparently that's who it was, although I gather it is still to be officially confirmed. Well, there will obviously have to be an inquest after the post-mortem so I really cannot add to that which you already know. I expect you have the whole story anyway," said Jonathon.

"You had better prepare yourself for the onslaught then Jonathon," said Tim, with a mischievous look upon his face.

"Whatever do you mean?" replied Jonathon, not horror stricken but close to it.

"The news papers my friend. The news papers will have a field day with a story like this and I'll bet it won't be long before they get their molars into it. Not just the local papers either but the nationals as well. I can see the headlines now,—'DEAD MAN WALKS TO A WATERY GRAVE'—they will love it. Make you out to be quite a celebrity I should think; but don't forget to make 'em pay heavily for the story though; you could make a fortune Jonathon."

The realisation of such a distinct possibility only added to Jonathon's already ceaseless anxiety but he pulled himself together quickly.

"Then it's just as well that we're leaving the village for a few days," he said, forcing a wide smile to waft over his face. "At least, by keeping a low profile for a short time we might escape some of the hullabaloo --- and who knows, perhaps things may have simmered down a bit by the time we come back and maybe even have returned to some semblance of normality."

"Anyway getting back to you. When are you planning on leaving the country?"

"Next week, and about time too or so the family thinks. Pops suddenly came up with the wherewithal so I'm off post haste. As you said, they're a mite dissatisfied with me lazing about the place so I guess they are more or less pushing me out. Canada seemed to me to be the place where it's all happening these days so I'm off there—can't wait I can assure you." A genuine expression of setting forth into the wide blue yonder accompanied his declaration.

"Anyway getting back to the lengthy and complicated saga of the moment. If as you say there is to be an inquest, which I don't doubt for one minute that there will be, then I'll lay a wager that there will also be a full enquiry as well. I can't see any coroner accepting a dead man coming to life and then killing himself once again, he'll think that more than a little bizarre don't you think? Well anyone would—and as it was you who originally found this Watts fellow you must be number one witness and will be required to be present each and every step of the way. Best of luck old chap; it looks as though you're in for a pretty rummy time."

"Anyhow, I must dash Jonathon; I fully intended to pop in to see you before I went but as you are away tomorrow."

The two friends shook hands and clasped each other fondly.

"I shall be calling in to have a chat with the colonel when I'm passing, your mother too, so you had better keep in touch with them, OK? Look after yourself Tim and drop me a line sometime when you have sorted yourself out and I'll keep you posted from this end."

"Good Luck Jonathon—not that you ever need it," said Tim. And with that they went their separate ways.

The moment Tim had left him, Jonathon's brain felt more encumbered. The sum total of these lingering mental disturbances was causing total panic within his mind and so he quickly opted for more time to cogitate. Immediately doing an about turn he retraced his steps to and past by the police station. He would take a round about trip to his home which would add a full hour to which otherwise would have been no more than a short jaunt. *'I simply cannot spend the rest of the afternoon chatting to two ladies, no matter how pleasant the conversation might be, who are hyped up about a couple of weeks holiday in Devon; not with all this going on in my head,'* he thought. He passed by the White Horse, where the drowned man enjoyed his beer, passed the Travers' residence just as Tim was entering the front door and on toward the little Methodist Chapel where he and the two mothers worshiped each Sunday.

Ernie Wright, who was one of the church lay preachers and also the Sunday school superintendent, was walking his high-nelly bicycle across the small chapel gravelled car park as Jonathon approached.

"Hello Jonathon m'boy," said the short corpulent man, with a broad grin on his round florid face. "I haven't seen you since you've been back from university. How did the course go? Biology, wasn't it? Passed with flying colours I reckon, knowing you as well as I do."

"Hello Mr Wright, it's good to see you again. Yes all my university days are now well and truly over I'm relieved to say, although I suppose I did enjoy them while they lasted," said Jonathon. "So, how are you keeping these days," he added.

"You probably heard about my problem Jonathon. Had to spend quite a spell in Ipswich hospital you know. The old water works have been playing up. That's the sort of thing that happens when you get to my age you know. Had to have an operation Jonathon, unpleasant it was—still I'm glad to be out of there I can tell you," said Mr Wright, in earnest.

"Yes we were all sorry to hear about your problem. Seems that you have had quite an awful time of it; still, you are certainly looking pretty good now Mr Wright," said Jonathon.

The little man beamed.

"Thank you Jonathon, yes I feel pretty fit all things considered," he said. "But I'm still rather stiff you know, much more so than I expected to be; too much lounging around I expect. That's why I cycled up to the chapel this morning, thought a little exercise might do me good. Actually I'm glad I bumped into you—I wonder—would you care to read a passage of scripture for us next Sunday morning? I shall be leading the service myself—and as you do read so very well I thought you might like to do me the honour."

"Mr. Wright, I would love to have read for you but the family and I are planning a short trip down to Devon, in fact we shall be leaving early tomorrow morning—so you see it will be quite out of the question. I'm so sorry, perhaps some other time," replied Jonathon.

"Never you mind yourself about that Jonathon I can read the lesson myself. I just thought that it would have been nice for you to do it seeing as how we are both in circulation once again at the same time so to speak.

"I've just this minute been chatting to Frank Bain, he told me about poor old Herbie. Sorry state of affairs and no mistake. Me and old Herbie --- well --- we went to school together you know. Not a bad kid on the whole --- played up a bit --- a few pranks but nothing too serious. Got caned a lot though --- but then we all did back in them days. But there was always something odd about the lad, never seemed quite the ticket if you catch my meaning. Still, we've all got to meet our maker one day and that's for sure and old Herbie, well, he's chosen his own path there, such a pity though --- to go before you're called, I mean. Still, as I say --- it's a sorry state of affairs.

"Well I must be off for my dinner, should be ready by the time I get home --- I hope so anyway, as the old stomach is rumbling something chronic. Now you take good care of yourself young Jonathon, have a nice holiday and give my regards to your grandmother."

With a little difficulty Mr Wright mounted his bicycle and peddled off up the road muttering to himself as he went and wobbling all over the road leaving Jonathon wondering if Frank Bain, the chapel handyman, had had a short back and sides or just a trim that morning.

Jonathon slowly skirted round the north side of the village passing Eld's corner and The Dial public clock. He then headed westward toward the Gandish Road which would eventually lead to Burnt Oak crossroads, then down Flatford Lane to where The Mansion stood and for all of this time in walking the problematic thoughts still tormented his mind, with no obvious answers.

Lady Barbara was busying herself in the kitchen when her grandson walked in.

"Hello dear," she said, looking up, "how did your visit with that rather pleasant Sergeant Pedley go? No problems I trust."

"Very well indeed thanks, taking all things into account. He's quite happy for us to leave the village for a while but I shall have to ring him to give the hotel's address and number. I bumped into Ernie Wright as I was passing the chapel and it seem that Mr Watts was always a bit strange even from the time he was a small boy, apparently they schooled together.

"I also met up with Tim and he is of the opinion that things could become more than a little unpleasant when the newspapers get wind of the incident. Do you know I hadn't even considered they might be interested? But *you* had, hadn't you grandmama? You realised that the situation would become a little tense, didn't you? That's why you suggested we go away for a break --- right? Thanks --- I appreciate it."

"That's alright darling. There are times when a short break from reality is essential, when it is important for the three of us to stand back and take a concerted look at the situation. So let's say no more about the ghastly business for the present and concentrate on sterner things like deciding what to prepare for dinner."

— CHAPTER SEVEN —

After a relevantly uneventful night; although Jonathon knew that disturbed sleep patterns would be the norm for him for a long while to come, the Fisher Family were ready for the off. With a sturdy breakfast beneath their belts the longish journey ahead would seem no more than a quick outing and everything would be brightness and light. That is --- except for the weather. Somehow someone had neglected to organise a more sunny aspect to the commencement of the day and so it was with some consternation that the small party, although trying to make light of the meteorological conditions, got finally underway.

As predicted by Lady B., there was quite sufficient room to accommodate the tall young man's seemingly endless legs beneath the steering wheel of the big black Bentley and more than enough room for the two beautiful ladies to be seated in the front of the car next to the driver and the roomy boot, filled to the top with their various pieces of luggage, completed the holiday conveyance.

They moved along the road unhurried in the London direction quite happily, at least the two ladies seemed happy enough chatting away ten to the dozen. Jonathon however seemed bent on more contrite matters viz. the Watts saga and appeared to be wasting valuable energy pondering matters about which he had no control.

His mother was not slow in noticing this non-fulfilment of chirpiness and purpose and decided to mention the fact.

"Jonathon, the reason why we are going away for a few days is to enable us to firmly leave our sordid and unhappy involvement in a suicide incident back in Bergholt where it truly belongs. Now we cannot possibly enter into the holiday spirit if you are continually pondering about that wretched affair. Why can't you leave all the worrying to the police darling --- after all that is what they are paid to do?"

Jonathon didn't answer for awhile not being overly keen at being firmly told how to conduct himself even though the meaning of the assertion was perfectly clear and accurate.

"Mother, I apologise if my silence offends you," he said, after a certain delay, "but you must appreciate the emotional disturbance that pulling a body from murky waters can have on a chap. It is not something that happens every day and it takes a bit of getting used to, that's all. However, given time, I expect to be able to chuckle once again, and to exchange the odd quip, but in the meantime I'm afraid I have some thinking to do."

Felicity coloured up with embarrassment.

"Darling I'm sorry if I was too harsh, I didn't mean to be. It's just that it pains me to see you taking the worries of the world upon your shoulders. I know it's not easy for you, I just wanted to make it so --- that's all."

Jonathon gently squeezed his mother's hand. "Don't worry" he said, "everything's fine."

The overnight rain had left everywhere damp and dismal and the low velvety grey clouds did nothing to brighten up the early morning as the journey progressed. Banks of even darker mantles billowed before them issuing a thunderous applause as the heavy, noisy rain pelted endlessly against the windscreen with its pivoting blades.

The two ladies entertained themselves with idle chatter about this and that but being particularly careful to avoid the subject that might bring about any unnecessary gloom and despondency whilst Jonathon concentrated upon his driving, at times peering closely through the falling rain.

The Bentley made steady progress despite the water drenched roads and it was not until they approached the Hampshire border that the inclement weather began to break and soon isolated patches of blue started to appear in the otherwise gloomy sky, bringing a change for the better and gladdening the hearts and minds of the Bentley's travellers.

A couple of miles past the turning to Basingstoke, Lady Barbara caught her breath awhile as she noticed a signpost skip quickly past the car and then another caused a smile to play upon the lips of the very nice lady.

"Jonathon," she said, excitedly at last. "In half a mile or so we should meet with a signpost pointing to a little village called Sutton Scotney, be a darling and take us there would you? It will be only a mile or so out of our way and as we are in no rush perhaps we might afford the place a visit. There is a delightful little stream that flows through the village where watercress grows in abundance, at least it used to when I was a girl. I should so much like for you both to see it, perhaps we might pick a bunch to eat with our picnic later." The lady seemed taken with the idea and smiled elatedly.

"Yes of course grandmama, its no problem at all. I'm sure we could all do with a short break anyway; I know I could. Sutton Scotney, that sounds a rustic sort of place --- just the right sort of name for a quaint Hampshire hamlet."

"That's precisely what it is dear, and it's the place where I spent many happy times when I was a young girl oh so many years ago," answered Lady B. looking thoughtful.

Jonathon slowed down a little straining his eyes for the landmark ahead. "Ah, would this be the sign post we are looking for?" he said as they approached the white pointer.

"That's the one," said Lady B., with a limp hand resting gently on her mouth, "yes, that's the one," she repeated.

Slowing down almost to a halt, the Bentley took the immediate left turning and threaded its way down a narrow twisting road with tall blackthorn hedges lining either side. Eventually, a tiny, pretty, sparsely built up village presented itself with cottages peeping out behind tall oaks but with no semblance of order or design. Cottages with thatched roofs, cottages with slated roofs each a picture of antiquity and charm each one unique, and no doubt, with a story to tell.

A large village green came into view where all of the past centuries' children had played and where their youths had courted avidly was evidently still well used today. Although well trimmed, patches of newly set grass could be seen where worn turf had turned to brown. It was still in need of further repair in places and would have it too, come the autumn. The road which bordered the green had three lanes sprouting from it at irregular intervals and angles, narrow lanes, the depths of which could not be seen from the green because of their twisty ways.

"If you park the Bentley there," said Lady B., pointing to a much worn and improvised parking area, "we should be quite safe and in nobody's way. That's it Jonathon—good --that's fine," she added, as she directed operations.

The two ladies got out of the car elegantly straightening their casual clothing as they completed the move. Jonathon, however remained where he was.

"Aren't you coming with us Jonathon?" asked Felicity, noticing that her son was making no attempt at all to stir.

"Mother, if you don't mind I would much rather have a catnap in the car. Four hours of concentrated driving can be pretty tiring. Anyway, I don't expect you will be long, it has turned half past eleven now and we estimated a luncheon break around noon," said Jonathon.

"Quite right," put in Lady B., "we will only be about ten minutes; the stream is just down that tiny lane over there." The lady pointed to the smallest of the three lanes.

"Are you sure you won't come with us darling," said Felicity, looking at her son anxiously and hoping he had not been upset by her earlier remarks.

"Mother, please stop worrying; I shall be fine here. As I have said, a catnap will be just what I need; so off you go the pair of you and enjoy yourselves, OK," said Jonathon.

The two engaging ladies walked arm in arm toward the narrowest lane with Felicity looking anxiously back over her shoulder a couple of times before the big black Bentley eventually disappeared from view.

About two thirds of the way down, immediately where the lane joined the pretty stream where the watercress could be seen growing in abundance with fresh new green leaves delicately covering the surface of the water, the couple stopped. A pretty fair haired young lady, about sixteen years of age and dressed in a long pink floral frock, seemed to be experiencing some harassment in a most hostile way by three acutely overweight youths who were plainly obstructing her path. The young lady was looking more than a little alarmed and somewhat distraught as she clasped her hands in front of her, anxiously and continuously wringing her fingers. The youths had their backs to the two ladies and so Felicity and her mother moved a few paces closer so that they might be able to accurately assess the situation.

"You better get out of my way Sam Wingfield, my brother Bill will be along directly and he won't take kindly to you talkin' to me one little bit, that he won't," said the young lady, in her broad Hampshire dialect.

"Sure we'll get out o' your way, just as soon as you pay us the price Flo Marks," said the largest of the three youths.

"You'll get nothin' from me—do you hear me—you're nothin' but a load of bullies—tha's what you are." The young lady's words were disjointed and troubled.

"Now don't you be like that young Flo, all us want is a kiss apiece that's the going rate ain't it lads?" said the grinning, most obnoxious Sam Wingfield with a lustfully determined look upon his fat face. He moved toward the girl, now paralysed with fear, and reached out as if to grab at her. Felicity, sensing Flo's fearfulness, started forward hoping to avert an assault on the young lady. But her mother's gentle restraining hand upon her arm cut short her move just as six young men appeared behind Flo carrying homemade cricket bats and six pointed stumps.

"Whats going on Flo?" asked the leading young man, who was the biggest of the sextet and about the same height as the three adversaries.

"It's these three Wingfield boys Bill. They won't let me pass so's I can go on up to the green and Sam threatened me if I didn't give them all a kiss," said Flo, suddenly sounding less distressed.

"Did they now? Well we'll soon see about that," said Bill, with a grin on his face that was neither pleasant nor indeed unpleasant. At first he failed to recognise the three youths but eventually their identity became more obvious.

"Well if it isn't the wonky Wingfield twins. Haven't seen you two about these parts for quite a while. How're you two doin'? Keeping out of mischief I hope; still I doubt it, doubt it very much indeed. I see you've got your big brother Sam with you and all. Let you out at last have they Sam? Not out on good behaviour. I'm sure of that. Seems as though you like clink so much that you're longing for another visit," said Bill, the grin on his pleasant face widening even further.

"What's it got t'do with you Bill Marks?" put forward Sam Wingfield, looking slightly worried.

"Just this," said Bill, his grin immediately disappearing. "If you don't get out of here very fast, even in the next ten seconds, you'll be finding yourself laying back in the water again like what you did a couple of years back, remember? It weren't pleasant for you then and it won't be very pleasant for you now. Do you get my drift?"

"Oh yeah? It'll take more than you to put us there Bill Marks," said Sam Wingfield, smirking.

As Sam Wingfield spoke, the smallest of the six idled his way past the three and casually knelt down behind Sam on all fours. Bill, suddenly moving forward made as if to aim a blow to Sam's head; and Sam, wishing to avoid a confrontation, moved hastily backwards stumbling over the crouching young lad and toppled over into the sludge and muddy stream. Howls of laughter from Bill Marks and his friends followed, much to the dismay of the three Wingfields who cried out vociferously. The twins, in desperate panic, tried to extricate their brother from the slimy water; both were getting their feet soaking wet and their legs splattered with mud.

"You'll be sorry for this Bill Marks," shouted a most distraught Sam Wingfield, with the utmost of disdain. "I'll get even with you, you see if I don't," he further added.

"Why, what did I do?" retorted Bill mockingly, his wide grin once more returning to his face. "You did it yourself Sam Wingfield, I never even touched you."

The three bullies beat a hasty retreat toward the two ladies who stood suppressing their delight with cupped hands over their mouths.

"What are you two grinning at?" shouted one of the twins, as he rudely barged into Felicity knocking her sideways into the arms of her mother.

"Oi, where's your manners?" yelled Bill, as he ran up to Felicity filled with apprehension for the beautiful lady's safety. "I'm sorry about that ma'am, are you alright?" he asked, kindly.

"Yes we are both quite alright; thank you for your concern young man," said Lady B., still smiling.

"Never you mind yourselves about those three idiots, they ain't got a ha'p'orth of manners between the lot of them and that's for certain," said Bill. "You sound as if you're a couple of toffs. Visiting the house are you, old Eld's place?"

The question brought a look of surprise to the face of Lady B., a question she hadn't quite expected but one that brought her much delight.

"No not exactly—at least I hadn't considered visiting the place—but I suppose now that we are this close it would be churlish not to see the old house once again. Akworth, isn't it? The name I mean. Akworth House—if I remember correctly." The Lady's eyes glistened as she spoke. "Do you know where it is? Do you know how we might get there?"

"Course I do. Take you there myself if you like, it's not far," offered Bill, obligingly. Then turning to his friends who had moved further up the lane he called, "be back in a minute, I've just got an errand to run. You be setting up the wickets OK! I shan't be long." Then back to the ladies he said, "You follow me I'll soon show you where it is."

The lane narrowed gradually and eventually came to an abrupt end at a sharp bend. From there it continued as a stone and muddy path with puddles of rain water covering its full width in places. As they cautiously picked their way between and over the puddles, Lady Barbara ventured to ask if she had heard correctly what Bill had said a few minutes earlier. "Has that awful boy really been in prison or were you cruelly goading him?" she asked hesitantly.

"Who, Sam? Yeah he's been in and out of jail or some borstal ever since he left school. They're orphans see. Mum and dad died about ten years ago; leastways their dad did; their mother died not long after. Sam was about eight at the time, I remember, Peter and Paul a couple of years younger. They haven't had a chance really, got dragged up by a bitch of an aunt who had no liking for them. But I haven't seen any of them for quite a while but it seems they have to learn some manners the hard way; maybe we shall have to teach the blighters a thing or two if they're going to go around being a nuisance to everyone.

"Here we are then—Just around this corner and you'll see the old place. You must have missed the huge gateway to the drive—it comes out onto the main London Road before the turning to the village—this is only the side entrance to the house and not used by many of its visitors."

The trio came to the end of the pathway and were faced with a wooden rickety gate in need of some attention. Here they stopped a while and stared at the ageing Tudor house of considerable size and beauty and although the greying white paintwork was flaking in a few places there was still a sufficient contrast to the black vertical and curved structural supports to provide a scene of elegance and charm. On the whole, the exterior appeared to be reasonably well maintained with the attractive irregularly faced leaded light windows reflecting the brightness of the mid-day sun's rays.

There she is, nice place don't you think," said Bill, as proudly as if he had built the house himself.

"Yes Bill, it is a very pleasant sight indeed and just how I remember it," said the very nice lady, as she produced a silver coin from her handbag. "Here you are Bill this is for you. You have been most kind to the both of us and I thank you most sincerely. The lady handed over a new fifty pence piece to the outstretched hand of the young man, and he, being extremely delighted, promptly pocked the money with a smile.

"Thank you ma'am, you really shouldn't have bothered. Still I shall be able to go out tonight and get myself drunk," he said, with a distinct twinkle in his eye.

Looks of complete disapproval filled the ladies faces.

"I'm only kidding, I'm not really that daft," said Bill, laughing merrily. But the two ladies were not so sure and exchanged a hesitant smile as the young man turned to retrace his steps back toward the village green.

— CHAPTER EIGHT —

Mother and daughter walked casually up to and around the house, still with arms linked one with the other, until they found the six wide steps at the front of the building that led directly to the large iron studded old oak panelled door. Lady Barbara carefully mounted the wet steps and pulled at the handle of the ancient doorbell and then waited patiently for a response. None came. She looked round at Felicity and raised her eyebrows then turned her attention once again to the doorbell handle which she tugged with more force. This time they could hear footsteps, not from inside the house however but crossing the gravelled pathway behind them. They turned round immediately.

"Good morning ladies, can I help you?" The laconic words of greeting came from a buxom, ageing woman of around seventy years, maybe a little more, with a pleasant enough face and who was supporting herself with an ebony walking stick upon which she was leaning heavily. Her attitude seemed slightly tense and somewhat sullen probably at being so disturbed and not even a flicker of a smile presented itself upon her face.

"Oh yes, good morning. I should very much like to see Mr. Nigel Eld," said Lady B., quite abruptly and taking on an air of dominance as she usually did when meeting someone for the first time.

"I'm very sorry but that won't be at all possible; you see Sir Nigel passed away over two years ago," said the woman, relaxing a little with the merest hint of a smile. She shifted her weight from one leg to the other as if she was experiencing some considerable discomfort, and all the time clutching at the handle of her stick with both hands.

"I see," responded Lady B., tersely. "And may I ask who owns the house at this present time." Despite the obvious delicate turn the conversation had now taken Lady B. refused to give an inch in her dominant stance and looked into the woman's eyes without batting a lid.

"As a matter of fact, *I* do," she answered, regaining her laconic dialogue and more than willing to stare out this most unwelcome and irritating individual. "My name is Ada Hutchins," she continued. "And may I ask to whom I am speaking?"

Standing riveted to the spot where she stood at the top of the steps and with the emergence of a smile, lighting the features of her face until it glowed, it slowly widened and developed into a most un-lady-like chortle. The very nice lady put both her hands up to her face then threw up her arms in complete amazement.

"My dear Mrs Hutchins is it really you?" she said, with words barely audible at first and then more loudly. She skipped down the steps her arms outstretched then taking the ageing lady in her arms repeated the words over and over again. "Is it *really* you?"

Mrs Ada Hutchins seemed temporarily stupefied. Her mouth gaped open and her eyes bulged like a bullfrog, quite as if she was about to fit. She explored every corner, every crevice of her mind in an effort to bring to mind the identity of this mad woman who was mauling her with insane efficiency. But nothing was revealed.

"Madam," she said at last, "do I know you?" The question could have, should have been uttered sooner but she had no control over that—even her balance was almost beyond her, so determined was the attack. And her voice was weak so that she had to pose the question a second time.

"Madam, please, do I know you?"

"Yes you do," said Lady Barbara trying desperately to contain her emotional excitement. "I'm the not now so little girl who stayed here with you for many marvellous months over fifty years ago. Who pestered the living daylights out of you, and --"

"-- and who wanted oh so much to grow up to be a lady," interrupted Mrs Hutchins with a plethora of feverish delight. "Barbara, my dear sweet Barbara, how absolutely wonderful it is to see you again, and after all this time."

The two ladies embraced each other with renewed vigour and with heart felt emotions amid floods of tears that issued from the reddening eyes of both faces. They were locked together thus for a full two minutes until Mrs Hutchins suddenly broke away from Lady B's vice like grip still retaining her expression of complete elation.

"You bad, wicked girl, how dare you stay away from me for all that time, didn't you realise just how much I would miss you? Well I can tell you I did, very much indeed. We both missed and pined for you, Sir Nigel as much as myself; yes we both missed you and not even a letter from you. All we could think was that you were so taken up with your new home that we, the old fuddy-duddies that we so obviously were, had been swept completely from your mind without a second thought. But we didn't blame you; you were young with exciting prospects ahead of you. We had no right to be kept within your mind but we kept you within ours I can tell you that, and for a very long time indeed."

"Yes I know I have been so selfish and neglectful and to those who have never deserved such treatment; I'm so sorry, so very sorry. But you see I needed to find my own identity and firmly establish it especially after loosing both my parents and I couldn't expect to use the two of you as surrogate replacements, that wouldn't have been fair. But, yes you are quite right I should have kept in touch, that was the least I could have done, and I'm so very sorry," said Lady B., tearfully.

"So you've realised it have you, your dream? There is no need to answer that, for I can see that you have, you are a lady and you deserve to be I'm sure. Now you come round to the back of the house with me the both of you to my kitchen; we can be comfortable there and I shall make you both a nice cup of tea, we've such a lot to catch up on haven't we?" said Mrs Hutchins. Then nodding in Felicity's direction she added, "so this is your younger sister is it, I didn't realise you had a sister, I always thought of you as an only child, except for your step brother of course. Well, aren't you going to introduce us Barbara? I can see how alike you both are and I've a daughter about the same age," said Mrs Hutchins, her eyes still not yet recovered from the reddening of her tearfulness.

"Good heavens no! But I shall certainly accept the compliment," said the very nice lady beaming with delight at the thought. "This is my only child, my daughter Felicity. She's ----" Lady B., was quickly interrupted by a timely cough from Felicity before the very nice lady had a chance to divulge or even hint at her daughter's age --- "yes well," went on Lady B. "I should think your daughter to be somewhat younger than mine, after all she has a son who is twenty three."

"Oh my God, we've forgotten all about Jonathon, he'll be so worried that we've been gone for so long. We really ought to be getting back to him mama," said Felicity, looking immediately agitated.

"Yes you are quite right darling, of course we must be getting back," said Lady B. Then turning to the mistress of the house, "Mrs Hutchins we really oughtn't to stay any longer, as much as we would like to. You see we are on our way to Brixham to visit my brother Jack and he will be expecting us to arrive early this evening; I'm so sorry. You see this was only an impromptu visit, I had no intention in calling on you today at all; I never even considered you would still be here. I saw a couple of road signs along the top road which sparked off some wistfulness on my behalf and I just had to show Felicity the watercress beds—and well—events sort of took over. Before I realised it the past flooded my mind and I just had to see the house once again but with no intention of coming in at all. But the need to walk the paths once more was far too compelling. Out of character all this nostalgic nonsense, quite out of character I can assure you."

"Out of character? What stuff and nonsense, it most certainly is not that. Barbara, do you mean that I am to lose you now that I have found you once again at last? Surely that cannot be. You must stay off on you're way back home, please say you will; I shall find it devastating not to see you again. My daughter Susan is coming home next weekend with some friends of hers from university. You must join us–she would love to meet you all I'm sure of that–stay a few days with me Barbara, I implore you! As I said we have such a lot to catch up on and we can do it then at our leisure please say you will," begged Mrs Hutchins.

Lady B. didn't hesitate, "yes of course that would be lovely, wouldn't it Felicity?"

Her daughter smiled and nodded approvingly.

Ada Hutchins ignored the outstretched hand that Felicity offered and embraced her warmly. "You are extremely beautiful my dear, I can't wait to see you again," she said.

"Thank you Mrs Hutchins, I shall certainly look forward to seeing you again as well—and to meeting your daughter," replied Felicity, graciously.

Mrs Hutchins linked arms with Lady Barbara and together they walked, ever so slowly, back to the side gate with Felicity bringing up the rear. There they said their farewells most reluctantly before mother and daughter ambled back up the narrow twisting lane in silence and without a backward glance. Mrs Hutchins on the other hand stood at the gate leaning against it holding her stick in one hand and waving ceaselessly with the other. She tried to smile but found it to be quite impossible. Instead she swallowed deeply and wiped a tear from her eye as the couple rounded the corner and disappeared from view. Then she returned to Akworth House alone.

— CHAPTER NINE —

Jonathon waited outside the Bentley pensively eyeing the entrance to the tiny lane down which the mothers had disappeared over an hour ago. Although he had expected the two ladies to have returned before this time he had no thoughts of conducting a search just yet in case they had decided to return to the car by another route. He was feeling much less tired after his short catnap and was wondering what could possibly have prompted such interest in keeping the duo completely occupied for so long when all at once the two ladies appeared arms linked as when they had left and with happy smiling faces. With a sigh of relief followed by a huge grin passing over his bronzed handsome face he acknowledged the ladies repeated waving by slightly raising his own hand. Not wishing to appear overly concerned, he didn't question how a ten minute jaunt could have been extended to an hour long excursion; instead he tried to appear nonchalant and greeted his mothers quite casually.

"Sorry we have been so long darling but we managed somehow to have forgotten the time by getting ourselves rather diverted," apologised his mother, still smiling happily, "I do hope you haven't been unduly worried about us."

"Nope, not at all, only hope you both enjoyed the trip; you both certainly look as though you did," answered Jonathon, benignly, then added, "I'm ravenous. Shall we eat here? It seems a nice enough spot."

"No not here Jonathon. There is a place about two miles further on and just off the main road which would be rather more appropriate," said Lady B., as they all entered the car once again and taking on an unexpected subdued posture. She said very little as they drove out of the village and restricted her remarks to the passing scenery and the now brilliantly sunny day. And Felicity, not wishing to impose herself upon her mother's meditation, confined her conversation to her son and was full of chatter.

"The watercress beds were simply lovely and fresh with an abundance of young leafy plants," she was saying. "And it was such a pity that we didn't get around to picking you any Jonathon. But what with the fiasco that took place as soon as we arrived at the stream its not at all surprising that it slipped our minds."

Felicity then went on to relate to her son all that ensued after their arrival describing in detail how a big bully found his way into a quagmire, much to Jonathon's amusement, and how a most pleasant young man of the immediate locality had kindly escorted them both to Akworth House and all that followed.

"It sounds a most interesting visit mother and well worth the small diversion it took to get you both there and I'm sure it will be most interesting to stop over at Sutton Scotney on the way back to Bergholt if the place is as interesting as you say it is," said Jonathon, eagerly looking forward to exploring the house and surrounding village himself.

The Bentley was brought to a standstill when it reached a sizeable expanse of closely cut grassland in the centre of which stood an impressively huge copper beech tree in full coppery leaf and beyond this magnificent specimen, by twenty or so yards and growing in a steep gully, was a thick, tall hawthorn hedgerow dressed in its springtime leaf of the palest green. Beyond the hedge, which served as the foreground to an impressive panoramic picture, could be seen a patchwork quilt of the most beautiful Hampshire fields. Some ploughed, some unploughed and rich with scarlet poppies, some a vibrant yellow with oilseed rape growing its oil-rich seed, and some pale green with wheat or barley, all forming a pattern of intense splendour. The colourful view, stretching out mile upon mile as far as the eye could see, was stunning and caused the trio to stand in awe with bated breath and bathe in its loveliness.

After a while of taking in the view Jonathon lifted the heavy wicker hamper from the Bentley's boot as the ladies spread tartan blankets upon the grass to sprawl on and erected folded chairs to sit on, so that a choice might be made available. And after a champagne cork had been withdrawn, amid exclamations of 'splendid' and 'superb' and fits of raucous laughter had filled the air, they seated themselves, the ladies in chairs and Jonathon slouched on one of the blankets; and there they ate heartily the food that had been so graciously prepared for them as if they hadn't eaten for hours.

More than half the quantity of dainty sandwiches were enthusiastically devoured with portions of pheasant, home cured ham and salad all prepared to perfection by May George. The delicious custard and mock-cream topped trifles which she had so daintily concocted were a complete success and were all washed down with the sparkling champagne.

The sumptuous feast was eaten and enjoyed in style well within the hour. Then Jonathon, feeling that he had over indulged a little, decided to stretch his legs and taking leave of the ladies he wandered through a gateway in the tall hedge to a large field of brightly coloured blood red poppies. Here he stood and watched as a pair of skylarks soared high in the sky above him each battling for height and vocal supremacy the one over the other until they were out of sight and only their tiny shrill voices seemed never ending; he smiled at them in appreciation for the pleasure they gave.

He walked for a bit, then sprinted across the lush green mead strewn with the scarlet poppies and yellow ragwort and when he had reached the far side of the meadow he rested for a moment and examined more wild flowers that grew there in abundance. Then he casually strolled back again.

As he neared the tall hawthorn hedgerow once more his attention was captured by the roar of a badly out of tune car engine coming from the roadway which he had travelled an hour earlier. Then the screeching of tyres, as the vehicle braked heavily on the smooth surface of the tarmac, reverberated to where he stood. Being perfectly still for a moment and wondering what lunatic could be driving so recklessly he waited and listened to the slamming of doors and then the voices of youths as they walked the distance between the road and the area where his mothers sat.

"Well if it isn't the two posh nosy parkers. Didn't get very far did you?" The loud mocking voice was easily discernable from where Jonathon stood hidden behind the hedge.

"Sam Wingfield isn't it?" Jonathon heard his mother's nervous questioning voice as it identified the youth.

"Tha's right first time missus. Got a good memory you has. Now s'pose you give us what Flow Marks refused us eh?" said the tantalizing obnoxious youth, endeavouring to fill his victim with the utmost fear.

"I think you had better leave young man and take your two brothers away with you," intervened Lady B. instantly with utmost self-assured assertiveness and with the merest touch of sarcasm in her voice. "This lady's son will be returning very shortly and I can assure you that you will like him a good deal less than you liked Bill Marks," she added

Lady Barbara's words didn't seem to have much effect on the Wingfield youths with their amoral attitude. They chuckled amongst themselves each giving the other a great deal of artificial encouragement.

"Little lad is he? 'Bout four or five I reckon. Must be if he's your son. Been for a quick pee behind the hedge has he? Little kids can do that can't they, still, so can the bigger ones, you show 'em Pete." The disgusting remarks of the objectionable Sam Wingfield had the desired effect upon both ladies for they cringed with fright and wished that Jonathon would soon appear especially as the remark was followed by the trio's sneers and rowdy laughter.

At last Jonathon decided he had heard quite enough. He stood in the gateway to his full height filled with complete annoyance and stared at the three delinquents.

"No, I'm not as small as you seem to imagine, so if I were you I would get back into that heap you call a car and go home as the lady has already suggested before you all get hurt," said Jonathon, coolly.

At this Sam Wingfield donned a most truculent sneer and looked at his brothers from one to the other and then started the ritual once again this time more nervously.

"Big man ain't he? Still I've seen these big men 'afore. They look big, they talk big, but underneath it all—they're pussy cats. Come on, there's three of us, let's take 'im on then we can 'ave our way with her," he said, glancing at Felicity wantonly.

Sam Wingfield then advanced nervously at first, toward Jonathon and then taking courage glared up into his face, and said: "Come on then big man, let's see what you're made of shall us?"

"Now, I do hope that you are not going to force me into doing something that's contrary to my nature and against my Christian ethics and which you most assuredly will regret," said Jonathon, still remaining very cool.

"You hear that Sam? Seems as though he's a Christian as well as bein' a pussy cat and you know what Christians are supposed to do if you give 'em a smack, Their supposed to turn the other cheek ain't they?" said Paul Wingfield, the slightly slimmer of the twins.

"Yeah," said the oldest brother, "tha's right. We'll see if it works then shall us."

And with that he dealt Jonathon a ferocious blow to the cheek with his open hand. Jonathon controlled himself and failed to flinch; it was as if his face had turned to marble. The lout clutched at his hand that seemed to be damaged in the exercise. Reaching out with his right hand and taking hold of the lapels of Sam Wingfield's jacket he lifted the overweight lout a few inches clear of the ground.

"I certainly am a Christian but that doesn't mean I am willing to be your punch bag," said Jonathon. Then placing his left hand by Sam Wingfield's knees, he proceeded to lift the frightened youth above his head as easily as if he had been a child. Amazement then filled the twin's faces as their voices croaked with fear.

"Put him down mister," one said in terror, "he didn't mean no harm."

"Now are you all going quietly or must your brothers disentangle you from that bramble bush over there. It's your choice but I must warn you that it won't be very pleasant," said Jonathon.

"No sir, please put me down sir --- we're sorry alright? Just a bit of fun, no harm meant. Come on—put me down—pleases put me down sir—we'll go quiet like," quaked the frightened voice.

Jonathon replaced Wingfield onto the ground feet first and stared at him incessantly.

"Well, off you go then," said Jonathon, sternly. "Don't stand around gawping at me. Just think yourselves lucky this time and try to learn from your experience otherwise you will find yourselves in a much worse predicament if you should have the misfortune to meet up with me again."

The three brothers took to their heels with all speed stopping occasionally to see if they were completely safe and not being followed, then on again until they had reached the comparative safety of their old wreck of a car just as a white police vehicle arrived and pulled up in front of them. Two police officers alighted from the shiny car and spoke to the three Wingfields.

"Thought we told you three lads to get that rubbish off the road; it's a menace to the community. If I see you in it again you'll be prosecuted. Do I make myself clear?" said the tallish policeman.

"Yes officer we will, 'course we will," said the oldest brother. And with that they clambered into the wreck and were gone.

The two police officers now turned their attention to the picnickers, chattered awhile, then strolled across, not in an official manner at all, but indifferently, as if they were about to meet some old acquaintances. Their uniforms appeared most comical and not as smart as one would have expected. The trousers in particular, if they had exchanged them the one with the other would then have looked reasonable but as it was the taller, skinny one wore his trousers at half-mast while the shorter and more dumpy officer's trousers gathered around his boots. They carefully removed their hats as they approached.

"Good morning ladïes," said the taller of the two, and they both nodded to Lady Barbara and Felicity in turn. And turning to Jonathon and looking up at him they merely murmured:

"Sir," and that was about the best they could manage.

"I do hope them three Wingfield lads haven't been causing a nuisance madam," said the tallish thin policeman. "I know they can be quite a handful when they put their minds to it."

"Not at all officer," said Jonathon, clearly ignoring the fact that the policeman's remarks had been directed at his grandmother and not at himself. "They were fine, really, a little short on manners but apart from that they were fine."

"And who might you be?" asked the talking policeman abruptly and not taking kindly to Jonathon's intervention.

"Oh I'm sorry officer how rude of me," said Jonathon smiling, "I should have introduced the three of us. This is the Lady Barbara Fisher Jones, her daughter Felicity Fisher and my name is Jonathon Fisher."

"Yes this is my grandson," intervened Lady B.

"Oh I see grandmother and grandson is it?" said the officer disbelievingly. "And I 'spect you'll be telling me next that this young lady is the gentleman's mother," he laughed, pointing to the seated Felicity and all the while looking directly at Lady Barbara and grinning with uncertainty.

"I thought that my grandson had made that perfectly clear officer," said Lady B., amused at the officer's obvious dilemma.

"Not at all madam," returned the officer. "All I've got so far is that you are the young gentleman's grandmother and that this here is your daughter. You could have a dozen daughters for all I know but as for this couple being mother and son, well, seems a bit unlikely to me. What say you Sid?" said the officer turning to his partner and still grinning.

"Jeremy," said the dumpy policeman, excitedly as he at last managed to find his tongue. "It's 'im ain't it? It's that giant bloke, you know—in the Chronicle this morning. That bloke who saved a drowning suicide man who died twice. It's 'im ain't it?"

"Sid you are not making a good deal of sense," said Jeremy, clipping his buddy gently around the ear.

"Ow, what's that for?" asked Sid, looking slightly displeased.

"That's for not making any real sense at all," replied Jeremy. Now you start again and this time—please make at least some sense my little friend."

"Look, don't you remember Jeremy? I showed you that article in this morning's paper about someone in Suffolk who rescued a suicide bloke, and then when he went for help the idiot went and did it again. You must remember Jeremy. His name was Jonathon—a Jonathon someone or other, that was it, Jonathon Fisher—I'm sure that's 'im" The excitement rose in the squat policeman's voice as he spoke and suddenly the light dawned on the face of Jeremy as well.

"Good heavens Sid I do believe you are right—I do remember—remember it well—that I do." Then turning to Jonathon he asked, "well sir, are you he?" The question was put in a most official manner.

"Yes you are quite right officer." Jonathon answered the question with a huge smile and holding both hands above his head as if surrendering. "I am he."

"Well strike me pink—I'll go to the foot of our stairs. On the run then, are you?" he asked.

"No, not at all," answered Jonathon, feeling a little peeved at being subjected to unwarranted questioning. "As a matter of fact we are at this point in time on our way to visit some of our relations at Brixham in Devon."

"Oh are you now? Well you can't. Leastways not 'til we get the all clear from Police Headquarters you can't," said Jeremy, filled with complete satisfaction. Then turning to his partner he said: "you go over to the car and get H.Q. on the blower Sid. Tell them who we've come across and ask them what they want us to do with them. I'll wait here and keep these nice people company and maybe have a sandwich or two, I'm sure they won't mind offering me a bite to eat," he said, glancing at the very nice lady.

Sid replaced his hat and hurried back to the brand new panda car chuckling to himself as he went, filled with his own importance and very pleased at, what he considered to be, his astute perceptibility, but not in those exact words.

Twenty minutes and six sandwiches later Sid hurried back again. This time looking out of breath, disappointed and most disheartened.

"It's alright Jeremy; they got through to Suffolk who said we were to let 'em go. I must say that our lot didn't seem too happy with the decision, but what can you do when someone else gives the orders?" said Sid.

"Never mind Sid don't take it too personally. We has to do what we has to do," said Jeremy. "Well that seems to be that," he said with a disillusioned tone to his voice. Then perking up he added, "still 'haps we better get in touch with Devon though, just to be on the safe side like—they ought to be aware who it is who's visiting their borders, ought to be told who it is who's visiting like, ought to know who to expect, now didn't they?"

They both walked away not at all sure if the matter was completely finished or not, then feeling rejected because they knew that it was. They had walked half of the distance to their car when Jeremy stopped, turned round and walked a few paces back again.

"Now don't you people stay off here on the way back to Suffolk. Didn't you see the 'NO PICNICKERS' sign as you drove in here? Blind are you? And make sure you tidies up after yourselves and don't leave no litter about the place. Mustn't expect other people to clear up after us now must we?" said the tallish officer, with an abundance of sarcasm.

They then continued with their stroll after they had once again nodded to the two ladies and with the murmuring of a lengthy 'yeees' to Jonathon they were gone as instantly as they had arrived.

Lady Barbara sighed a sigh of relief and then smiled a smile of reassurance at her offspring.

"Well, now that the Keystone Cops have departed perhaps we might at last resume our journey to Devon. Quite an unpleasant little fiasco wasn't it? So glad it didn't go on for any longer. And yes I did notice the 'no picnickers' sign as we drove in; just in case it did cross either of your minds to ask. But really, I couldn't possibly have considered it to have been meant for us, now could I?" said the very nice lady.

The drive for the rest of the journey was practically uneventful, yes they did notice a broken down wreck of a car by the side of the road not much further than a half of a mile from where they had stopped to eat and with three shameless youths standing to the side of it just staring with eyes and mouths gaping at the flawless Bentley as it passed. And even though the Fisher trio was in the best of high spirits, the Good Samaritan bit did not enter their minds at all.

— CHAPTER TEN —

As the big black Bentley was approaching the Torquay area of Devon, Jonathon seemed totally engrossed not only in driving the Bentley in a safe and reliable manner but also in pondering what mischief the two Sutton Scotney policemen might cause by informing the Devon force of the families imminent arrival; and not at all certain that a word of notification to the local press was beyond their capability.

"We have no idea at all what sort of mischievous welcoming committee those two complete nitwits may have unwittingly arranged for us do we?" he said, at length. "Here we are the three of us minding our own business and just looking for a spot of the jolly old peace and quiet and not attention seeking in the slightest when who knows what may pop up. I should have thought that the last thing we need right now is a visit from some story hungry reporter or be intimidated by the local constabulary looking for something to brighten up their otherwise dreary day for them. If anyone has been alerted then obviously they will be looking for some tall chap accompanied by two beautiful young ladies, will they not? Well now, if they notice two lovely ladies flitting about the place but minus the tall fellow, then their suspicions may be far less aroused," said Jonathon outwardly chuckling at the thought. "I think that perhaps the two of you would be much safer if you went on ahead as planned but without me. Book in at the Northcliff Hotel, make yourselves comfortable and I will turn up a little later and join you both for dinner. How does that sound?" said Jonathon, looking far less serious than he felt.

"It makes sense to me Jonathon. We are here to relax and enjoy ourselves, as you say, what do we want with more intrusion on our privacy? We've had quite enough of that already. What do you think Felicity?" said Lady B.

Felicity wasn't quite so sure.

"But what about you Jonathon," she said, not at all certain how this was all going to pan out. "I sincerely hope that you are not intending to walk to Brixham from here; the thought of it leaves me aghast, it's much too far, even for you."

"Good heavens no mother, I'm certainly not up to a walk of twenty to thirty miles. No, I shall enter the water at Rockend and surface at Berry Head. Yes I intend to swim Torbay. It certainly won't take me very long to do it and I should be there about an hour after your arrival. Look, you both know I have completed the swim a couple of times before and besides, the exercise will do me the world of good and just what I need after being cramped up behind the steering wheel of a car for most of the day," said Jonathon getting quite excited at the prospect.

"I really don't like the idea of you swimming the bay one little bit darling. Oh I know you are more than capable of doing that short distance but not after such a long and tiresome journey. I tell you, I just do not like it at all, and to my mind it would be unnecessary and most unwise."

Felicity was uncompromising in her attitude. As far as she was concerned Jonathon was behaving illogically and he should most certainly complete the journey with them. Nobody would see the party as it arrived at the hotel, she reasoned, so what was all the fuss about? It was obvious to her that Jonathon was using the ploy as an excuse to have a swim; he would do almost anything for such an opportunity as she knew full well and much to Jonathon's consternation she told him so.

"Quit worrying mother, so what if I do look forward to a swim in the briny, there is nothing wrong in that. But I still feel it to be safer if we arrive in Brixham separately holding fast to the reasons I've already given," he said. "You skirt around Paignton to Brixham and I shall meet you both later for dinner, I shall be famished so please order me the largest mixed grill they can possibly dish up," said Jonathon, grinning.

He stopped the Bentley, got out and went round to the large boot and took out his waterproof shoulder bag which contained his swimming gear. He then walked to the front of the car and kissed the ladies goodbye; once more reassuring his rather anxious and perturbed mother that all was well. Felicity then climbed into the driver's seat discontented and drove the Bentley away; much to fast for Jonathon's liking.

It was late in the afternoon when the young Adonis took his leisurely stroll to the area of Rockend; where he found a secluded spot and changed into his trunks without being disturbed. He folded his clothes neatly and placed them into the water proof bag which he securely strapped to his back; put on his underwater goggles and dived into the refreshing water.

It felt good to be immersed in the calm sparkling sea once again, enjoying the warmth of the late May sunshine as it played upon his strong tanned body. It had been a full year since he had experienced the swell of the waves pitching and lurching in complete command, and battling himself against such an awe invoking element was both challenging and exciting and provided a frightening, more sinister sort of challenge to him than his beloved Stour ever could. The river was a friendly, more gentle experience, while the sea was hostile thrilling and unpredictable.

Jonathon surged speedily ahead through the clear, calm, almost tranquil waters of Torbay, using the gyrating power of body and limb. Soon, in no time at all really, he was halfway across the length of the bay with scarcely a breathing respite to break the crossing. He stopped and floated on his back awhile watching some common gulls as they swooped and squabbled over titbits they had gathered from a small launch that was anchored a half mile or so out to sea. He watched the launch as it bobbed up and down with the swell of the waves and noticing some movement onboard he lifted his goggles to the top of his head so that he might observe the scene more clearly.

Two divers were entering the water backwards from the launch, he could see that much, but as they reached the surface of the sea they obviously disappeared from view. He thought how exhilarating the divers must be finding the experience with full underwater regalia in calm clear water. Then he noticed two other people at the prow of the launch sliding an indiscernibly long object into the water where the two divers were reckoned to be. This action promoted some interest to Jonathon's mind and he wondered what kind of manoeuvre was being carried out.

He decided to position himself under the waves to see if the divers might pass his way so that he may join in, or witness any subterfuge taking place, if indeed that is what it was. He quickly repositioned his goggles and dived just beneath the waves, swam around, and waited glancing in the direction of the launch hoping for a glimpse of the divers.

He didn't have long to wait, however, for very soon they came into view; as silhouettes at first and then more clearly moving fast with flipper fitted feet and complete underwater paraphernalia. Their wetsuits and face masks were black and oxygen cylinders were strapped securely to their backs with fitted belts around their waists from which hung instruments of various means.

One person at the front and the other at the rear, one pushing and one steadying what looked to be a long sled-like craft laden with a quantity of parcels and packages each enclosed in waterproof wrapping and strapped securely to the sled. They travelled so deeply in the water that they almost scraped the fine gravel and sand on the ocean floor; walking, crawling and swimming all at the same time but in perfect unison as if the exercise had been practiced to a polished performance. They floated the lengthy craft along at a goodly pace toward the sun baked shore where a narrow flat beach, completely hidden by huge chalky rocks that had fallen from the cliffs many years ago, provided the perfect landing for such a craft.

Throughout all of this time, Jonathon had resurfaced no more than a couple of times in order to regenerate the life sustaining air without drawing attention to himself. Now he was quietly floating on top of the gentle waves and watching closely as the two divers dragged the craft slowly out of the water and onto the shore a couple of hundred yards from where Jonathon was keeping watch. Then, as if from nowhere there appeared two other figures, each clad in in thick seafarer's jumpers and black trousers, half covered by thigh high wading boots and with dark woollen bobble hats upon their heads. Jonathon smiled at the uniformity of the garb considering they would look well in some Hollywood war time movie.

The four men together, pulled the sled further up the beach and commenced to unload its cargo, placing it neatly and carefully in stacks. As soon as the unloading had been completed the two divers re-entered the sea and promptly disappeared beneath its crest and watched by Jonathon they made their way back to the launch pulling the now empty sled behind them.

Jonathon didn't see the going of the two men on the beach only the parcels that were left behind but he felt he had certainly seen enough to realise that no matter what the divers had transported on the sled that afternoon, the whole of the operation had been carried out quite furtively to his way of thinking and therefore was somewhat irregular and sinister and needed checking out at once.

With his pulse racing Jonathon restarted his swim to Brixham and swimming mostly beneath the surface of the waves he covered the remaining couple of miles at an incredible speed, surfacing at Berry Head as planned. He dried himself on the towel he had carried in his shoulder bag and dressed quickly. Within fifteen minutes he was in the foyer of the Northcliff Hotel making room enquiries.

As instructed by Lady B., the hotel porter had taken Jonathon's suitcase to room 107 and placed it on the case rack at the foot of the bed. Once inside the room, Jonathon opened his case and selected his toiletry requisite bag, and, removing his clothing once more, he went to the bathroom.

After taking a shower, bathing in the deepest of piping hot baths, and then showering once again he dried himself and fell limply on top of the bed. With his hands supporting his blonde head from behind and his eyes staring up toward the very high ceiling he experienced the now familiar feeling of total bewilderment. *'Everything seems to be happening with strange rapidity. I enjoy excitement'* he told himself, *'that isn't the problem. The drawback to the problem is the speed, the expeditiousness of events, everything is moving far to fast, too efficiently. First the death of Watts, then the problem at Sutton Scotney with the wayward youths and the police, now the discovery of a probable smuggling racket. Where will it all end? Certainly not yet'* he told himself, convinced that more was to follow, much more.

He dressed, at length, into his smart dinner suit and searched for the ladies. He found them both relaxing in the busy lounge each holding a large aperitif which they sipped appreciatively waiting patiently to be called in to dinner. After gathering a much needed drink for himself, Jonathon joined the mothers and when completely settled he began to unfold the afternoon's drama in meticulous detail.

"Well there is only one course of action open to you as far as I can see Jonathon, the incident has to be reported to the proper authorities without delay if they are to stand half a chance in apprehending those responsible; otherwise who knows how far the villains might get; if indeed they are villains," reasoned Lady B., and looking at Jonathon in a thoughtful and most serious manner.

"Done that grandmama, I telephoned the local police as soon as I reached the hotel. Of course, I failed to leave my name and the address of this place, not wanting to get too involved, hoping that the whole thing might blow over fairly quickly I suppose. Still, it doesn't usually work that way does it? These things tend to drift on and on once the police get their hooks into you. Anyway, they did sound extremely interested I'll give them that. I expect they will have contacted the coast guards straight away to have the launch intercepted and then sent the Hampshire equivalent of the flying squad down to the cove to see what's going on down there. They seemed to have some idea of the place I was trying to describe, only hope the police are not too late that's all.

"But the puzzling thing is why would anyone unload a cargo of obvious contraband in broad daylight? Perhaps it's not so obvious, perhaps it's not contraband after all, perhaps it's some completely innocent underwater exercise being carried out by the S.B.S. or some club. What a surprise they will get when the cops turn up," exclaimed Jonathon, grinning widely at the possibilities. "Anyway," he continued hopefully, "I'm sure it would be a good idea to tune in to the local late night news, you never know, there may well be a report on the strange incident then at least we would have some idea as to what's going on."

Felicity raised the index finger of her right hand.

"I understand perfectly why anyone would use the daytime as a cover for any untoward activities of this nature," she said. "Think about it, if they carried out the exercise at night then that would mean lighting being used to some extent and they would risk arousing almost everyone's suspicions. Where as, if everything is carried out in the daytime nobody would give them a second look. That's why they decided to use divers I suppose and not any other method in getting the stuff ashore."

"What a clever girl you are darling," said her mother, full of maternal admiration. "Of course you are perfectly right, it makes complete sense, doesn't it Jonathon?"

Just then the waiter who had been hovering and waiting for a lull in the conversation walked over to the trio and told them that their table was ready.

Throughout dinner the conversation was largely centred on the launch episode with each in turn expounding various theories regarding smugglers and smuggling, past and present, various contraband items that could only find their way into the country by this method and even a suitable punishment which is or should be applied. Mainly the conversation was quite light and good humoured although occasionally it did take a turn in becoming slightly more serious.

"Looking back I suppose I was a little hasty in leaving the scene as quickly as I did; but because I had seen the divers returning to the launch I automatically assumed that I had witnessed the first trip of many. What a pity it would be if that was the one and only one. That would mean that the launch would have had ample opportunity to get out of the vicinity and for the people on shore more than enough time to be on their way," said Jonathon, thoughtfully.

"No Jonathon, I'm sure you did exactly the right thing in leaving when you did, and I am equally certain that more than one trip took place. Why else would they have placed the packages in neat piles if there was no more to follow? Surely they would have taken them away immediately and loaded them directly into their truck or whatever it was they were using for transportation," said Lady B.

"In any event, we are sure to find out what this is all about soon enough. Rarely do the authorities sit on news of this sort. They like to use the media and the public to their advantage whenever possible especially in cases like this," chirped in Felicity.

"What's the time now?" queried Lady B.

Both Jonathon and Felicity looked at their watches simultaneously.

"Nine forty five," returned Felicity.

"Well the late local news starts at ten sharp so perhaps it might be a good idea for all of us to take coffee and brandy in my room. That way we can watch the television together," said Lady B.

Jonathon summoned the wine waiter straight away and instructed him to serve coffee and brandy for three in Lady Barbara's suit and then followed the ladies from the table.

At two minutes to ten the television in Lady Barbara's suit was switched on and the appropriate channel selected. And at two minutes past ten the three learned:

"---- That two men had been arrested while in possession of a substance or substances unknown and that a motor launch and its crew had been apprehended under suspicious circumstances. All of the information leading to the conclusion of the arrests was made possible with information given to the police by an anonymous member of the public. The Brixham police are anxious that this person should get in touch with them again as soon as possible, in order to clarify the sequence of events that took place this afternoon."

The three looked at each other dumbfounded.

"Well where precisely do we go from here?" smiled Jonathon, the question being lost in flights of fancy, for none held the answer for certain.

"I am just as much at a loss for words as you are," said the very nice lady, looking more perplexed than anyone and eyeing the blank screen of the television pensively.

"I'm at a loss too," added a vexed Felicity. "Perhaps the only clear way forward would be for us to contact the police, put them fully in the picture, as far as we are able, and hopefully find out the whole story; but somehow I doubt that will happen. Obviously, for some reason best known to them, they are feeling rather hesitant in disclosing anything further at this stage. I mean, what on earth are we supposed to make out of the morsel of information that they have just given out?"

"One thing is for certain, I am not about to present myself as a sitting target at any police station. You can safely bet that there is an organised syndicate of sorts involved in all of this who have also watched this scanty report and you can also gamble they will be looking for retribution of one kind or another for spoiling their fun. Probably eying the police station as we speak to see who turns up and then maybe carry out their own investigation on the unfortunate individual. Not me, no chance—no chance at all," Jonathon thought deeply for a while. "I wonder if perhaps it would be possible for me to meet with the police on neutral territory as it were. That way I should be able to secure myself a good deal more anonymity. Yes, that's it, much more sensible," said Jonathon aloud but mainly for his own ears.

"Anyhow, I think we had better sleep on it; nothing more to be done tonight and perhaps things will look a deal less involved in the morning," he concluded.

They each agreed and drifted off to their separate bedrooms hoping, above all else, for a goodnights sleep.

Jonathon's night was anything but restful. He spent most of it mulling over the recent events including those he had left in Suffolk, and finally gave up on all hope of sleep. In the early hours he went for a swim in the hotel's indoor pool; which was always kept open for those guests who might be suffering from insomnia, and spent an interesting half hour in conversation with a chirpy pool attendant who didn't appear to be overly concerned that his night was being disturbed.

"The hotel proprietor doesn't mind me sleeping in the office. In fact nine out of ten nights I manage to sleep right through. So long as I'm available to look out for anyone who wants a dip, no one cares," said the attendant, blinking his eyes open.

After enjoying a mug of hot sweet tea the two sat down together for a chat. The attendant was a young man of twenty two or so, quite tall and well built with a mass of dark wavy hair.

"Did you happen to see the ten o'clock news last night by any chance?" Jonathon ventured to ask.

"Do you mean the bit about the local smuggling goings on?" returned the attendant, as he slurped at his tea.

"Yes that's the one," said Jonathon. "Is there much of that sort of thing going on these days? Of course I realise in days gone by smuggling went on most of the time along many of our coast lines but I should have thought that with modern trading and co-operation between Britain and the continent most activities of that nature would have ceased long ago, or am I being extremely naïve?"

"Afraid you are. It still happens today, from time to time, but not to quite the same extent as it used to." The attendant became enlivened with the topic of conversation.

"All the latest crazes which are unable to enter the country legally manage to find their way in via the black market and that involves an extensive smuggling racket," he continued. "The current problem for the authorities is drugs of course. This is a perfect coast line for dropping off the stuff; what with the railway line skirting round the bay and Churston railway station being only a stones throw away. Why, only a couple of months ago there were sixteen arrests made and a sizeable quantity of heroin seized. It doesn't always make the top national papers of course but there are always rumours flying about down here.

"I've a brother who is stationed locally, only a PC mind but he's usually in the know. Actually, we watched the news together tonight but he didn't seem to know what was going on, not this time he didn't. He was unable to make any comments at all on the subject, which is most unusual for him. I reckon this is different somehow. Someone is stopping the rumours at source; someone's worried about something. Protecting themselves more than likely, or someone else, that's what I reckon. Someone's involved with something they shouldn't be that's why doors have been firmly closed. We'll probably never know, but it seems weird to me."

After a short time Jonathon wandered back to his room, went through his usual ablution routine and prepared himself for his full English.

— CHAPTER ELEVEN —

Jonathon and Felicity were already seated at the breakfast table when Lady Barbara put in her appearance looking every inch the stylish noblewoman she purported to be. And after exchanging early morning pleasantries with the others, she, like Jonathon, settled to do justice to an immodest breakfast.

"So how is our adventurer feeling this morning?" asked Lady B., playfully of Jonathon. "Hope you slept well after all that concentrated driving and exercise yesterday. For me, I must say, it was rather pleasant to obtain a full eight hours and most invigorating to take the sea air first thing."

"Don't tell me you have been out already this morning mama; I find that very difficult to believe," said Felicity, contending her mother's integrity.

"I most certainly have my dear, and do so very often. How else do you think I manage to keep in shape?" Lady B. was indeed in good shape even in her advancing years she still looked a good thirty of them younger.

"Anyway enough of me," she resumed, "you failed to answer me Jonathon. Did you have a peaceful night?"

Jonathon produced a look indicating that the opposite was accurate and told the two mothers that he had spent a good half hour in the company of a young pool attendant who was well versed in the knowledge of the entire unseemly goings on in and for miles around Brixham.

"Well did you draw any conclusions from the tête-à-tête with your young attendant chum or was the conversation without resolve?" queried Lady B., desirously. "Surely you must have formulated some sort of plan of action by now."

"The way forward hasn't changed at all as far as I can see. I still think it would be most unwise for me to present myself at the police station this morning and so I am intent on telephoning the man in charge to hopefully arrange for a more clandestine get together. But there is certainly no need for the three of us to get involved, after all said and done, your knowledge is second hand at best so I intend handling matters myself.

"The conversation with the pool attendant was fairly interesting; it seems that smuggling is still quite a prevalent industry especially in these parts, only he firmly believes there to be something unique about this little escapade. Secrecy on behalf of the local police has entered the equation. As you mentioned yesterday mother, the police don't usually withhold information of this sort from the public. Mostly they consider the more Joe public is involved the better the chances they have in solving the problem. But this time it seems, everything, except for basics, has been kept under wraps. The attendant considers it probable that someone might suffer some huge embarrassment, someone important maybe, if the press were to have free range to bandy the story about as they usually do.

"Anyway I intend to find out exactly what's going on; after all I am an interested party, comparatively speaking, so hopefully the police will be forthcoming—we'll have to wait and see," said Jonathon, trying to sound more optimistic as his oration developed.

"When you watched those four people unloading the packages and stacking them up one upon the other, what were your immediate thoughts Jonathon? Did they seem very heavy, I mean, did anyone struggle with them at all? Were they of similar shape and size or were they a hodgepodge of different shapes and sizes?" asked Felicity.

"It was quite difficult to see really—remember I was still a fair distance away, and I had to keep low in the water for fear of being spotted," answered Jonathon probing his mind. "But yes," he said at length. "I should say they were roughly the same shape and size but they certainly didn't appear to carry very much weight. Even so, the packages were handled with great care, almost as if they were bombs or something. But that doesn't really give us much to go on does it?" answered Jonathon.

"Certainly not kegs of brandy then," laughed Felicity.

Jonathon smiled, "no not that," he said.

"It's not a bit of use our guessing you know, we might just as well wait until you have spoken to the police and see what they are willing to tell us. I know we keep going around in circles saying that maybe we'll soon find out, but why should they tell us? Why should you have privileged information Jonathon?"

They each finished their breakfast in relative silence then as they were about to leave the table Lady B. said they ought to fulfil the reason for their visit to Brixham in the first place before they had been so distracted.

"Well, it may seem rather ill-mannered to come all this way and not visit my one and only step brother. I'm sure he would be most upset and probably never speak to me again. Now there's a thought," laughed Lady B. "Felicity, perhaps you and I should walk to Jack's home and maybe meet with Jonathon there later, after he has concluded his business with the local police. Let's hope that neither visit will be too drawn out, we need the opportunity to bask in this lovely sunshine don't we. Now is every one happy about that, does that meet with every ones approval?"

Jonathon walked slowly back to his room sat down in the armchair leaned his head against the headrest and gazed at the walls. Half an hour later he leant forward picked up the telephone receiver and dialled the number of the local constabulary.

The warm air was filled with the sound of deranged screeching from flocks of herring gulls, as they fought each other incessantly for oddments of food, when Jonathon walked slowly down to Brixham quay at eleven that morning. The friendly exchanges of harmless banter between tanned local fishermen as they sat repairing their nets was always an entertaining feature of the harbour and one that Jonathon had repeatedly found to be so very fascinating. However, on this particular sunny morning, he was just a little disappointed to find the tide out and the small harbour almost deserted. His eyes strayed casually into the various shop windows as he strolled along, each competing vigorously with their neighbour in the retail of a miscellany of memorabilia. He wandered meditatively through to the entrance of the anchorage and upon reaching the farthest point he turned his gaze to the sea's far horizon scanning it for nothing in particular.

After a period of time he turned his attention from the sea once more and refocused his eyes to watch the tall figure of a middle aged man as he approached from the town end of the quay. The man was sturdily built but not overweight and looked reasonably fit for one of his age. He was immaculately dressed in a dark grey suit that fitted as though it had been tailor made and he walked upright with a gate that was both long and measured. He sidled up to Jonathon, a wide grin upon his face and with an extended hand he greeted the taller man cordially.

"Superintendent Dobson," he said, using a deep formal voice.

Jonathon took the hand in his and greeted the stranger politely but without announcing his own name; that could wait, he thought.

"So what's all the secrecy for then me 'andsome?" The superintendent spoke with a broad Devonshire brogue that was reassuring and friendly. "You shy o' police stations then are you?"

"Not at all," replied Jonathon, smiling. "Just exercising my right to be cautious, that's all."

"Quite right too. 'Twill pay to be careful these days that it will," said the superintendent, fixing his eyes directly into Jonathon's without a flicker of his own.

"Well now, I 'spect you'll be wantin' to know what's going on—why we put that sort of SOS out for you on the news last night? Well the top and bottom of the matter is we want to express our gratitude, yes that's it, and we want to thank you for what you did. Took a lot of courage that did and a lot of important and wealthy people are in your debt this morning 'cause of it. So, 'twould be churlish of us not to recognise the fact now wouldn't it? Some has even asked us for your identity so as they can thank you more personal like. Up 'til now we haven't been able to say much about you even if we wanted to, on account of the fact of you wanting to remain anonymous, not giving your name over the phone like, and we'll respect that, course we will—even though we know who you are." Jonathon felt less than amazed at this disclosure but kept a steady look. "Oh yes, we knows who you are alright," rejoined the superintendent. "Got a brief phone call from Hampshire yesterday saying as how we should expect you like—you're building up quite a reputation for yourself from all accounts young man. But I shan't give your name to no one—no, not at all. 'Twould be more than my job's worth to do that and no mistake—'less o'course you says I can," said superintendent.

"Thank you superintendent," said Jonathon, still smiling. "I'm pleased to accept your vote of thanks, but you must be in no doubt about my wishing to remain anonymous. I do not wish for my name to be given out to anyone, I hope you and your associates will understand that. I merely did what I considered to be the right and proper thing to do at the time—what most people would have done in my place I'm sure. But as for anyone thinking they owe me a debt of gratitude, no, certainly not," said Jonathon, adamantly.

"Well if that's the way you are wanting it young man then we will say no more about the matter. But it beats me as to what you are afraid of, a big chap like you. After all you did a great service, no not to just a few people but to the nation as a whole so to speak. That's why I'm here you see—could have sent a police constable, but no, the powers that be they insisted that I do it myself. Still I can do no more than thank you, and I've already done that. Deserves recognition though to my way of thinking that you do. But I'm not here to put pressure on you, so we'll say no more. 'Twill be a sorry day indeed when we stop expressing our thanks, hope it never 'appens. I'll bid you farewell now young man, it's been a privilege meeting you, hope our paths will cross again someday," said the superintendent, as he turned to go.

All at once Jonathon felt rather perplexed and realised he had been well and truly bamboozled by the superintendent and that he was no further forward in gaining the knowledge he sought than he had been at the beginning of the meeting.

"Just a minute superintendent," called Jonathon, firmly. "Before you take your leave, you mentioned I had done a service to the nation; now that sounds a trifle over the top to me. All I did was to report an incident which I considered was being carried out under suspicious circumstances, no act of heroism here or anything close to it, yet you heap praises upon me as if I'd saved the lives of the entire royal family. So, what exactly was in those packages superintendent? What is it that has caused you to come all this way to meet with me this morning? Nothing else better to do with your valuable time superintendent?"

The superintendent came abruptly to a full stop and spun round to face Jonathon once again and continued with his wide grin.

"So you are inquisitive enough to want to know that, are you? But not enough to step forward like what you should. Well Jonathon Fisher, I can't divulge that bit of information, no not even to yourself see. Oh dear me no, can't do that, more than my job's worth that would be me 'andsome. That's for someone else to do see? G'bye then." And with that he left; and a most bewildered young man remained staring at the policeman's back as he went.

After quite some little while of pondering Jonathon finally decided to leave in favour of finding the ladies and so with the acrid smell of fish and the sea filling his nostrils he left the quayside and walked back through the town.

— CHAPTER TWELVE —

Number thirteen Hollyhock Close was only a ten minute walk away from the harbour; even so, climbing the extremely steep hillside from the town was an invigorating exercise for the athletic young man.

The Payne's residence was unusually large for the local area, with extensive outbuildings at the rear of the property, one of which was used by Jack Payne as a workshop where he carried out all manner of repair work and the production of all sorts of miscellaneous items. It was here that Jonathon found his uncle idly chatting away to his mothers.

The uncle's enflamed eyes lit up as Jonathon entered the disorganised workshop.

"Well if it isn't my favourite great nephew," said Jack Payne, as he wiped away from his eyes some aggravating specks of sawdust that had been bothering him.

"Hello Uncle Jack, good to see you once again," said Jonathon, cheerily. "How are you? Must say you're looking in pretty good shape."

"As well as can be expected you know Jonathon, just able to sit up and take a little nourishment," laughed Jack, as his large red face creased to the nape of his neck.

Jack Payne was a substantial man standing well over six feet with a huge corpulent figure, a bespectacled face and a head that was completely devoid of hair. He had a jovial nature, laughing at almost anything and was always pleased to receive visitors, which were varied and often.

"Goodness Jack," said his stepsister Lady B. "You've been using that old stock in phrase joke for as long as I can remember. Don't you think it about time it was used up? It must have whiskers on it by now," criticized Lady B., with a discrete chuckle.

Jack Payne ignored the impolite remark and turned his attention to his beautiful niece.

"Anyway what about this young lad of yours Felicity, will he ever stop growing? It beats me what you feed him on up there in Suffolk."

"I think he has just about stopped trying to reach the sky at last uncle," answered Felicity. "But I have to say he does have a strong liking for his food."

The boring enquiries that one expects on occasions of this nature poured out, compelling all central characters to yawn and run for shelter.

"And how did you get on at university Jonathon," this was the second of the many tedious questions Jonathon was fast tiring of. *'Why was everyone so blasted interested anyway,'* he thought to himself.

"Only no one has said if you've finished or not," rejoined Jack Payne, labouring the enquiry.

"Very well thank you Uncle Jack," said Jonathon blandly. *'Please don't ask me how I got on,'* once again to himself.

"And how did you fair, pass everything did you?"

"Yes luckily," came the reply.

"Why are you being so modest Jonathon?"

'Really grandmama you are as bad as your brother, why on earth can't you drop the subject in favour of something moderately interesting?' Thought Jonathon, feeling as if he would prefer to go up in a puff of smoke or vanish into thin air and he was beginning to wish he could do either.

"He did extremely well actually Jack."

'Why oh why couldn't this woman let it go? Doesn't she realise how embarrassing it is for everyone?'

"Finished with a first class honours degree in biology as you probably know and then went on to do his masters last year." Lady B. would have gone on and on about her grandson's great academic achievements had Jonathon, knowingly, not knocked over a pot of paint so that the subject might be changed. But it didn't happen. After Jonathon had apologised for the apparent mishap and his uncle had told him not to worry, as if he did, the subject was encouraged to rejuvenate itself.

Fifteen minutes later with a "well done m'boy" from Uncle Jack the subject was at last dropped, very much to Jonathon's relief and the situation resumed a more acceptable theme.

It had not escaped Jonathon's notice that his meeting with the police earlier had not been alluded to since his arrival. *'Could this be something the ladies were deliberately playing down not wishing to admit my own involvement in the escapade for some reason best known to them?'* he asked himself. *'Or maybe they feel that the relative just talks too much to anyone willing to listen and considered diplomacy to be more appropriate.'*

Jack Payne had spend the biggest part of his working life as a mechanical inventor confining his talents to domestic appliances with several patented items to his credit, all of which had little or no fascination for Jonathon; he being at one with mother nature's machinery rather than that of mans. However, Jonathon did appreciate that there was a place for certain innovative contraptions to enable the cogs of life to run more smoothly and with this in his mind he posed a question to his uncle that he had been turning over in his head for some considerable time.

"How are things on the invention scene uncle?" asked Jonathon, cautiously. "Are you still keeping busy since your retirement?"

"Things have been pretty quiet on the whole as you might well imagine," said Jack, wiping his large hands on an oily cloth. "Manufacturing companies are seeking alternative sources for their new design work. At last they appear to be getting the message that I'm not interested anymore. So I'm confined to using the gadgets instead of inventing them. You're aunt, she keeps me busy and out of mischief so I'm never at a loss for something to do. Oh I potter about the old workshop most of the time but don't get myself involved in anything too serious. Why do you ask Jonathon? Got something in mind have you?"

"As a matter of fact something did enter my head some time ago which I thought may well appeal to you. As you probably know I'm interest in freshwater biology mostly river and pond life and I need an apparatus which would enable me to stay under water for longer periods of time. Something small and less cumbersome than the conventional oxygen cylinders," said Jonathon.

"Well now, there have been great improvements in underwater technology since the war. Underwater–sub aqua clubs I believe they're called are springing up all over the place and very popular the sport is becoming too. I do believe that one is being set up here in Brixham—I shall have to check that out. The equipment they use is the most up to date available, I've seen pictures of it as I suppose you have yourself Jonathon, still seems a mite cumbersome though doesn't it? I don't know what else can be done though really–not if you're looking for something less awkward and as small as you say to give you more freedom. Don't think it's possible to compress oxygen that much. Look, you leave it with me, I shall hike around to see what I can come up with—something may spring to mind—it usually does.

"Now let's see if we can rustle up some refreshments for everyone, come on, let's find Eileen, she'll have something in mind no doubt," said Jack, licking his lips.

The family spent the whole afternoon enjoying the warmth of the day just walking and talking about this and that, about times past and about those yet to come, but not once did anyone mention the smuggling incident, even though the previous night's news reader had made the matter public knowledge. And not once were they hounded by reporters of any description.

Not until that evening, when the Fisher family had found themselves once more in the Northcliff Hotel and once again enjoying an aperitif before their evening meal did the subject get an airing. Jonathon had spent some time in telling the mothers about his meeting with the superintendent, of how the details and nature of the smuggled items had not been revealed to him and how certain unidentified people were seemingly queuing up to express their appreciation.

Lady B. suddenly stood up almost spilling the drink she was about to sip. Then she resumed her seated posture at once and composed herself.

"Let's go over the events once again shall we? Something has sprung to mind. I believe you mentioned Jonathon, that the packages were of similar size and shape, that they were quite light in weight and that they were fairly flat," said the very nice lady excitedly.

"I don't remember saying that the packages were flat at all grandmama. But now that you mention it, perhaps they were flattish. They were certainly not cube shaped anyway, but maybe halfway between the two," interrupted Jonathon.

The lady's excitement gave way to a more pensive look then almost at once she changed back again and continued with her original excited appearance.

"Well all of this, plus your interview with the police this morning, despite it's seemingly negative outcome, clearly points in one direction and confirms my opinion," said Lady B., her voice maintaining it's usual steadiness of tone suddenly erupted into a verbal crescendo, startling her offspring alarmingly.

"Paintings!" she exclaimed, with exhilaration. "Why ever didn't it come to me before? The wretched solution has been hovering around in my head all day long but just would not present itself. Small paintings, perhaps miniatures of sorts, it has to be, no other explanation fits. There must have been many works of art gone missing over the years. Some thefts have made the headlines others have not. Some of these pictures were stolen under the noses of careless owners, some misappropriated in other dubious ways. But all have been taken away from this country in order to swell the collections of greedy, selfish people in many parts of the world. Not necessarily major works I'll grant you, but works important enough to arouse the self-indulgent interest of fanatical collectors, especially those situated on the continent; the trip across the channel is just too easy you see—yes that must be it," concluded the very nice lady with a triumphant expression on her face.

"But why bring them back again into the country from where they were taken in the first place and en masse at that?

"It just doesn't add up somehow," said a doubtful Felicity.

"Oh I should think that one of the so called 'collectors' has died thus leaving the heir, who may not share his predecessor's fanaticism, with a major problem to sort out. I suppose the pictures have been returned to this country for redistribution, some probably bound for America and others for sale on the black market here in this country. How unfortunate it was for them that Jonathon happened to be passing by at the time," said a more restrained Lady B.

"OK, I'm with you so far, but why the secrecy with the authorities?" asked Jonathon.

"Insurance, that will be the insurance. Don't you see? If anyone has something valuable stolen, then the obvious course of action would be to make a claim on the appropriate insurance company, right? Now let us just suppose, for argument's sake, that all or part of the stolen items be they paintings or anything else for that matter, turn up say fifty years later, or maybe even longer, would anyone hand back the insurance claim? The police obviously don't think so. You or I probably would, but I guess that we would be in the minority and it has to be faced that there are indeed many unscrupulous people who would not. My guess is that the biggest majority of people wouldn't even consider it. Look, we are not talking of just a few pounds here, we are probably talking of millions, absolutely fortunes; and that explains the reticence we are finding on behalf of the authorities," said Lady B., placing her hands to her lips in prayer like fashion thoughtfully.

Felicity was still looking most dubious about the explanation her mother had just stated.

"But surely the police have an obligation to throw this sort of matter into the public arena," she said, "especially if what you say is correct and that so much money is involved."

"Yes of course they do; but don't let's allow ourselves to be deceived. Policemen, of whatever rank, are human beings first and foremost and as such they can be bought, if the price is right. Yes, corruption is not too strong a word I think," said Lady B.

"Well if that's the way of things, then maybe I should step forward and at least try to put a stop to this nonsense," said Jonathon.

"I fancy this needs to be thought through a little more thoroughly before we take any further action," rejoined Lady Barbara. "You see there is another category of victims; these being the owners who did not have their pictures insured in the first place. For them it would be a most genuine embarrassment indeed and it would be very difficult for them to have their property returned, especially as the police seem to be in no hurry to make the public fully aware of the situation by stating precisely the nature of the contraband be it paintings or something else. I doubt very much if the amiable Superintendent Dobson wanted merely to extend his gratitude to you Jonathon; what stuff and nonsense. His aim was to positively identify you and to find out if you had any idea at all exactly what was being smuggled. How relieved he must have felt to find you wanted no part in any seedy reward even if it was only a verbal or written gratification. He really didn't try hard to convince you, did he? If his intentions were indeed genuine he should have been quite emphatic about you stepping forward for recognition, even to the point of ignoring your insistence on anonymity, there are ways you know.

"What joy he must have felt to discover that you had no conception of the contents of those waterproof packages. If I am right, then he would have been rather busy this afternoon contacting those owners who he considers might be able to identify and prove ownership. I'm certain he will be doing a thorough job of it, relying of course upon those pictures that slip the net. Yes the more I think about it the more I am convinced that it would be prudent to wait awhile, just a few days, maybe a week or two before we make our move," said a very convinced and satisfied Lady Barbara.

Both Felicity and Jonathon recognised their mother's ingenuity and her masterly approach to the solution, presupposing that the assumption was correct in the first place of course but it did sound, to them, to be flawless, for the time being anyway. Even so, a worried look did briefly appear on the daughter's face which she failed to disguise, she being inclined to express her doubts at any given opportunity.

"You said that you considered it more appropriate for us to wait a few days before we make our move. Well I personally fail to see what good that would do. Surely it would be much better if we strike now and catch them unawares," said Felicity.

"Not at all darling. Actually I'm inclined to favour a couple of weeks minimum. That should give sufficient time for the jelly to set so to speak. We, acting to soon, will enable the worms to wriggle out by playing innocent before they have committed themselves. Yes, I think we can safely wait until we are back in Bergholt, when we will be able to seek some professional advice from someone who knows what course of action is to be taken.

"In the meantime, I suggest that we enjoy what is left of our short break before we head for Sutton Scotney," said the very nice lady.

Two days later the trio called in again at the Payne's house to pay their further respects and to say their goodbyes.

"When will we be seeing you all again," asked Jack.

"We'll try not to leave it quite so long next time," said Lady B. "maybe before Christmas --- of course you are both always welcome to visit with us, you know that. You never have! And now that you both have time on your hands there is no real excuse is there?"

"Yes I know B --- I know --- but you also know me! Always been a terrible stick in the mud, haven't left these Brixham boundaries in years. Still we'll surprise you all one of these days, you see if we don't.

"Now when I've made some sort of progress with the little exercise young Jonathon here has presented me with I'll give you a ring then perhaps you will pop down again to see if it's what you are looking for," said Jack.

Lady B. Felicity and Jonathon piled into the freshly laundered Bentley and moved smoothly away with Jonathon at the wheel and the two ladies waving sedately from the window.

— CHAPTER THIRTEEN —

The long haul back to Sutton Scotney from Devon was pleasant enough and everyone in the big black Bentley were relaxed as they cruised along at fifty miles an hour. The weather was clement and the company congenial and all were looking forward to spending an interesting weekend with Ada Hutchins at Akworth House.

"Have you ever met Susan Hutchins mama," enquired Felicity, knowing full well that her mother had not but wishing to open a conversation about the family they were about to meet.

"No dear of course I haven't. I thought you appreciated the fact that I didn't even know that Ada Hutchins was married, she certainly wasn't when we first met all those years ago and we have never been in touch with one another since those halcyon days. I've always thought of her as a devout spinster with no gentleman callers at all. I must say, life is full of surprises," answered Lady B.

Felicity's ploy in ferreting for Akworth intelligence was soon terminated in favour of sterner issues.

"Would anyone care to stop for a break and maybe take on board some light refreshment? Any noses need powdering?" asked Jonathon, light heartedly as they sped through the Devon countryside and into Dorset.

"Excellent idea darling that would be wonderful. Where are we exactly?" asked Felicity

"We are approaching Tollpuddle mother the place is steeped in history so it might make for an interesting stop," said Jonathon, trying to sound helpful. "Look, there's a quaint little public house coming up on our left; I'll pull in there so that we may fortify ourselves, that's if no one has any objections."

The big black Bentley glided majestically to a halt in an allotted parking area to the side of the inn and the eager passengers and Jonathon eased themselves from the car and walked slowly to the front of the building admiring the exquisite surroundings as they went.

The Owl's Nest appeared to be a popular inn of some considerable age and character. Its low thatched roof hung wide of the white cob walls on which thick variegated ivy clung with a congregation of house sparrows playing and squabbling noisily within its vines.

Eventually the trio entered a small hallway by way of a heavily painted open outer doorway that looked as though its woodwork had not been exposed to the light of day since the time it was first decorated. The hallway led directly to the long narrow lounge tastefully decorated with age old elegance but which had a certain lingering musty smell about it and the well trodden, uneven wear on the flagstones seemed to give fair warning to any unwary customers. A collection of gleaming horse brasses hung neatly from beetle-bored beams and an assortment of elegant figurines and a variety of paintings of owls of every pose completed the old-world charm of the public house.

Lady Barbara, being the first to enter the inner sanctum for the house's elite customers, chose a round table next to the small latticed window for them to sit and promptly occupied the seat facing the blue cloudless sky with her back to the other tables in the room. Felicity and Jonathon were seated either side of her and each began to search through the menu which was decorated with a handsome tawny owl upon its glossy cover.

"Did either of you notice the name of this place when we arrived?" asked Felicity, mischievously.

"Yes I did mother, it is called The Owl's Nest, hence the picture that you see before you," replied Jonathon, aiding his mother with her tongue in cheek question.

"That's what I thought, so why the picture of an owl in flight?" mussed Felicity, smiling.

"I really don't know mother, does it matter? Now are we hungry thirsty or both? Speaking for myself I feel famished. However, not to spoil the jolly old appetite for dinner later I shall opt for a couple of roast beef sandwiches with lashings of mustard, all washed down with a glass of cool ale," said Jonathon, voraciously.

"Yes that does sound rather appetising but just the single sandwich for me. What about you mama, does that appeal?" said Felicity, closing her menu.

"Yes please that will be lovely, the same as Felicity please Jonathon," replied Lady B.

"But first the powder room I think would be in order," said Felicity, rising from the table and straightening her skirt. She glanced out of the corner of her eye around her as she hastened to the ladies room while Jonathon walked casually to the bar to order luncheon.

As Felicity glided across the room, three pairs of eyes followed her every step, focused intently on the closed door she had entered and then stared at her unerringly as she made the return trip. Jonathon rejoined the table at the same time as his mother with a perplexed look on his face. Mother and son seated themselves comfortably then Jonathon leant forward to speak.

"Did you happen to notice those three gentlemen in the opposite corner mother? Their eyes didn't leave you for one second as you crossed the room. I am fully aware of your stunning beauty but that was most impolite by any standards. Maybe a quiet word with them wouldn't go amiss," said Jonathon, looking extremely annoyed.

Before Jonathon was able to get fully to his feet his mother prevented his further movements with a delicate restraining motion of her hand.

"No don't do that darling, I really didn't see them at all and I certainly do not see the need for you to make a fuss," said Felicity with a sympathetic smile.

Jonathon and his mother sat sideways on to the three strangers and Lady B. had her back to them but neither turned their heads to glance across the room in that direction.

Jonathon now felt churned up inside because of what he adjudged to be a rude intrusion upon his mother's privacy and was very quick to respond.

"All the same mother, I refuse to just stand around and watch any man demonstrating brash discourtesy to either of you," he said.

At last Lady B. decided to take a hand in quelling what she considered to be no more than a harmless irritation, determining that Jonathon was making far too much fuss and mountains and mole hills sprang to mind.

"Jonathon, both your mother and indeed myself have had to tolerate bad behaviour from a motley section of the male population ever since our adolescence and we have completely learned how to handle situations of this nature. Trifling bad manners really do not bother us in the slightest, so please exercise some restraint and calm yourself," said an affable Lady B.

A sudden movement from the table opposite caused Jonathon to turn his head.

"Well let's see if this bothers you then," said Jonathon, grinning. "One of the three has left the table and is heading in our direction.

The man who crossed the floor slowly but deliberately toward the Fisher table was tall, sturdily proportioned but not overweight, with blonde, wavy, well groomed hair. He was casually dressed but smart and with an estimated age of forty-five years he possessed appealing looks.

Jonathon rose from his chair as the man approached and extended his hand in a polite and friendly manner.

"Jonathon Fisher, how may I be of service to you sir?" asked Jonathon, determined not to allow his uneasy feelings show.

"Joseph John Cabin," replied the tall stranger, a little nervous at first and looking straight into the eyes of the taller man. "I thank you but you cannot, be of service to me, that is. I needed to offer my sincere apologies to the young lady for our unforgivable display of bad behaviour when she crossed the room a moment ago. Staring at her like three pubescent juveniles, quite abysmal conduct, unforgivable. But not without some justification I hasten to add, after all, it is extremely rare that one sees beauty that is able to delight the senses as well as the mind. And for there to be two such beautiful creatures gracing this relic of a place and at the same time as it were—extraordinary, even unprecedented I should say," said Cabin in a most charming way.

"Most gallant of you Mr Cabin even if it is more than a little over the top," replied Felicity, just as the sandwiches and beer was delivered to the table. "However, my mother and I both thank you for the compliments; and now if you would be kind enough to excuse us we should very much like to partake of our refreshments," said Felicity, completely unflustered.

"Yes of course, please pardon the intrusion," said Cabin, and began to leave as if to return to his friends, feeling somewhat taken aback by Felicity's curt response to his excessive compliment. Then turning back once again he queried the statement. "Your mother?" he said hesitantly. "Surely you must be mocking me."

"Now why should I wish to mock you Mr Cabin? This is the Lady Barbara Fisher-Jones, my mother. And this is Jonathon Fisher my son. And now, if you please?" said Felicity, deliberately not disclosing her own name and with a feeling of considerable elation.

A look of total bewilderment swept across Cabin's imposing face almost twisting it into a state of distortion.

"Yes—yes of course," he said. And then as an after thought added, "so sorry," he walked away to his table and to the safety of his friends, dumbstruck.

Once again enjoying the privacy of their luncheon the Fishers talked quietly among themselves relieved that the friendly intrusion was at last at an end.

"Well darling," said Lady B. happily, "that was very fittingly handled. But I always thought that you abhorred pomposity in all its shapes and guises. But to my way of thinking that was indeed an admirable demonstration of the subject."

"Not at all mama," returned Felicity with the merest hint of self-satisfaction still evident in her beautiful eyes. "I was just putting on the style a little that was all. Particularly effective when the wolves are howling I always find."

"Putting on the style? Rubbish, balderdash and brick dust mother. You were flirting with the man, playing at being hard to get I should say," interjected an aroused Jonathon.

"That is no way for a Christian man to speak to his mother Jonathon, you should show some respect," retorted Felicity, laughing.

"Well now, putting on the style, flirting, or just plain pomposity, it doesn't matter which it was as it had little or no effect, because our friend Cabin is returning hoping for more rebuttals it seems while his two companions are leaving. Now would you like me to politely show him the door mother or are you still happy to battle it out on your own?" said a vexed Jonathon.

"No darling, no scenes if you please. Let me handle this," replied Felicity, by this time looking a little anxious.

Joseph Cabin's stride faltered briefly as he approached the Fisher table once again. The look on his face was, to some measure, showing a nervous strain and his complexion appeared slightly pallid with small beads of perspiration clearly visible on his forehead.

"I'm sorry, but I seem to have got off on the wrong foot with you," started Joseph Cabin, his voice seemed laboured and he spoke with difficulty.

"Not sorry yet again," interposed Lady B., turning her head toward the intruder. "Mr Cabin, you are in mortal danger of spending the rest of your life apologising if you are not at all careful. What is it this time? Not more compliments I hope." A hint of a sardonic smile played upon the very nice ladies mouth.

"Yes, most unfortunate—I mean, no not at all—look, please take my card; if ever I can be of assistance to any of you—at any time at all, then—please do not hesitate to call me," stammered Cabin, as he forced a small business card into Felicity's hand and left hastily.

Seconds later, Jonathon turned his head sideways in the direction of the small latticed window to watch a very new, very bright red Jaguar car as it moved slowly out of the car park, with a distraught Joseph Cabin looking back from the rear seat.

"I'm sure he would have been a most pleasant gentleman, given the opportunity. He seemed slightly nervous to me and allowed himself to be easily intimidated; unwittingly I'm sure. Anyway, what is printed on the card Felicity, anything of interest?" asked Lady B.

"It says 'Jones Cabin and Jones. A firm of solicitors. Presented by Joseph J Cabin.' It also carries a Colchester address and telephone number." Felicity read the card over once more then placed it carefully in her purse.

"I must say the name doesn't ring any bells with me, it must be a fairly new partnership. I thought I was aware of all the solicitors in both Ipswich and Colchester, as I say; it must be a new firm just starting up. Dear, dear, what an opportunity we have missed; we might easily have obtained some free advice on the smuggling saga from him—what a pity," said Lady B., with mocked disappointment.

"Well all is not completely lost, he did say we were to contact him if any of us felt that he could be of service didn't he? Well we could easily do that if we've a mind to, after all, Colchester is only eleven miles away from Bergholt," said Felicity.

Jonathon looked directly at his mother and then at his grandmother in a mode of total disbelief.

"Am I to understand that your intentions are to pursue this acquaintance mother? To put it bluntly I certainly should feel more than a little disappointed in you if you were to go chasing after this Cabin fellow. After all we do have certain standards and principles to maintain—well don't we?" said Jonathon, clearly worried.

"Certainly not darling. It was just that mama intimated that we had lost a golden opportunity for some free advice and I merely pointed out to her that we hadn't, that was all. You clearly have drawn an instant dislike to Mr Cabin and I can understand that. But really Jonathon, you have to stop worrying about me. As you so often point out, you are now an adult and more than capable of looking after yourself. Well the same applies to me," retorted Felicity, feeling quietly annoyed.

"Touché," responded Jonathon, with a grin and said no more about the matter.

As soon as they had eaten the food and drank the ale the Fishers departed The Owl's Nest, settled themselves comfortably inside the Bentley and resumed the trip to Sutton Scotney.

— CHAPTER FOURTEEN —

The remainder of the journey was accomplished under some duress, not only was Felicity still feeling Jonathon's intrusion into her private thoughts to be unwarranted and insensitive but she also seemed to have taken a liking to Joseph Cabin with his curious hypersensitivity which undoubtedly would never be aired. So she continued the afternoon in relative silence while her mother and her son had all but forgotten the episode at the Owl's Nest.

Jonathon passed the turning he had taken four days earlier that had led them to the village green and instead he took the following turning right leading through the wide wrought iron gates of Akworth House.

The driveway to the large, ancient residence was mainly of stone and shingle, with sizeable potholes that needed filling and which caused the suspension on the Bentley to groan in protest at having to deal with such an obstacle course even though its pace was steady. The rough track, for that is the only real description one could possibly use, was hardly a proper built-up road as it was covered by a thin layer of tarmac only in part and did not do justice to the place to which it was obliged to serve. It was three hundred yards long at the very least with a large lake on the left hand side surrounded by lawns and landscaped with a variety of trees interspersed with a multitude of shrubs. The lush, but untidy grass was repeated on the right hand side also, splashed with overgrown crimson rhododendrons in full bloom.

The car drew up to the front of the house, just as Ada Hutchins was walking, with much difficulty, across the gravel to greet her guests. The lady of the house appeared to look somewhat older, more tired to Lady B. than when they met a few days ago even though the huge smile she carried on her wrinkled face was continuous; and she appeared to have greater difficulty in the way she walked, now using both her hands to support her bosomy body on the strong ebony stick.

"Oh how wonderful to see you all, welcome, welcome," she called, before anyone could leave the car. Lady B. was the first one out closely followed by her daughter; both smoothing their clothes quickly as they did so. Mrs Hutchins immediately threw her arms around Lady B. being particularly careful to hold on to her stick with one hand, and the very nice lady responded with equal eagerness. But it wasn't until Felicity had nearly been wrestled to the ground that Jonathon decided to risk a gentle bear hug or two himself. He quietly exited the car and casually wandered round to be greeted by his hostess.

"This is my son Jonathon, Mrs Hutchins," said Felicity, with a look on her face that betrayed the love she felt for her son; even though she did consider him to be overstepping the mark at times. "We are moderately proud of him," she added, with a hint of a smile.

"And so you should be my dear, what an incredible specimen of manhood he most certainly is. Hello Jonathon, I'm so very pleased to meet you," she said, taking his hand in the both of hers to steady herself and looking up into his grey blue eyes.

"Likewise Mrs Hutchins," replied Jonathon, bending down to kiss her cheek.

"Ada, please, you must all call me Ada," she said, as she beamed all over her wrinkled face. Then turning to Jonathon again she continued, "you really are a fine looking man Jonathon, and handsome with it. I can certainly see how good looks run in the Fisher family."

Jonathon smiled politely and walked towards the Bentley's boot in order to remove the luggage but Ada, noticing his action intervened at once.

"Please leave the suitcases where they are Jonathon. We haven't a chauffeur or a butler anymore but we do employ a handyman who will be more than capable of carrying your cases up to your rooms. Now then, first things first—a good hot cup of tea I think, to bring you all up to scratch after your long and tiring journey. Everything is ready for you and the kettle about boiled so if you'll all follow me," said Ada, as she hobbled away, carefully supported by the very nice lady.

They all walked around the side of the house, paying little attention to the weather worn heavy front door where the two ladies had first met with Ada. Lady B. did steal a glance, however, and registered its dejected appearance as she longed to use that familiar portal.

Slowly they made their way into a spacious kitchen where a huge black kettle was singing merrily away on the Aga cooker hob. The back wall of the kitchen seemed to be totally covered with a massive Welsh dresser festooned with pink and blue willow patterned china among a fine collection of brass jugs and jelly moulds. The wide floor appeared to be relatively new with beige ceramic tiles occupying its full width and upon which stood the enormous kitchen table that completed every old fashioned kitchen in bygone days. Its bleached, scrub worn surface had a grain which stood proud, emphasising its character and the continual labour of love that had been regularly plied ungrudgingly to its façade over the many years. The whole room had a warm glow about it bringing security to any who sat within its homely walls. Even the variegated spider plant dangled its young down the dainty whitewashed walls as a friendly gesture to all who entered. This was indeed a sanctuary to bring solace to the most troubled of souls and rest to the tired soma.

Two hundred, it seemed, freshly and meticulously cut sandwiches overflowed the two large white meat dishes in the centre of the table; mixed sandwiches, filled with chicken, ham, egg and beef. Sandwiches to titillate the most insensitive of pallets, sandwiches enough to feed the village. And biscuits too and fancy home-made cakes aplenty for all to enjoy. This was a trial run before the main event, a period of time during which hostess and guests could become better acquainted. A large blue enamel teapot, already primed with Ceylon's finest leaves was filled with boiling water from the black kettle. They all sat around the table and began to demolish the sandwiches and to drink the tea.

After they had had their fill of food and had emptied the pot for a second time, Felicity suggested that she and Jonathon might explore the gardens to allow Lady B. and Ada some privacy to chat over old times and revel in nostalgia and maybe bring each other up to date.

"What a truly lovely family you have Barbara, and so devoted to one another too it seems," said Ada, after mother and son had left the room to explore the garden.

"Yes, I like to think so. But as in all families we have our moments. What about your daughter Susan, when can we expect to meet her? I certainly hope that we will be able to do so before we return to Suffolk," said Lady B., piercingly searching for the answer to Ada's mystery in Susan.

"Unfortunately there has been a change in plan Barbara; she won't be arriving here until next Tuesday, but at least she will be staying with me for the remainder of the week. Actually, I was hoping that you might consider extending your stay for a few more days or for as long as you want to, of course. It's going to be so good to have you around the old place once again and I should so much like you all to meet Susan, she's such a wonderful girl. Oh I know I shouldn't say so but she really is, I love her so very much and I know that Felicity and Susan will get on well together. So what do you say, will you all stay a little longer than you had planned?" implored the hostess, with a hopeful gaze.

Lady B. looked past the head of Ada to where a small spider was crawling up the white washed wall and smiled to herself speculating what secrets were known to spiders.

"I really don't see why we shouldn't extend our stay by a few more days Ada. As far as I am aware, neither Felicity nor I have anything we need rush home to take care of. I'm not so sure about Jonathon however; he has a boring hearing to attend soon, not at all sure when exactly, but one telephone call should settle it," said Lady B.

"I couldn't help but notice the curiosity in your face when you asked about Susan just then Barbara. You were wondering what has happened to my dear daughter's father weren't you. Well it's only right that you should know, and not only that but I really would like you to know, if you understand my meaning. Oh dear, I'm really not putting this at all well am I?" said Ada, fidgeting with a circular earring, swivelling it backwards and forwards in the lobe of her ear. "You see Sir Nigel and I were very fond of one another. Oh no, we weren't together, as they say today, when you visited here that long hot summer all those years ago. But after you went away, you seem to have left a void within the hearts of both of us. So, gradually over the years we became closer to one another—very close—and eventually we became two lovers, oh—not in a sordid way at all, but in the truest sense.

"We never did get married, however; I don't think his family would have approved; you know, the class thing. But we really did love each other, he me and I him.

"And so, just twenty-five years ago, I was able to present him with a beautiful little daughter. She was only five pounds when she was born and we had some difficulty with her for the first six months, being totally confined to the maternity hospital for all that time. But gradually she gained her strength and I was able to bring her home. Oh, what a day that was Barbara, we were the most proud parents imaginable. He was so happy, my, but he was happy and I was too of course, but especially him. You see, after his wife had died, that was long before I came to live here, he never dreamt he would ever have a child of his own; she was barren you see, and so you can guess the effect that Susan's arrival had on him. They were inseparable, Barbara, quite inseparable. At times I thought that she meant more to him than I did, well maybe she did, I don't know. All I do know is that we were so very happy together, just the three of us.

"We lost him just over two years ago, the weather was bitterly cold that year and we were ankle deep in snow for most of the winter, but it wasn't the weather that killed him. One minute he was fit and well, the next he had a massive heart attack. We called the ambulance of course and he was still alive when they took him but he didn't survive the journey, yes he was dead on arrival as the hospital put it. We were devastated, probably me more than Susan but she did take it bad, I know she did. But I still miss him Barbara; miss him more than I can say: I expect I always will.

"He left everything to Susan in his will you know, the whole estate, everything. He left me nothing. Oh yes, I am able to stay here until I meet up with him again, but Susan inherited his fortune and this place, nobody else had a mention even his brothers and their children in Suffolk near where you live, they didn't get a mention either; must have had their noses put out I should think, serve them right that's what I say, they're a snobbish bunch at the best of times." Ada forced a smile and wiped a tear as it stole down her face and paused awhile before she continued.

"Where was I?" she said, at last. "Oh I know. This place! It's all but worn out now Barbara, like me it's getting old and needs some money spending on it if it's going to live a little longer, especially the inside. Susan said she would see to it, 'sort things out,' that's what she said and I know she will, she's like that, wants everything to be properly looked after you know; like her father in that respect.

"Anyway that's enough about me and my worries. How about you? Why isn't Felicity's father with you, or Felicity's husband for that matter?"

"Well now, since you have opened up all your family secrets to me, I suppose it only right that I reciprocate; although anyone but yourself would get a totally different version of the story from me, I can assure you of that.

"It seems that both Felicity and I are very alike in as much as we both have a child as a result of some loneliness, a warm summer's day and a moment of lustful weakness; although champagne did play a minor role in Felicity's case I believe, which regrettably, I cannot claim in mine. And as far as the worthy gentlemen are concerned, they are completely unaware of their fatherhood; that is as far as we know they are unaware, and long may it remain so. We are both complete individuals you see and do not appear to need the male gender in our lives, except for our darling Jonathon of course, and he seems to be a complete person also; at least I have never heard him speak the name of any other female companion," said Lady B., being careful not to disclose too much personal information.

Ada fidgeted some more with her earring uneasily, all the time concerned that her personal account outweighed that of her guest by a considerable measure and worrying if her indiscretion could bring about some hindrance to the reunion which she hoped would prove to be lasting. Also her concern bordered on the moral comparison between Lady B. and Felicity's conception with that of her own.

"That sounds very cosy to me Barbara," was all the response that came from Ada for that immediate instant and so she lapsed into yet another moment of silence, pondering how to continue without seeming to be censuring her guests in any way.

"I'm sure it doesn't matter how our children reach us only that we love them and share the happiness they bring," said Ada, at last, conscious of the fact that she had avoided displaying her own true thoughts of disapproval. "And yours are certainly providing you with love and happiness Barbara; I can clearly see that in all your happy smiling faces when you are together. Still one never knows exactly what may loom up around the corner–there is still enough time yet for both you and Felicity to find the man of your dreams.

"Anyway, let's put men aside for a moment and concentrate on the two of us shall we? Perhaps I should give you a guided tour of the house, I'm sure your memory will have deserted you after all the years that have past since you were last here," said Ada.

"Yes that would be lovely, but may we enter the house from the front door? I have been hoping that my memory of the place is still intact and after all, that is how we always entered the house when last I was here and never via the kitchen," said Lady B., trying to suppress any undignified excitement.

"Yes of course we can. I made sure that it was unlocked before you arrived; we hardly ever use it these days you see, but everywhere should be clean and tidy, so come along, you follow me," returned Ada, gathering her ebony stick and walking slowly toward the door quite unable to contain her enthusiasm.

They left the cosy kitchen and wandered out into the immediate garden and followed the gravelled path they had walked earlier and arrived at the front door just as a familiar figure was struggling with two heavy suit cases.

"Bill Marks," exclaimed the very nice lady, with marked surprise. "You didn't tell me that you worked here. How very nice to see you again, how are you?"

The blushing young man was equally taken aback.

"You didn't ask madam, but yes I do work here—and might I add how nice it is to see you as well," said Bill, resting the cases for a while.

"You are in need of help with those hefty cases Bill. My grandson will be along shortly, why don't you wait for him to give you a hand?" said Lady B. quite concerned.

"No no madam, I shall be alright. Have to earn me keep y'know," said Bill, picking up the two suitcases once again and entered the house by the large oak door that Ada was shakily holding open for him.

Lady B. promptly mounted the steps to stand beside and support her host.

"What a very agreeable young man he is," said Lady B., smiling broadly and nodding her head after Bill entered the house. "It was he who first directed us to Akworth House you know."

"Yes that's right, Bill told me all about it the next day. He is a lovely lad Barbara, keeping me amused with his tales and local gossip, he's quite a card that one. I don't know if I should believe him half of the time though, what with some of the things he comes out with. I don't mean that he tells fibs of course, just elaborates on the truth a bit to make me laugh, that's all. But he is a treasure to have about the place, he really is," said Ada, grinning as she held tightly to the arm of Lady B.

The two ladies waited awhile for Bill to return and soon he was seen panting and puffing mostly for effect.

"That's the lot now Mrs H., so if there's nothing else for me to do I'll be making me way off home," said Bill still a little flushed from the exertion.

"Yes that's fine Bill, no nothing more to keep you. Perhaps we'll see you again tomorrow," said Ada.

As soon as Bill had hastily departed, the two ladies entered the large dreary hall where they were immediately presented with the wide, once polished, staircase and balustrade which rose from the left hand side. The wooden railing, supported by its balusters extended across the top of the hall, bordering and protecting an obviously wide landing and the red patterned, dowdy carpet, covering the floor of the hall and centre of the stairway, was badly worn in places and in dire need of cleaning. The walls also, did nothing to brighten the sombre vestibule, being covered with drab ancient oak wall panels and a few badly positioned oil paintings of little credit or colour.

A lone, dull crystal chandelier hung from the high, grey white, water stained ceiling with its ornate plasterwork was slightly tilted and like the carpet below was in desperate need of repair. In fact the whole place echoed the need for attention, crying out for a drink of soapy water. But the dubious character and atmosphere of the place brought vivid memories of a happy childhood flooding back, swamping the mind of Lady B.

"Nothing has changed Ada, it's still as wonderful as I remember it," said the very nice lady, looking all around her with the dampened eyes of a child.

They walked ever so slowly through all the downstairs rooms with Lady B. uncritically exploring every nook and corner, absorbing intently and with relish everything that evoked nostalgic memories of her childhood visit. And in each room the pattern of damp stained linings of drapes was repeated. The drapes, which covered all the tall dusty windows, were rotting and torn with age and occasionally hung in shreds at the edges. Only the high quality of the original fabric was holding them together now. A dank, musty smell lingered around each of the dust defiled rooms and the tightly closed windows offered no solution in any way to the completely airless problem. All of this had been respectfully ignored by the very nice lady and the fixed smile upon her lovely face gave a heart warming feeling to her aging hostess.

After they had completed the tour of the downstairs rooms they returned, almost reverently, to the dismal hall and carefully climbed the stairs to the first of the three floors; Lady B. being particularly diligent in offering Ada all the physical support she needed.

"How many bedrooms do you have?" asked Lady B., as they neared the top of the stairs.

"There are just ten that we use regularly," said Ada, counting in her mind. "What with Susan's friends from the university often visiting the place with her at odd weekends and at holidays we need them all. Yes the place really comes alive when they're all here and that's a fact. Actually I seem to remember her saying that a couple of her mates would be coming down with her next Tuesday. Anyway, there are two other smaller rooms on the third floor; the attic is what we always called it, where you used to play when it was raining if you remember Barbara. And we still have that big doll's house that you loved so much."

Lady B. smiled widely then searched her mind for a name.

"And what about Miranda? Is she still in existence?" she asked, delighted that the name came so freely to her mind.

"Yes, she's still up there somewhere I expect. Fancy you remembering that old dolls name after all this time. You carried that old doll of mine everywhere you went, didn't you my dear," said Ada, feeling a trifle maudlin.

After they had finished their reminiscing, they went down the stairs again to the drawing room to wait for Felicity and Jonathon.

— CHAPTER FIFTEEN —

The moment Lady Barbara and Ada walked into the drawing room once again, the much used memory seemed now to be playing havoc with Lady B.'s mind. *'Now what was it that prevented me from noticing when I first stepped into this room,'* she asked herself, as she placed two closed fingers to her temples. She turned temporarily to her friend and then diverted her attention to the walls of the room.

"Ada, something is missing from this room. I clearly remember the walls simply dripping with pictures when I was here last and now there is but a handful," she said, her expression indicating her alarmed feelings.

"Yes you are quite right Barbara. We possessed quite a collection of very fine watercolours didn't we? Those were my special favourites. Well six months before Sir Nigel died we lost them all. Unfortunately someone broke in when we were away for the weekend and took all the small paintings. Why only the small pictures were taken I have no idea, someone had a fetish for them I expect. The strange thing was we didn't go away that often, so I immediately thought that the thieves must have known we weren't here; they must have found that out somehow. And stranger still, the pictures weren't all that valuable, not as paintings go, that is. Sir Nigel had them all valued a few years previous, that would have been about 1964 and the most expensive of them then was only about five thousand pounds. But I suppose that in to-days market the most important of them would probably have doubled in price, maybe even more who knows. But they were truly a delightful little collection; at least I thought they were anyhow. Funny really, Sir Nigel always promised them to me when he died. He said he would rather they belonged to someone who really appreciated them for their art sake and not just for the value they held. Still they're all gone now and it's no use me crying over spilt milk, now is it?" said Ada, remorsefully.

Lady B. placed a comforting arm around her friend as her senses became more alert at the talk of the theft but felt she needed to know more without appearing to be overly curious.

"How many pictures were taken Ada?" she asked, casually. "Were there many?"

"There was twenty-five in all," replied Ada. "Mostly wonderful Victorian watercolours of rural England but there were two oil portraits as well, one of Sir Nigel's mother and one of his late sister which we both admired. But those two were of little value and only of interest to the family really, I shouldn't have thought they would have been of much interest to anyone else, they weren't painted by a famous artist or anything, you see."

Lady B.'s attention was held and her interest grew by the second.

"And were they marked in any way, you know to prove ownership as it were?" she asked, as she felt her pulse racing and her excitement mounting.

"Oh yes my dear. Sir Nigel was most particular about that sort of thing; all of the frames of his pictures are embossed with the letters 'NE' on the back. But they will have been discarded by now and reframed I expect," said Ada, staring at her friend with a degree of curiosity.

Just then, mother and son returned from their walk and entered the drawing room from the doorway that led in from the kitchen; plainly delighted with their garden ramble.

"Hello you two, caught up on the years have you? What truly magnificent gardens you have here Ada," said an elated Felicity, refreshing her memory by gazing out of the window. "The rhododendrons and azaleas are particularly beautiful and being under planted by the rich carpet of bluebells produces quite a luxurious effect, the blueness seem to be everywhere. How many acres are there? Quite a few I should imagine, the grounds seem to be never ending."

Ada smiled discretely. "Do you know I'm not at all certain? Somewhere in the region of eight or nine I should think, maybe even more. You will have to ask Susan when she arrives; she will know the answer I'm sure. Anyway, I'm glad you approve of our little plot, it always seems to be appreciated by our visitors."

Jonathon produced a look of eagerness equal to that of his mother. Actually all three Fishers were horticulturalists at heart and enjoyed their own gardens back in Suffolk with enormous passion.

"We have a small lake back home Ada but yours, being so wide and long dwarfs ours into being but a mere puddle. The water looks very clear and bright and blue quite the cleanest lake I've seen," said Jonathon. "I expect you have it treated to maintain such a high standard. I noticed a couple of small fish darting about the place I suppose it's alive with them, am I right? And it looks pretty deep to me. Any idea just how deep it is?" Jonathon's avid joy at seeing the lake was not totally unexpected and the enthusiasm he expressed seemed to delight Ada Hutchins.

"I'm so glad you approve Jonathon. Actually, there are three ponds, that's what Sir Nigel always called them, and the largest, which was probably the one you are talking about, is about twenty feet deep in the centre and shelves down rather steeply once it starts. The two smaller ones can't be seen from the drive; you have to take quite a walk to see those. But Sir Nigel always maintained that the three are connected by underground tunnels of some sort or another but I don't think he was ever able to find anything to give the theory any support. I think myself that that was a myth put about by the locals over the years for whatever reason, but of course no one knows for sure. A small spring does flow into the smallest pond at the top and then keeps the others well topped up so I suppose they are connected in that sense but as for there being tunnels linking them together, as I say, I very much doubt it.

"Each pond is well stocked with fish despite the fact that they are fairly rich in minerals; fish don't usually take kindly to mineral rich water, or so I am led to believe. But there is plenty of fish including Cyprinus carpio, that's the common carp to the unenlightened; showing off I'm afraid, that's the only Latin name I can remember," said Ada, laughing at her own statement. "But you don't often see carp; I think they mainly stay down on the bottom filling their bellies down there I should think."

"What about pike?" asked Jonathon. "Surely there has to be pike lurking about close to the weed beds."

"Yes Jonathon there most certainly is quite a few of those, I know, I've seen them myself. Vicious looking creatures with their big sharp teeth aren't they.

"And did you notice the water lilies? The yellow ones are my special favourites although they are all lovely in their own way," said Ada, happily.

Normally Lady B. enthused with the best of ardent garden lovers, always willing to be caught up in conversation over horticultural matters. But this time however, Lady B. listened impatiently to the now, arduous conversation and throughout this period she waited for a lull during which she might be able to pursue the more important subject of the missing art collection and at last the opportunity presented itself.

"Before your return, Ada was telling me about some pictures that were stolen from this very room a couple of years ago. It seems there were twenty-five in all; not overly valuable it's true but certainly valuable enough to be of interest to some discerning person," she said, hoping for a positive response from the others.

"Really," exclaimed Felicity, alertly surprised. "Well then, perhaps we had better tell Ada of Jonathon's discovery and of your own suspicions mama, who knows, there may well be a link."

The Fisher family looked at one another quizzically and agreed that nothing would be lost in divulging the whole story. And so Lady B. related the chronicle to a wide eyed Ada whose attention was held completely and without her interruption.

"Well I'm blessed," said Ada, when Lady B had at last finished. "So, are you saying that there may well be some possibility of you getting my pictures back for me then?" asked a most enthralled Ada. "Oh how wonderful to think that I may have my pictures returned and after all this time. I'm so thrilled. So what do you think we ought to do now?"

"Well, firstly we certainly shouldn't go building up too many hopes, not at this stage Ada. You see we are assuming a great deal at this point; pure speculation on our part you see with nothing really tangible to go on as the police were not prepared to qualify or make clear to Jonathon precisely what was being off loaded onto the beach a few afternoons ago."

"By the way Ada were the pictures insured?" asked Felicity, interrupting her mother with the important point.

"No unfortunately they weren't. Sir Nigel, for some unknown reason didn't include them with the rest of the pictures. I remember Susan trying to make a claim and the insurance company said they were not covered as they weren't itemised. We were so disappointed as we thought every picture in the house was covered, and they are, but not the watercolours and the two small portraits," answered Ada.

"Well I'm not sure what the others think but as far as I can see it is now imperative that we return to Devon. In the light of what Ada has just told us we must hope that our assumptions are correct and hinge all of our assurance on a speculation," said Lady B. determined to do all she could to recoup her old friends losses. "Yes," she continued, "we must return to Brixham as soon as ever possible, even tomorrow and taking Ada here with us and have a quiet word with the illustrious Superintendent Dobson. If, and I admit it is a big if, if Ada's pictures are indeed at Brixham Police Station, then it is up to us to see that they are returned to her with minimum delay. It appears you were right all along Felicity we shouldn't have waited any longer, not now anyway," said Lady B., touching her daughter's arm.

Felicity's smile was very slight and she inclined her head in acknowledgement to her mother, but said nothing.

Jonathon was mulling over matters in his own mind without speaking and as though inspired by a sudden notion he rose from his seat and paced awhile.

"How pleasant it would be if we could have surprised the said gentleman before he had had the opportunity to think up some crazy story of his own. But of course, if one thinks about it, he has no real need to do even that; I mean, he needn't feel obliged to see us at all, if he's not so inclined," He deliberated once again. "Perhaps it would be in our interest to find out if he will be prepared or even available to see us, especially on a Saturday. How utterly futile it would be and how stupid we would look turning up for an appointment that was never going to happen and with a wasted trip as well. Yes, maybe telephoning him would be the right course of action, much as I hate the idea."

"Yes you are right of course Jonathon; although like you, I was rather hoping to have arrived unannounced myself and with the very same idea in mind. But your telephone call would be the right course of action, I can see that now," said Lady B., looking slightly disappointed. "Oh and by the way, while you are using the telephone, do you think it might be an idea to have a word with Sergeant Pedley in Bergholt, just to gain his approval in our staying here a couple of days longer. He will need this address and telephone number anyway and I have promised Ada that we would stay on to meet with Susan. I'm sure he will have no objections at all and he will appreciate being kept informed of our exact whereabouts."

After adjourning to the kitchen and procuring Ada's permission to use the phone, Jonathon quickly dialled the number of the East Bergholt Police Station and was relieved to hear the Suffolk voice of Sergeant Pedley.

"What's that you say Jonathon? Stutton what?"

Jonathon repeated the address and telephone number once again smiling broadly.

"Oh right, I got it that time," said the sergeant, confirming the accuracy of Jonathon's instructions. "Yeah, that'll be OK. There's bin a bit of a delay this end and the post-mortem won't be takin' place now for another couple of days, so you've got plenty o' time afore the coroners git their hands on it. But keep in touch will you as things change from day to day. 'Haps you'll pop in and see me when you git back." The sergeants Suffolk accent was like music to Jonathon's ears.

He replaced the receiver and then lifting it again he dialled the number of the Brixham Police.

"I'm afraid that Superintendent Dobson won't be in his office tomorrow morning, in fact he won't be back in his office now until next Monday. Can I take a message?" offered W.P.C. Balaam in response to Jonathon's request.

"Yes you may," replied Jonathon politely. "Please get in touch with the superintendent at once and express the importance of me seeing him tomorrow morning. And then would you kindly ring me back at this number with his response."

"Yes of course sir. May I ask who it is who's calling?" questioned the W.P.C.

"Jonathon Fisher," said Jonathon, replacing the receiver.

— CHAPTER SIXTEEN —

The four continued debating the possible outcome of the forthcoming twenty-four hours with Ada's eagerness mounting by the second, when, precisely ten minutes after Jonathon had completed his two calls, the black telephone rang, almost dislodging it from the small baroque table on which it was standing. Ada Hutchins rose from her chair and unsteadily hobbled over to the phone then after the preliminaries she turned to her guests and said,

"I think it's for you Jonathon; a police call from Brixham I believe."

"Hello me 'andsome, how be you getting' on then? Now I do believe that you be wantin' to see me tomorrow, is that right?" It was the unmistakable tone of Superintendent Dobson.

"Yes indeed superintendent. Something of the utmost urgency has arisen about which I need a discussion with you and I must add that I am not prepared to accept delaying tactics on your behalf," said Jonathon, forcefully.

"Well now, changed your mind 'ave you me 'andsome? Lookin' for some reward after all eh?" said the policeman, with the utmost sarcasm in his voice and ignoring Jonathon's feistiness.

"Not at all, but time is of the essence superintendent and the matter is exceedingly important," replied Jonathon, hoping that he wasn't going to be fobbed off with a barrage of excuses.

"Well I don't know, don't know at all. I'm not usually at the station on a Saturday not unless it's of paramount importance; an emergency like; and I don't 'spect that anything you 'ave to say come any where near that, now do it me 'andsome? 'Haps you better say what's on your mind 'ere an' now like, so's I can judge if I should accommodate you or not." The superintendent was seemingly toying with Jonathon. *'Probably hoping I would drop my insistence and opt for a more reasonable time.'* he thought.

"Superintendent, I have already stressed the acute urgency surrounding the expectations of a meeting with you so you will have to judge the merit of such a meeting upon that which I have already stated," said Jonathon, retaining his insistence of the high-priority upon which he placed his request.

"Alright then I'll see you," said the superintendent, relenting at last to Jonathon's petition. "I'll make an exception in your case Jonathon Fisher, so long as you be 'ere at my office afore noonday tomorrow. Though why I'm obligin' you, I shall never know. Noonday tomorrow it is then me 'andsome and don't you be late, you 'ear me?" replied the policeman, at last.

Four people with firmly fixed faces marched stolidly into the superintendent's rather small office at eleven fifty-five on the following morning and were immediately followed by an incensed Superintendent Dobson with the air of one who might easily have trodden in something unsavoury out in the street so tepid was his demeanour and his welcome.

"Jonathon!" His tone was raised and was all but equalled by the look he gave to each person in turn as he glared at them with unnerving ferocity; at least that was the effect which he hoped to achieve but it had little or no impact on the Fishers determined attitude. He continued: "I must say I'm surprised at the crowd you've brought along with you Jonathon. Needed moral support I dare say, is that right?" He paused awhile, taking stock. "No, I most certainly didn't expect you to turn up with the whole of the blinkin' family that I didn't. Anyway, seein' as how you're all here you had better introduce me to everyone," said the unsmiling policeman.

After this ritual had been completed without the formality of shaking anyone's hands the superintendent continued once again.

"Now what's this delegation all about Jonathon? I should appreciate you comin' straight to the point; my days off are mighty precious to me, that they be; and not only that but I'm due at the nineteenth hole in a little while," he said, and finished by allowing the hint of a smile to pass his lips.

"Very well then," said Jonathon, "I shall come directly to the crux of the matter. I need to know the answer to the question that I asked you when last we met. I need to know what it was that was being smuggled onto these shores five days ago and I need to know it now."

"Do you indeed? So this is what it's all about is it? Well I told you the last time we met that I didn't 'ave permission to tell you that; that was for someone else to tell you and not me. Well, I grant you that things have changed a mite since we spoke a few days ago. You see I've 'ad a word with my chief an' he seems to think that there is no harm in you're knowin' what it's all about, should you 'appen to ask like, but he's left it completely up to me. I however don't agree with 'im one little bit, that I don't, so I be still reluctant to change me position on the matter. No, I'm not prepared to go any further than I already 'ave, no not at all," said the superintendent, maintaining a rather haughty manner which the Fishers found to be obnoxious and totally inexcusable.

Jonathon briefly weighed up the situation and decided that attack to be the best way forward; after all he had nothing to lose.

"I can't say that I am not disappointed in your attitude because I am. You see we have our own suspicions as to what was being brought ashore and we are all firmly agreed about that event. So, maybe it would be more appropriate if we speak directly to your chief and maybe he will be rather more forthcoming than you obviously appear to be at the moment superintendent," said Jonathon, with all the assertiveness he could muster.

The superintendent was clearly ruffled by the proposal and raised a hand to his mouth indicating his indecisiveness.

"Hold you fast there me 'andsome. You say you reckon you know all the answers do you? Well now, why don't you just tell me what it was they were smugglin' an' we'll take it from there shall us?" said the superintendent, in an even more serious tone but now trying hard to produce a smile but without too much success.

Jonathon's smile was much more successful however and he allowed it to intimidate his adversary to the limit.

"I really do not see the point of that at all. To my way of thinking it would be much more advantageous for me to arrange an interview with the chief superintendent now, or as soon as possible, so that we can sort this matter out once and for all. From what you have told me, he would appear to be so much more amicable than yourself and one from whom we would gain the utmost sympathy, cooperation and support," said Jonathon, continuing with his smile to its greatest effect.

The tall policeman resorted almost to a panic and was certainly too flustered to put up very much resistance. He contemplated the ceiling, the walls and the floor and with no help from any inanimate object he finally admitted defeat.

"Alright, alright we don't want no cat and mouse games here now do we?" he said, at last. "So I'll tell you if you must know. Them were pictures OK? Some were small some were miniatures. Some had bin out of the country for a long time, some not so long. But they're all British pictures by British artists, some old some not so old but they're all beautifully preserved, bin looked after perfect like. And it's up to me and my team to sort 'em all out and to return 'em to their rightful owners. So now you can see why we've bin so cagey; didn't want 'em fallin' into the wrong hands now did us? 'Twill be the easiest thing in the world for anyone to turn up 'ere and stake their claim like, yeah, easiest thing in the world that it would be. No, they mustn't go to anyone except their rightful owners. There are hundreds of 'em, oils, watercolours, pastels, and pencil drawin's you name 'em there 'ere. So you can see the quandary we're in; you see some of 'em 'as bin out of the country so long their original owners are dead, in fact most of 'em I should think, so you can see we 'ave a big problem on our 'ands. At the minute we're sortin' and cataloguing' 'em and tha's goin' to take quite a while I can tell you, even though we 'ave expert advice."

When the superintendent had at last finished his report he mopped his brow while the Fishers stared at one another in complete relief.

Jonathon was the first to speak, his face sparkling with shear delight.

"Bingo," he exclaimed, joyously. "Right first time grandmama. You couldn't have been more accurate even if you'd tried."

The policeman looked over at his visitors, vexed and in a state of uneasiness and all at once his ferocity had disappeared and was replaced with one of dubiousness.

"Whatever do you mean?" he said nervously. "Surely you are not about to tell me that pictures were on your minds all along are you? I don't believe it. Reckon you be pullin' me leg to some extent am I right?—Tha's not possible, not possible at all," he said looking at the Fishers as they moved their heads slowly with a positive expression.

"Oh yes it is superintendent, I can assure you of that," said Jonathon, almost arrogantly. "You see this lady is Mrs Ada Hutchins and was housekeeper and heir to the late Sir Nigel Eld, and it was Sir Nigel who had a quantity of small paintings stolen from Akworth House in Hampshire just over two years ago. The pictures were bequeathed to this lady by Sir Nigel but unfortunately they were stolen just prior to the gentleman's death. And according to medical opinion, the incident played no small part in Sir Nigel's demise, he being so distraught by the whole beastly business." (Jonathon considered that some embellishment of the facts at the above juncture to be most appropriate). "You see, superintendent, Mrs Hutchins had always expressed a fondness for the pictures to Sir Nigel and so they were promised to her upon the event of his death. So you can clearly see the importance of the pictures being returned to Akworth House with the minimal amount of delay possible," said Jonathon, underlining the significance of his words with an impromptu gesticulation of his hands.

The superintendent looked slightly abashed at the statement Jonathon had made and appeared to regret, to some extent, the entrenched attitude he had originally taken and still found himself in, but from which he now had to crawl out unexpectedly.

"Well now, that throws a totally different light on the matter, that it do, a different light entirely I should say," he said, with raised eyebrows. And then as an afterthought: "I 'spose you do 'ave a positive means of identifyin' the pictures should any of 'em be among the lot that we are holdin' 'ere. Oh-ah m'dears, must 'ave that an' no mistake, most important that be."

Evidently, the superintendent was quite comfortable with being entrenched for he now appeared to be digging himself further in the mire rather than taking his opportunity to escape and appeared very eager to control the situation once again.

The challenge was answered immediately.

"Yes indeed superintendent," returned Jonathon, with a grin, "Mrs Hutchins has made an accurate list of the pictures concerned, together with the appropriate artist's names. And oh yes, there may well be the owners initials NE on the rear of each of the frames. I think that should be sufficient identification superintendent, don't you?"

Jonathon, who by this time was enjoying the contretemps and dissension that existed between he and the tall policeman, walked over to the ladies embracing each in turn and expressed his ardent support and optimism of a successful outcome to Ada in particular.

This move by Jonathon didn't go unnoticed by Superintendent Dobson.

"Now don't you all go buildin' your 'opes up, I 'aven't confirmed if any of the pictures are 'ere at all yet, and it may well be that they're not," he said, contemptuously. "Anyway it may take me quite a while to be able to say yes or no, like. Perhaps you better give me the list so as I can check it against our own lists we 'ave compiled so far. --- So the list if you please Jonathon!"

The superintendent seemed more relaxed at this point, hoping that he had at last managed to express a more lenient attitude than before by changing sides somewhat. He even chanced a movement to his mouth which didn't quite have the desired effect, as he extended his hand.

"Certainly," said Jonathon, still with his mouth turned up at the edges. "Perhaps you would have your secretary make a copy of the list which I shall keep; after you have signed it of course. Then you may retain the original for your personal use and eventually for your files."

The superintendent's face at last broke into a wide and not unpleasant smile which seemed to suit the tall policeman very well.

"Certainly me 'andsome, that'll be just fine," he said. "But I must say you be a mite cautious; still, you were that the last time we met weren't you? When the sortin' 'as bin finished and they 'ave all bin catalogued I shall need to go through 'em all to compare your list with mine, so to speak. Shouldn't take too long but I doubt I shall 'ave any news for you yet awhile, probably not 'til next week, so you'll all 'ave to wait patient like to see if your lot are among 'em. Now if you would be good enough to leave me your particulars—address an' telephone number an' all that—then I shall be able to get in touch with you just as soon as I 'ave anything to report."

A supercilious grin now replaced the pleasant smile upon the tall policeman's face as the Fishers left the small office. No hands were shaken, no words of farewell spoken but the small family and their friend felt positively optimistic and satisfied that the meeting had been successful.

— CHAPTER SEVENTEEN —

Optimism had entered the hearts and minds of the babbling quartet as they enjoyed the harmonious return trip to Hampshire that Saturday afternoon. The heavens seemed bluer than they had an hour ago, even though grey clouds hovered over the horizon. Yet still, the clouds that had been suspended over the Fisher family's minds prior to, and indeed during, the now seemingly conclusive visit had vanished in a trice. All the hitherto speculations that had plagued them over the past twenty-four hours were now gone and a state of complete euphoria had taken their place.

The three ladies heaped much commendation upon Jonathon's ability in the handling of the interview with the superintendent, so much so that the big man was beginning to feel somewhat embarrassed by the approbation.

"The situation was its own acclaim," he said, trying to parry the praise and concentrate on the road. "There was really no two ways in achieving the result we did; only dogged perseverance in helping the man see reason; he had to in the end you know and I'm certain he knew that only too well. I don't think he really appreciated our point of view right up to the end and it wasn't until he admitted going against his superior's opinion that his argument broke down and he had to exercise good sense and reason. Once he had confessed to that, he was unable to maintain his own composure. A pity it had to come to that, one hates to see a man in authority do an about turn and frankly admit he was being slightly obtuse. Still, we are the beneficiaries; or rather Ada is, hopefully. Even so, I'm not now at all certain that he was, or indeed is, involved in anything illegal; no chicanery going on or anything like it, as we once thought; just a policeman doing a job of work to the best of his ability in protecting the public interest. I suppose that there will be a few unclaimed works looking for a new home but the superintendent doesn't appear to me to be the type of man who would get involved in misappropriating pictures."

Lady B. wasn't quite so sure; after all it was she who laid the question against the police in the first place.

"I'm not really certain on that point Jonathon; I don't seem to be able to share your optimism in the police being completely unimpeachable. As I have said before, first and foremost the force is made up of human beings, and as such, like the rest of us, is not completely immune to perversity. If the chance does present itself to misappropriating pictures, as you have so succinctly put it, then certain members of the force would not, or maybe could not, resist the temptation, and who is to say that our Superintendent Dobson isn't one of those," said Lady B.

After awhile the subject was dropped with each party reserving the right to their own private opinion. Only Ada refrained from entering the debate, she being only concerned about her precious paintings. Debating didn't seem to hold an appeal for Ada, for even if she had had an opinion which she didn't seem to have, she wouldn't have entered the affray.

The sun was low in the sky when the Bentley arrived back at Akworth House and the three huge blue cedars, that graced the immediate surroundings of the place, cast wide chilling shadows over the dramatically impressive building making it look strangely foreboding and cold and caused a shudder to traverse Felicity's spine. As the car drew to a halt, a green woodpecker, aggravated by the patter of the car's engine, flew noiselessly from one of the big oak trees that stood behind the cedars to another in search of an alternative roost for the night conscious of its creature comfort.

The foursome entered the house by the now familiar doorway to the warmth of the welcoming kitchen all chatting and glad to be back. The moment they were all inside Ada filled the black kettle with water and placed it on the Aga for a brew of her special blend of tea.

"I intend cooking us a lovely meal tonight; after all you have done for me today, I think you all deserve one," said Ada, as she busied herself with the ingredients for a roast dinner. She found each of her guests a task to do so that they could all contribute toward the meal while the kettle boiled.

Halfway through eating the dinner the telephone rang. Ada answered it as quickly as her arthritic legs allowed and spoke warmly to her daughter. After she had finished her conversation she returned slowly to her place at the table.

"I expect you all guessed that that was Susan on the phone. It seems she can't wait to meet you all after I told her you were here yesterday and so she intends joining us tomorrow about midday instead of Tuesday, as she originally planned. She told me she would be bringing one of her friends down with her and some more may turn up later; should be quite a lovely party from all accounts," said Ada, excitedly.

Jonathon toyed with his fork and moved his food about his plate plucking up some courage before he posed what he considered to be a possible impertinent question.

"Ada," he said, at last, "do you think it would be impolite of me to ask if I may help myself to a dip in the large lake tomorrow sometime—if at all possible?"

Ada placed her knife and fork down and finished her mouthful before answering.

"Dear me no, of course it isn't an impolite question to ask Jonathon, the very idea. You use the ponds all you like and whenever you like, no need for you to ask, you just help yourself. Sir Nigel used them all the time as a swimming pool. He loved his early morning swim, all weathers, it made no odds to him, he didn't mind the cold you see. Now Susan she don't swim in them hardly at all; reckons the water is far too cold. Well maybe it is I don't know or maybe it's just her being too lily livered. So yes, I should be delighted to have you use them, it will be like old times for me. There is a diving board at this end of the largest pond, canoes as well. Now that's what Susan likes best, the canoes; reckon she feels safer in one of them. So have fun while you are down here with me I shall be delighted," answered Ada happily.

It had been the Fisher family's unfailing Sabbath ritual to attend worship in the little Methodist Chapel when they were at home. Lady B. had joined the church when she first came to the village and Felicity also was encouraged both as a child and throughout adulthood to worship there, which she did with eagerness. Jonathon as well, when he came along, was most earnest with his religious conviction and so it was that the whole family eventually became ardent members of the Methodist movement joining in with every facet of church membership.

Not wishing to neglect Sunday worship the family decided to use the local C. of E. church as the Methodists were not represented locally. The following morning then, at ten o'clock sharp and after persuading Ada to join them, they left Akworth House and idled along to the local village place of worship. The sun shone down upon the little party as they took the quiet back lane they had used when first they visited Akworth, passed the watercress stream, where the Wingfield's had been confronted by Bill Marks and on to the tiny village of Sutton Scotney.

The local C. of E. church was small and quaintly ancient with a bell tower that housed but a single bell that tolled continuously until all the pews were filled to capacity. Then, when the vicar came on stage, and not until, the bell ceased to function and a quietened hush descended reverently over the small congregation.

At the appointed moment, everyone listened intently to the Reverend Oram's evocative sermon, with not a single head in the place drooping with boredom; although there were diverse and varying opinions as to the validity of the homily which was being presented. The religious discourse, intended for spiritual edification rather than for instruction, seemed to the Fishers to be debateable; and on the way back to Akworth after the service was over, Felicity couldn't resist expounding her views upon the reverend gentleman's edifying remarks.

"All that hogwash about earning the respect of others does not go down at all well with me," she said, not more than twenty yards from the church. "To my way of thinking, respect should be obligatory and should be instilled in children at a very early age. Yes, children should be taught to respect their peers, their elders and indeed other people's property as soon as they are able to string two words together. I mean, what on earth is the use of bolting the stable door, as it were. Once learned never forgotten, that's my motto. After all, that's what you taught me mama and through me, Jonathon as well."

All of Felicity's remarks were addressed to her mother although the other two listened on with some degree of interest.

"Yes dear, I do agree with you up to a certain point but we have to remember a child's innocence, say, up until the age of puberty, don't you think? During that period we have to earn their respect in the hope that what they are taught at mother's knee will eventually sink in," said Lady B.

"But what about those who have little or no tuition at mother's knee, as you put it. Take those awful Wingfield boys for instance. How on earth can one possibly earn their respect, and that is what that clown of a vicar is expecting from his congregation. The Wingfields and those like them seem to be delinquents from the day they were born and totally incapable of paying respect to man or beast for that matter," said an embittered Felicity with her face flushing to match her words.

"One earns their respect slowly with love and tolerance I suppose darling. After all, the rudest of all children are newly born babes with their disgusting habits of fouling themselves at both ends and at the same time more often than not and screaming loudly to get their own way at the drop of a hat. But they thrive on love and tolerance do they not? Remember, we know nothing when we are born and have the most revolting manners but gradually we are taught right from wrong, what people will tolerate and what they will not and with patience, understanding, and a great deal of love from our parents and the people about us, we get there. And if there is no tuition when children are young then we still have to persevere in our endeavours to earn their respect," said Lady B.

The discussion continued between mother and daughter all the way back to Akworth House, and beyond; with Felicity battling for respect to be an automatic response from one person to another and not requiring that it should be earned in any way at all; while Lady B. sided with the vicar that where ever possible respect could only be received with the perseverance in working for it.

Jonathon was beginning to find the friendly debate a tad boring and so as soon as lunch had been eaten he decided that the time was more than right for him to experience Akworth's calming waters. He checked once more with Ada stating his desire to swim the large lake, went to his room to collect his swimming gear, and then set off with the minimum of delay.

The mid afternoon sky was bright and cloudless with warmth in the May sunshine that streamed down upon the colourful gardens. Everywhere he looked indicated to Jonathon the promise of yet another hot summer that was on its way. He hummed a tune to one of the hymns he had sung earlier in church quietly to himself and admired the sparkling azure lake set out before him as he sauntered along.

Gradually the sound of conversation and laughter mixed with the splashing of water drifted up from the far end of the lake breaking the tranquillity of the moment for the tall young man. He stopped for a short period and looked hesitantly toward the spot from where the disturbance was coming and observed the naked figures of three lads as they jumped, frolicked and cavorted in the water; quite innocently pitching, what appeared to be, a large beach-ball or pigs bladder, from one to the other; then scrambling and splashing to retrieve it when it was missed.

Jonathon walked casually round the far side of the lake, totally concealed by the dense rhododendron and azalea shrubs, to where three bundles of clothing lay half hidden beneath the branches of a sweetly scented yellow azalea bush. He stood and watched silently for quite awhile, a smile broadening on his handsome face as the three Wingfield lads, in innocence, continued their raucous jollification; quite unaware of their observer's presence. Jonathon knew very well what he must do of course but he was feeling rather reluctant to spoil the Wingfield's enjoyment and waited a little while longer.

"Hi there," he said, at length. "You look as though you might be having a good time but do you mind coming out of the water for a moment? I have to talk to you."

The three lads were obviously startled by the sudden intrusion and at first looked as though they might decide to ignore the request. But when they saw who it was demanding their attention, they decided to move to the order at once, well—more or less; the memory of the previous unfortunate and unforgettable encounter had been etched on their minds and was clearly visible in the expression on their faces.

"We didn't mean no 'arm mister, honest we didn't. We just fancied a swim that was all," said Paul, one of the twins, looking rather anxious.

"No, I'm quite certain that you didn't mean any harm. But the plain truth of the matter is ---" Jonathon hesitated. "Look, you cannot go around just helping yourselves to using other peoples property no matter how much the idea might appeal. You see, these are private grounds in which you find yourselves, as I suspect you very well know, and my guess is that you haven't had the owners consent to use the lake in the first place." Jonathon's words were kindly enough and didn't carry any malice in them.

"No we 'aven't, but we ain't done no damage neither so I don't see what all the fuss is about," said Sam, feigning a defiant note to his voice.

The three Wingfields hadn't yet completely withdrawn themselves from the water and retained their dignity by still remaining waist high in the lake.

"Well, maybe you haven't; but don't you see that it is all a question of respect. Now, you wouldn't take kindly to me helping myself to something that is rightfully yours, now would you? So the same thing applies here, you shouldn't be helping yourselves to a swim in this lake; if you take my meaning," said Jonathon, calmly and without reproach.

All at once the debate between the mothers came flooding back to him. If Felicity was right in her assumptions then he should now be sending the lads packing with a flea in their ear, in order to teach them some respect and also some better manners in obeying, without question, what they already should know. But on the other hand, if Lady B.'s opinion was more fitting then his own action, thus far, in endeavouring to earn their respect by patiently instructing them in the rights and wrongs of this particular situation would be deemed to be more appropriate. Jonathon decided upon the latter.

"Do you understand exactly what it is that I am trying to get over to you?" asked Jonathon, propitiously.

The Wingfields looked vague; whether deliberately or not, Jonathon had no way of knowing.

"Alright then, let me put it another way." He thought for awhile as if seeking inspiration. "OK, this lake is full of weeds, long sturdy weeds and therefore most dangerous—right? It is also extremely deep in parts. Now if one of you got into difficulty and maybe got caught up in the weeds and was drowned—heaven forbid, then the owner of the estate would feel in someway to blame; probably for not policing the lakes properly. Now, I am not the owner of this estate but I am pretty certain that she would not welcome you here at all. So I think that it is about time you made yourselves scarce don't you? In other words, you should all collect your clothes and get the hell out of here, and be quick about it. And I'm going to add a little rider to that—DON'T COME BACK!" The final three words were stern and loud and quite powerful enough to put the fear of God into the three Wingfields for they stood rigid and still as if petrified. But although Jonathon felt as though he had at last reached their mentality with the demands he had made, they still failed to move and seemed to be staring past him rather than at him. Even so, Jonathon continued in his demands of the three lads with some force; words which were now veering toward his mother's opinion; but still the three remained.

"Look you three idiots, I shall give you just one minute in which to get dressed before I physically remove the lot of you," he said, with a stern look of determination on his face and with a sudden movement of splashing and fear the Wingfields were out of the lake; and grabbing their clothes as they fled; they didn't look back.

"Bravo, well done that man. It took a little time but you got there in the end." The feminine voice came from behind him as he spontaneously spun round to see a pretty young woman smiling down at him from the vantage point of the lake's embankment.

— CHAPTER EIGHTEEN —

The pretty young woman moved slowly and cautiously toward Jonathon half stumbling as she did so and Jonathon, taking hold of her outstretched hand led her to the safety of the more level ground at the lake's margin.

"Thanks," she said, looking up into Jonathon's face with a questioning expression upon her own as if wanting to ridicule the height of the man; and thinking better of it, she stored it at the back of her mind for future reference.

"I'm Susan Hutchins," she said. Then realising that her dainty hand was still being firmly clasped in Jonathon's oversized strong fist, she added, "mind if I have it back please?"

Jonathon looked puzzled.

"My hand you oaf, you've still got hold of my hand," she said.

"Oh, so sorry," he said. "Still thinking about those wayward lads," he lied.

"So, you must be the gorgeous Jonathon Fisher; at least that's how mummy described you to me the other day. I arrived home about ten minutes ago and she suggested I might find you here so I thought I would give you a pleasant surprise; now wasn't that kind of me?"

Susan's voice, in fact her whole demeanour seemed frivolous and superficial to Jonathon; even though he was taken with her good looks, at first glance. But not being one for jumping to conclusions or making rash character assessments especially when meeting someone for the first time, he merely smiled and took the offered hand again, this time in a friendly greeting.

"Hello Susan, I'm pleased to meet you," he said, holding on to the petite hand a little longer than was necessary and feeling his legs go just a shade shaky.

"Sorry about the bother you had with those hideous boys." She spoke the final two words in a derisory tone as if she looked on them disparagingly or as if she had had some experience of the wayward lads in the past. She continued:

"They have never been over here before, not to my knowledge anyway but I have heard rumours about them; a bad lot from all accounts. But I can see that I shall have to get a few pertinent notices made, warning people to keep out, so that there can be no mistake about this being private property; at least that would be a start to policing this place properly, wouldn't it?" she said mockingly.

"Look, I'm terribly sorry but I didn't mean to imply that your mother wasn't doing the job appropriately—I was merely trying to get a point across to the Wingfield lads—that was all," said Jonathon contritely.

"Yes, I know you were, no apology necessary. But you are quite right, people should be under no illusions about Akworth or who owns it. It is private property and it belongs to me, so you see it is my responsibility to make certain that the public, in all its guises, are made aware of the beastly fact. One must nip these things in the bud before they get out of hand or I shall see the place turned into a play ground or a lido for all and sundry," she said, waving her arms about her to illustrate the width and breadth of the estate.

Changing tack and mood, her face suddenly lit up as if she had thought of some idea which was quite unprepared. And removing the blue and yellow wrap she had about her, she revealed her scantily clad pulchritudinous figure and to Jonathon's amazement she dived into the lake without hesitation.

Jonathon, realising that Ada's words were somewhat inaccurate in her estimation of her daughter's probabilities, laughed quietly to himself, stripped off his own clothing and dived into the water after her, surfacing some twenty yards beyond an amazed Susan before she had had a chance to turn.

"Show off!" she screamed. "How did you manage to do that?—Fitted with an outboard motor or something are you?" she giggled merrily. And with all the unrestrained fervour of a child, she splashed the big man, squealing and laughing as if she was having the time of her life; which indeed she was. The two new friends amused themselves in the water for over an hour with Susan more than proving her adeptness as a swimmer and as a seeker of pleasure and to Jonathon's amazement and utter delight, they seemed to compliment each other with immediate rapport but not once did she attempt to follow Jonathon by swimming below the water's surface.

"Perhaps it's about time we joined the rest of the party, I should hate for them to think that we had deserted them already," said Jonathon, well after the full hour was up, and quickly removed himself from the sparkling water and towelled himself dry.

"Oh, do we have to Jon?" Susan's question was asked with disappointment, as a child might petition its father so crestfallen was she to find that the afternoon's enjoyment was already at an end and not wanting for one moment that it should be

"To be perfectly honest I shouldn't have minded staying here for the rest of the day. I know the sun has lost its warmth just a little but that shouldn't worry a big man like you Jon, surely. Mind if I borrow your towel?" she asked, as she joined him on the bank. "I didn't think to grab one before I came over; too intent on getting changed quickly I suppose.

You know Jon; I haven't enjoyed myself half as much as I have with you this afternoon, not for a very long time. Thanks! Only hope we can do it again before we both go our separate ways," said Susan, flinging Jonathon's towel back to him playfully.

"Likewise," said Jonathon, happily drying his hair once more, "I've enjoyed myself immensely too, and I'm game for a swim any time; I could spend the whole of each and every day in the water but I guess there are other things in life."

When they were both dry and dressed and once again looking reasonably presentable, they started off around the lake in the direction of the house, comfortably chit chatting to one another continuously as though they were old friends replenishing a long lost relationship.

"I was most surprised to hear you say that you were in fact the mistress of Akworth, Susan. Don't know why, but I automatically assumed that after your father had died your mother would have been left in sole charge of the place; it seemed to me to have been the natural course of events and what happens in most regulated families," said Jonathon, thinking that there had to be a fundamental reason for Ada's exclusion and was hoping for some enlightenment on the subject. But he was disappointed with what seemed to him to be a deft way of avoiding the issue.

"Hardly surprising you would think that Jon," she answered, tossing her head as if to aerate her blonde locks, "considering I'm so seldom here, now that I'm at university for the greater part of the year and only come home for a few weekends and holidays. I suppose to most people mummy would be considered to be holding the reigns as it were, or at least giving the impression to be. Anyway, I suppose it's just as well, all things considered, she does give that impression; and in all fairness to her she does do a bit, enough to occupy her mind anyway and enough to keep the grey matter turning over to stop her from going totally doolally; and at the same time it frees me of unnecessary worry, to think of her here, in charge. But daddy left me as sole heir to his estate when he died, so in reality, it is I who settle all the major decisions, not that there are many to make. Anyway when things get out of hand there's always David to help me out. He's an absolute treasure and always more than willing to oblige, thank goodness," she said, glancing at Jonathon to notice his confused look. "Sorry," she rejoined. "David is the family solicitor, a useful sort of chap to have around and he's often here offering me his friendly advice. Actually he did mention he might pop in this afternoon when I told him I would be home. Got a couple of letters to the council he wants me to sign; boring routine stuff really and nothing to get excited about. But I should like you to meet him all the same; even though he's well over forty I'm sure you'd both get on. On second thoughts perhaps not, you're much too tall, too young and too lovely; David is a touch jealous do you see and tries to treat me as his ward.

Somehow I suspect he quite fancies me, although he hasn't said as much, but one senses these things. Still, he has no chance, no chance at all, far too old for my liking. What about you Jon?" she touched her mouth with her left hand as though she wanted to suppress something already spoken. "Sorry, but I hope you don't mind me calling you Jon. Jonathon sounds rather formal and stuffy to me. Anyway, what about you? Are you seeing anyone at the moment?" She asked the question attempting to exercise as much familiarity with the tall young man as she thought he would consider acceptable.

At once Jonathon imagined he heard alarm bells ringing and so he attempted to evade a potentially embarrassing inquisition.

"I'm rather in between relationships at the moment," said Jonathon, amazed at the speed in which Susan was capable of moving to make herself completely familiar at an intimate level. "I did get friendly with a girl at university last year," he continued, "but it didn't develop into much and we haven't been in touch since then. I expect we were both of the same opinion so I guess we just let it go. Personally, I feel there is plenty of time yet before I even consider settling down to one partner, even though I might find the idea appealing at times. I expect someday a girl will come along who I feel I can't live without but until that happens I guess I'll muddle through on my own. Anyway I need to devote my thoughts and energy to developing a proper career first; that has to be my main objective, the rest can wait."

Although Susan considered she had not gone out of her way to making a pass at her newly found friend she still felt slightly rebuffed at his repulsed reply but said nothing. Instead she decided to quickly fall in line.

"Oh yes, me too." she said, without further hesitation. "We've both got yonks to go before we feel the need to settle down. But I suppose it would be rather pleasant to have someone special on the sidelines, so to speak; without being totally committed of course," she hastily added.

Jonathon pondered awhile before offering his reply. "Yes, I suppose so, although I have never really felt the need for a sideline person, being close to the family ladies it rather defeats the object." He thought awhile longer, then: "but yes, I do see your point of view. I suppose it would be rather pleasing to have that extra someone to send a Christmas card to and maybe share the odd moment with," he said, smiling.

They walked slowly back to the house as the orange sun was sinking lower in the pale blue sky, both wrapt in light-hearted conversation, with Susan's highly infectious laughter reverberating around the grounds.

"Hello you two, you seem to be hitting it off rather nicely." It was Ada's homely voice that greeted them as they approached the gravelled area to the front of the house.

The figures of Lady B., Felicity and of course Ada emerged from behind a large cream rhododendron shrub all smiling and in a jovial mood. The three had obviously been engaged in the close study of the massive flowers that fully covered the shrub in creamed profusion.

"You were in such a rush to get over to the ponds when you arrived Susan that you didn't give me the opportunity to introduce you to our guests, so come over here and meet them now," said Ada. Susan moved closer to the two ladies who remained where they were standing. "This is Lady Barbara and this is her daughter Felicity, ladies this is my precious daughter Susan," said Ada with pride. (Obviously she was very proud of her daughter but equally proud to be associated with two of the most beautiful of ladies).

"Oh, hello Barbara, hello Felicity, so nice to meet you both. Mummy has told me so much about you that I feel I know the two of you already," said Susan.

Inwardly, Lady B. resented the familiarity considerably but assuming Ada had referred to her in that manner failed to acknowledge the presumptuousness. Instead she stepped forward and embraced Susan fondly, kissing her on both her cheeks. Felicity and Susan exchanged glances and shook hands cautiously each half expecting the other to develop the greeting. In the end it was Felicity who took the initiative.

"I understand from your mother you are studying law at Colchester University Susan. Colchester is only a few miles from where we live so perhaps we might see something of you in future. How are you finding the syllabus? It always seem to me to be a very complex subject to take on and one that is under constant review," she said, trying her level best to be kindhearted to someone she considered might well be of an imperious nature. Unlike her son, Felicity was quick to weigh up peoples personalities.

"Yes, I suppose it might appear to be somewhat involved, to the uninitiated, but having a penchant for the subject does make all the difference you know. Some of my friends are finding the going jolly tough, not because they are lacking in any ability of course, but purely and simply because they are not in love with the subject. Actually, it was one of these friends who was supposed to be coming here to Akworth with me this morning, but she had to excuse herself because she needed the time to catch up on some intensive reading," said Susan.

"Yes I was wondering where your friend had got to dear. But you disappeared so quickly when you arrived that I forgot to ask," said Ada.

"Sorry about that mummy, but I noticed Jon by the big pond as I idled down the driveway, and thought it might be amusing to surprise him. Actually we've had heaps of fun together this afternoon haven't we Jon?" returned Susan, directing her attention to Jonathon.

Both Lady B. and Felicity smarted at the sound of their son's name being shortened so distastefully. But it was the very nice lady, who, ignoring her own feelings immediately changed the subject before Jonathon had a chance to reply.

"Jonathon," she emphasized the name a little, "well the three of us really, have been extremely busy over the past few days down at Brixham. We visited Devon last week and quite accidentally stumbled across some untoward activities taking place. However, as things have transpired it would appear that both your mother and you may, hopefully, benefit rather nicely," said Lady B.

An excitedly enthusiastic Ada, interrupted Lady B.'s flow. "Oh yes Susan," she said, setting off at a pace. "You'll never guess what these wonderful people have found for us. You remember the pictures daddy promised to me that were stolen just before daddy passed away? Well, it seems that Jonathon may have discovered them quite by chance. Of course we won't be absolutely certain for a day or two yet but everything does look very hopeful. Isn't that wonderful news darling?" said Ada.

"Well yes, it is good news indeed, if it is as you say. How did you find the paintings Jon?" asked Susan, rather sceptically and with a curious expression that matched the suspicious intimation in her words perfectly.

It wasn't until Jonathon had sketched out the Brixham events, placing the major credit on his grandmother's deductions, his mother's supporting role and almost totally ignoring his own part in the affair, that Susan lifted the incredulous look from her face and replaced it with one of stunned amazement.

"Anyway, the bottom line is that we are now to expect a telephone call from the Devon Police telling us that they have something positive to report. So you can guess we are all on tender hooks until the call comes through," said Jonathon, winding up the full report.

"Gosh what a fantastic yarn; it's unreal," said a much changed Susan. "Just wait until I tell all of my mates back at Colchester, they'll never believe it. They'll be even more amazed than I am at this very moment, as I say it's quite fantastic. What clever people you are."

"Hold on just a minute Susan. We are not one hundred percent certain that the Akworth collection is among those that Jonathon saw and now currently being held by the police. I do not wish to dampen your enthusiasm but we do have to recognise the need for total police confidentiality, you of all people ought to know that. We must certainly not, and I repeat, not, attempt to pre-empt their decision as to when to go public; not at any cost, most important! Otherwise we might well find ourselves out of favour with our friend Superintendent Dobson, and that would never do," said Lady B., sternly and looking directly into the eyes of Susan.

"Of course, yes, I do understand," returned Susan, trying to look as if she meant it. "Understand perfectly. So mums the word is it?—But all the same, it's still a great story isn't it?"

Almost as soon as Susan had finished her enthusiastic commendation to the Fisher family, the loud roar of a car's engine that could be heard from the top of the stony driveway compelled the little group to turn as one to look at the bright red sports car as it motored toward them at speed, totally ignoring the potholes and divots of the drive's surface.

"Oh it's David everyone; he said he would try to call in to see me today. And it looks as though he's brought a couple of his cronies with him. Oh Barbara," she whimpered like a small adolescent asking a special favour. "Do you think we might tell him the news? After all, he is a solicitor and knows full well how to keep his mouth shut." The excitement in her eyes abated when she turned to Lady B. for the answer. The stern face told her all she needed to know and so she looked up to the heavens and added; "don't you worry yourself, I shan't say a word."

— CHAPTER NINETEEN —

The bright red car skidded to an abrupt halt in front of the small, now smiling group, with David West at the wheel and his two friends crammed in, one on the back shelf and the other in the passenger seat. The Akworth's solicitor was quickly out of the sporty Jaguar car and was immediately followed by his two male associates who were promptly and eagerly received by Susan who had walked over to them in haste.

"Hello Susan, how the devil are you?" said David, embracing his lovely client. "Just popped in on our way back from Bournemouth as promised to get these wretched letters signed. Brought along a couple of my old buddies, this is Dennis and the good looking one is Joe. Hope you don't mind them tagging along. But I see you already have visitors of your own; won't you introduce us?"

They ambled over to where the ladies and Jonathon stood and everyone was introduced in turn. After all the pleasantries had been completed, David turned to Susan and taking her by the arm, started to lead her toward the house.

"If we might go inside awhile Susan, there are a couple of points I should like your approval on before I ask you to sign, only take a couple of minutes, I'm sure Dennis and Joe will be happy enough in this most delicious company," he said, eyeing the ladies as he spoke.

After solicitor and client had left, Joe Cabin walked casually over to Felicity looking worried but affected a faint smile to conceal his anguish.

"Felicity would you mind awfully if I spoke to you for a minute or two?" he asked quietly, so that no one else might hear.

"You are doing aren't you Mr Cabin?" retorted Felicity, smiling falsely.

"No not here, not like this; I mean privately, if that's alright. Perhaps we might walk awhile, there is something I feel I must discuss with you," said Joe, still maintaining a low voice and looking even more nervous.

Lady B, glancing over in the couples direction noticed a degree of uneasiness in Felicity's countenance and felt the need to make her own presence felt.

"Not apologising yet again I hope Mr Cabin," she said, cutting in on the obvious private conversation he was having with her daughter.

"No, not at all Lady Barbara. Joe, please call me Joe. I wonder, would you excuse us for awhile? There is something I have to say to Felicity, something which I must take the opportunity in saying now." Joe's faint smile broadened as he looked from Lady B. to Jonathon knowing he had not fully explained to them his intention. And taking Felicity's arm gently in his hand he casually and slowly walked her up the driveway and out of earshot of the small gathering as they looked on aimlessly.

Felicity felt a little apprehensive at being held by this relative stranger's hand, no matter how caringly and disentangled her arm at once while wondering why she was being singled out for such personalized attention. It seemed possible to her that the man was merely looking for some romantic interlude in his drab life. *'Well if that is what he is looking for, he should think again; this lady is certainly not available to fulfil his lustful desires.'* She smiled inwardly to herself not dismissing entirely the obvious but unsolicited compliment he was paying her and inwardly rehearsed the speech of rejection she would use when required. *'If the situation gets a little out of hand I always have Jonathon to fall back on,'* she thought, reassuring herself.

Not until Joe considered they had obtained complete privacy did he further speak and then not until a few silent moments had passed did a single word pass from his lips. Eventually they stopped and he turned to face Felicity as his own self assurance returned. He had hoped for an extended amorous liaison but he was now unsure that it would happen.

"Felicity, you do remember me don't you? Or are you just being recalcitrant?" he asked.

"No Joe, I'm not being obstinate at all, or difficult or uncooperative; you see I do know what the word means," she answered, mockingly. "Why on earth should I remember someone I have never met before?—Oh yes—a couple of days ago our paths did cross for a very brief moment in that public house, what was it called? The Flying Owl—no The Owls Nest—yes that was it, when you were rather rude to me and felt you had to apologise for being so. But apart from that immature and unfortunate incident, no, I cannot ever recall having the misfortune of meeting you before. Please enlighten me." Felicity's attitude was indeed gathering a marked degree of obstinacy, or impudence at the very least.

"Allow me to take you way back in time, say twenty to twenty-five years ago, to a lovely spot we called Touchy Hill in the Suffolk village of East Bergholt," said Joe, his voice was calm and even.

Felicity let out a gasp as she felt her legs grow unsteady and Joe's firm bracing hand grab out to hold her secure.

"But that was Joseph Jones—not you," she said weakly, desperately trying to overcome her shock.

"It still is. I altered it to Cabin when I joined the firm ten years ago. Jones, Jones and Jones would have looked rather ludicrous as a firm of solicitors, don't you think?" said Joe laughing and looking rather pleased with himself.

"But you've changed," offered Felicity still weak.

"You haven't," returned Joe.

"Why didn't you—why didn't you see me again, after," Felicity hesitated—"well after that champagne afternoon? Do you mean to tell me you have waited all this time—it must be twenty-four years—before contacting me, when we lived only eleven miles from each other? Oh go away Joe, get out of my sight. Go this very minute and don't ever try to see me again. I am thoroughly ashamed of you and of the fact that I ever knew you. You nauseate me Joe, you got me drunk on champagne, took what you wanted and then you ran away like some scared rabbit," said Felicity, her initial shock being replaced with anger.

"Now you hold on a moment, you stop right there. OK I admit I was frightened at first, hell who wouldn't be? But we were young Felicity—not much more than children—we all were. After quite sometime, when I came to my senses, I realised I needed to see you—to talk with you. But by that time it was too late you had already moved to Australia, so all I could --." Joe was immediately interrupted by a furious Felicity who stepped back and surveyed her adversary with a look of mocking disbelief.

"Joe, you were at least twenty-three at the time, you dismal apology for a man, I would hardly call that below the age of pubescence which is how most people define a child these days and as for me moving to Australia,—poppycock. Well it's all plainly obvious to me, just more of your fanciful excuses to avoid your moral responsibilities, I'm quite sure of that, you louse," said Felicity angrily and feeling her hackles rise with every word.

"What?—do you mean that you're mothers emigration plans were put off—abandoned?" said Joe, putting forward an air of complete surprise.

"Off? They were never on and well you know it. We have never even considered moving to Australia or any other country for that matter. Just where do you get these stupid ideas Joe? Who could possibly have put such a notion as improbable as that into your tiny mind?—If indeed anyone did" said Felicity quite exasperated by this time.

"Humphrey Powell, that's who," he said, with a sneer on his face. "Yes, good old Humphrey Powell. And to think that for all these years—all these years," he repeated, "I have been an utter and complete fool. I have only just realised it—what an idiot—what a total ignoramus I have been," he said woefully.

"Well you can't expect me to argue with that," taunted a smiling Felicity.

"You may laugh Felicity, but really, really I don't know why I'm so surprised. After all, Humphrey was always crazy about you. Well let's face it we all were, you must have known that. But it was me who cared; it was me who wanted you for keeps and it was me who spent the past twenty-five years in complete celibacy just hoping—yes—hoping for the day when we would eventually meet again. Felicity, I have not even looked at another woman in all of that long time—that is until I saw you the other day at The Owls Nest and I felt I couldn't speak to you then, but at least I knew you were in this country. And now I know you never even left it—what a rotter—what a bounder, Humphrey Powel I mean. He deliberately lied to me so that he could have you for himself. When I meet up with that imbecile again I shall certainly teach him a thing or two you may rely on that. Still, I expect I shall be wasting both time and effort—I expect you have been seeing each other for all of this time—am I right? I even expect that he is the father of your son—well is he?" Joe was now displaying all the raging signs of anger, frustration and anguish a wronged man might resort to using, but which didn't appear to impress Felicity in the slightest.

"What utter nonsense, if you think that I believe all that garbage then you must be a bigger fool than you say you are," she retorted jeeringly. "I haven't seen Humphrey Powel more than half a dozen times since I last saw you, and then only to exchange the time of day which was never very pleasant if I remember rightly."

"Well then, perhaps your son is mine, is that it? Is that my son standing over there Felicity?" he asked. His torment appeared to be building to a crescendo as crocodile tears glistened in his eyes and which Felicity was pleased to ignore.

"What nonsense, Joe you really are the limit. Your male ego seems to be getting the better of you, please do control yourself or I shall feel obliged to call Jonathon over to set you straight. Do you really consider that you and Humphrey Powel to be the only tall blonde males in the world? You are so conceited Joe you're beyond belief. Anyway, as far as I recall, neither you nor your friend Humphrey Powel were particularly strong swimmers," returned Felicity thinking she had discovered some loophole in Joe's claim.

"Swimming? What on earth has swimming got to do with anything?" asked Joe curiously and not too quietly.

"Just this, as I myself am not one of the world's greatest swimmers, then one would have expected Jonathon's father to have been. You see Jonathon swam perfectly well from the moment he was born," said Felicity smiling.

"What absolute twaddle; don't you know that thousands of babies are able to swim the moment they are born, in fact I should think that most of them can if they are given the opportunity. It's a throw back Felicity, a throw back to our ancestry, that's all," said Joe gaining a little confidence.

"Well you can think just what you like, all I know is, you are the most obnoxious man I have ever met or likely to meet come to that. So if you will excuse me I should very much like to join my family," said Felicity huffily.

A panic attack of regret seemed to come over Joe immediately Felicity intimated that the conversation was at an end.

"Look Felicity, I'm sorry if I have offended you in any way, or if I came on a bit too strong, then I apologise, really I do. All I want is for us to have the opportunity to get to know each other once again, that's all. Please don't dismiss me out of hand, just give me a chance that is all I ask," pleaded Joe, his male ego was clearly showing; he being unaccustomed to such rejection, or so it seemed.

"Mr Cabin, Jones, or whatever your name happens to be, I have said it before and I shall say it once again; go away now, this very minute and please do not try to contact me again. I have managed very well without you over the past years so I am damn sure I can continue through the rest of my life without you equally as well. Thank you for the offer Mr Cabin, but no thanks, and goodbye," said Felicity, who turned quickly before he saw her fighting back the tiny tear of anger that was beginning to swell in her eye, and walked hurriedly back to where her son and mother stood anxiously waiting.

"Are you alright mother? You are looking just a trifle upset, is everything OK?" asked Jonathon concerned, as he placed a comforting arm around his mother's shoulders.

"Yes darling I'm fine, really I am, shall we go inside?" she said as she forced a smile from her sad but furious face. As she walked toward the house with mother and son on either side of her and Ada bringing up the rear they didn't turn to see J.J.Cabin standing with his friend, looking tired and rejected, beside the very red Jaguar.

As Felicity and her ensemble neared the entrance to the kitchen, Susan and David came out of the house exchanging frivolous banter and both giggling like children.

"Oh hello you lot; finished with the garden have you?" laughed Susan. "Look, I'll just see David and his chums off the premises then I'll join you all for drinks," said Susan, who sounded as if she had had one or two already.

"Sounds like a good idea Susan, I'll see to it. Goodbye David, see you again soon I expect," said Ada cordially, as David West excused himself politely, exchanged farewells with the Fishers and walked to the car.

The small group entered the kitchen, allowing Felicity her privacy by refraining from any pertinent questions that may have been on their lips.

After a little while Susan walked in, still encapsulated in a frivolous mood and found everyone in the drawing room talking together without purpose and sipping their drinks.

"Well that's the council sorted out, a very clever chap is our David and most informative as well. Actually he was telling me of your chance meeting in The Owls Nest over in Tollpuddle and how his friend, Joe Cabin, seemed to think he recognised Felicity from way back. Is that true Felicity or did he have his wires crossed? Chap's often do you know, they think it to be some clever chat up line," asked Susan inquisitively. All eyes went to Felicity.

"Yes we did meet briefly a long time ago but I failed to recognise him. People change so with the years don't they? Or at least some people do. But I'm afraid that his wolf baying didn't impress me in the slightest," said Felicity defensively.

"But you have to admit he is rather dishy, a little old maybe but still rather dishy all the same," returned Susan teasingly, adding as an afterthought, "well, are you going to see each other when you return to Suffolk?"

"Lord, I certainly hope not. I'm afraid I do not share your enthusiasm about Mr Cabin—you see I really am not at all interested in self opinionated people, be they male or female," said Felicity crisply, dismissing Susan's remarks with a coolish gesture.

Lady B. beamed noticeably, but the subject was dropped in a moment.

— CHAPTER TWENTY —

The early morning after Felicity's brief and unfortunate encounter with Joseph Cabin, saw Jonathon hastily preparing himself for a much longed for solo swim in the large lake. And so, while the whole of the household at Akworth was still dormant from a late night of discussions on various topics of conversation, the big man stole stealthy from his comfortable room and made his way to the most scintillating of waters. He continuously looked back over his shoulder toward the windows of the silent house to reassure himself of his own solitude but failed to notice the twitching curtains at Susan's room as the lovely blonde young lady eyed him as he walked the gravelled drive.

When he had reached the diving board, he stripped off his clothing and plunged into the chilly lake, shuddering slightly as the bracing water enveloped his powerfully built body. Staying well below the lake's shiny surface awhile, and only periodically replenishing his air supply, he swam its full length then turned to swim back again. About halfway down the return length, as he was surfacing for a breath, he looked back and was momentarily surprised to notice an object reflecting the sunlight through the clear blue waters on the lakes muddy bottom close to where the steep shelving commenced. Without hesitation Jonathon gulped in some much needed air and dived back again some twelve feet to where the corner of a box-like object protruded through the silt, clay and gravel mix of the lake's foundation. For a full two minutes he tugged at the corner of what appeared to be a metal box about six inches thick, the length and breadth not being visible, attempting desperately to ease it from its secure anchorage but without success. Before long his chest told him of it's dire need for a replenishment to it's spent oxygen supply and so he surfaced slowly once again to breath deeply the wonderfully fresh, clean Hampshire air. He carefully noted the precise location of his find before swimming back to the diving board, where he could see Susan waiting for him.

"Good morning big man, and what exactly do you mean by swimming the lake without inviting me?" Susan's teasing question was light hearted enough and brought a wide smile to his handsome face.

"Hi Susan. Well if you insist on hugging your pillow for half of the day what do you expect? Sorry if I disturbed your beauty sleep though—didn't mean to; in fact I tried to make my hurried exit as quiet as poss. purposefully not to disturb anyone," said Jonathon, as he exited the water, deliberately ignoring the fact that his intention was to get some quality time for himself before anyone was up and about, so that he might be able to focus on some serious swimming for a change.

"Forget it, no harm done," she said. "Mind if we swim together? It looks a tad cold to me." She dipped her toe into the cool water. "Eek! Its ruddy freezing! Still I expect it's OK once I get in there—here goes." and with that she belly flopped into the water with quite a bang.

"You OK," shouted Jonathon noticing the bad entry.

"Yeah, I'm good," she returned, shouting and gurgling some water. "Bad dive wasn't it? I knew it would be as soon as I left the board. Still, I didn't hurt myself. Come on back in Jon, you land lubber; I'll race you to the far end and back again."

"I don't think so," shouted Jonathon, "lets play." And he dived to the bottom of the lake as he spoke.

The couple played around in the water much as they had done the previous day but this time with Jonathon taking every opportunity to dive down to check and tug at the box then resurfacing in various parts of the lake each time. This seemed to puzzle, with some amusement, the ever enquiring Susan, who was a good enough swimmer but lacked the confidence to venture beneath the waters sparkling surface except when diving from the board.

Jonathon continued, laboriously and secretly, to ply his considerable strength to the now only half buried box and after several more strenuous attempts, managed to free it completely from the vice like grip of the stony clay bottom. The result of his disguised actions was complete. Susan was none the wiser as to what was going on under the water and Jonathon was able to surreptitiously carry the container to a much shallower part of the lake, to the edge that was closest to the drive. And there he left it amongst the reed where he knew he would be able to retrieve it at some later point in time, when hopefully he would be on his own. Although he was well aware that the lake belonged to Susan and that, presumably, anything that was in the lake belonged to her also, he felt a certain interest in the box; something about how the thing was buried absorbed his mind, so much so that he needed the opportunity to examine the container without an audience.

After an hour or so of their watery high jinks, with intermittent periods of serious swimming, the couple decided to return to the house to prepare breakfast for everyone.

They towelled themselves dry then began to walk slowly back as they had the previous day just chit chatting to each other with entertaining wordplay.

"How do you manage to stay under the water for so long Jon? You seem to be down there for simply ages. Do you think that I could ever do it? Would you teach me please?" Susan's usual child like questioning imploring Jonathon to accommodate her was innocent and spontaneous and she fondly slipped her hand through his arm as she asked them.

"Well, mostly it's through hours of practice; remember I swim in the Stour almost every day of my life, but I guess a decent sized pair of lungs does help. I was fortunate in as much as the Good Lord kindly bestowed upon me the wherewithal to apply myself, quite naturally, to the water. But sure—I'll certainly help you all I can to get started Susan, the rest will be up to you and the amount of free time that you are prepared to devote to practicing," answered Jonathon.

"Jon, you said the Good Lord gave you the lungs to help you swim. Do you often go on about things of that nature, you know, about God and stuff. I mean, are you really as religious as you appear to be or is it just some craze you've taken to?" asked Susan, pleasantly.

Jonathon tightened her arm to his body.

"What's this Susan, twenty questions?" laughed the big man. "I do hope I am. The alternative seems pretty bleak to me. And if you are a thinking sort of person as I hope I am, then you certainly need something more positive to conjure with," returned Jonathon happily.

Susan clutched hold of her own hand with that of her free one drawing herself even closer to Jonathon.

"Maybe you're right when you put it like that," she stated. "So, I can't be much of a thinking person can I? You see, I don't give the thinking side to life any time at all, not really; except for my studies and reading of course. I just seem to live for the moment and take each day as it comes, enjoying myself mostly. You see, I don't know too many thinking people, not in the context in which you are talking anyhow. Perhaps I should find some and give more thought to good old God and stuff, that way maybe I'll get more out of life and be a better person." She laughed at the thought. "The trouble is I always seem to need things being proven to me, I don't seem to be able to take things for granted, if you see what I mean. Take this faith stuff, it goes completely over my head I'm afraid. Oh I know there are scores of people who claim to have it but surely it's just pie in the sky isn't it? I'm afraid I would need something more tangible to believe in than just myths, and you cannot prove any of it can you? Not religion, not God not any of it. Even the creation theory can't be proven can it?" Susan was soberly putting all of these questions to her new friend who was listening intently to what she had to say.

"Oh I am sure you can. In fact the bible positively encourages us to 'prove all things.' And the alternative to the 'creation theory' as you put it, I prefer to use the term 'creation fact,' is an accident and I have yet to see order come out of accidents—let alone millions of them in succession and all of them highly dubious to say the least," said Jonathon, with a serious look to his face.

"Yes I quite agree with you about accidents, heavens, I think almost everyone would agree with you on that. But that is not proving the creation theory to me now is it?" Susan laughed inwardly and mischievously at the sober debate she had gotten them both into.

"Let's see now; what I am about to say is not off the cuff Susan, I've heard this illustration used many times before as a demonstration in defence of creationists. There is a fish called the archer fish. Now this little fish, of which there are several species, is a freshwater fish native to Asia, Australia and other places—which I forget—oh yes the Philippines. Now this little fish earns its keep by spurting water from its mouth at insects that have settled on nearby foliage. It's a pretty good shot as well, it has to be, bearing in mind its eyes are below the surface of the water when it aims and so has to allow for light refraction into the bargain.

"Now then, up until the time it supposedly had evolved this complicated method of catching its food, it must have had some other method of catching its tea, right? So why did it change? It had to have been able to successfully spurt water whereby it caught its food, immediately, or it starved to death. But it didn't starve to death, because it is still alive today, living very happily thank you very much and doing what it did from day one. It must have had this remarkable ability from the day it was created, that's the point; and it is all part of natures wonderful design don't you think?" said Jonathon.

"Good heavens," said Susan, "I've never even heard of an archer fish. But if what you say is true, and I don't doubt it for a single minute, then yes, it certainly gives one food for thought. Why isn't this sort of thing made more public, well I suppose it is but its just not given the same interpretation as you have put on it," said Susan.

Jonathon thought awhile.

"I'm not saying there is no room for changes in nature at all, of course there is, we see it all the time. But I'm certain that the change mechanism, the ability to change, is in built. Take micro organisms for example, they seem to be able to change extremely quickly, for as soon as we think we have one flu bug under control then the little blighters change and we are presented with yet another format of the same virus. Now, I'm not at all au fait with the mechanics of flu bugs, not many people are, I suspect. But they certainly do not need millions of years in which to adopt a new configuration, so the ability to change has to be part of their design. Also some birds seem to change. The Galapagos Cormorant, being so isolated, has no natural enemies and doesn't use its wings as it once did. So gradually it's losing them. Not an example for evolutionist merely a question of 'use them or lose them.' Animals as well, they do not usually interbreed, at least not without the intervention of us humans and even the domestic dog, while they are prolific cross breeders, still remain true to their own kind; still dogs," said Jonathon.

Susan was captivated by Jonathon's role as a creationist champion and seemed almost converted to the cause.

The couple walked unhurriedly back toward the house in fascinating conversation, completely relishing each other's society talking of cats and bugs and dogs and things, when all at once a tired old fox sauntered across their path quite oblivious to the couple and only intent on the lifeless rabbit that it clutched tightly between its jaws.

This seemingly barbaric exhibition on behalf of a beast of the countryside upon one of its fellow creatures filled Susan with nausea, producing an inarticulate moment; during which she pointed at the animal with one hand and at the sky with the other then interchanging the one for the other she repeated the action. When she had found her voice once more, she screeched, not loudly but loud enough, then she regulated her voice to its normal pitch halfway through the verbal expression.

"Now that little spectacle has thrown me completely. How on earth can a loving all-powerful God allow a savage fox to kill a poor innocent little rabbit? It just doesn't make sense," she said, sadly.

Jonathon smiled and comforted his friend.

"But that is precisely why; you have said it yourself. The fox is a wild savage, Susan, and does exactly what he has always done in order to keep his own species alive and well. He does what he has been created to do, to keep the smaller animal population under control and his own breed thriving. If we didn't have foxes and all the other beasts of prey, we would be overrun with rabbits and all sorts of other vermin. But it is nature's way that provides the balance and only man's intervention that can bring about an imbalance. Please don't allow yourself to be put off Susan, it is all OK."

Jonathon and Susan eventually arrived back at the house, entered the kitchen and started the preparations for a massive breakfast for five, when in walked Ada.

"Hello you two, you're up bright and early this morning, I don't need to ask what you've been up to," she said.

Susan glanced at Jonathon and smiled. It was wasted.

"Are you suitably refreshed after your swim?" the elderly cripple asked.

"Yes thank you mummy, Jon and I have had a fabulous time together," responded the daughter happily.

Ada paused from what she was doing and looked up earnestly.

"Darling, I'm not at all sure about the Jon bit. I don't think Jonathon's mother would approve of you shortening names willy-nilly like that, especially Jonathon's name. Or his grandmother come to that, I don't think she would appreciate the familiarity either," said Ada disapprovingly.

"OK mummy, I will only get familiar with him when we are alone then," chuckled Susan.

— CHAPTER TWENTY-ONE —

The Monday morning breakfast started as a jolly affair, not only because the two younger members of the little gathering were so chatty and lively after their exhilarating early morning swim but also because they had unexpectedly prepared a most acceptable meal for everyone. However it was soon spoiled by quite an innocuous remark made by Ada concerning her daughter that seemed quite out of character.

"I can't understand why you don't always get up for an early morning swim when you are at home Susan," said Ada glancing around the table as she unwittingly informed every one of her daughter's morning sluggish habits. "You could easily adopt this sort of routine whenever you come home—and prepare and serve my breakfast as well, it wouldn't hurt you, you know, especially as my legs are so poorly" she fixed a derisory smile on Susan as her words sank in.

Susan was mortified by her mothers pointed remarks especially as they were made in front of the man upon whom she had hoped to make a favourable impression. She quickly tried to change the subject before anyone else decided to offer her mother any support as she glared at her mother with an ever darkening expression. But she would not take issue with her mother for the moment that would come later. She decided that by ignoring the remarks was far the better way of handling such a slight. And so she cast a smiling glance in Jonathon's direction for some immediate relief instead.

"Jonathon," she ventured casually and as naturally as she was able, "I have to pay a visit to the village shops and post office a little later this morning. Would you care to go with me? We could make an interesting morning of it."

Susan, being ever hopeful of an agreeable and positive response, was most disappointed when the big man failed to answer. No one else paid any attention at all to the question, although they clearly heard it. Everyone's eyes became suddenly fixed on Susan; not because of the content of the invitation, no, that would have been totally expected. But what was this? Did everyone hear her correctly? Susan, actually using Jonathon's name without feeling the need to shorten it? Most surprising! Nevertheless, the invitation was not met with the favourable response that Susan had taken for granted or indeed hoped for as afore mentioned. After he had relapsed into this brief silence, pondering this unforeseen invitation, Jonathon made an unrehearsed and feeble reply, hastily excusing him from the excursion and thereby freeing him for a more important mission. But instead of expressing her extreme disappointment at the response in what would have been her own objectionable manner, her lips broke into a forced grin and she ran her fingers through her blonde silken hair as if the refusal was of no consequence.

Even so, the Fisher ladies were not slow in noticing the whole occurrence the moment Ada had posed the disparaging remark and Susan's reaction to it and also noted the somewhat strained relationship that now existed between the two and filed the information away for future discussion.

Jonathon, on the other hand, ignored the whole episode. He had a much more important matter that was plaguing his sub-conscious and which had been niggling away for most of the breakfast time; for even after enjoying the most satisfying of meals the thought provoking steel container was still on his mind.

And so, after a suitable period of time, he politely excused himself from the breakfast table and made his way to his small bedroom where he patiently waited for Susan to depart. This time it was the big man's turn to spy through curtained windows to scour the gravelled drive below. And in no time at all he watched Susan as she entered her car taking a quick look toward his window as she seated herself. The lovely blonde girl took a further glimpse as she turned the car round and headed up the drive toward the main road.

When he was completely satisfied that all risk had left the premises with Susan's departure, and that his own privacy was now complete, Jonathon quietly exited his room and stealthily made his way down the wide carpeted stairway and out through the big front oaken doorway. He furtively made his way up the stony driveway toward the lake with hurried looping strides, all the while concerned that his mission was being carried out with the utmost secrecy.

Once at the lake's side, he quickly removed his size fourteen shoes and socks and rolled up his trousers to above his knees. He waded into the water, then realising that it was deeper than he had imagined, he gave an extra couple of turns to his dampened trousers then continued to retrieve the muddy steel box that he had successfully secreted earlier and waded back again through the weeded margin. The box was a deal lighter than he imagined it to be when he had towed it through the water earlier that morning but it was quite difficult to handle because of the wet slippery mud that was partially caked to its metallic surface. He placed the container on the short dry grass and commenced rubbing it back and forth to dislodge some of the debris. Not satisfied with that, he scooped water in his large hands and further washed the thing to a state of acceptable cleanness then dried it off on the grass once more.

The sealed watertight lid proved difficult to remove and the big man fished in his pocket for his hefty polished handled shut knife which he used as a leaver to good effect. A little more effort and the lid left the box's base to reveal, carefully wrapped in plastic sheeting and perfectly dry in the baize lined box, two small oil paintings lying side by side in perfect condition. The first one that Jonathon removed was of an elderly lady with a serene look upon her furrowed face and a crimson shawl around her shoulders held in place by a large blue cream cameo broach. She wore a double string of pearls choking her throat that were so realistically painted they stood out above all else. The whole of the picture was beautifully executed in a traditional style with each dainty brush stroke almost invisible to the eye and the detail of the subject so perfectly defined that it commanded approbation.

Jonathon wrapped the picture carefully once again and replaced it in its housing. He removed the second picture which had been painted in a similar style to that of the first and caught his breath when he saw the perfect likeness of Susan staring back at him from the flawless canvas. Her hypnotic eyes were of the same shade of the deepest blue and the beguiling red mouth smiled with an iridescence that sent shivers down the big man's spine. Only the hair was different to that of Susan's, the artist had painted his subject with a slightly darker shade but the mysterious resemblance was unmistakable. Jonathon stared, captivated by the image and touched its surface with gentleness before he wrapped and replaced it beside the other. With reluctance, he repositioned and secured the shiny lid, rolled down his trousers and replaced his socks and shoes. He picked up the box carefully and hurried back toward the house to where the big black Bentley was parked. He fumbled for the keys, not wishing to put his prize down, unlocked the boot and safely deposited the stainless steel box in side. He was relocking the car's boot when he heard his mother call out to him.

"Oh there you are darling, we were wondering where you had disappeared to," said Felicity.

Lady Barbara followed her daughter out of the house and linked arms with her as they strolled toward Jonathon both looking happy and glowing.

Lady B., noticing a concerned look on the big man's face touched Jonathon's arm with gentleness.

"Everything alright Jonathon?" she asked, concerned at Jonathon's lack of spirit.

"Walk with me," he said under his breath.

The trio made their way to the back of the house to a spot in the tidy kitchen garden where they were completely hidden from view. Here they stopped while Jonathon related to the ladies the episode of the box in the lake. He was listened to most attentively and not once was he interrupted.

The two beautiful ladies looked from one to the other in complete perplexity and utter amazement and then relapsed into a condition of deep thoughtful silence before Felicity spoke out with a hint of authoritative reckoning.

"Well there can be no prizes for guessing who it was that placed the box in the lake," said Felicity succinctly, "or who hid it so securely; it must have been Sir Nigel himself; no other would have had the cunning intelligence for such an operation. But why? That is the question we now have to ask ourselves. It is possible that he owed a debt that he needed to be kept a total secret. Something about which he was deeply ashamed and so he engineered the robbery himself to obtain the money with which to pay it off. Let's face it, he was a very wealthy man, very wealthy indeed, and could have raised any amount without even noticing it, and certainly the sum total of the paintings would have been no problem to him at all." Felicity's reasoning sounded both authentic and explicit and gained support from the rest of the family.

"Yes darling, you could possibly be right there. He would not like to have lost paintings of close relatives and especially if they are as grand as you say Jonathon. Pictures of his dear mother and sister could never be replaced, any other subject possibly could. As Ada has admitted, the family portraits would have been of very little value to any collector no matter how good they are, simply because they were not painted by a well known artist. So, the obvious thing to do would be to hide them where nobody would think to look for them, and what better place? The lake would keep his secret for years and years and then he could have resurrected them at some future date and feign their recovery in some obscure art gallery," said Lady B., hastily adding the credible additional hypothesis to her daughter's foundation of the brief assertion with similar plausibility.

"I appreciate we are jumping the gun here a little, but I wonder if he enjoyed the horses at all. I mean, most people of his station do. Maybe he was a compulsive gambler, owed a bit of money and wasn't at all proud of his weakness," said Felicity. "Just a thought," she added, "but maybe we should find out one way or the other."

"But does my discovery of the two oils mean that the rest of the pictures were not stolen after all? Only if that is the case then obviously the police will not be forthcoming with the water colours will they?" enquired Jonathon.

"Oh, I think we are pretty safe there Jonathon. My guess is that he invited the robbery; probably organised the whole thing himself and was conveniently absent from Akworth House on the weekend of the break in. Obviously he wouldn't have expected the full value of the paintings but certainly enough to cover his immediate requirements. My reckoning is that he left his own fortune intact for reasons best known to himself, but one of them being for his darling daughter's benefit and at the expense of Ada's. He obviously doted on Susan but could not have been that enamoured with her poor mother or he would have found some other way of raising the cash. And I must say that the picture of mother daughter relations at the breakfast table earlier did not provide the illustration of the most perfect of bonding that separately and individually they wish to portray. Anyway, that aside. What we have so far speculated has now to be substantiated and so I shall take your advice Felicity and sound out Ada, maybe she will be able to throw some light on the matter. Perhaps she will know if her dear husband was in debt or not, or at least know if he was a gambler; I don't see that he would have been able to keep that sort of thing to himself," said Lady B.

They ambled to the front of the house once again still pondering the various possibilities that confronted them. As they neared the car parking area they stopped and Lady B. turned to her two children.

"Look, do you mind occupying yourselves in the garden for a while? Susan being away at the moment provides an excellent opportunity for me to have a quiet word with Ada in private. Should Susan return before me perhaps you would keep her talking out here in the garden. The last thing I shall need is for her to interrupt me while I'm talking to her mother and offer her the opportunity to take up the cause on her father's behalf."

Mother and son looked at each other and nodded their heads while Lady B. left them and hurried into the house.

Lady B. found Ada busying herself in the kitchen, seated at the table and carefully polishing a brass ornament. She went to the kettle and promptly filled it ready for boiling.

"Would you like a cup Ada?" asked Lady B. cheerfully.

"That would be lovely dear, I'm just about finished with these ornaments," answered Ada, holding up and admiring the results of her labours.

The kettle boiled, Lady B. brewed the tea, sat opposite Ada at the table and the two began to chat.

The weather was the starting point of the conversation, followed by the garden and then on to the children. Slowly the build up was taking shape quite nicely as far as the very nice lady was concerned and it was all too easy for her to manipulate the conversation any way she wanted. Lady B. paid particular attention to Jonathon's swimming proficiency and other sports she thought he was interested in and some he wasn't and then related the subject to Susan asking if the daughter shared common interests to that of her grandson.

"How about Susan, is she attracted by the sporting fever that seems to be gripping the nation these days?" she asked confidently; not considering for one moment that Susan was capable of anything that demanded any form of exertion.

"Dear me no," said Ada, a little surprised. "Susan is very like me in that respect. She inherited her father's family good looks but not his passion for sport. Now Sir Nigel, he loved all sports especially the 'gee-gees' as he used to call them."

Lady B. couldn't believe her luck as she feigned a temporary look of puzzlement.

"Gee-gees, right, I get it now. You mean horse racing don't you? But horse racing, to my way of thinking, isn't strictly a sport at all; even though it's sometimes regarded as the sport of kings. No, it's more an opportunity for the godless gamblers of this world to indulge themselves, I should say."

"Yes, how right you are Barbara, my very own thoughts exactly. Sir Nigel used to gamble regularly but he always tried to hide it from me; he knew I would disapprove you see. But many a time I would overhear him placing his bets on the telephone. He used a betting agent to do this you see but he never confided in me, not at all. It's a cruel sport you know Barbara, I've seen it on the television, they beat those horses unmercifully sometimes; I hated it so much," said Ada.

All was becoming clear and in a very short time at that.

'But the fact that Sir Nigel gambled on horses didn't make the man a sore looser,' she thought.

"And Sir Nigel, did he often win his bets? Only I've heard of people making an absolute fortune at the races," ventured Lady B. carefully.

"I couldn't tell you my dear, but to my own way of thinking there is usually only one winner and that's the bookmakers. As I've already said, he didn't confide in me, so I have no idea if he won or lost. One thing is for certain, he couldn't have lost very heavily, if at all, because he left his daughter a very wealthy woman indeed," said Ada.

"Did Sir Nigel ever actually go to the races?" enquired Lady B.

"Only about twice a year and then only to Windsor or Sandown Park. We had a chauffeur in those days and he would drive Sir Nigel there. They used to make a day of it just the two of them, quite enjoyed themselves from all accounts. Obviously I was never invited along, just Sir Nigel and Patrick O'Keefe went on their own; quite friendly they were in those days, went everywhere together. But Sir Nigel was an armchair gambler really. He spent hours in front of the television with a copy of the Sporting Life spread out in front of him studying the form of the horses and then using the telephone to place his silly bets," said Ada.

Lady B. was fascinated by the way that the conversation was progressing and desired to know a lot more but without appearing to be unduly inquisitive.

"What happened to the chauffeur after Sir Nigel died Ada? You obviously didn't keep him on." It was the casual tone of her voice that allayed any suspicions that Ada may have had about her being cross-examined, and she suspected nothing.

"He has his own business down in the village now; a garage, and quite a busy little place it is from all accounts. He got it going when Sir Nigel was still with us; but I'm sure I don't know where he got the money from to get it all started up; I expect Sir Nigel must have helped him because he never earned a fortune chauffeuring for us and that's the truth. You see, he had a mechanical background when he first came here, and he always looked after Sir Nigel's cars for him as if they were his own; kept them polished up wonderfully he did, made a much better job of them than I've made on these brasses. I suppose it was to be expected that he would have his own business some day and I'm pleased for him. Yes, he's making a real go of it, so Bill Marks tells me, though Susan doesn't use him at all. She always takes her car, when it needs looking at, to a place in Basingstoke, I believe," said Ada.

The untimely ringing of the telephone interrupted the flow of the conversation. Ada hobbled round the table to answer it, hanging fiercely onto her ebony stick with pained expression.

"---- Could you please hold the line for just a moment while I see if I can find him for you," said Ada, smiling into the phone's mouth piece as if she thought she was being observed by the caller. Then she turned to Lady Barbara.

"It's a call from a Superintendent Dobson in Brixham for Jonathon. Do you know where he is Barbara?"

"I believe he's in the garden with Felicity, Perhaps I should take the call; we don't want the gentleman being kept waiting, now do we?" said Lady B., taking the receiver from Ada's hand as she hobbled away not wishing to intrude.

"Lady Barbara Fisher-Jones speaking, I'm afraid that Jonathon is unable to take your call at this precise moment superintendent; perhaps I might be able to help you. You may remember that we met a couple of days ago, Saturday morning to be exact."

"Ah yeah, I remember you. You alright me 'andsome?" said the superintendent, who seemed to be delighted at being reacquainted with the very nice lady.

"I'm fine thank you. Do you have any news about the pictures Superintendent?" asked Lady B. hopefully, and with her dainty fingers crossed.

"Oh yeah, we got all of 'em here. Well all of 'em 'cept the two oil paintin's of the two ladies you wrote down on your list," said the policeman sounding most delighted with his disclosure.

Surprise surprise' thought Lady B. "Oh I'm so pleased she exclaimed aloud, "does this mean that we may return to Devon once again to collect them?"

"Yeah, you can if you want to. 'Course we can always deliver 'em to your door so t'speak. But if you do come down 'ere then the lady owner, she'll 'ave to come as well, so she can sign for 'em like. Can't go given' 'em to just anyone see, no that would never do," said the superintendent laughing raucously.

"I understand perfectly," said Lady B. looking a little concerned. "So we will see you around midday tomorrow, if that's alright."

"I shall look forward t'that, that I shall. Good day t'you 'til tomorrow then." The superintendent sounded a very happy policeman, very happy indeed.

Lady B. replaced the telephone receiver as Ada entered the kitchen.

"Good news Ada, the Devonshire police have recovered your paintings and they are safe and sound in Brixham so we can pop down and pick them up tomorrow, if that's alright with you," said the very nice lady looking more happy than she felt deep down.

"Oh that is good news indeed Barbara. I can't thank you enough for what you've done for me," said a most relieved Ada.

"I will just pop out into the garden to find Felicity and Jonathon, I'm sure that they will be equally as pleased to receive the glad tidings," said Lady B. as she hurried away before giving Ada the opportunity to invite herself along.

— CHAPTER TWENTY-TWO —

Felicity and Jonathon were wandering around one of the two large greenhouses marvelling at the wonderful collection of orchids that were banked up on either side of the walkway when Lady B. called to them.

The disturbed expression on the lady's face as she entered the greenhouse, immediately filled both mother and son with apprehension.

"What on earth is the matter mama, you look as if the world's caved in or something equally unlikely," said Felicity, making light of what appeared to be an impending dire catastrophe.

"Now we do have a problem on our hands," said an ashen faced Lady B. "The Akworth watercolours have all been recovered and we may pick them up midday tomorrow. But, and this is the problem, Ada has to be there to sign as having taken possession of them. So she will know that the two portraits are, to all intense and purposes, still missing when to her mind they were the only two that were of no real value to anyone except the family."

"Yes I can see the dilemma. We won't now have the opportunity of placing the oils with the other twenty-three then," said Felicity.

"I don't really see what all the fuss is about. Surely all we have to do is to sell the oils to some art dealer and slyly get Ada to buy them back again," said Jonathon, adding "there must be alternative ways."

"What and loose the profit margin the dealer would be making? See sense darling that's no practical solution. Even if we could find a dealer willing to take them in the first place, they could easily be sold before Ada even stepped into the gallery? No, that's not even a starter Jonathon," said his mother looking cynically at her son.

"OK, I can see that no third party can be involved, so perhaps we could take a letter from Ada saying that she is indisposed and giving us permission to act on her behalf; surely that's not impossible and would have the desired effect," returned Jonathon.

"The police are quite adamant that Ada is the only person qualified to sign and they are more than willing to deliver the pictures here themselves, so obviously that would be their reply to that one," said Lady B.

"Look, if I have a word with the superintendent and explain the situation to him he may be persuaded to include the two oils; I'm sure he could be a helpful sort of chap if he put his mind to it," offered Jonathon.

"No, that wouldn't do either. You would be inviting an enquiry which will implicate Sir Nigel and that in turn would devastate poor Ada and Susan, and we wouldn't wish to do that now would we? No the only way is to come clean and clearly state to our hosts that you found the two oils in the big lake; or any of the lakes come to that. Of course we shall withhold all of our own suspicions in so much as to how the two oil paintings came to be there, and allow them to draw their own conclusions. No doubt they will be able to conjure up some plausible excuse with which the noble gentleman may be completely exonerated," said Lady B.

"Of course they may be just a tiny bit curious as to why nothing was mentioned when I actually found the box, don't you think?" said Jonathon, pensively.

"That shouldn't pose a real problem. You will be conveniently returning from the lake with box in hand just as Susan is returning from the village. I know that I told Ada that you were in the garden with your mother when the call from Brixham came through, but if she remembers that ... well ... then we will have to fudge it somehow. You had better be quick Jonathon your admirer might return any moment now," said Lady B.

Without answering his grandmother Jonathon hastened from the greenhouse and headed back in the direction of the car-park not running but taking the longest of lengthy strides possible.

"And make sure that the box is dripping wet as well Jonathon," called out his mother, unsure if the big man had heard the request or no.

Jonathon went straight to the Bentley, fished inside his waterproof haversack and slung the damp towel, he found there, around his neck. He picked up the box in two hands and quickly ran to the lake, almost stumbling as he went. He dipped the box into the water and covered it with mud and weeds. As soon as he was satisfied with the result he rested on the grass mid way up the lake's side and waited for Susan to return.

Ten long minutes passed before the purring sound of a car could be heard as it entered the gateway to the Akworth drive heralding Susan's arrival and prompting the big man to casually walk along the green verge that ran the length of the of the drive in the direction of the house. He stopped awhile holding his thumb in the air just as if he were a hitch-hiker patiently waiting for an opportune lift.

The car skidded to a noisy halt on the very loose gravel causing stones to fly in all directions.

"Not been for yet another swim without me have you Jon? That is not on you know big fellow, not on at all. You might have waited for me," she whinged.

"Look I didn't tell you to go to the shops, post office or the hairdressers. I can see that that's where you've been—looks pretty good to me Susan. Still we'll soon have that messed up for you if we go swimming later," said Jonathon, trying to be as relaxed as possible.

"What's that you're carrying Jon? Bring it here so I can take a look!"

"Don't know what it is—just an old box I found buried at the bottom of the lake."

"Let's see," said Susan inquisitively, getting out of the car and walking round to where the big man stood.

Jonathon held out the box for Susan to take. She placed it down on the ground and rubbed it on the grass as Jonathon had done earlier then tried to lift the lid without success.

"Here let me help you," said Jonathon bending down beside her and removing the lid with exaggerated effort. Aware that the lid had come away far too easily, Jonathon cleaned it again on the grass and picked handfuls of the stuff to divert attention, allowing Susan to investigate the secret contents without his help.

Susan's face turned ashen as she gazed at the substance of the box's contents. She selected the painting of her aunt and stood up holding it in her hands at half arms length. Then her balance left her for a brief moment as she stared in wonder, but she didn't fall. Jonathon had moved in quickly to support her as she gazed continuously, her eyes not letting the picture go.

"You OK Susan? What's the matter? Just a picture of a woman isn't it?" asked the big man.

"No Jon, it isn't just a picture of a woman." Her words were strained. "Not just the picture of a woman at all. It's the picture of my father's late sister who died the day I was born."

She replaced the portrait in its housing and lifted the likeness of her grandmother, searching with her eyes every inch of canvas as she had the other.

"This Jon, is the portrait of my father's mother, my grandmother. She couldn't accept her daughter's death and died the following year. Both of these pictures I have loved since I was a small child Jon and they were both stolen from Akworth along with the watercolours." She turned her head to Jonathon and smiled.

"Thank you Jon, thank you with all of my heart for bringing them back to me."

Then she placed the picture back into its holder and replaced the lid. She turned again to the man who stood beside her and reaching up to him pulled his face to hers and kissed him gently whispering her thanks once more.

"Perhaps you had better rest awhile, you have had quite a shock Susan although you are looking much better now."

"No Jon, I shall be alright but my mind is buzzing with the thoughts of how this box came to be in the pond. What do you think Jon? How come it was in there?" Susan's voice trembled a little as she tried diligently to apply her mind to the troubling speculation.

"No idea, perhaps the thieves realised their worth and wouldn't be bothered with them and so tossed them into the lake as they were passing; who knows?" said Jonathon, feeling slightly guilty by the question.

"But why take them in the first place then? Surely they must have seen at once exactly what they were, so why go to all the trouble in placing them into a perfectly tailor-made container like this. Doesn't make sense. Seems more than a little suspicious to me Jon. Come on, hop in the car, I'll give you a lift," said Susan looking very worried but in charge of her senses once again.

Jonathon clambered into the passenger seat tucking his long legs away as best he could at the same time nursing the troublesome box painfully. He was feeling rather guilty at the disingenuous pretence he had undertaken and wondered how much further he would have to travel down that slippery slope before honesty became paramount once more.

"Bye the way, we had a phone call from the police in Devon a couple of hours ago, the other pictures have turned up and we are allowed to pick them up tomorrow." Jonathon could easily have bitten his tongue as soon as he said it. He thought maybe he shouldn't have but he felt he needed to give her some cheer at least after the shock she had just experienced. *'It's to late now, I've said it,'* he thought to himself.

The response was immediate and with a high degree of surprise.

"Gosh, that's a coincidence. That means we have the complete set back again. Mummy will be pleased, after all they do really belong to her you know as daddy said she should always have them," said Susan, as she again braked hard to skid on the loose gravel in front of the house.

Jonathon breathed a sigh of relief; he now felt certain that he had gotten away with his faux pas.

The couple got out of the car and walked toward the rear of the house, entered the kitchen and found the three ladies deep in conversation around the kitchen table.

"You'll never guess what Jonathon has just found in the big pond mummy," said Susan as she placed the still wet box onto the wooden tabletop.

"Voila!" she exclaimed with delighted utterance as she removed the lid of the stainless steel container once more. "How about that—is that wonderful or is that wonderful?"

Each of the two paintings were carefully removed and placed onto the dry table for all to see and admire. Ada was quite speechless with wonder, and gently wiped a tear that had unexpectedly meandered down her cheek.

"Good heavens," she said at last, bracing herself.

Both Lady B. and Felicity had feigned an exaggerated gasp of surprise simultaneously but remained silent.

Ada picked up each picture in turn absorbing their beauty, and fingering them with loving gentleness.

"How ever did you manage to find them Jonathon?" she asked, still caressing the canvases with care. "I thought they would have been with the rest of the pictures; what a lovely surprise, how wonderful. Sir Nigel would have been delighted I'm sure. But how do you think they came to be in the big pond and in such good condition after all this time?"

"Jonathon wonders if the thieves decided that the two oils weren't worth bothering about and slung them into the pond on their way out. But something worries me about that theory. Why would they pack them into a special container in the first place? I mean they didn't take them with their eyes closed did they?" said Susan, her radiant face was now beginning to change as she began to unravel the box's mystery on her own. "You can see the box has been specially made to the precise dimensions," she went on, "so that the pictures couldn't move about and get damaged. Look how snugly they fit!"

"Amateurs," broke in Lady B. offering to relieve what she considered to be a tricky situation. "Probably decided that twenty-five were too many to handle and promptly discarded the ones that were going to fetch the least money."

"Yes that must be it, no other explanation," chimed in Ada. "Look, the important thing is that we have them back safe and sound." She paused awhile before continuing the after thought that was on her mind. "No need to mention to the police that we have found the two oils that would only complicate matters."

"Complicate Matters?" Susan was astounded at her mother's reasoning and she stood up to confront her. "I realise that you are jealous of daddy's affection for me you demonstrated that fact at the breakfast table this morning by showing just how much you despise me. But why mummy? Why are you protecting him now? You know very well that daddy must have been implicated in all of this it's as plain as day and that's the real reason why you don't want the police involved, isn't it mummy?

"Look, these people have been kind in doing us a very great service and at no small risk to themselves, especially Jonathon. THE TRUTH mummy, you owe them that much," screamed Susan, her face temporarily flushing with anger. And then calmed down again as Felicity placed a soothing hand on her arm before she continued once more. "Mummy don't you think it about time you came clean about daddy and that monster Bernard Yates? They were no good, either of them, and you know that as well as I do."

"Bernard Yates? Who the devil is Bernard Yates?" requested Felicity, most insistently.

"Bernard Yates is the real name of our erstwhile butler come chauffeur, Patrick O'Keefe," said Susan. "And he is the vilest, most vicious animal to walk God's earth. He was involved in a crooked casino in London for many years, until my father rescued him and brought him here, supposedly until things cooled down; but the only problem was, he stayed. I wouldn't put anything past that man, he even wanted me. And so my father, yes my dear daddy told me to be nice to him. My own father saying that to me. Can you believe it? I wouldn't of course and so my father threatened me by saying he would cut me out of his will. Fortunately for me he died before he had had the opportunity to alter his testament. And so it was me who inherited the family fortunes and this place, much to the disappointment of Bernard Yates. But it was my father who set the man up in business you may be sure of that, because he was all but penniless when he came to Hampshire; the rival gang who threw him out and took over his dubious business saw to that. He seemed to have some sort of a hold over my father, no idea what, but certainly something. Anyway I'll bet he kept in touch with his usual contacts in the gambling fraternity after his move down here, and he and daddy must have made and lost fortunes on the horses.

"Jonathon, where exactly did you discover this stupid box?" Susan asked the question at the end of her tiring statement and indicated that she was beginning to wilt but recovered her faculty when she fetched herself a large drink. No one else was asked.

"On the far side of the lake, more than three quarters buried in the clay and silt," replied Jonathon as Susan returned to the table. "Anyway Susan, after thinking about it, I'm pretty sure that the box would have floated had it been idly thrown into the water and could not possibly have sunk without first filling up with water. But it is perfectly dry inside as you can see for yourself, take a look."

Susan brushed her hand across the entire felt lining of the case and lid thoroughly.

"Yes it is, it's completely dry. And in any case no one could possibly have thrown the wretched thing as far into the pond as that and make it stay there, not without it being weighted, not from the driveway side of the pond anyway as Jonathon has already pointed out. So it must have been deliberately planted there, and there was only one person who was capable of doing that." Susan's voice was dry and she sipped the amber liquid freely. "Daddy, clearly, he must have put it there himself, hoping to get it back much later. He didn't fancy the idea of loosing the pictures, they were far to precious to him, and he couldn't run the risk of leaving them hanging on the drawing room wall or anywhere else in the house for that matter in case the police found them and started asking embarrassing questions as they were part and parcel of the collection, so he did the most obvious thing."

For all of this time Ada sat rigidly in her armchair at the table's head supporting her chin with both of her hands and looking morosely downcast.

Tears welled in her aging eyes as at last she stirred herself and put the kettle on as if to offer the only remedy she knew.

"Susan, I hate you talking about your father in that way," she said, as she placed the kettle on the hob. "He loved you beyond reason, much more than he cared for me and the way you talk about him, anyone would think him to be a most hardened criminal instead of the kind and most generous man he really was."

"Mummy you know that I am right. Just look how he treated you all those years, confining you to the kitchen like some sainted skivvy. Yes, you are right he did dote on me, indeed to the exclusion of you. He didn't even have the courage to acknowledge you by offering to make you his wife did he? Mummy I hate to say it, but he used you—used you to get me. There I've said it, but it's true all the same."

Ada hobbled out of the kitchen with tears streaming down her wrinkled face. Susan immediately started after her but Lady B. intervened.

"No Susan, you leave this to me, I shall go after her. I think it is about time you both left this place," she said, as she went out of the door.

After the very nice lady had left the kitchen, a silence, like that when an imminent darkening storm was about to burst, fell upon the room.

Felicity gazed at Susan in bewilderment, then to her son, then back again to Susan.

"It's no good you looking at me like that Felicity, these things have to be faced up to, you must understand that," said Susan.

"Susan dear, I'm not looking at you with animosity in my heart;" she said quietly. "I'm looking at you because I feel such sorrow. Sorrow for your mother; sorrow for you. You see, if what has been said is confirmed, then sorrow is all there is left, nothing else can now be done," said Felicity maternally.

"I don't want your pity Felicity just your understanding. Barbara was right in what she said when she left, it is time we rid ourselves of this place. We don't really belong here anymore; if we ever did," said Susan as the inevitable tears began to form.

Jonathon, seeing Susan's gathering misery rose from his seat to place a comforting arm around her shoulders.

"Try not to distress yourself too much Susan. I'm sure that things aren't as black as they may appear," he said, offering a clean handkerchief.

"Not as black as they may appear? Exactly how much blacker do you suppose they could be Jon? My own father betrayed me when I thought he loved me and he stole from the only woman who ever loved him, and oh so very, very much. And for what? Just because he yearned for the excitement of some stupid animals running round a field. It was crazy, him getting himself in debt like that and then needing to hide it so that he could go on being the much admired village squire that he thought himself to be. Oh yes, he thought he was well liked alright. If only he had known just how much the villagers despised him, yes all of them. So you see he had no real reason to hide his weakness from anyone," said Susan, blowing her nose on the tear drenched handkerchief as her mother returned to the kitchen closely followed by Lady B. Susan got up from her seat and ran to her mother throwing her arms around her neck.

"Mummy I'm sorry, so very, very sorry. I didn't mean to hurt you like that," she sobbed.

"It's alright my darling; please don't you torment yourself anymore. You were right to say what you did and I was wrong in protecting him the way I did, for so long. But when he died I truly thought that I should have died too, and if it wasn't for you—well let's not go down that road. I didn't realise that your father had been so unkind to you Susan, I really didn't. If only I had known everything at the time, but then, I don't expect that I should have believed you anyway. But it is all in the past now my darling and that is where we must leave it," said Ada, wiping her own face as she spoke.

"I have had a long chat with Lady Barbara," she continued, "and she has persuaded me to leave Akworth and spend some time with her and her family in Bergholt. And I shall go too, if they all agree to have me. As for the pictures, well they don't seem so important anymore. So I intend to sell them all and eventually buy myself a little cottage in Suffolk with the proceeds; I really couldn't have them on the walls of any future home you know.

"But you my darling, you stay here if you want to. This place will make a fine home for you and some of your university friends. Then eventually you could turn it into a lovely hotel or something. Anyway that is what I have decided I must do and I'm sure there will be enough money left over to keep me out of the poor house for awhile," she laughed and cried at the same time. "It will be lovely being near my Barbara and I know she will care for me."

"Mother that is enough of this nonsense. If you think that I am going to live without you just yet—well then, you are sadly mistaken. Wherever you go I shall go. I'm sure that I could be as equally happy in Bergholt as anywhere else come to that. Besides the place is almost on the doorstep of the university so I score all round."

Lady B. and Felicity both stepped forward to give mother and daughter a hug while Jonathon walked to the kettle to fix the tea. Susan, noticing his action called out, "I think something a little stronger is called for Jon—sorry Jonathon," she said, filling the room with laughter.

The telephone's loud ringing tone interrupted the ladies babbling voices and was quickly answered by Felicity.

"Jonathon, it's for you, Sergeant Pedley from Bergholt no less."

"Hello sergeant, Jonathon Fisher here," said Jonathon.

"Hello Jonathon sorry to interrupt you're day but I 'ad to let you know that everythin's changed an' the inquest is now scheduled for next Monday mornin' so you 'ad better be home in plenty o'time," said the sergeant.

"Where and exactly what time will you need me?" asked Jonathon.

"Well the hearin' is to be held at the Coroners Court in Colchester at eleven in the mornin'. So if you would present yourself, say, an hour afore that, that will be great."

"Thank you very much I shall be there," said Jonathon. Then turning to the ladies he announced the inevitable.

"Afraid I shall have to return to Bergholt on Sunday as the hearing is to be held the following day and I mustn't be late for that, no matter what happens."

— CHAPTER TWENTY-THREE —

The third trip to Brixham was pleasant enough even though three journeys in as many days seemed tedious in the extreme to Jonathon. But the trip was of vital importance, to Ada anyway, and bearing in mind the lack of time available to undertake such an excursion before he left the county for Suffolk, he attended to the drive with surprising self-assured calmness and good grace, dispelling all need to dwell upon the past day's emotional revelation completely.

Ada retrieved her pictures thankfully much to the delight of everyone concerned and was offered the most cordial of felicitations by the beaming superintendent who had a distinct note of regret in his voice when the time came for parting.

"So, I don't 'spose I shall be a seein' of you agin then Jonathon, not now that you 'ave all the pictures back in the fold, all safe an' sound like," he said, feeling a little maudlin and somewhat stretched for words.

"Oh I don't know about that superintendent," said Jonathon, as he shook the policeman's hand firmly; relieved to have the whole episode behind him and finished with in a complete and satisfactory manner.

"We have relations who live here in Brixham who we usually meet up with a couple of times a year so if you are that desperate to see us we could always pop in to see you," said Jonathon, smiling at the inference of his remark.

"Is that right now? Well, when you do come down agin you make sure you do just that and I shall be glad to stand you all a bit o' lunch. Now don't you all forget! You mustn't also forget there are still a lot of people out there who feel they be indebted to you Jonathon. Well, even this mornin' I got a call from a gentleman who wanted your identity so's he could thank you personal like," said the superintendent, in such a way as to project his longing to tell the world of Jonathon Fisher.

"Superintendent, I just cannot emphasise enough the enormity of my need for complete anonymity in regard to this matter. You do fully understand that I hope. No one, but no one, must learn of our secret," said Jonathon, in profound earnestness and which caused the tall policeman to widen a grin upon his already exuberant face.

"Now don't you go worrying yourself about that none me 'andsome, your little secret's safe with me that it is," said the superintendent, now dissolved into accelerated laughter.

The return trip to Hampshire was as equally pedestrian as was the ride to Devon. Everyone was happy enough and smiling. All the pictures had been safely stowed away in the Bentley's boot with no anxiety at all in anyone's mind. Felicity and Susan were ensconced in the front of the vehicle alongside Jonathon while the very nice lady occupied the rear bench seat quietly focused and chatting from time to time with Ada about all things mawkish.

Now it so happened that in order to regain the ancient heart of the village of Sutton Scotney, where Akworth stood in all its splendour, that the big black Bentley had to pass by the village's peripheral housing estate where an extensive garage stood close by. All of this was to the west side of the village and so removed from the place as to form little or no actual part of it, except that it was included by reason of a prominent introductory sign stationed at the edge of the road.

The afore mentioned extensive garage, which served the entirety of the local community's automotive needs, appeared to be well organised and efficient—at least that was the impression the casual passer by was bound to receive by the orderly looks of the place. For this particular garage, had prominently arrayed, and within the reaches of its forecourt, flags and bunting and an outsized sign emblazoned in neon lighting of various colours, and the name 'O'KEEFE AUTOS' notably illuminated and was grossly over displayed so that no one could possibly fail to discern or to recognise the garish establishment for what it was, or for that matter who owned this particular motor port.

It may be well worth noting at this juncture that the O'Keefe Autos business, principally, had a distinguished local reputation for being fair in their charges, expert in their mechanical skills and expeditious and professional in all assignments carried out within the motor repair and servicing industry; all of which no doubt, would have been strongly repudiated by Susan Hutchins, were she to be asked; she, quite rightly, being bias against to a very high degree.

"It's probably a good idea for me to fill up with petrol now grandmama," suggested Jonathon, as he slowly turned the wheels of the Bentley into the garage's immaculate forecourt. "Then I shall not have to bother with that chore on Sunday morning. It's always a bore retracing a couple of miles just to fill the tank and as I intend leaving for home as early as possible on that day, everything then will be ready for the off."

As Jonathon pulled up beside the first available 'four star' pump of six, a thickset man of medium height, smartly dressed and in his late forties with a mass of red, curling wiry hair turned back to speak to someone as he came out of a double door marked 'reception.' Continuing his walk and looking round as if to admire the big black Bentley as he strode, he clearly recognised Susan sitting between Jonathon and his mother, for a pained look of dissent registered upon his face which in reality appeared to be closer to anger than not, as the deep reddening of his features spread instantly from the back of his thick neck. His beady eyes furtively scanned the remainder of the Bentley's occupants and with a devious dipping of his head he hastened round the corner of the building and instantly disappeared from view.

Susan's scrutinization of the well dressed gentleman with the mass of red hair unsettled the lovely young woman considerably, so much so that she instantly turned her head to Jonathon in a discreet downward motion as if hoping not to be recognised.

"That Jonathon, if you hadn't guessed, was Bernard Yates alias Patrick O'Keefe," whispered Susan, her hand cupped over her mouth.

"Yes Susan, I did gather that much by the attitude of the man," responded Jonathon. "A sneaky looking character if ever I saw one. Still we mustn't judge a person by his looks I suppose; hopefully he now has a changed disposition since you last knew him."

"Coo, I doubt that," retorted Susan in a derisive manner.

"Let's find out shall we?" said Jonathon, turning round to face his grandmother. "How about if we check to see if the car is in need of a service grandmama? Or a change of oil and plugs at least."

"But Jonathon the car has had a complete overhaul, just before we left Bergholt if you remember. I should think it most unlikely that the engine requires any further attention already would you?" said the very nice lady, with a puzzled look on her face.

"Precisely, but I should like that as an excuse to test the man's honesty," replied Jonathon, getting out of the car as the pump attendant approached.

"Would you be good enough to fill her up please," he said, tossing the man the keys, then ambled over to the reception area.

A short gaunt looking man, dressed in grey oil stained overalls sat immediately behind the large modern till, totally engrossed in an erotic 'Beautiful Briton's' girly magazine. He looked up quickly and concealed the magazine under his seat as Jonathon entered.

"Good afternoon," said Jonathon. "I have quite a long journey to make soon and I wondered if it would be an inconvenience for you to have a look at the Bentley's engine for me, before I get underway."

"Not at all sir, let me see now," said the gaunt looking man, as he reached for a smart looking appointments book. "There is a suitable appointment on Wednesday afternoon, that's in a day's time. It seems we have had a cancellation and I certainly could fit you in then if that would suit you sir. Otherwise we wouldn't be able to look at it until next week sometime. What needs doing sir? A full service is it?

"No, a full service certainly isn't necessary but maybe if you could check the oil and plugs and maybe give the engine the once over for me that will be fine," said Jonathon. He gave the mechanic his address and telephone number, settled the bill for the petrol and left.

Resuming his position behind the wheel of the Bentley and looking in the rear view mirror, Jonathon slowly pulled away. Coming out of another doorway further down the line of doors he noticed the sullen features of Bernard Yates glaring after the Bentley as it moved off the forecourt.

"Our Mr Yates doesn't look at all pleased with himself Susan, I wonder what his problem can be?" remarked Jonathon, blandly.

"Oh I know exactly what his problem is. He's peeved because he lost the fortune he had hoped to gain a couple of years ago, and he can't forget it."

The party arrived back at Akworth soon after five that evening in high spirits and with relaxed laughter filling the cosy kitchen. After the most excellent of meals had been consumed, Susan invited Jonathon to take a turn round the gardens with her; the excuse being that a gentle stroll might aid the digestive process after such a lavish meal; not that Susan required an excuse for anything she had made up her mind to do, as everyone was now beginning to suspect. And so it was that the merry pair sauntered off on their own into the grounds full of the joys, as it were, and leaving the three remaining ladies to clear away and see to the dishes; which they were very pleased so to do.

The bright rounded evening sun sat low in the sky blue sky and the end of day air was filled with the perfume of the sweet smelling azalea shrubs which grew in pronounced abundance around the grounds in the most vibrant yellows and oranges imaginable.

As soon as the young couple were completely out of sight of the house, Susan casually slipped her arm through Jonathon's, totally uninvited, squeezing tightly and leaning her body firmly against his, slowing the big man down to a pace that suited her. He tried desperately not to reciprocate the fervent favour but relented after awhile as he felt his adrenalin rise within his veins and drew her ever closer.

"Jon," she said, reverting back to old habits, "I have to return to Colchester myself on Sunday afternoon as I have an important lecture to attend pretty early Monday morning. And although I realise I cannot travel in the Bentley with you, I wondered if we might go together in convoy; it would be so much nicer knowing we were close together, and maybe we might stop somewhere on the way for a farewell bite to eat."

"Splendid idea Susan. You could possibly stay over at our place we have heaps of room and then we could travel to Colchester early on Monday morning, again in convoy if that would suit you."

Susan's eyes lit up at this promising opportunity and in truth, she couldn't believe her ears. *'What is this man of Christian ethics really proposing, a night of romance or a night of unending debauchery? Surely neither!'* She played along in complete innocence hoping for more signs of what she desired, not realising that the man walking beside her had nothing attuned to her thoughts on his mind at all, only friendly fellowship the one with the other.

"Yes that would be good," she remarked, in the faked purity of naivety, then instantly changed the subject hoping that the man was already committed to his suggestion.

"This has been quite a trip for you Jon hasn't it?" she said, still quaking in her shoes and feeling the palms of her hands moisten. "What with finding the twenty-five stolen pictures, frightening off cowardly lads from the pond and travelling back and forth to Devon a dozen times; yes quite an exciting and interesting few days I should say." She paused a moment not finding the right way to continue—and then blundered—"Best of all though, for me anyway, was us meeting each other. I'm so glad it happened Jon. I wonder—would you be the one on the side lines for me?" she asked assertively and immediately wished she hadn't. *'Damn and blast, where the hell did that come from? He'll think I am pushing too hard, far too hard'* she thought to herself feeling the back of her neck blush in frenzied agitation.

Warning bells rang out loud and clear in Jonathon's head for a second time but on this occasion he paid them little attention.

"Susan I shall be delighted to be there for you. Perhaps we could meet up from time to ti --" He caught himself mid stream. "Well we most certainly will do won't we? Seeing that we will probably be living in the same house together for a while; I mean, it would be pretty difficult for us not to meet up; wouldn't it?" he stammered just a little, eventually laughing off the situation as they continued walking.

Feeling relieved that her own faux pas had passed her by unscathed she felt more confident in teasing the big man without restraint.

"Jonathon Fisher I do believe you are playing at hard to get," she quipped laughingly.

"Not at all Susan, but I did tell you before that I'm not yet ready for a serious relationship, I have other priorities that I must attend to first. I thought that you had agreed with me on that one," said Jonathon, feeling completely in control of the situation.

"Yes of course I do, but a girl needs to feel that she is wanted occasionally you know," she said.

The couple continued walking far beyond the large lake and eventually arrived at one of the lesser stretches of water.

In many ways the smaller lakes seemed more interesting to Jonathon; much closer to a natural setting, providing natures inherited habitat for all the wild life that dwelt therein and a closeness and conviviality that seemed to escape the larger. Beautiful bull rushes adorned the edgings, and banks upon banks of rhododendron shrubs rose up on every side laden with crimson and ivory blooms all interspersed with the ubiquitous blue bells and azalea bushes. Indeed, a complete haven for wild life was presented before the couple, as they stood perfectly still in absolute wonderment. Coots and moorhens and mallards had nested in the reeded borders and ground hollows and were dashing about, with young chicks serenely following mother hen as they ventured in and out of the seclusion of the embankment. One mallard duckling, finding itself being left behind by its siblings, decided to catch up with the rest of the family group and swam quickly, almost running on the water's surface as it did so. The two humans looked at each other smiled and simultaneously sympathized a longish aah. The two pair of nesting mute swans that glided nonchalantly over the lake held their long necks in a gentle 'S' shape also added their contribution to the most congenial atmosphere of nature's palace, producing an unsurpassed splendour of spontaneity and beauty that thrilled the very heart of the young couple as they stood in silent awe.

"Jon, do let's have a swim right here and now in the smallest pond. I'm sure the ducks wont mind or even notice us," said Susan, breaking the beautiful spellbinding stillness in an instant.

"Unfortunately we didn't bring our swimming togs with us," replied Jonathon with a dubious glance.

"Who cares," shrieked Susan. "No one's about; let's skinny dip." And with a further shriek she commenced abandoning her clothes not waiting for approval or consent.

The complete shock of the statement brought about a feeling of immediate sobriety and a state of panic stricken terror swept instantly over the big man as he physically attempted to control Susan's insistence in being unclothed.

"Susan, stop that at once! Have you no shame, no self respect?" he said, with such a sanctimonious vigour that it brought a look of dismay to the lovely blonde woman's face, compelling the eagerness within her to subside.

"Jonathon Fisher why don't you stop being such a boring prig? Where the hell is your sense of adventure man? Most people would have jumped at a chance like this but not you, oh no not the 'oh so perfect' Jonathon Fisher," said Susan, feeling the fervour of her spirit draining fast. But she waited awhile for a change of heart within the big man, which sadly for her didn't appear to be imminent.

Gradually Jonathon's inflamed level-headedness gave way to a more genteel mode although he felt some forthright words of retribution would not go amiss.

"Susan, there seem to be a couple of lessons missing from your moral preparedness and upbringing. Firstly the human body is to be respected, kept private if you like between man and wife. Secondly one doesn't go around flaunting one's private parts to any old Tom Dick or Harry who might be available to witness the erotic show," said Jonathon, rather pompously.

"One and the same thing I should have thought," retorted Susan with a derisive jeer. "Anyway, I do respect my body—rather proud of it as a matter of fact. And you are not any old Tom Dick or Harry are you? I thought we meant more to each other than that Jon—much more. You are the guy on the side lines for me, remember?" Susan was in a fit of pique but tried not to show her annoyance, wanting matters resolved between them and for normal service to be resumed as soon as possible.

But Jonathon was having none of it. If she wanted to be in some sort of relationship with him, then she had to show some decorum and customary protocol—even though the relationship may be no more than that of friends.

"No Susan that will not do, it's not as simple as you make out. Supposing that it wasn't me who was walking with you this evening. Supposing it was–say–David West or someone else more likely. Would you be skinny dipping with him?" A moment's pause. "Yes I guess you would—you probably have already. Susan you are nothing but a promiscuous, spoilt child, wanting your own way in every thing that springs to your minuscule mind." Jonathon was feverishly enraged and felt tainted by a splattering of jealousy as he marched off toward the house.

"Jon, wait a minute, please. Don't go back just yet, not like this. No of course I haven't been skinny dipping—not ever, not with anyone, let alone with David West. It's just that the girls at uni often talk about it and I thought that it might be fun that was all. Jon please don't let us fall out over this. I do see your point of view upon reflection, honest I do and what is more, I agree with it. I do want so much for us to be friends Jon and I should hate my foolishness to stand in the way and spoil everything. Please Jon—please."

Her supposed begging for the big man to return certainly had the desired effect, for Jonathon turned round, took a few large paces back to where Susan was standing and putting his hands around her tiny waist lifted her up to his lofty height and kissed her tenderly but firmly on the mouth. He then replaced her, dove like, onto terra firma and released her. It was the releasing bit that caused the problem, it was late or rather he released her far too early, for her legs buckled beneath her and she slipped inelegantly to the grassy floor. Jonathon smiled compassionately and helped her to her feet.

"And I suppose that is within your book of rules on ethical behaviour is it Jonathon Fisher," said Susan weekly but with the most delicate of smiles.

"Yes it most certainly is. It's rule one hundred and sixty one and deals with preventing someone who you are beggining to care about from making a complete ass of themselves."

Jonathon smiled warmly into Susan's eyes and kissed her once again. Still feeling fragile and legless Susan held onto the big man tightly.

"And are you beginning to care Jon?" she said.

"Looks that way," said Jonathon pulling away from her and brushing aside the pertinent question as they returned slowly back to the house hand in hand.

But tender imaginings had already entered Susan's mind; thoughts about which she felt that Jonathon might not readily approve—not yet anyway.

The evening, by this time had quietly settled in when the affectionate couple eventually arrived at the kitchen door. They promptly separated as Jonathon lifted the latch. But a knowing wink of the eye from him was all the reassurance that Susan needed.

— CHAPTER TWENTY-FOUR —

After enjoying all the restful sleep he needed to replace the energy he had used during the previous days exhausting activities and with a feeling of emancipation flooding his mind because the unsavoury affair of the stolen paintings had now been categorically resolved, Jonathon rose from his long comfortable bed feeling the need for some physical activity to re-energise his spiritual batteries. And as was his wont at this particular time of day back at his East Bergholt home in Suffolk to obtain such a requirement by swimming his ever beloved Stour, he now opted for the next best available undertaking, viz. swimming the large Akworth Lake. He quickly dressed and gathered his swimming gear ready to make his way to the large lake once again where he anticipated some untroubled time in the silvery water which seemed to have eluded him of late.

The time, as he glanced at his watch, was a little before five thirty, and so he hurriedly left the house on this extremely agreeable Wednesday morning. And not at all certain if the inhabitants of Akworth House were firmly asleep in the cosy land of nod at this unearthly hour, he silently walked on the soft grassy verge so as not to noisily disturb the gravel of the driveway. He quickly glanced over his shoulder a couple of times, as he had done on the previous early morning jaunt, to scan the upstairs windows where inquisitive eyes might be observing furtively or who may have been inadvertently disturbed by his unadvertised departure; even though the silence he was observing was primarily for the consideration of others.

The early morning chorus, chirruped continuously by his various feathered friends, was about reaching its climax, and he listened intently as he recognised his favourite songs drifting over the cool tranquil air and being echoed so melodiously in the broad leafed trees beyond. Small trill voices and louder slightly harsher cries all blended together to form a sound so celestially harmonious as to delight any ear patient enough and attuned sufficiently to attentively listen.

He walked unhurriedly to the waters edge stopped and turned looking back toward the big house, searching for any sign of movement and to assure himself of the complete privacy he was selfishly looking for. *'I'm in luck this time'* he told himself *'no one has seen me,'* he seemed to be quite certain in his mind. But as in the past, his movements had not been unobserved and his freedom from intrusion was to elude him once again, maybe. Nevertheless, ignorance being ever blissful, he was relaxed and uninhibited and with no obvious worry on his mind he entered silently the peaceful shining waters.

The underground link between the lakes that Ada had mentioned and which she had so quickly dismissed as being mythically orientated by villagers of a bygone age was the excuse his mind was dwelling on; an underground cavern seemed unlikely but who knows? And so he dived to the lakes base foundation to search for the unblemished truth, even to the far reaches of the waters expanse hoping to find a tunnel, a pipe, anything that would do to prove the link; but nothing. After scouring the length of the entire lake's edging on its farthest side, not once but two times, and finding nothing more than a few rodent holes, and them being above the waters level, he gave up. Taking thought and not wishing to waste a moment of this golden opportunity Jonathon abandoned the whole exercise in favour of one more energetic; the activity of power swimming. *'This will charge the batteries even quicker,'* he thought to himself. And so, by timing each one hundred yard length meticulously with the aid of his chronometer, he set off at a pace. Jonathon was feeling fit and healthy, and deeply satisfied both within himself and with the improved performance he was putting up. As with all athletic types, it is always found to be most pleasing to notice even the smallest of advancements in particular capabilities.

   On the twelfth length Jonathon was beginning to tire slightly and slowed down a fraction to pace himself when suddenly a splatter, an unexpected splash in the water's surface occurred about a yard in front of him. He stopped for a brief moment when a second splatter occurred, this time only inches away and to the left. Then another, and still more rained down at regular intervals. Too late it registered what was happening to him as an enormous thud exploded in his head and blood started to gush from the back of his aching cranium. At last, realising that he had been hit and the impending danger of being hit yet again, Jonathon quickly dived beneath the surface of the water and to the safety of its welcoming depths. A ghastly feeling of complete insecurity overwhelmed the young Adonis as he employed the sum total of his considerable strength of body and power of mind to gain that end of the lake where he knew the diving board would be. He swam remorselessly; at times losing totally his sense of direction but at last his weakened fingers touched the grassy bank and the relative security of its dark green velvety mantle.

   With the final vestige of his abundant strength now all but exhausted, Jonathon gainfully and painfully struggled out of the reddening water, and nearing a state of complete collapse he laid himself helplessly down on the soft green bank as a benevolent mist clouded his weary mind.

   Unbeknown to Jonathon, minutes, that felt not unlike the passage of days had past before a gentle hand tried to help him to his feet and with already spent strength he stirred a little and after a fearsome struggle he managed slowly to move one knee beneath him and as soon as he gained that creditable pose he fell back again into the arms of the welcoming, friendly grass. Through the nebulous blur that surrounded his wretchedly numbed brain, he vaguely heard the distant anxious voice of Susan repeatedly calling out his name like some distant mythological spirit of nature come to bring him succour or some apocryphal Aphrodite come to encourage his love. Gradually and surely the foggy dew began to clear once again as he blinked his eyes in an effort to gain control of his battle weary mind; it was indeed a battle and a battle he temporarily won. He lie there still, unable to move, now unable to blink anymore, just looking up into Susan's tear filled eyes, while her silken hand tenderly soothed and caressed his throbbing bleeding head and all the time he longed for some remedy, a respite even, to this hopeless predicament he was in.

As Jonathon's motionless body lie prostrate on the dew damp grass, a newly arrived voice jarred his head. A much harsher voice from that of Susan's rang in his ears but one that instantly instilled a marked degree of confidence to his muddled mind. The form of the man that overshadowed him spoke with a hesitant but distinct Hampshire tongue.

"Everythin' a'right then?" it said, in a disturbed but concerned manner, "can I help at all?"

"No Bill, everything is not alright. Jonathon has been hit and—and he's in a terrible state. Run quickly to the house—fetch help—an ambulance Bill—quickly—quickly. Go on—hurry!" Jonathon vaguely heard Susan's disjointed voice sobbing out her vital orders as the hazy clouds of obliviousness overshadowed him again and he was out off the battle once more.

When he eventually regained consciousness, Jonathon found himself in the clean, white crisp sheets of a hospital bed, surrounded by an elderly, comparatively speaking, white coated doctor looking down at him quite unconcerned and two immaculately turned out nurses who were. Jonathon trying to stir was immediately rebuked by one of the nurses who urged him assertively to lay still and relax.

The doctor moved more closely to Jonathon so that he unmistakably was heard by his patient.

"That is one hell of a haematoma you have there young man, very nasty indeed, but not at all life threatening I can assure you of that. Anyway, we'll whip you away in a moment or two, take a few pictures of your bonce just to make certain that nothing is broken and then we'll leave you to rest in peace. Now you are bound to feel a bit shaky even dizzy at times and probably have a bit of a headache but try not to worry too much about that, nothing that a couple of painkillers can't sort out for you. The best thing you can do is to rest and lie as still as you are able and allow the nurses to look after you—I'm pretty certain they will love doing that," said the kindly doctor as he winked and smiled in a fatherly way toward the young man.

After the ex-rays had been summarily completed with no obvious difficulty, Jonathon was steadily wheeled back to the accident ward where his mother and grandmother sat apprehensively awaiting his return. In turn they had walked round the bed in his absence, patting and smoothing the pillows in a finicky and exacting manner while their eyes occasionally cast furtive glances at the door and they had successively walked to it eyeing the corridor in each direction seeking signs of their son's arrival. When at last he did emerge and had been safely deposited within the crisp white sheets of his bed once again their craving anxieties became vocalised, especially that of his doting mother.

"Darling how are you?—We've all been so worried about you—are you alright darling?—What did the doctors say?—were the ex-rays satisfactory?—is your poor head aching darling?—please speak to us Jonathon—we are so worried," Felicity's overwrought utterances bombarded Jonathon continuously and as her feverish voice almost reached a state of hysteria the big man raised his hand for peace and solitude and smiled reassuringly.

"Mother, if you slow down a couple of seconds perhaps I shall be able to put both your minds at rest. I'm fine, really I am. Just a bump on the head that's all. My skull seems to be intact, no fractures or anything, so there is no need for you to worry or be alarmed about. But because I have suffered a degree of unconsciousness, they are rather keen to keep me under observation and monitor my progress for the next twenty-four hours. After that, I shall certainly be fit enough to return to a normal active existence. So you can make all necessary arrangements to get me out of here tomorrow morning, OK? So please stop your worrying."

Although Jonathon's bandaged, injured head was causing him an amount of sore discomfort, the analgesic capsules administered a few moments earlier had not yet taken satisfactory effect, he did not allow this to impede his enthusiasm to rid himself of this unfortunate situation and so his words were both candid and sure; he wanted out of here tomorrow and no mistake and with as little fuss as possible.

"Jonathon dear, I can understand very well your anxiety at being in this place and your urgency in getting back to normality with us but I do feel that if more time is considered necessary for you to make a full recovery then the opportunity should be taken. I would hate for you to discharge yourself which, to me, is what you are implying. Everything seems reasonably under control and satisfactory as far as it goes but like you I shall not be happy until you are safe with us once again but that doesn't mean we want you to do something you may regret later. Still you are alive, that's the main thing and I have no doubt that with the required amount of rest you will be you're old self again in no time at all.

"It was those three awful Wingfield boys who were responsible you know Jonathon, we are well aware of that. They attacked you with catapults loaded with steel ball bearings; the wicked thugs. Bill Marks noticed the three of them leaving the grounds by the back lane as he came to work earlier this morning. He told us that they seemed in rather a hurry and didn't stop to speak although it was obvious that they had seen him. Much too anxious to leave the scene I expect. Bill said they often go about the village armed with those dreadful weapons causing all sorts of damage and mayhem; even the police know about their pranks and apparently have tried to stop them on many occasions. Anyway we have notified the local police so I am sure it won't be long before those ruffians are put into police custody. I only hope they get their just desserts, that's all," said Lady B. withdrawing all her right-mindedness regarding the earning of respect she had expresses before and was now seemingly seeking defiant retribution for the abuse to her grandson.

Felicity, noting her mothers remarks smiled inwardly and bit her tongue saying nothing untoward, instead she continued the report -

"Luckily, Susan noticed you leaving the house this morning and after she had suitably attired herself she followed you to the lake feeling at the time rather 'put out' was how she described it. She was wonderful Jonathon. She stayed with you all the time, nursing your poor head and desperately trying to keep you conscious until the ambulance arrived but without success. Apparently Bill noticed you both and ran to see if there was a problem. Then he tore off to the house 'sprinting like the very devil' was how he put it, used the kitchen telephone to summon the ambulance and then sprinted back again to you. What a lovely boy he is, isn't he mama," she said, glancing at her mother who smiled and nodded an agreeable nod. "Anyway," Felicity continued, "no one else in the house was alive do you see, and it wasn't until the ambulance alarm bells rang out that the house was eventually brought to life. Susan came to the hospital with you and Bill went back to the house by which time we were all awake and fully dressed. He told us as much of the story as he knew and we immediately rang the hospital for a report on you and then we telephoned the police station as mama has already said. Afterwards we came to the hospital as quickly as we possibly could; leaving Ada to man the phone in case we were needed. Anyway, I sincerely hope they have now caught those awful boys and that they will be sent to prison and the key thrown away, hopefully to the bottom of the lake." Felicity had all but regained her poise after her initial state of shock and had filled her most beautiful face with an emotional smile.

"Where is Susan now?" asked Jonathon, trying to sound as insouciant as possible, not wishing for the mothers to get any unwarranted notions into the development of any relations or feelings the unfortunate episode might have unwittingly brought to the surface.

"She is outside darling, in the waiting room, anxious to see you I am sure, but unfortunately the rules are only two visitors per patient at any one time so we claimed first option. Do you wish to see her Jonathon?" Felicity looked a little uncertain as her hankering need was to spend as much time with her son as she possibly could.

"Yes of course, how could I not? But when we have finished mother, no hurry," replied Jonathon, reading his mothers thoughts so lucidly.

Just then, one of the staff nurses who had received Jonathon onto the ward when he had first arrived returned to his bedside, jovially chatting to the visitors before turning her attentions to Jonathon. She was rangy, about five feet ten, not overly attractive but eager in every sense.

"Hello again Jonathon, how's the head feeling? I should think that your skull must be made of cast iron the way it coped with such a blow; any normal nut would have easily cracked from a much smaller knock than the one yours received and that's for sure.

"Jonathon the police are on the telephone asking me if it would be alright for them to pop in this afternoon to have a chat with you. Now I know all too well what their chats can be like, so if you're not up to it just give me the word and I shall tell them to wait until you have been discharged. I'm sure they won't gain much in their enquiries even if they saw you this very minute so a few hours longer will make little difference."

"No, I'm fine, really nurse. I would much rather get the whole thing over now, than allow the blessed thing to drag on. So yes, let them come in please," said Jonathon.

The nurse returned immediately after she had further spoken to the police and after fussing about and diligently studying the T.P.R. charts that were clipped to the foot of the bed she drew the curtains around asking the two ladies if they would mind stepping out for a few minutes; which they felt obliged to do.

"The police mentioned to me a second ago that they had apprehended the young rascals they think did this to you Jonathon," she said when they were quite alone, "complete with their nasty weapons too I should think. What a wicked thing to do, have they nothing else to occupy their minds I wonder? Still, you are already on the mend and we expect you to make a splendid recovery. Now I have to record your T.P.R. yet again; I realise it is boring for you but it has to be done so just relax."

With careful in depth attentiveness the nurse took the handsome young man's temperature, his pulse and his respirations then she clumsily wrapping the strap of the sphygmomanometer around his upper arm so inappropriately that the task had to be attempted twice, she eventually and quite unnecessarily recorded his blood pressure. And with an unmistakable utterance of satisfaction she penned the results of her examination onto the afore mentioned chart, drew back the curtain once again, gave Jonathon a smile while she fluttered her eyelashes and left, allowing the two ladies to return to their son's side.

"You know, I really don't see why the nurses get so damned flustered over recording a few observations," said Jonathon feeling a little peeved at all the fuss.

Lady B. looked at her grandson and smiled raising one eyebrow very slightly.

"Don't you dear," she said.

— CHAPTER TWENTY-FIVE —

By far the biggest majority of fit and healthy young men who unfortunately find themselves incarcerated within the confines of a hospital ward, no matter how short the visit is promised to be, do tend to feel the experience most tedious and uninspiring, craving for the social aspect of life and even finding the hum-drum outlook of gainful employment more preferable. Jonathon was no exception. The minutes passed as hours and the hours like unto days for the young Adonis as he lay upon a bed too hard for his particular comfort.

He had been left alone for a short while as the shift of his entertainers, come overseers, changed; the two mothers deciding to relinquish their places at his side in favour of Susan and a pleasantly warm cup of tea.

Susan entered the ward looking tired and forlorn and not at all the bubbly creature Jonathon had come to know. She kissed the big man's cheek with barely a greeting and occupied the chair that his mother, Felicity, had vacated still without a commencement of conversation.

"Honestly Susan, the way mother said goodbye one would think she was under the impression that she would never set eyes on me again.

"Anyway, how are you after conducting your 'Florence Nightingale' demonstration earlier? More than a little shaken I expect, if that peaky look on your physiognomy is anything to go by." Jonathon's greeting was too flippant and waggish for Susan's liking but she abandoned all admonishments and without a smile said:

"'Honestly Susan' nothing. Jon, you have given me the biggest shock of my life. Why do you insist on swimming all by yourself instead of involving me? It wouldn't have happened had I been there, and you know it. Oh I'm sorry," she hastily added, "I know it wasn't your fault, but my God, what a morning it has been, I haven't been able to think of anything or concentrate on anything but you. Anyway, I do seem to be getting up to scratch at last, thanks to the tea they offer you in this place. Did I say tea? More like washing up water if you ask me, little wonder it has a reviving effect.

"I have to say you seem bright and breezy Jon, good colour too all things considered, or is it your permanent tan that's deceiving me?" said Susan, still grim faced but trying to lighten up.

"Are they treating you well Jon? I expect the nurses can't keep their hands off you, am I right?" The semblance of a smile broke through at last although still a little weak and watery.

"Can I bring you anything Jon? How about some lovely grapes? I do so like grapes. I could sit on the side of your bed and eat them all for you."

Susan's attempt at humour seemed empty even to her, but she had made the effort and grinning at her own poor witticism, fruitlessly hoped it might be contagious.

"Susan I shall definitely be out of here tomorrow so there is no need to bring anything in to me. You know, I'm a little concerned about the Wingfield lads Susan, I don't expect you have seen them at all have you?" Jonathon's concern about these wayward individuals astonished Susan greatly.

"What on earth are you concerned about those louts for Jon? They are trouble with a capital T and deserve all they get in the way of punishment," she said, shaking her head.

Jonathon ignored Susan's assertion and stared out of the window for a brief moment searching his mind for the words he had been ruminating.

"I've been told that they are in police custody and I'm not entirely clear what the situation is with them. Look I have given the matter a great deal of thought since I've been in here, in fact I have thought of little else and I have come to the conclusion that there is little to be gained by bringing official charges against them and so I intend to forget about the whole affair," said Jonathon, who sounded resolute enough but this weird statement brought a look of despair in Susan's pretty face.

"What?—Jon, have you lost your reasoning? That bump on the head must have addled your brains or worse. Of course you must bring charges against these idiots; they are lunatics Jon and should be locked away." Susan was equally as adamant in her opinion as was Jonathon in his. To her mind Jonathon was in the cursed state of an ethical dilemma, probably brought about by some religious persuasion or the bump on the head.

"Anyway, the police will be in later for one of their cosy little chats so maybe I shall speak to them about it," said Jonathon, attempting to abandon the subject. But Susan wasn't playing ball, she being intent on convincing Jonathon of the error of his convictions.

"Jon, please listen to me for a minute. These lads are very dangerous you must see that. It could easily be me who is next on their hit list, or maybe mummy who they decide to attack or even some other innocent and unfortunate target. The only safe place, for all our sakes, is for them to be behind locked doors," said Susan, raising her voice a tad.

"Susan these lads just haven't had a chance in life. It seems to me they have been on the wrong road ever since the day they were born, with no proper upbringing, parental control or guidance at all. I'm told that Sam has been in and out of jail ever since I don't know when, and that doesn't seem to have been any help to him at all, now does it? Any more visits to prison and he will be beyond redemption, believe you me. And his two brothers appear to be just as bad; they seem to be following Sam down that same rocky road completely un-blinkered. Susan, there simply has to be a better way of tackling this problem, another way, any other way besides incarcerating three young men for six months. Oh I am fully aware that the prison authorities mean well and on the whole they do a good job, I'm quite sure of that. But what I mean is, the prison administration can provide all the rehabilitation programmes under the sun, and they do, but when it comes down to it, the real problem is the locking away bit and living with the type of people who are only too willing to teach young offenders more tricks than they already know. I truly believe in the old adage that there is some good in all of us, no matter how difficult it is to find. But it has to be found, yes Susan, even in the Wingfield boys," said Jonathon, earnestly pronouncing his thoughts completely, and in every respect his attitude was never going to change, no, not at all.

"Well the magnanimous Jonathon Fisher has spoken and he seems to have his mind made up without hesitation, with no reservations and without proper debate either. I have to hand it to you Jon, you most certainly do provide a very convincing argument for your causes, but then, that shouldn't come as a complete surprise to me as I have found you in that convincing mode before haven't I? However, the proof of the pudding, as they say, will be if you are able to convince the police of your intentions but I think that that will be quite a different matter myself, and not an easy one for you to overcome?"

Susan's scepticism was rather difficult to swallow for Jonathon but she wouldn't be the only one to convince; the family had already stated precisely where they stood regarding the Wingfields and Susan was quite right, the police too would be formidable opponents for the young man to overcome.

Abandoning the awkward subject and after a few valued moments of exchanging harmless banter with Susan the two mothers put in an appearance at the door, much against the rules, and they entered and joined in some frivolous repartee to keep light the entertainment for the injured man. Both Lady B. and Felicity were now looking more refreshed and much happier than when they left and each anticipated going back to Akworth for lunch.

"Susan, we have decided we are leaving now that we have been completely assured of Jonathon's wellbeing and are wondering if you would like to go back with us or perhaps you would choose to stay with Jonathon awhile longer; it's up to you, we can always pick you up later, in say a couple of hours or so, if you would prefer to stay," said Lady B.

"Thanks Barbara, yes I will go with you both now, if that's alright. I have done all I have to do and said all I have to say and I am quite satisfied that the patient will live; he's in good hands anyway," said Susan glancing toward a pretty nurse who was supposed to be attending to another patient's needs but who was finding great difficulty in applying herself to the task in hand and kept looking in Jonathon's direction whenever the opportunity presented itself.

Lady B. following Susan's gaze, appreciated the difficulty the nurse was finding in her concentration. Then she looked back at her grandson and smiled.

"Just a moment ago we were both assured by a very amicable but not so young a doctor that you are on the mend Jonathon, and short of an unexpected major relapse we shall be able to collect you in the morning, so you can guess we are jolly pleased about that," said Lady B., getting up to go.

They all said their goodbyes and Susan being the last in the queue kissed Jonathon fully on the mouth, much to Felicity's astonishment.

It was three in the afternoon when the two police officers eventually put in their appearance on the casualty ward both looking unremarkable and unrefined in their uniforms; in a word, scruffy.

The sun was shining through the large open casement window directly into Jonathon's eyes causing the big man some considerable annoyance. A pretty nurse, noticing her patient's difficulty at being powerless to move out of its dazzling rays, wandered over and adjusted the green blind by pulling it down sufficiently to provide a shadow precisely where it was needed and touched his hand tenderly as she did so. Jonathon smiled and thanked his attentive carer then looked over in the direction of the double doorway as the two inelegant police officers entered.

"Oh no, not Sid and Jeremy again" said Jonathon under his breath. "The Laurel and Hardy of the Hampshire force." He tried desperately to conceal his gleeful amusement as the two policemen looked around the ward scrutinising each bed in turn before approaching his.

"So we meet once again Mr Fisher," said Jeremy, with the merest flicker of a smile on his quivering mouth.

"Blimey it's 'im agin," said sizeable Sid, looking down at the patient and then up at his much taller partner.

"I've just said that you dumpling. Sid, must you repeat everything I say?" asked Jeremy, without actually turning his head.

"Sorry Jeremy," said Sid, sinking into his boots.

Jonathon fought back the same compunction to laugh aloud at the two-part comedy act in blue, as he had when they immediately entered the ward. But, so that his own composure might be completely maintained he offered them his brightest of afternoon greetings and hoped they were in good spirits.

"Now don't you go worrin' your head about our state of health young man; you're the one who's sick, remember? So how's the bonce comin' along?" he said, closely examining the bandaged head with uttermost interest but seeing no hint of a wound.

"I 'ave it on good authority that you're now in a fit state to answer a few questions and to make a statement. Well that's what we're 'ere for anyway aint it Sid?"

Sid made no attempt at a reply to his partner's question but instead he searched the ward for a chair not unlike the one Jeremy was now sitting on, and upon which he might stash his own fat backside for the duration of the visit. (Felicity having tidied the seating arrangements before her departure).

"So 'haps we can get started straight away then," said Jeremy, comfortably settling himself.

After Sid was also suitably installed, he took out his official notebook with a flourish and also a ballpoint pen which he licked as if it were a pencil thereby staining his lower lip which matched the colour of his uniform perfectly.

"Now we've had a word with those Wingfield cretins an' they say they pelted you with their catapults thinkin' you were ducks," said Jeremy. "Now how they come to mistake you for ducks I really don't know. Could 'ave bin a trick o' the light I s'pose, that bein' so early in the mornin' like. Anyway we had to hear their side o' the story afore we goes an' arrest 'em proper like. So now we need to 'ear your side o' things, what you 'ave to say OK? Sid 'ere shall be writin' down what you say, so not too quickly now if you don't mind 'cause he can't write fast," said Jeremy.

Jonathon went over the morning events in some detail, slowly and deliberately, from the time he rose from his bed in the morning to the time he found himself in bed once again; obviously omitting any parts which had been filled in by others. Everything appeared to be completely satisfactory and the inquisitors appeared pleased with the interview to the extreme, that is, up to the moment when Jonathon declared that he had no intention in pressing charges.

"What? Not pressin' charges?" said Jeremy. The policeman was furious and he let it be known that he was furious. "I be furious young man," he said. "Do you realise what it is you are a sayin'? They tried to kill you with their ruddy catapults an' now you say you're not pressin' charges. Now you listen to me young man, you 'ave to press charges, do you hear me?" Jeremy was getting most enflamed by this time and he let it be known that he was getting inflamed. "I be gettin' most enflamed with this situation, I surely do," he said. "They'll be thinkin' that you be scared of 'em. Scared to death of 'em tha's what they will think. An' you know what? They'll make your life a misery not knowin' what they be up to next, so you 'ave to press charges." Jeremy was most adamant in his assertions and continued in this vein for some considerable time.

Jonathon on the other hand felt relaxed and defiant knowing full well that his physical fear of anyone was non existent.

"On the contrary officer," he said smiling, "I'm quite sure the Wingfields are under no illusions on the point of my being in fear of them. You see they have tried to intimidate me before and have found to their cost that I am not to be trifled with."

"But all the more reason not to let the blighters off the hook. Well if you do, then you must have a very good reason that's what I think; so 'haps you better talk to me about it," suggested Jeremy.

"No, not at all. There is nothing to talk about. You see I have given the matter some considerable thought and I have come to the conclusion that no good purpose can be served by sending them to prison and that is precisely what would happen if I did bring an action against them. So no, definitely not," said Jonathon, with a spiritual passion of determination set fully upon his features.

On the face of it, Jeremy had all but given up the cause as he scoured Jonathon's face hoping for a last minute break through but finding none he said:

"Well now—we've taken your statement, so if you would be good enough to read it through careful like an' sign it on the bottom, I shall be grateful. But don't you think for one moment that this is the last you be hearin' of the matter, oh dear me no. My chief, he'll be wantin' a few words with you I'll be bound," said a despondent and disappointed Jeremy.

"Oh yeah, he'll be wantin' a few words with you an' no mistake," chipped in Sid, smiling broadly.

"Alright, alright Sid, I've said all that's needed to be said thank you very much. So we'll push off now an' make out our report sir," said Jeremy, as the two police constables made their way slowly to the door marked exit. As he placed his hand upon the handle of the door he briefly hesitated as if he had forgotten something of some importance and turned to Jonathon.

"Anyway we're glad you be lookin' so well like, young man, not so sure that Sam's boss will be as pleased though. Cheerio then, be a seein' of you sir," said Jeremy, smiling smugly to himself.

"Just one moment officer, who exactly is Sam's boss?" Jonathon asked the question eagerly hoping for an immediate answer and he wasn't disappointed.

"Oh didn't you know? Why, it's Mr O'Keefe, friend of Miss Hutchins I believe," responded the officer still smiling.

The name triggered an instant thought in Jonathon's mind.

"The service on the Bentley," he said aloud. "I must remind mother about the service on the Bentley."

He called over the pretty nurse, who had appropriately relieved him from the sun's glare, and asked if he might use the portable telephone.

She wheeled the contraption over to him from the far end of the ward and plugged it in beside his bed. He deposited a five new pence piece into the slot and dialled the number of Akworth House. After some time the voice of Ada sounded only just audible as she repeated the number Jonathon had dialled. He asked the old lady if the two mothers had arrived back yet.

"Not yet Jonathon," came the reply, "I believe they had to take the car to the garage on the way back from seeing you. They may be waiting for it to be looked at or be walking back, not at all sure which. Anyway they will be some little time yet I should think."

A relieved Jonathon replaced the receiver and the pretty nurse giggled as she returned the telephone to its station.

— CHAPTER TWENTY-SIX —

The remaining hours of Jonathon's stay at the hospital were spent in a state of daunting apprehension, wondering all of the time if it was Patrick O'Keefe himself who had perpetrated the attack on him as some bizarre vendetta against Susan and all because of the Eld inheritance he had failed to obtain. *'If indeed that was the case, then what am I, Jonathon Fisher, doing by allowing my attackers off Scot free? How could I be so stupid?'* he thought to himself. *'People have tried to kill me and here am I saying come on lads take another pop at me. How crazy is that? It was somehow different earlier before the fatuous fringe of the Hampshire police decided to stir up my mind for me,'* he rationalised warily. *'It was juvenile pranks then, but now the rules have changed completely. Suddenly, and without warning a once full time racketeer has now taken the limelight centre stage. He, the one time leader of some crime syndicate, has set himself in direct opposition to me.'*

Two massive questions now loomed up before the young titan. One: where would his Christian chivalry lead him if he decided to perform a shift, a 'U turn,' and level indictments against the Wingfields after all? And two: how could he possibly face a formidable adversary like O'Keefe and still keep his Christian ethics unblemished. *'One step at a time,'* he told himself. Getting out of hospital and back to a semblance of normality was his first priority; uncovering the reality of O'Keefe's involvement would be next, he would re-assess the remainder of the situation later.

Felicity Fisher was on time. She picked up her son from the hospital promptly at eleven o'clock the following morning as arranged with undiluted gratitude for all the care the hospital staff had displayed in assisting her beloved son.

The rain fell heavily as the, bandage free, big man settled himself in the passenger seat beside his mother, his long legs being moderately contorted to accommodate them but not uncomfortably so. And with the windscreen wiper blades activated in full rotating action, they set off for Akworth House.

"How did the Bentley acquit herself at the garage yesterday mother," asked Jonathon, eager to learn the truth about the ultimate in garage functioning.

"Much as you had anticipated darling. Fourteen pounds for a new set of plugs and an oil change, except the plugs were not changed because I took the trouble to secretly mark them before the car went in, and the marked plugs are still there. I have no idea at all if the oil was changed because that was done before we left home and so I would have expected that to be still fairly clean anyway. Personally I doubt they even bothered to inspect the dip stick," said Felicity, cynically.

Jonathon looked at his mother, whistled through his teeth and scratched the part of his head that was without damage.

"That's a tidy sum for doing nothing isn't it? So the rogue is still a rogue then, despite what everyone seems to think about the man and his garage. Perhaps we should call in on the way back so that I can confront him with a few pertinent questions and demand a few clear answers," said Jonathon, amused as he cogitated the report.

And so the couple did just that, at least Jonathon did, while his mother preferred the safety of the Bentley knowing what her son was capable of when confronted with evil.

The forecourt of the garage was completely deserted when the big black Bentley pulled up in front of the doorway to the reception area and Jonathon unhurriedly exited the car through the pouring rain and casually strode into the office.

The same grey oil stained overalls hung on the same gaunt faced mechanic behind the polished till, still scanning the same seedy pages of the same sleazy magazine which was promptly despatched as soon as Jonathon made his entrance.

"Good morning sir, what can I do for you this lovely morning," said the gaunt faced mechanic as he looked out at the rain as it pelted against the ever so clean window pane.

"A quick word with the proprietor if you please," was the terse but polite reply.

"Certainly sir, I'll just see if he's available. What name shall I say?" asked the gaunt man.

"The name is Jonathon Fisher and I'm a little short on time," said Jonathon, warming nicely to the occasion.

The grey oil stained overalls effectively disappeared through a narrow doorway then reappeared via the same channel just thirty seconds later.

"Afraid the boss is far too busy to see anyone at the moment, perhaps you could call back later this afternoon," suggested the mechanic, looking slightly awkward.

"No, I most certainly could not," said Jonathon quite brusquely, and brushing the gaunt man to one side entered the O'Keefe inner sanctum breezily.

Patrick O'Keefe, who was seated behind an enormous desk, was partially hidden by the mountain of clutter which was heaped up upon its surface in the most untidy manner possible, and not at all in keeping with the structured appearance of the remaining part of his business. He looked up unsettled, not once but twice and straightened himself as the imposing figure of the big man entered the room.

"Thought I told my man that I was not to be disturbed; far to busy to see anyone this morning, so you'll have to come back later." He snapped the words with his mouth but the remainder of his features betrayed the uncertain discomfort he felt within.

"Don't worry about that, I shan't take up much of your time Mr O'Keefe—or should I call you Bernard Yates?" The uncertainty in the man's features became more pronounced as Jonathon continued.

"Now I want you to listen very carefully to what I have to say to you," he continued with the same threatening trend to his voice, "very carefully indeed. You have a young thug working here for you by the name of Wingfield. This person and his two mindless brothers did their level best to injure me yesterday but with limited success I hasten to add. If they try anything like it again they will, in truth, rue the day that they were born—and so will you O'Keefe. You see I have it on good authority that it was you who perpetrated the whole episode," went on Jonathon with increasing fervour. "Now that was, without doubt, one very big mistake for you to make." said Jonathon, leaning over with his knuckles placed firmly on the untidy desk, and with faces almost touching, he stared directly into the Irishman's bulging eyes.

"I'm sure I don't know what it is that you're talking about. 'Tis true, to be sure, that young Sam works here from time to time, cleaning my cars for me an' all. But I'm also sure he's the meekest boy in the world so he is, and wouldn't hurt a hair on a fly," said O'Keefe lapsing into a slight Irish accent but still choosing his words most carefully.

Jonathon felt aggravated at hearing the false character reference being painstakingly spouted out by the Irishman; as he himself had had first hand experience of Wingfield's irrational behavioural patterns and downright thuggery capabilities. And so he moved slowly to the end of the garage owner's heavy oak desk and with his eyes steadily and continuously piercing those of O'Keefe's, he placed the index finger of each hand beneath the desk's top and lifted it steadily so that the untidy heap on top of the desk became an even untidier heap on the floor.

"I'm not here to bandy words with you O'Keefe, do you hear me? Now I shall be away for a few days so you had better make sure you keep a tight rein on that young hooligan if you know what's good for you. One, just one step out of line and I shall be back here and on to you like a ton of bricks. Do I make myself clear O'Keefe?" said Jonathon, as he made his way to the door. He stopped suddenly and turned to face O'Keefe once again.

"Oh, and one other thing, you owe my mother fourteen pounds, the plugs in the Bentley were not changed neither was the oil. You see we took the precaution to mark the plugs before we handed the vehicle over to you;

they're still marked. And the special pink oil that I use is still pink. Do you get my meaning O'Keefe?" said Jonathon, bringing the cosy tete-a-tete with his very sickened prey to a close.

"Yes of course sir, my mechanic must have made a terrible mistake. Look here's the money, take it, gladly," said O'Keefe, trembling as he fumbled for his wallet.

"Not now man, save it. You can hand it to the court authorities later. How does defrauding the public sound? Got a certain ring to it, don't you think?" said Jonathon, as he closed the door while the beads of perspiration that had surfaced upon the Irishman's forehead started to trickle down his face.

Felicity sat anxiously studying the reception doorway as her son came out into the now bright sunlight. She leant over to unlock the door as he casually ambled over to the car in a seemingly carefree fashion and waited as he slid into the passenger seat beside her.

"Jonathon darling, are you alright?" Her voice sounded tense and worried. "I thought after you had left me that you shouldn't be having a confrontation with that horrid man this morning, not so soon after coming out of the hospital. After all, the money is of little consequence compared to your health and safety."

"Quit worrying mother everything is fine, it's all sorted out. I don't think we will be hearing from Mr Yates for quite sometime.

Jonathon was graciously invited to the local police station the following morning and despite his uneasiness about the situation and the dilemma which had plagued him for much of the night, he informed the station sergeant in a bold and innovative way that he was quite adamant about not pressing charges against the Wingfields. And after much debating over the rights and wrongs in allowing potential criminals to be free from public prosecution he left the constabulary with a thoughtful mind and with the infestation of unease still lingering within him.

Walking across the small, almost empty car park, Jonathon noticed a movement at the far side of the Bentley. He reached the car and to his surprise found Sam Wingfield waiting by the driver's door nervously fidgeting with his hands in his pockets and looking rather distraught. But because of the propitious decision he had made within the walls of the police station a few seconds ago regarding this very person, Jonathon decided to be as amicable as possible and not allow himself to falter into making hasty revelations.

"Hello Sam, you waiting for me?" asked Jonathon cordially but with a puzzled look upon his face.

"Yeah, I seen you go into the police station like and I been waitin' 'ere for you 'til you come out," said Sam.

"So what was it that you wanted to see me about Sam?" asked Jonathon, still looking puzzled.

"Well it's about yest'day an' us peltin' you with our catapults like." (The word 'like' that Sam used every now and then seemed to Jonathon to be a nervous inclusion and not something he would normally say). Sam continued quite monotonously:

"Well I just wanted to say sorry like, an' ask you not to summons us like. But as you've already been into the cop shop I s'pose I'm too late. Y'see, I've already been to prison twice an' the next time they'll be keepin' me in for a long stretch like an' tha's for sure. I don't wanna go back there no more—an' I don't know what to do like. I'm really sorry Mr Fisher, honest I am an' it won't happen ag'in honest it won't. But if I'm too late, well I might as well push off," said Sam, turning as if to leave.

Jonathon stood motionless and thought for awhile before replying.

"Just a moment Sam," he said. "I'm a little puzzled at what you have just said. If you are as remorseful as you make out, then why on earth did you do it in the first place? Did someone tell you to do it Sam?"

"No sir, I don't take no orders from no one," said Sam.

"You sure about that Sam?" asked Jonathon.

"Yeah, I'm sure," said Sam hesitantly.

"You're lying aren't you Sam?" said Jonathon.

"No sir—why would I do that?" answered Sam.

"Probably because you're afraid. Are you frightened Sam? Are you frightened of upsetting someone?" asked Jonathon.

"No sir, I done it on me own. No one told me to do it—I just did it on me own." Sam grew extremely restless and flustered at the continuous inquisition.

"How old are you Sam?" Jonathon wasn't letting up.

"I'm twenty in August," said Sam.

"Well Sam, you are the only nineteen year old lad that I know who gets out of bed before six in the morning when he doesn't have to," said Jonathon. "Most young men of our age would stay in bed until lunch time if they thought they could get away with it."

"Yeah? Well I'm different, tha's all," said Sam.

"No Sam, you're not different, you're just not telling me the truth, now are you? You are currently employed by a Mr Patrick O'Keefe at O'Keefe Autos aren't you Sam? Cleaning cars on the odd occasions is that right?" said Jonathon, changing tack a little.

"How the heck d'you knows that then?" asked a surprised Sam rather hastily.

"He told me so, that's how I know. How do you get on with Mr O'Keefe, Sam?" said Jonathon.

"He's alright I s'pose," said Sam.

"Was it Mr O'Keefe who told you to attack me with your catapults Sam? After all, that is where you get your supply of ball bearings from, isn't it Sam, the garage?" said Jonathon.

"Why you askin' me all these questions for? You're not the blinkin' police are you? I thought only the police asked questions," said Sam, getting increasingly irritated.

"OK Sam," said Jonathon, turning, pretending to be stroppy, "if that's the way you prefer it, then maybe it should be the police who asks the questions; it suits me. You have made it abundantly clear that you are not prepared to cooperate with me and tell me the truth, so perhaps it would be better if we have a word with them, perhaps you will be more willing to tell them exactly what it is that's going on. Come on then Sam, let us both go inside and speak to the police, I'm sure they will be delighted to ask you a few questions without me interfering."

Jonathon took hold of Sam's arm very firmly and started to march him off to the police station.

"Alright, alright I shall tell you then. But first you 'ave to promise me you won't be pressin' charges against me," said a panic stricken Sam, trying to divert his attentions to his trouser pockets.

"No deal Sam, you tell me what is going on right this minute or we both go inside the station and you can tell them. What is it to be Sam, me or the police? It's up to you," said an unwavering Jonathon, holding Sam's right arm unbearably tight.

"Alright if you must know, but let go me arm first, you're hurtin' me," said Sam, wincing.

Jonathon released his grip a little but still held onto Sam's arm so that there could be no escape.

"Come on then, tell me Sam," said Jonathon.

Sam hesitated once his arm was loosened somewhat, but when the big man tightened his fingers again, he was prompted into speech.

"O'Keefe, he says it might be a good idea if you weren't around like. Said if I scared you off that he'd give me a good few quid. Said as how he knew you swam early like, most mornin's, said as how he'd seen you hisself. Said as how you'd soon get the message. I said to 'im as how there would be no chance of you bein' scared off like—said you ain't afraid o' nothin' nor nobody—I tell 'im all that but still 'e won't listen like. Said as if I wanted to keep me job I'd know what to do. But I knew I wont be able to put the wind up you sir, I knew you wouldn't be scared off—I was blasted stupid to even try. I told 'im all o' this, but O'Keefe 'e wouldn't 'ave it, 'e don't take no for an answer not ever 'e don't. Just keep on sayin' as if I wanted t' keep me job I'd know what t' do an' I should get on an' do it. I 'ope as how you understand like, an' I'm sorry—honest I am but if I'm goin' t' go down for this well tha's how it'll 'ave t' be—I deserves it. But me two brothers—well they ain't got no form, not yet they ain't—so if we could say I did it on me own like—an' leave them out of it—how would that be sir? Would you agree t' that?" said Sam, at last.

By the time the young thug had finished pleading his cause, his face had grown flushed and the fidgeting had started over. But Jonathon ignoring the fidgets and the flushes thought he could discern a new bright complexion within Sam. A slight, vague appearance of the good in him that he hoped is present in all mankind even the most evil of men. He stood there quietly for some little time; a few minutes went before the big man was able to gather himself. But in the end his words failed to reflect his frame of mind.

"It's no good is it Sam?" he said at last. "I mean—you are never going to change are you? You will never make anything like a responsible human being will you Sam?"

"I don't know sir. Sometimes I think I would like to be a proper person an' do good things like, but bad thoughts, they keep comin' to my mind like an' bad things, they keep hapenin' to me an' everythin' go wrong. But it's me own fault I knows that, it's always me own fault," said Sam, almost tearfully.

"How much does Mr O'Keefe pay you for cleaning his cars Sam?" asked Jonathon, after a thoughtful silence.

"A bob a knob—tha's the goin' rate. Why do you ask," said Sam.

"Well it seems to me Sam, that your biggest problem is a lack of respect," said Jonathon with informality. "You appear to have none at all for other people or their property and precious little for yourself. The only people you seem to care about at all are your two brothers. Now there is nothing wrong with that and in point of fact, in some ways, it might be your saving grace. But there ought to be room for others in your existence as well Sam. Even so, I think it is possible for you to turn things around, it's never too late you know, if you have the will to do it. I think that if you have something in your life about which you might derive a sense of pride, something that would take up a lot of thought and a great deal of your energy then these bad things you were telling me about will eventually stop happening."

Jonathon, by this time, was looking to find his way to Sam's new bright complexion, amplifying it to make it more brilliant, more discernable and easier to shape.

"Sam, I think it about time you gave Mr O'Keefe the sack. Instead you should wash and clean cars for Samuel Wingfield Car Cleaning Company," said Jonathon as broad grins decorated the faces of both young men at the very thought.

"You could start by cleaning my car both inside and out for the realistic price of twenty new pence. And then you may use my name as a reference by which to obtain other clients. Now the very first time you clean a car for a new customer you charge twenty new pence for inside and out. If they refuse to pay the agreed price because they are dissatisfied with the result of your work then you are to charge them nothing at all and use it as an experience to do better next time; unless of course they allow you to do the job again. That way you will always make sure you provide a first class service first time. Well, what do you say Sam? Are you up to giving it a try?"

"Well yeah, tha' sounds great but I don't see as how I shall be able to clean many cars in clink, do you?" said Sam, disconsolately.

"Now you listen to me Sam. If you promise me to work hard at what we have just been talking about, then I for my part will promise not to bring charges against you. I will go even further, I shall make certain that your brothers are not prosecuted either. It's up to you Sam. You make your life a success or you make it a failure, you choose. And you must do the same for those twin brothers of yours. Teach them the difference between right and wrong and you will be teaching yourself at the same time. Bye then Sam, and I hope that good fortune will attend you at all times," said Jonathon, delighted at the outcome of a difficult set of circumstances.

"Thanks Mr Fisher I shall be doin' me very best," said Sam, as he skipped away child like.

It took less than one minute for Sam to come running back to where Jonathon was still standing.

"When did you say I could make a start on your car Mr Fisher?" he asked, quite out of breath.

"I didn't Sam. So let's say later this afternoon shall we?"

— CHAPTER TWENTY-SEVEN —

The water was almost tepid when Jonathon and Susan enjoyed their final convivial swim together early that Sunday morning. The sky was almost clear with just a few pieces of wispy, watery, vapour filaments and tufted streaks of cirrus clouds floating high in the atmosphere. And the sun reflected a brightness of a turquoise tint off the surface of the beautiful lake that produced a warmth that lingered over the entire area of the water; even where the leafy blades patterned by the rhododendrons and imposing pines were mirrored.

As mentioned this was to be the young couple's final swim together in the Akworth waters and so they desperately needed it to be an hour of uninterrupted pleasure, a diversion that would stay in their minds for many years to come whether together or apart. And they certainly needed to erase the past unpleasantness that unfortunately lingered, and plant a more happy memory that could be looked back on as good old fashioned fun.

And so it was—to a large extent it was precisely that. Howbeit, the hour long session was mostly taken with Jonathon in deep despair as he attempted to teach Susan the rudiments of swimming beneath the water's surface. From time to time she had taken in copious amounts of the wet stuff in making a brave effort, but it wasn't to be. Complete success eluded the pretty young woman at every stage for when she had successfully managed to get the front half of her body to cooperate with her wishes in ducking down beneath the surface, the back half wilfully refused to follow suit and her bottom was left trailing behind like some glowing buoyant float bobbing about on the water warning of navigational difficulties.

The intended single hour of happiness had turned into two when they eventually returned to the house and with bloodshot eyes Susan prepared some tasty breakfast which they enjoyed together before joining the rest of the family group for Sunday worship in the now familiar local Anglican Church.

Not unsurprisingly, the allotted period for the service had overrun by more than thirty minutes that day, with Susan squirming and wriggling for most of the time in lassitude and boredom. And with periods of irritated glances in her direction by several of the congregation, she was, with not an immodest sigh of relief, most delighted when the final blessing was bestowed upon her, together with the rest of the congregation of course, and for the first and final time the experience of Sunday worship at last was over.

Because the service had been so prolonged by almost half again, the small congregation, not without cause, were eager to escape the ancient church in favour of various culinary duties at their individual abodes. And so, a certain milling about in the tiny vestibule took place as the people, all hoping for a speedy exit, jammed the doorway to such an extent that an orderly outward flow didn't occur at once, and the Fisher party, along with everybody else, were somewhat delayed. Nevertheless, Jonathon, by using his considerable height advantage, looked across the heads of the crush and through the open doorway and was most surprised to see, his now ally, Sam Wingfield and the twin brothers, sitting on the ancient church wall idly watching the congregation as they slowly left the place. Using his weight and his height he managed to manoeuvre his way, rather rudely at times, to the front of the queue and almost totally ignoring the outstretched hand of the reverend gentleman he hurriedly made his way to where the three lads sat.

"Hello you guys," he said frivolously, "everything alright?" The question wasn't meant as an enquiry into their personal wellbeing but rather as a polite introduction to conversation as is the norm these days; mostly without the 'everything.'

"Yeah, everythin's just great thanks," said Sam, as he relinquished his seat and almost stumbled down the grassy embankment as he did so.

"Oops!" he said laughing as he regained his pose. "I told these two what you said last Friday as you come out of the cop shop, as how you wouldn't be bringin' any charges against us like and they thought they ought to say thanks. Not my suggestion—it come from them. Anyway, I guessed you would be at church this mornin', today bein' Sunday like; see, I remembered as how you were a Christian who turned the other cheek." A broad grin encompassed his wide face as he recalled the Fisher's picnic of a few days previous.

"Well that's good. Saying thank you is always a right and proper thing to do; even when there is really no need," said Jonathon piously. "So how is the car valeting service coming along Sam? Have you been able to make a start yet other than the cleaning job you did for me on my car?"

"Yeah I have, an' a pretty good start it is an' all. Miss Hammond, she let me clean her car inside an' out yest'day, but I still only charged her ten pence though, as she don't 'ave much like. Still, one good thing's come of it as she now wants one of us to do her garden for her once a week as well as clean her car, so that'll be good won't it? Then I cleaned Mr an' Mrs Clifton's car, they were really pleased; said as how I can do it every week if I want to. Anyway, I 'spect there'll be plenty of others as well, given time. Anyway, we just wanted t'say thanks like an' that I will clean your car every Saturday if you want us to, I shall only charge you half price like, seein' as how you've been so blinkin' kind to us," said Sam, enthusiasm issuing from his whole being.

"Sam, I'm really sorry, but I don't expect to be around here for very much longer." Sam's eyes lit suddenly at this information. "But hopefully I shall be back again soon and when I do, yes, that will be fine I shall certainly like you to clean it for me and I'm sure that Miss Hutchins will be agreeable for you to clean her car as well, why don't we go over and ask her?" said Jonathon, turning his head toward the church to notice the ladies leaving. When he turned back again the Wingfields had gone.

'Much too embarrassed to take the business proposal any further I suppose,' he thought to himself anxiously. Even so, Jonathon felt quietly encouraged by Sam's attitude and walked back to Akworth filled with hope and the expectancy that here at last were three ne'er do wells that might just amount to something after all.

Jonathon and Susan left Akworth House around one thirty that afternoon for their respective destinations of East Bergholt and Colchester. The skies were now filled with dark grey threatening clouds which didn't help Susan's feeling of despondency in the slightest as she weighed up the prospects of being parted from the man for whom she had gradually come to have such amatory feelings and extreme high regard. *'There is however tonight,'* she thought to herself as they motored in convoy on the main road to London and while the rain began to fall by the buckets full. *'He has never again mentioned the proposal he made to me when we were walking in the garden the other evening. I expect he has forgotten all about that. Typical man,'* she mused.

Jonathon, on the other hand, had his mind fixed firmly on other matters; the morrows hearing being uppermost and the wondering of what possible judgements the coroner might pronounce upon the untimely event of Mr Watts's demise. Nothing of Susan's ponderings had entered his head since the stroll and she was not incorrect in supposing that the incident in the garden had been totally washed from his mind.

As planned the couple drove steadily in their separate cars, still in convoy, as far as Colchester where Susan was undertaking the reading for her law degree. Also as planned the couple stopped a few miles short of Susan's turning to the university at the small village of Marks Tey where a fine public house stood to welcome weary worn travellers who felt the need for a refreshing break to their tiring journey.

The big black Bentley turned slowly into The Spaniard Inn car park and Jonathon situated his vehicle nearest the exit knowing he had a further eleven miles to journey before he reached The Mansion in Bergholt and planned on making a hasty getaway from the place after they had been refreshed. He was closely followed by Susan in her new beige Ford Fiesta who parked neatly beside him and sounded her horn to let the young man know she had arrived.

They entered the pleasant empty saloon bar, discreetly holding hands, where they ordered a plate full of freshly cut pieces of chunky bread placed together and generously filled with cheese and pickle and a glass of the finest ale with which to wash down the not so dainty sandwiches.

"How's the head after driving all this way Jon?" asked Susan, when they had comfortably seated themselves in the corner of the room. "I must say the swelling has gone down considerably in fact it's hardly noticeable being hidden so well in those blonde wavy locks of yours."

"Yes, its OK thanks," answered Jonathon brightly, "no sign of any aches or pains at all I'm glad to say. Luckily I seem to have a pretty good recovery capability; another couple of days and the bloody marks will have vanished all together and be gone for good, I hope.

"Susan, I feel I really haven't thanked you properly for all you've done for me over the past few days. If it hadn't have been for you and your promptness in fetching the ambulance, well I don't know what sort of state I would be in right now; if in any state at all. Anyway, I just want you to know how much I appreciate all you did."

"Don't say another word Jon, please, or you will have me in tears. You know very well that I did nothing that anyone else wouldn't have, besides I hope you would have helped me in the same way had our rolls been totally reversed—well wouldn't you?" One of Susan's eyebrows rose immediately as she spoke the final three words and she smiled as the leading question left her lips.

"Maybe," answered the young Adonis returning Susan's smile with interest. "But all the same I'm still in your debt Susan and I thank you so very much."

"Well if you are feeling so indebted and matey toward me how come you have said nothing further on the proposal you put to me in the garden the other evening?" said Susan, endeavouring not to sound pushy. This defect, however, as on other occasions was not entirely missing.

"What proposal was this?" questioned the young man scratching his head yet again this time accompanied by a look of complete bewilderment.

"Oh I see, feigning amnesia now are we; probably due to the knock on the head I suppose."

"Susan, I have no idea of any proposal that I have supposedly made to you. I'm afraid I am completely at a loss and you will have to remind me."

"Oh forget it Jon, *you* obviously have anyway."

"No Susan, I can't forget it. If I have made a promise to you then you certainly must remind me what it is otherwise I won't be able to fulfil it."

"OK! You invited me to your home for the night and that we might travel to Colchester tomorrow morning at the same time and in convoy, remember?"

"Good heavens is that all? I really thought it was going to be something of some major importance. Of course I think it to be a splendid idea. I would welcome the opportunity of cooking for you and for us to spend the evening together, no reason on earth why we shouldn't, it might be fun and it will certainly help me to take my mind off tomorrow's ghastly coroners hearing. So yes, when we leave, just follow me it will be great," said Jonathon.

"Well if you are sure Jon, only I wouldn't like you to feel I have foisted myself upon you if you are not entirely sure," said Susan, with her fingers crossed beneath the table.

And so it was decided. Susan, feeling that she had gained the all important romantic assignation with the man she simply doted on and with whom she hoped to build a long and lasting relationship without losing to much of her all important self esteem, was quietly happy and inwardly most content.

Jonathon on the other hand was feeling more than a little denigrated and although he realised that the idea of the 'night together' was irrefutably his very own in the first place, it was, in truth, an 'on the spur of the moment' conception which came about when he was definitely in a most awkward and untoward situation and one not of his own making either. Now he felt he had been manipulated in the highest degree by one of the most calculating, devious and guileful of the female species, and one who was going to have her own way no matter what or who was going to foot the bill be it himself or some other poor unsuspecting devil. Nevertheless, he had made the proposal and he would see it through in good grace, no matter what; well perhaps not no matter what, but more probable, within reason.

After they had eaten only a couple of the sandwiches but had had their fill of ale Susan decided it was now time to make a fresh start for Bergholt; the weather at the moment being most suitable for a genial drive and the promise of a pleasurable evening ahead clearly written on her mind. And so without further delay they left the inn; noticeably this time without the aid of each other's supporting hands and entered their respective vehicles without saying too much.

Although the remainder of the journey was relatively short, being a mere eleven miles as afore mentioned, the motoring time involved was quite enough to allow the most welcome and tranquil of evenings to descend out of the unwelcome grey and lofty clouds that had hitherto filled the skies. And the undoubted promise of a night of sheer bliss filled the heart of the lovely young woman, so much so that she literally jumped for joy, after she had exited her modest motor, and scanned the pleasurable features of the sylvan gardens of The Mansion with much approbation.

They walked together now as they had when they walked together into the Spaniard Inn just an hour or so before, hand in hand and chit chatting about everything and nothing, laughing and smiling as they always seemed to do when they were on their own. In through the front oaken door and into the immodest lounge Jonathon escorted his guest with an air of pride and satisfaction in what he regarded as the most homely but imposing of homes. They seated themselves comfortably after Jonathon had poured two of the most generous of martini cocktails and together they sipped and chatted and laughed for further moments. And after encouraging his lovely young guest to remain relaxed exactly where she was he reluctantly drifted off into the kitchen to prepare a special dinner for two.

As it turned out the dinner for two was not at all special. Jonathon, not being the most capable of cooks managed to mess up and burn almost everything he put his hand to, so much so that in the end Susan had to rescue the event by binning everything and by miraculously preparing the most delicious of omelettes that Jonathon had ever tasted. The wine, however, Jonathon did manage to get right without too much difficulty; and the cheese and biscuits, he did rather excel himself in that department also. Oh, and the clearing away and the washing up, he was indeed first rate here as well—well he loaded the plates and glasses on the spacious drainer and promised to operate the washing up liquid and washing up cloth in the morning when he would deal with the breakfast crockery at the same time.

The couple were feeling rather more than a little squiffy after their second brandy as they walked the garden in the evening air, and twice Susan tripped and had to be supported by the big man, who wasn't at all sure if the trips were some sort of tactical ploy or no, he being ever mindful of the lovely young woman's devious capabilities. And after walking the whole of the garden and around the small lake a couple of times and as the dampening air was beginning to feel slightly chilly, Susan, not unexpectedly decided it was time to go inside.

Jonathon, upon entering the lounge played some lively classical music, softly but loud enough to fill the vacant background while the couple conversed the one with the other; their words flowing gaily at times, more soberly at others until suddenly, becoming somewhat bored with the conversation and feeling that insufficient progress was being made in the direction she had planned, Susan impulsively and with out warning stood up and taking Jonathon by his fingers pulled him to his feet; deciding they should take to the floor in a dance routine she had recently learned and that the music playing was perfectly appropriate. After some debate the couple held each other in an attitude which faintly resembled that of a couple of ballroom dancers and slowly Jonathon was pushed, nudged, and propelled into all sorts of improbable contortions until Susan finally realised that Jonathon's dancing was no better than his cooking.

"Come on Jon; do try not to be quite so clumsy. Look, put your arm around my waist a little more tightly and hold me as if you were enjoying it. There that's better. Now move your feet one at a time and try listening to the music," she said happily.

Just being held closely to him was more than she had dared to hope for a few seconds ago, but now all at once her eagerness seem to take control as she moulded her body into his and placing her arm around his neck, with her slender hand she pulled the big man's head down, down to where her lips were waiting to meet his. The embrace was not totally one sided for the big man felt his adrenalin rise within his veins as it had before but he knew he must not allow the situation to get out of hand. But how on earth could he stop it when he needed her so much. With a single deft movement Susan took hold of his hand and placed it delicately upon her firm round breast holding it fast so that it could not easily be removed and pressing her mouth avidly into his she entwined her body around his lifting her tiny feet completely from the floor. With complete unwillingness Jonathon took advantage of the situation in which Susan had placed him and lifted her bodily, placing her on the black leather chesterfield and stood breathlessly away from her and making a determined effort to appear composed he bent down and kissed her cheek. Immediately a ray of comfort darted across her face which she dashed at once. In its stead she smiled lovingly upon his face.

"I'm so sorry Jon," she offered meekly, "but I couldn't control the moment. Please don't think too badly of me."

"How could I possibly think badly of you Susan? I was as much to blame as you; if indeed blame is the right word to use. It was a wonderful moment but one that must be left for awhile and gathered again at some more appropriate moment when we are better suited to do it justice."

— CHAPTER TWENTY-EIGHT —

The couple breakfasted at the reasonable hour of seven-thirty the following morning. Jonathon had already been for his early morning swim in the river and Susan was just about finished cooking the eggs and bacon as the big man walked through the doorway to the kitchen.

"Hi Susan," he said, as he kissed the lovely young woman's cheek. (She wanted more than a peck, much more.) "Is there time enough for me to take a quick shower before breakfast: if I'm really quick." The tone of his voice had an ambivalent expression as though he failed to know exactly what had been required of him in the way of a greeting.

He thought he had done enough.

Clearly Susan didn't. For the dispirited look on her face was one of extreme disappointment—indeed displeasure. Jonathon noticed it—at last. "Take two," he said, as he went outside again then re-entered after a period of ten seconds.

"Hi Susan," he said, taking the lovely young woman in his arms and bruising her lips with his. "Did you sleep well my beloved?" he quipped, causing hilarious laughter from the two of them.

"I love you Jonathon Fisher," she said, without taking thought.

"No you don't," said he, "you just want my body."

She failed to disagree.

Jonathon went off for his quickest of quick showers then re-appeared some minutes later attired in a dark grey pinstriped suit, white shirt and formal tie.

"You are looking very smart this morning Jon, for the benefit of the coroner no doubt," she said, feeling somewhat underdressed herself; she being clothed in an overly bright chunky sweater which covered her bottom and almost down to her knees, (appropriately in vogue for students and for wearing during university study only), over a pair of the whitest of white jeans.

"Thanks," he said, "one has to look the part I suppose, still you're looking the part as well; most attractive I must say."

They sat down to breakfast and began to exchange words in a more formal mode of conversation.

"When will you be going down to Hampshire again Jon?" she asked warily. "Not going to leave it too long I hope."

"I shall have to see how things pan out at the coroner's court this morning. There may well be a full investigation in which case I expect I shall have to hang around for a few days to assist the police. But hopefully I shall be back for the weekend.

"I suppose your mother will be putting Akworth on the market pretty soon or will it be you handling things?" asked Jonathon inquisitively.

"Neither actually, I shall place the whole of the sale in the hands of David West. It will be he who deals with everything; he'll be keeping me up to date with the agent's progress and any offers that may come along in due course, but what I need to avoid is for the house to be left empty for any length of time. The last thing I need at the moment is for the place to be vandalised in any way at all. Oh, I know you think that the Wingfields are little angels at the moment, Jon, but really they can not be trusted in the slightest. It would be just my luck for them to start helping themselves to anything they fancied, be it from the house itself or from the gardens. Fortunately the three mums seem to get on very well together so hopefully they will all stay at Akworth until it is finally off my hands," said Susan, suddenly looking very concerned and worried, "and that could take months you know. And as for that Bernard Yates, well, we will have to be particularly careful as far as he's concerned. He is a ruthless individual and he will stop at nothing to get his own back on me. Please promise me Jon that you will take care as far as he's concerned, I should hate for anything more too happen to you on my account."

"Quit worrying Susan you seem to be better at it than my mother. Of course I shall be vigilant and with fingers crossed it will all be over before you know it. Anyway I shall be pleased to flit between the two places from time to time; maybe I might pick you up some weekends and we could travel down together," said Jonathon with yet another 'spur of the moment' suggestion while trying to reassure the lovely young woman.

Susan was about to put forward her own suggestion, namely, that she might stay here at The Mansion with Jonathon and travel to and from Colchester on a daily basis. However, she checked her thoughts and held her tongue firmly in a controlled and proper manner.

Jonathon loaded the large white sink with all the various plates and dishes both from breakfast and from the previous evening's memorable meal and washed them before the couple left and after exchanging their fond farewells they journeyed to Colchester in tandem.

Colchester's Monday morning is, without exception, both tediously irksome and most of all slow moving with the street market holding up the piling traffic in every direction. And this particular Monday morning, the morning of the inquest into the death of H. Watts Esq. was no exception.

Jonathon had waved at Susan as she turned off for her schooling and had parked the big black Bentley safely in the coroner's car park half an hour after he had left Bergholt. And so with one full hour still to spare before his crucial appointment he decided to while away the time by walking the streets of this most ancient Roman town. He entered Head Street from the High Street, paused a moment outside Joy's fuller figure store and smiled mannerly at the blushing petite redhead as she applied her artistry to a display in the front window of the small arcade. Then as he neared Tindal Street he heard his name being called out from across the road. Stopping and turning, as anyone would, he noticed the tall fair haired figure of a man crossing the street and beaming all over his striking face. To Jonathon's absolute horror J.J.Cabin drew level and commenced to walk along side him.

"Hi Jonathon, I was hoping to bump into you," he said, offering his hand in a friendly greeting. "How are you? I must say you're looking pretty good to me. Life being particularly kind to you at the moment is it? Well it certainly looks that way." J.J.Cabin had an air about him that exuded confidence and amicability but which was wasted on the younger man, for the moment.

Jonathon took the offered hand without hesitation although he failed to enjoy being accosted in this particular manner and showed his abhorrent feelings by the intentional disinterestedness he displayed upon his face.

"Mr Cabin!" he exclaimed. "Fancy meeting you here. Yep, I'm fine thanks, all things considered." Jonathon tried not to sound overjoyed at meeting up with the man and felt he may have overplayed his part in the greeting somewhat.

"I take it that you are here for the inquest into the death of Mr Watts right?" said Cabin, the sickly smile, supporting the supposition, spread instantly over his fine features. "Being a solicitor," he added pompously, "I tend to keep abreast of the day to day goings on in the jolly old coroner's court; it's surprising what bits of useful information one can glean from so doing, and I happened to notice that the inquest on the Bergholt man was scheduled for this morning. Naturally the old curiosity was somewhat aroused and after making a few discreet inquiries I found you to be one of the key witnesses, if not *the* key witness. Well, you can guess what a surprise that was." Suddenly his overbearing attitude changed and a more ambivalent and caring tone escaped his mouth as he continued. "I have a free day today Jonathon and I was wondering if you wouldn't mind my tagging along as it were. I promise not to be a nuisance or get in the way or anything and my being there with you might help to relieve the monotony. What do you say?"

Jonathon was stumped what could he say? He could hardly be rude and throw the considered proposal back in the solicitor's face. He thought awhile, carefully mulling over the suggestion. *'It mayn't be such a bad idea after all, at least he would be able to explain procedures and the like,'* but one thing bothered the young man; if indeed Cabin was supposed to be on a day away from the office why on earth was he dressed so formally. He quickly put the thought behind him.

"Yes, Mr Cabin that will be good, I don't mind your company in the slightest and perhaps you will be able to explain to me exactly what is going on," he said at last slightly dropping the barriers.

Of course the tall, smart solicitor was totally delighted at the acceptance and he extended his hand once again to illustrate the fact.

"Ah, that's great, most pleased about that Jonathon. Oh, by the by—one thing that is most important though—the name—its Joe to you—OK?— Look, I am on my way to grab a bite to eat if you would care to join me. The Clover Café isn't far away—it's a bit of a dingy place I know, but they do make the most delicious of toasted bacon sandwiches there. Do you fancy it?—we have plenty of time," he said.

Jonathon eagerly accepted the offer even though he had not long consumed a most enormous breakfast with Susan at The Mansion. And so they walked together almost to the bottom of Tindal Street until they reached the colourless entrance to a most gloomy looking café. They went staunchly in and occupied the un-wiped table for two immediately next to the entrance and ordered their already chosen fancy, which incidentally was served upon immaculately clean plates.

Jonathon found it surprisingly easy to converse with Joe and his mother's name wasn't mentioned at all, at least, not after the initial enquiry into the two ladies' well being. This omission on behalf of the solicitor astonished the young Adonis as his first reaction when stepping into the café was one of foreboding, he being quite certain within his mind that Joe's prime intention was to ally himself to Jonathon in order to talk about his hopes in gaining a relationship with Felicity. *'How wrong I was,'* he thought himself.

"Have you been to a coroner's court before Jonathon?" Joe asked.

"No, not at all," replied the young man. "Of course, like most people I have read about them in the press from time to time but my experience of them is absolutely zero. How long have coroners been in existence," he asked, trying to sound interested in a subject which had very little appeal.

"Well now, the office of coroners is extremely ancient and if my law school memories serve me correctly can be traced back to the days of William the Conqueror. There's obviously been a few changes since then Jonathon, today, professional people who have achieved qualifications as doctor, solicitor or barrister can hold the office and we seem to be most fortunate here as our coroner, Dr J.B.McCall, is not only a practising GP but is a barrister as well. Apparently he spent many years studying medicine after becoming totally disillusioned with the law. Anyway, I'm pretty certain that it will indeed be the doctor who will enthusiastically oversee proceedings this morning, so hopefully we could be in for an interesting time."

The two big men retraced their steps back to the centre of town and entered the court where Sergeant Pedley was impatiently waiting for Jonathon, walking back and forth and now and then nervously glancing at his watch.

"So you made it then Jonathon, must say I was beginnin' to wonder if you would, you bein' such an important witness an' all. Thought I told you t'be here an hour afore hand, you've left it a bit late, still you're here now an' that's what count. Hello Mr Cabin. Didn't know you two knew each other," said the officer, perking up a little.

The two new friends nodded, looked at one another simultaneously and smiled lucidly.

"Life is full of surprises sergeant," said Joe Cabin happily and touched his young friend on the arm as if to reinforce the acquaintanceship. "Yes we certainly do know each other," he said, as if he had known Jonathon for many years and neglected to state the newness of the mutual attachment.

And so, in the fullness of time, and with the eminent Doctor J.B.McCall in total charge of the proceedings the inquest was duly opened and then adjourned without delay pending further enquiries to be carried out by the police and until the coroner's investigations had been accomplished. Jonathon glanced about him as he left the small courtroom his eager eyes examining the varied crowd hoping for a view of the balding head of the village sergeant. Jonathon entered the wide entrance hall where he eventually spotted the elusive sergeant in intense conversation with one of his fellow officers who was about to leave the building. Jonathon moved quickly before his target could occupy some other's auditory attention.

"That was a surprisingly short session Sergeant. How long do you think it will be before the matter in question will be completed?" asked Jonathon, feeling rather perturbed at purposely travelling such a long distance for such a short hearing.

"No tellin' but weeks rather than days I should think. Some enquiries, they go on for months sometimes—or even years. But I shouldn't think so—not in this case. No, give it a couple of weeks an' it'll all be wound up an' put t'bed, so to speak, you see if I'm not right," said the sergeant, looking amused at Jonathon's concern.

"So in that case, perhaps it will be in order for me to join my family back in Hampshire?" Jonathon's question was said optimistically, ever hopeful that the answer to his plight would be in the positive.

"Good gracious me no, you can't do that," came the feared terse reply.

"Why on earth not?"

"Look Jonathon, you can't leave the district 'til you've made a further statement to one of the coroner's officers an' tha's a fact. Some one will need to question you, you bein' the key witness an' all. Look, if you wait here a tick I'll ave a word with someone an' find out what the score is OK?" So saying, the sergeant left Jonathon hurriedly and disappeared through an open doorway marked private and carefully closed the door firmly behind him. One minute later, Joe Cabin joined Jonathon after chatting to one of his associates and noticed the worried frown on his companion's brow.

"What's the matter Jonathon?" asked the tall solicitor gaily.

"Not a lot Joe," Jonathon failed to smile. "It seems that I may have to stay in Suffolk until this stupid hearing is over or at least until the coroner's boys have had a word with me."

"No, surely not. You've given your signed and completed statement of everything you know to have happened, haven't you?" Jonathon nodded. "Well then, there's nothing left for you to add surely, is there?" said Joe reassuringly. "It's the village bobby, he has his wires crossed I should think; although I don't see why he should have because he is most erudite in the ways of the law and the function of the coroner's boys."

A full thirty minutes had elapsed before the sergeant reappeared and Jonathon was most glad of the tall solicitor's amity for all of that period. When at last he did present himself, the sergeant's face was beaming as though he had won the football pools or something equally as gratifyingly relevant.

"Sorry about that Jonathon," he said, when at last he came, "'ad to 'ave a word with the coroner's officer in charge and after he'd checked through your statement he seemed satisfied with what you'd said already. But he did want to go on a bit an' tha's what took so long. Anyway the top an' bottom of it is that so long as you 'aven't anything further to add you are free to go so long as you promise to make yourself available should anyone decide they've found some obscure an' unforeseen question they need the answer to.

"We'll be in touch then Jonathon; just as soon as we 'ave a proposed date for the new inquest or if, as I say, we need to speak to you further," concluded the sergeant happily, before he disappeared once again this time avidly licking his lips as he went.

— CHAPTER TWENTY-NINE —

Jonathon and Joe Cabin finally left the coroner's court with a degree of hesitancy each feeling rather reluctant to let the other go such was the inexplicable bond that now seemed to exist between them.

The two tall men communicated well with each other; quite as though they were acquaintances of long standing instead of the casual connection that truly existed between them. They slowly walked and talked along Sheepen Road, onto East Hill and then into the High Street once again where they altered their course and walked the street in the opposite direction to that which they had wandered earlier.

A most strange and foreign feeling was at this moment being exposed to Jonathon's mind. A sense of kinship, which he had never before felt with a fellow being quite so soon after the establishment of such an improbable association, now existed. The compelling urge to relate his whole life's story to this comparative stranger, but newly found friend, was upon him; to speak of his hopes, his fears, his aspirations and his dauntless ambitions; to open the pages of his very existence to be browsed over, examined, studied even criticised such was the young man's confidence in the older man's aura that was being displayed. Unceasingly, Jonathon opened up to Joe, who just listened attentively seemingly honoured and privileged to act as confidant to this very personable young man.

Eventually Jonathon reached the purpose for his visit to Colchester this day and the fateful morning when he found the hideous body in the river and the awful and perplexing conundrum as to how a seemingly dead body could resurrect itself in the space of half an hour and then to purposefully carry out its prime intention of suicide.

"I'm quite sure there must be a perfectly analytical explanation which any accomplished physiologist could clarify," said Jonathon, perplexedly. "But the only answer I can come up with is that the immediate shock of the cold water on a body, hot with booze, caused a type of metabolic change in the cells of his vital organs thereby necessitating them to temporarily close down in order to preserve life, thus making him to appear lifeless to the amateur and uninitiated observer."

Joe smiled and inclined his head in a gesture that indicated his supportive approval.

"Sounds more than feasible to me Jonathon. How could I possibly argue with that clear-cut explanation? After all, your qualifications take you much closer to these things than mine ever could," said Joe attentively. "Perhaps the coroner will think to engage the right sort of expert to explain how this thing is possible, presuming of course he accepts your version of events and not try to gloss over them. But yes, I'm sure that he will do his utmost to verify your statement but I must say it does sound rather complicated."

They walked the full length of the High Street which terminated outside the huge black wrought iron gates of Colchester's famed Norman castle; here they crossed the street and entered its grassy grounds.

The early afternoon sun shone brightly as the two men idled round the pleasant gardens and created a cosy warmth to the early summer air that had invited the scores of couples to drape themselves about the closely cropped green lawns in contented laziness; while the close by street discharged all the humdrum noise of a busy Monday afternoon's trading.

Jonathon was about to relate his Torbay crossing which led to the discovery and eventual recovery of the stolen watercolours when Joe abruptly intervened.

"Jonathon, I'm so sorry to interrupt this most interesting conversation but I have just spotted someone on the far lawn who I should very much like to have a quiet word with. Would you please be a good chap and excuse me for a couple of minutes, it is imperative that I don't miss this opportunity; I shan't be long and I'll catch up with you directly," said Joe quietly and with a distracted look upon his face.

"Yes of course Joe, that's OK," said Jonathon, his voice trailing off into infinity as his friend made his way to a couple that was sitting on the grass obviously engrossed in the calm of one another's company. Jonathon surveyed the scene as Joe, crouching down beside the couple, engaged the man in conversation. The two men then stood up and to Jonathon's utter amazement, the stranger towered above Joe by at least six inches. Jonathon was sure that he himself was taller than Joe by three inches which would have made the stranger at least six feet nine inches or even more. The two men then strode some distance from the young lady who remained seated on the grass and they began talking to each other in a somewhat heated manner. This continued for quite some time with much gesticulation taking place from both parties, when suddenly and without perceived provocation the stranger telegraphed a blow to Joe's head. Joe hastily retreated and the clumsy punch missed the lively Joe by a mile throwing the taller of the two tall men off balance. Joe instinctively retaliated by jabbing his protagonist in the solar plexus and as he doubled over, from the wind being temporarily knocked from his body, he was straightened up with a left uppercut to the jaw that Joe Louis himself would have been proud of. The very tall stranger fell to the ground like a ton of the most healthily fermented manure and lay there prostrate on the grass, although he did writhe about a little as Joe walked calmly away with a wry smile of satisfaction spreading over his deep set face. The young woman, seeing her companion's dire dilemma leapt quickly to her feet and aided the tall man into a sitting position, she appearing only slightly taller than he sitting and she standing, and soothed his scowling brow with cupped hands, while the out of it punch bag commenced to hurl obscene abuse in Joe's direction. Joe, ignoring the man's abstruse curses continued on his way with a backward wave of his hand.

Jonathon felt slightly bemused. Here was a new friend to whom he had, without the slightest hesitation, opened up the leaves of his very existence only to find him to be completely incompetent at handling a frustrating situation peaceably: no matter how provoked he may have been. And who was considered, prior to this demonstration, to be an even-tempered sort of person without an enemy in the world. But now, seemingly, he was found to have a very short fuse and was most adept at using his fists. '*Hmm,*' thought Jonathon, mulling the situation over in retrospect. '*It would appear I have a good deal to learn about people. I do hope I haven't found a serious flaw in Joe's character and one I may have to excuse. Still, it's imperative not to be too hasty in the judgemental department and I shall most certainly have to give him the benefit of the doubt.*' His thoughts were indeed worrying the young man considerably; but then, Jonathon appeared to be a perpetual worrier of late.

Soon the tall solicitor had made his way back to Jonathon's side and the two men continued their walking as before.

"Sorry about that Jonathon but some people just will not listen to reason no matter how elucidating one is," he said.

"No need to apologise to me Joe, and I'll not ask what it was all about. Obviously you both had your motives and you didn't exactly start the problem anyway but coped with it as you considered appropriate," replied Jonathon, hoping he wasn't condoning Joe's action in any way.

"I expect you would have handled the situation far better than I, Jonathon, and would not have involved yourself with physical violence in any shape or form. But unfortunately there are times when one has to resort to a little barbarity if,only to protect ones self esteem against bullies who know no better; and this was one such time. Anyway, let's both forget about the whole sordid and unsavoury incident shall we? You were telling me about your visit to Devon," said Joe, trying to regain some of the mood of their interrupted conversation.

Jonathon started from the beginning once again, endeavouring to bring Joe up to date with the recent events; including the recovery of the missing watercolours, Susan's sad disappointment in her father's involvement with Bernard Yates alias Patrick O'Keefe, plus every detail he could bring to mind, when Joe made a startling assertion.

"Jonathon, did you know that Bernard Yates has been on the police wanted list for a number of years now?" said Joe, regaining much of his aplomb. "They have been rather anxious to talk to the man with regard to many unsolved crimes including murder and gang warfare. Yes a most dangerous man is the illusive Bernard Yates. And did you also know that Sir Nigel Eld had relatives residing in your neck of the woods? I believe the family has had associations with East Bergholt for hundreds of years."

"Yes I knew that a prominent and affluent family with the same name live in my village but I hadn't realised that they had any connection with Sir Nigel, not sure if my grandmother is aware, she hasn't said anything to me. Anyway, you seem to be insinuating that there could be a possible link between Yates, Sir Nigel and East Bergholt or am I imagining things? Surely you are not saying that Bernard Yates had anything to do with the Watts affair are you?" asked a puzzled Jonathon, sceptically.

"I really don't know what I am saying at the moment but you must admit that the tie up is certainly there and it just maybe worth our while to look into the matter. Perhaps it might be a good idea to have a snoop around Mr Watts's old watering hole for starters, who knows what we may discover. The White Horse public house you said, wasn't it? Maybe we could call in there for a couple of drinks—what do you say?" said Joe, looking very pleased with himself.

"I am indeed up for that, its not far away. Don't know about you but I have plenty of time," said Jonathon.

The two men strode back to the coroner's small car park rather more quickly than when they left the place, both feeling most satisfied with Joe's inspirational input. They entered the big black Bentley and made their way along the A12 to Bergholt chatting convivially as they went.

It was still mid afternoon when they arrived in Bergholt and as the licensing laws, at this time, did not allow the trading in alcohol to commence until six thirty pm, Jonathon suggested that they should pay a visit to the part of the River Stour where Mr H. Watts met with his untimely death, so that Joe might fully acquaint himself with the miserably depressing scene. And so, parking the car at the top of the stony lane that led to the rickety bridge below they picked their way carefully down to the Dead River where the police ribbons still hung suspended from the stakes which cordoned off the dismal area. Jonathon searched the side of the embankment where he had seen the word 'BY' etched into its muddy surface and saw to his disappointment that the indentations had been attacked by the elements and that the letters had all but disappeared leaving only parts of the word still visible.

Joe stooped down to examine the indentation in the muddy surface more closely. Then standing again he looked directly at Jonathon accusingly.

"You see Jonathon," he said, "you, along with everyone else have assumed, quite wrongly to my way of thinking, that this was the poor old chap's parting gesture; assuming that he was unable to spell the simple word BYE correctly. But let's suppose, for a moment, that he wasn't saying that at all. Let's suppose that he was in fact trying to inform us of the identity of his assailant; Bernard Yates, for instance. Now that to me makes much more sense than your reasoning or it is nothing at all Jonathon."

"I'm sorry Joe, but I'm finding your hypothesis a little difficult to swallow; it is complete conjecture on your part. I mean, even if there was foul play, and nobody but nobody at all is thinking along those lines at the moment, nobody has even hinted at murder. But even if there was foul play, how on earth could he have known who his assailant was? He would hardly be in a position to ask, now would he? 'Oh pardon me sir but could you possibly tell me your name before you drown me in the river?' I don't think so Joe," said Jonathon, being more than a little contemptuous at Joe's suggestion.

"Jonathon, I am fully aware that the whole thing sounds pretty improbable. But let us, just for a moment, pretend it is true. Let us, if only to humour me, suppose that Mr Watts is standing here before you right now, this very minute, and suppose he explained it all to you, face to face, confirming precisely what happened on that fateful night and what his intentions were in scrawling those two letters in the muddy bank. It would still sound equally ludicrous wouldn't it? But you would have to believe him wouldn't you? What I am saying, Jonathon is we don't know. Everything is guess work, pure supposition but one thing is for certain, nothing can possibly be ruled out; not at this stage of the game. So, let's just wait and see what the White Horse can tell us, if anything, before we wipe the slate clean."

Jonathon reluctantly agreed and after Joe had seen all he wanted to see and had had his fill of the gruesome scene, they began to retrace their footsteps up the rough, rutted and unstable lane. Half way to the top they paused momentarily as Jonathon pointed to a small thatched cottage partly hidden by hawthorn bushes and standing in front of the great oaks that dwarfed the cottage into insignificance.

"That's the cottage where Mr Watts lived on his own," said Jonathon dolefully. The drab, poky little dwelling, to all appearances, was peacefully unaware of the tragedy that had befallen its owner, it was now waiting for a new resident to brighten it and give it back its life again. After a sympathetic pause Jonathon continued:

"The police are apparently of the opinion that Mr Watts was very much the worse for liquor that night, or rather early in the morning, and that he missed his turning as he careered down the lane, being so obviously out of control of his cycle at the time, and ended up in the river. They also consider the letters BY to be totally irrelevant and were not engraved by him at all. That to me is much more feasible than your theory Joe," said Jonathon.

The two tall men continued their walk to the top of the lane, entered the Bentley and headed for Flatford which was just a half mile further up the winding river and close to where Jonathon lived with the two mothers. Their attitude, the one with the other, was still much the same as when they entered the village and their differences in opinion was soon forgotten.

Flatford, is a most beautiful and resplendent setting, where the River Stour is spanned by a pictured bridge whose usefulness has been tested by ages beyond recall and where noisy rooks have raised their downy chicks since time in memorial in the bosom of the lofty elms that have stood nearby for centuries and that brush the sky when the easterly winds tear over the hills or across the dampened mead.

It was here in this magnificent place that the two men intended to fritter away the remaining time until the White Horse public house, which was situated further up the village, opened its doors for business. They parked the big black Bentley in the field car park opposite the quaint old Thatched Cottage café which juxtaposed the bridge, then wandered over to the bridge itself where scantily clad youngsters were plunging into the flowing river below. One small fair haired lad stood poised, unaided, on the top rail of the ancient bridge ready to launch himself into the turbid water. A larger, more robust lad and older by some years tried to entice the little lad down from off the rail by telling him and all who cared to listen that he, the fair haired lad, was unable to swim and not to be such a prat. But the crazy young bravado, ignoring the warning, instantly launched him into the water, surfacing some twenty yards away by the grassy green bank. Jonathon, ready to rescue the young idiot hurried to the rail of the bridge but had no need to inconvenience himself, for the youngster, obviously adept at performing the act, was scrambling out of the water grinning from ear to ear.

"Well show-offs come in all shapes and sizes," said Joe smiling, "but I'll bet that one will break more hearts than he does bones."

"I expect he's done that already; his mother's quite possibly," returned Jonathon.

They turned back to the quaintly old thatched café and ordered tea and fancy cakes then walked out into the tea gardens and sat and stared at the beauty of the river and the surrounding fields that were John Constable's very own. The river was busy for the time of the week and the time of year with rowing boats passing back and forth on their way to and from Dedham village, and a couple of men hopefully dangled fishing lines into the water. Looking through the standard rose bushes that edged the gardens they could clearly see the fair haired lad who had caused all the anxiety a few moments ago, still adamant about showing off to his mates and anyone else who cared to look.

"Strange how the very young, especially boys, love to make exhibitions of themselves; it's as though something deep within urges them on. The only problem is it can be extremely destructive as well as dangerous. I can well remember doing stupid things when I was younger; took away a precious and promising relationship and harmed my own life to a large extent," said Joe, sounding despondent as he spoke.

A pensive thought crossed Jonathon's mind and he paused a while before adding his comments.

"I suppose it could be nature's way of introducing the mating game to the adolescents," he said at last. "Maybe those who show-off the most possess a greater sex drive than those who don't indulge in the ritual. So perhaps you were a lot closer than you thought when you spoke about young Blondie breaking hearts."

The two tall men left the tea gardens, happily rested and each simultaneously glancing at his watch as they moved.

"It's still quite awhile before the White Horse is open so perhaps a quiet walk along the river on this pleasant afternoon might provide us with an interesting way to spend the time," suggested Jonathon.

"Sure, why not? It has been quite awhile since I was down here last and the exercise will do us both good," replied Joe enthusiastically.

The young divers and swimmers were nowhere to be seen as Jonathon and Joe retraced their steps over the bridge, then turning left they followed the river along the old towpath that the departed bargemen and their horses used to manoeuvre the barges in the bygone years. They passed the closed lock gates dripping with water through the wooden slats which prevented the backflow of water and stopped to admire the old watermill which once belonged to Golding Constable, the father of one of England's best loved artists, John Constable. The mill had been kept in good repair over the centuries and was now owned by the National Trust as a place of learning for students engrossed in biological study. The water still flowed by the mill, however, and streamed over the sluiceway to the large mill pool below. From this point the two men were able to see Willy Lott's Cottage that featured so prominently in Constable's Hay Wain, still being tenderly cared for despite its age.

The river was flowing quite fast as they strolled along the man-made path that led to a part of the river locally known as Judas Gap, and fishermen littered the riverbank hoping to catch the rainbow trout that had been introduced to the river from North America a few years earlier. They watched as one fisherman tried desperately to land quite a large fish, be it trout or no, none could tell, but was only successful in getting his feet wet; Joe nudged Jonathon and together they laughed quietly to themselves.

At Judas Gap, more youngsters were enjoying a late afternoon swim and the two tall men looked on enviously at the frivolous fun being enjoyed by the swimmers. After a few moments of spectatorial and entertaining pleasure they walked back the way they had come. Back to the picturesque bridge that arched the river by the pretty tea garden and the old thatched cottage; both feeling more at ease and both looking forward to a pint of ale in the White Horse public house.

— CHAPTER THIRTY —

The White Horse public house was an imposing building of clean red brick quite three storeys high with the whitest of window surrounds and was situated back from the road by some twenty yards. A small square of neatly cut grass, centrally situated to the front of the house, was surrounded by a heavy black chain, the alternate links in which encased spiked pieces of metal purposely fitted to prevent the children, or any other with such intentions, from sitting thereon thereby using the chains as a swing, and was held in place by four white posts with angled tops. In the centre of the lawn stood a tall white post supporting a decorative wrought iron frame for the elegant painting of a magnificent white stallion; unusually encased in glass. And a heavily gravelled car parking area encompassed the lawn and met with a row of joined garages to the right; the end wall of which faced the roadway. Three young lads stood with their backs to the wall, all facing the road endeavouring to dodge a tennis ball that was being hurled at their legs from across the far side of the narrow road by 'Blondie' the show-off from Flatford Bridge.

Jonathon stood awhile and smiled at the lads playing 'hit the legs' then politely asked Blondie to be careful not to harm the Bentley which was parked nearby. Assured that the motor would be reasonably safe, he and Joe entered the public house by the door marked 'Public Bar.'

The lone figure of an aging, balding, white haired man sat at a table close to the large bay window with its frosted glass directly opposite the tall polished bar where customers purchased their indulgences. Jonathon ordered three pints of the best Greene King ale from the burley barman then led Joe over to where the old regular sat toying with a pack of dog-eared playing cards; taking the pint mugs of cool ale with them as they went.

"Hello Charley, may we join you?" asked Jonathon, placing a mug of ale in front of the white haired man.

Charley raised his sparsely covered head and produced a wide grin exposing a set of toothless pink gums nodding incessantly to the two men as they sat and acknowledged the ale appreciatively.

"Joe this is Charley Brand, one of Bergholt's eminent characters. Charley this is a good friend of mine who accompanied me to Herbie Watts's inquest this morning," said Jonathon, as Joe offered his hand to the old timer.

"Daft ol' sod that Herbie, why'd he want an' go an' kill his self for? Still he al'as said he'd do it some day so I s'pose we shouldn't be surprised."

But it beats me how 'e could bring 'is self t'do it all the same." A slight flush mantled the cheeks of the old man betraying a degree of thoughtfulness as he gulped the first mouthful of his ale.

"Had you known him for long Charley?" asked Joe not wishing to cause any immediate embarrassment.

Charley looked up again somewhat surprised that the question had been asked and that everyone should have known the answer to that one.

"Course I 'ave, known 'im pretty well all me life. Went t'the same school together didn't us? Though I was a good few years older than 'e was. Scatty then as I remember, up t'no good all the time. Wouldn't take t'learnin' nothin' that 'e wouldn't. Everyone said e'd not amount t'much an' they was right weren't they? Don't believe 'e could even write 'is own name right up till the time 'e died." A tear glistened in Charley's eyes as he spoke but it didn't spill over the lid.

Both Joe and Jonathon sipped their ale and looked at each other thoughtfully not wishing to seem too inquisitive but still needing to learn as much about the fateful night as possible without causing any distress. Slowly Jonathon pried the answer that they both needed to know out of the old man.

"Was Herbie here in the evening—it happened?" asked Jonathon, delicately.

"Yeah, 'e rolled in 'ere 'bout 'alf past ten." The answer came immediately. "He'd 'ad quite a skin full afore 'e got 'ere though, I could tell that by the way 'e was staggerin' about; all over the place 'e were, but still 'e wanted more. Put away another three or four pints I shouldn't wonder, even though the landlord said 'ed 'ad enough."

Jonathon's attention was intensified by this information but he needed to know more.

"And were there many customers in that evening?" he asked.

"Yeah, there was more'n quite a few, almost a full 'ouse y'might say when 'e arrived. But it seemed t'empty pretty quick once ol' Herby started yappin' an' makin' a fool of 'is self though," said Charley, a faint smile hanging about his mouth as his memory of the evening was recalled.

"Anyone in here that was—unusual? I mean, were there any strangers, anyone you didn't know at all?" asked Joe, tact being the essence of the question.

"Only one bloke as I remember. Spoke with a sort of accent 'e did; I remember hearin' 'im talk when we was both up at the bar getting' drinks in at the same time. When I sit down ag'in next t'Herby, well that was when the daft ol' sod started goin' on ag'in. Reckoned as how he knew who the stranger was that stood at the bar. Said as how 'ed seen 'is picture in the paper not so long ago, or so 'e reckoned. Then 'e went on about this bloke bein' wanted by the police. Anyway, 'e wouldn't let it drop, kept goin' on an' on about it. Reckoned as 'ow he'd get a reward if 'e went to the police. Said he was damned if 'e wouldn't go there tomorrow an' tell 'em as 'ow he'd seen 'im, an' claim the reward. Well I could see this bloke keep lookin' over in our direction so it was pretty obvious 'e could 'ear what Herbie was a sayin' of. Herbie, 'e could see the bloke lookin' as well but that didn't stop the silly ol' fool, he just kept on, raisin' 'is voice all the time; made me feel sort of embarrassed 'e did I can tell you. Anyway, this bloke 'e finished up 'is drink an' left soon a'ter but even that didn't stop the idiot; 'e then went on about it to Pete Miller 'till kicking out time. They left together a'ter time was called, did Herbie an' Pete, I expect they both went round to Pete's house t'ave some of his home brew an' the rest I 'spect you know cause it was you who found 'im in the river," said Charley mopping his brow with a dark blue handkerchief as if to say that talking for so long was thirsty work. Joe took the hint immediately and replenished his glass after Jonathon had declined the offer of further alcohol.

"Charley, if you were asked would you be prepared to repeat what you have just told us to a court of law?" asked Joe, upon his return.

"What? Now you look 'ere, I don't want to get involved with no police investigation. After all 'e did drown 'is self didn't 'e? I mean, there was no one else involved was there? So why do you ask a damn fool question like that for," said Charley, clearly expressing his irritation with some force.

Jonathon touched the old man's arm in an effort to quell his anxiety.

"We don't know that yet Charley, not for certain," he said, dismally. "But if what you have just told us turn out to be true, then yes, there certainly are grounds for suspicion."

Jonathon drove Joe back to Colchester later and there existed an unusual quietness between the two men and for the first five minutes not a single word was spoken. Eventually Jonathon decided to break the silence.

"So your theory appears to be turning to reality by the minute Joe. So, what do you suppose our next step should be?" he asked.

"I'm not at all sure Jonathon; I suppose that logically our duty should take us hot foot to the police station but I am inclined to add—not yet. It's quite late and I am sure that nothing can be accomplished if we go there tonight. Perhaps it might be a good idea to save it till the morning and sleep on it 'till then. What do you say?"

The last part of Joe's phrase seemed to indicate to Jonathon that his friend was either tired or he was looking for Jonathon to expressly lead the way. Jonathon dallied before committing an answer.

"If you mean hanging onto the information that Charley Brand has just told us, then yes, I suppose there are no alarm bells sounding for an immediate rush. But to be perfectly honest I cannot see the matter looking any less obvious in the morning. One thing is certain however, that it is plainly our duty to inform the law of the whereabouts of Bernard Yates, before he decides to move on. We should have done that much earlier, in fact when you first mentioned that he was on their wanted list," said Jonathon, beginning to feel the need for immediate action.

"Yes you are right of course," said Joe. Then after a moments thought he added -

"You know, the more I think about that character the more I worry what exactly he might do next. From what you have told me about the man he is well aware that Susan Hutchins knows of his identity but because nothing untoward has happened thus far he feels relatively secure in his alias. Even so, since you threatened him over the car business the other day, I'm not so sure, not sure at all. Don't be deceived by his reaction to your threat to him Jonathon, he is definitely a very ruthless man and if cornered, would most certainly prove to be highly dangerous. Actually, I am inclined toward advising you to return to Hampshire as soon as you possibly can, if he knows that you are there at the ladies side, and believe me he will know or very soon find out, then he may think twice about taking action in closing Susan's mouth." Joe seemed most concerned even agitatedly uneasy as he fumbled for a cigarette from the pocket of his jacket.

"I agree," said Jonathon, equally concerned. "Luckily Susan is in university at the moment, so I'm not too worried about her immediate safety. The three mothers, well, they are entirely a different matter. Yates must realise, unless he has only half a brain, that there can be no secrets at all about his identity and so their safety is in jeopardy. I think that I must get back there right away; tonight Joe," said Jonathon.

"Good man, I hoped you would say that," was the prompt response. "I shall pay a visit to the Colchester police station first thing in the morning to have a chat with an old friend of mine there, informing him of Yates whereabouts; now that I know it. I also intend telephoning the Hampshire police as soon as I reach home instructing them to meet with you at Akworth House tonight. Then I propose taking a few days leave and will join you in Hampshire early tomorrow afternoon, if that will be alright. When I see our boys in blue tomorrow I shall tell them everything we have discussed together and what Mr Brand said this evening. Not certain if they will mind me telling them their job though, if they do, well, then they will have to lump it. At least they will be able to make up their own minds if you and I are reading into the incident of a drowned man something that isn't really there or not," said Joe, a smile at last being arrayed upon his face.

Jonathon also beamed a smile which was more of the nervous variety than that of a relaxed kind as he continually feared for the safety of his mothers.

"That's great Joe we shall all look forward to seeing you tomorrow. Good luck with the police," said Jonathon, and meaning it.

The two tall men then exchanged telephone numbers; Jonathon giving Joe the number to Akworth House, shook hands amicably then embraced one another as though they had held each other in high esteem for many years.

Jonathon reached Akworth House soon after midnight, there being little traffic about to hinder his progress and not wishing to disturb the ladies slumber he cut the engine at the gate allowing the light of the moon and the incline of the drive to direct and carry him to the resting place of the parking area.

As he quietly left the big black Bentley he unexpectedly noticed that no other car was in sight and wondered if the local constabulary had paid a visit earlier and had already left, they, being satisfied that the ladies were quite safe and in no immediate danger; if indeed they had bothered to show at all; he knowing that the only person to be really relied upon, as we all know from time to time, was himself.

The old house seemed uncannily eerie at this time of night and the moon cast sinister shadows that made the big man shudder. He closed the car door silently and made his way noiselessly to the rear of the house hoping that the latch would be off so that he might be able to access the kitchen without arousing anyone. From where he stood no lights could be seen in any window and the silhouettes of the lofty trees now caused pitch darkness to the path on which he trod causing the hairs on the nape of his neck to prickle in trepidation.

As he rounded the final corner, a tiny shaft of light issuing from a chink in the kitchen's heavy curtains shone narrowly across his path and filled the big man with hope that at least someone was about to let him in. Carefully picking his way to the small, slightly opened window he cast a brief glance inside through the tiny chink in the curtain and then a more focused look made him catch his breath in horror. The three ladies were seated at the table facing the window while the thickset figure of a man stood facing the frightened ladies with his broad back toward Jonathon. Jonathon manoeuvred his field of vision as much as he was able and saw a second figure of a man standing to the side of the kitchen close to the door that Jonathon had hoped to enter with a pistol in his hand which he held levelled at the ladies.

"Now, I shall be asking you just one more time." The unmistakable Irish brogue in Bernard Yates' voice sounded ominously menacing although somewhat shallow.

"Where—is your daughter?" he said restlessly.

Although his words were menacing they were also uneasy, almost stuttering, as though his patience were finally giving out thereby resigning the man to less attractive actions of persuasion.

As far as Jonathon could see, the Irishman was completely unarmed as he leant forward with both hands spread out upon the surface of the table to evenly support his considerable weight; but Jonathon wasn't completely sure. Ada was looking absolutely petrified as the probing question was being directly aimed at her; but it was Lady B. who answered the question.

"We have told you a dozen times already Mr Yates; we do not know where Susan is right now. All we know is that she left here about one o'clock Sunday afternoon with my grandson; she supposedly returning to university to attend to her studies and he to Colchester to deal with an outstanding business matter this morning. I really cannot see what else I can tell you, we certainly haven't heard from either of them since they left and in actual fact hadn't expected to. Anyway why do you wish to speak with her so urgently? You have had plenty of time to contact her in the past so why have you waited until now? Something happened has it Mr Yates? Something that now makes a meeting with Susan seem more imperative is that it? Well I can assure you Mr Yates that Susan has no desire to talk to you, not now, not ever. And for heavens sake do tell that imbecile Mr Wingfield to stop pointing that ghastly thing at us. He did quite enough damage with his wretched catapult the other day, so I am quite certain that he cannot be trusted with a weapon as dangerous as the pistol he is holding," said Lady B., endeavouring to exercise her authority over the situation.

Bernard Yates had other ideas about who was to be in charge of the proceedings, he knew full well that it was he who had to exercise control and he would do it yet, even if it took a most unspeakable threat or action on his part.

"I'll tell you why I need to see her shall I? She knows too much that's why. Since she decided to befriend Fisher she has found out things that are not good for her, so she has; things that are not good for me either. And people who know too much are unpredictable so they are, and not safe to have around. So, they have to be gotten rid of do you see? Just like the three of you knows too much an all, so you'll have to go, so you will. Cant be trusted, the none of you," said Yates now smirking. And the feeling that he was completely in charge gave him a sudden rush of adrenaline which lightened the load and inspired such confidence that he felt that he himself could cause anyone to die man or woman, just as he'd done it to that idiot in Suffolk and the others, oh so many others. Or better still; watch someone else do it for him. Yes he'd like that, that he would. What pleasure to be felt as he watched the agony. So much clearer that way too, study them, as they squirmed; watch them pleading for their very lives—such joy.

"But what about Sam Wingfield?"

The voice of Lady B. brought the Irishman instantly back from his wanderings. She went on -

"He knows all about you as well, doesn't he Mr Yates? And if you get rid of us, as you so delicately put it, then he will know even more. So is it your intention to get rid of him as well?"

Lady B. was obviously attempting to make a breach between Yates and Sam which the Irishman wasn't slow in noticing.

"Oh no, Sam's a good lad so he is, he'll do exactly what I tell him," he said. Then glancing over to Sam Wingfield he smiled wryly, and he thought awhile before adding -

"Anyway, it'll be Sam who does for you three then all I have to do is wait, wait for the prodigals to return. If what you're saying is right, then it won't take long. They'll try phoning you do you see, they're bound to do that sooner or later and when they find no one is answering their calls they'll soon come running and when they do—bingo—I shall be having them."

Jonathon looked directly into Sam's face; it looked edgy but somewhat excited probably at the thought of playing the role of high executioner.

'Sam oh Sam why did you have to lie to me, you almost made it, I would have helped.' The words flashed through Jonathon's mind and were gone in an instant.

Stooping below the window's sill, Jonathon quickly and silently made his way to the kitchen door. Bending down, with his eye to the keyhole he could clearly see through. The figure of Sam's body, in profile, was immediately the other side of the door and was looking fidgety as he shifted his weight from one leg to the other as though he was desperate to use the toilet. The gun was still in the youth's hand and pointing directly at the ladies. Jonathon contemplated the situation. He couldn't see where Yates was standing or even the mothers sitting, all he could see was Sam and the pistol. He had to wait, wait for the moment–the appropriate moment. He knew he would have to be quick after making his decision and that it would be a once only effort–there would be no second chance.

Then he saw it–the moment he was patiently waiting for. Sam was obviously experiencing a considerable irritation in his right leg, just below knee level for he lowered the pistol and in order to relieve the aggravating itch he scratched his leg with the tip of the barrel. Jonathon suddenly released all the pent up strength within his powerful body and launched himself at the wooden door as the hinges, latch and lock gave way immediately under the young man's incredible might. In an instant he grabbed Sam's wrist and squeezed it until he felt and heard the joint and bones shatter. Howls of agony issued from the mouth of the now disarmed bulky bumpkin which didn't affect Jonathon in the slightest. He merely picked him up as he had done on their first encounter and hurled him at Yates who was attempting a possible escape through the window. Jonathon casually walked over to the Irishman and locked his head in the crook of his arm stemming the flow of blood to the brain thus rendering the Irishman totally unconscious. It was almost immediate that the body went limp and Jonathon allowed it to slip noiselessly to the floor.

"Well done Jonathon, I didn't underestimate you after all," said a familiar voice, from behind him.

— CHAPTER THIRTY-ONE —

Jonathon spun round quickly to see the leering figure of Joseph John Cabin towering in the kitchen doorway resting languidly on the broken hanging door with his left hand and a small firearm in his right, which, being held devilishly steady, was deliberately aimed at the taller man's chest.

"Hi Joe, what are you doing here so soon? I wasn't expecting you until tomorrow; and point that stupid thing in another direction Joe, I don't take kindly to anyone who masquerade as halfwits playing with guns," said Jonathon, looking most surprised and agitated all at the same time.

"Who's playing," Joe's voice had a mocking ring to it the tone of which disturbed Jonathon a great deal; this certainly wasn't the voice of the Joe he had come to trust and value as a friend.

"And what am I doing here? Well I followed you here dear boy that's what, and a jolly good job I did too, by the looks of things. Allow me to explain; I'm sure you're all just dying to know anyway. You see, after I had received a telephone call from the Irishman, who is at this precise moment in time having a quiet nap face down there on the floor–a rest I might add that he definitely has not earned and therefore certainly doesn't deserve–after I received his call, panicking and complaining about his precious cover in danger of being blown by you people, I decided to take a hand in the proceedings myself. Oh I was well aware that you Jonathon was visiting Colchester today, sorry yesterday; I found that out a day or so ago. Well as soon as the coroner's thing had been announced it was pretty obvious that you would have to be called as the main witness. Anyway, I thought that it might be a good idea to stick close to you and sound you out as to the present state of play. And so I did just that and your divulgence into the goings on these past few days proved most useful both to support my anxiety and to inspire my next plan of action. Thanks for that Jonathon very good of you dear boy," said Cabin, grinning the full width of his face although sounding sickeningly cynical.

Jonathon felt completely dispirited by this time and was completely taken aback by the Cabin revelation and admission by implication of his conspiracy with Yates; it seems they all were, for the ladies were immediate in directing a look of dismay at one another although none offered to comment.

"Joe I really thought that we were friends. What a disappointment you have turned out to be. Do you know, I was even beginning to think you may be ---" Jonathon was rudely interrupted before he had the chance to complete his sentence.

"Your father?" Cabin laughed raucously at his own assumption. "Not a chance in hell young man."

He now seemed to find difficulty in controlling his mirth, and so his mirth was sustained a while longer. Eventually he regained control of his vocal cords and continued his speech.

"You know, I was pretty sure you would be a hard nut to crack Jonathon, you proved that just a while ago; but really—I didn't have you down as being a romantic simpleton as well," he said, as his sniggering got the better of him once again.

Jonathon was livid at the 'romantic simpleton' charge but would not lower himself to confirm or contradict the comment.

"Trying to exercise your own pathetically feeble ego are you Cabin? Endeavouring to score a few meaningless points, is that it? Well you put that gun down and we'll soon see what you are really made of and how many points you are in truth capable of scoring," said Jonathon, taking a step forward.

Cabin's response was to shake his gun-hand slightly, other than that he failed to budge; he just stood there stone faced while the young man's move was brought to a halt.

Nevertheless, Jonathon continued calmly:

"So, you knew all along that Yates had drowned Mr Watts, did you? I can see now why you were so damned cock sure of yourself; making out that you were arriving at the facts by some obscure reasoning and trying to sound the expert when all along you knew for certain what the answers were."

Cabin had realigned his original composure by now and exercised the width of his mouth once again by twisting it into an unconvincingly broad smirking smile.

"Anyway that aside," he said, "where was I?—Oh yes, I was about to enlighten you about our friend Bernard here wasn't I? Well the dear kind man has been keeping me very well informed since your arrival in Hampshire, very well indeed, he's on the ball I'll give him that, but that's about all he gets from me. I didn't whole heartedly approve of the rash Irish idiots action in killing Watts at first; but since our little visit to Bergholt I have seen the light as it were and I do see the need to get nosey people well out of the way when it's necessary and I was pleased, in that respect, to see he used his Irish initiative in the way he carried out the deed and all the more so because Watts had a big mouth and was about to use it; well Charley Brand more than proved that didn't he? You see, if Yates had been apprehended, then it would only have been a matter of time before I was dragged into the fray knowing for certain that he would have squealed like the proverbial stuck pig if it meant it would stand in his favour and save him a few years in jail."

Sam Wingfield was sitting in a corner completely isolated and nursing his broken wrist, quietly crying to himself of the pain and the fear of the dire consequences all of this would lead him to. The ladies also appeared to show signs of distress about the repugnant exchanges between Yates and Jonathon especially Ada who nervously leant against Lady B. and was receiving a steady pressure to her shoulder from the very nice lady's comforting arm and at the same time her hand was being soothed tenderly. Felicity, in spite of the fact that she also had caught the distress disorder was unmoved in position and seemed to be exercising a modicum of self control; although it has to be said the colour of her cheeks were not of the rosy hue one might have expected, in fact her face showed itself to be somewhat ashen as she watched and listened to her son verbally battling with the obnoxious Cabin.

"You will be telling me next that you were behind the art theft as well," said Jonathon, wisely deciding to keep Cabin talking for as long as possible now that he realised the police would not be arriving.

"Yes indeed, well, with the help of dear old Nigel and of course that useless heap there on the floor. Actually it was Nigel who first suggested he needed to lose some pictures a few years ago but it was me who organised the whole operation and I must say I was extremely proud of that little piece of ingenuity, especially as there were no problems in finding a buyer on the continent at that time. And when I learned about a huge quantity of pictures coming *back* into the country for redistribution, well, I was most eager to get involved with that as well. Then, low and behold I found out that Nigel's Akworth collection was to be among the same consignment; so bingo, two bites at the same cherry do you see; very appetising I must say and a rather pleasant way to capitalise on poor old Nigel's miserable misfortune even though he was well and truly under the sod, so to speak, poor fellow. And it would have all paid off rather nicely if it hadn't have been for your confounded interference you dolt. And I thought all was lost and it would have been too but for my dear old friend the Superintendent Frank Dobson, who gladly informed me that he had all the paintings in his safe keeping. But how to get them out of his safe keeping that was now the problem. You see I mistakenly thought too many people knew of the pictures specific whereabouts by this time, including yourselves. Then up you pop again getting more tiresome by the minute I can tell you. But because you wanted complete anonymity we were still in there with a chance to make a sizeable killing; didn't have to go public after all you see. Even with losing the pictures that had to be unavoidably returned to their owners, including the Akworth collection, there was still over three quarters of the haul left and they would still bring in more than ten million pounds if they were carefully placed I'm pretty sure of that.

"But then I saw you all at the Owl's Nest—well I couldn't believe my luck Jonathon, really I couldn't. A golden opportunity to get close to you all and to find out exactly what your plans were. I discovered, by way of Yates, that you were acquainted with the original owner of some of the pictures and that you were staying here at Akworth, which opened up all sorts of possibilities I can tell you, what a bonus! My hopes rose beyond all of my wildest dreams.

"Then came the wretched disappointing down turn in my fortunes, your mother here failed to acknowledge me as her one time lover so the closeness that I had hoped for seemed completely lost for ever. And then came yesterday, dear old yesterday. Jonathon you were an absolute doddle, I couldn't believe you could have been won over so easily; my closeness to you all was on again; talk about the ups and downs of a scenic railway, that is nothing by comparison.

"So here we are once again. Watts systematically out of the way, me on target to receive a handsome premium for all my labours–and you?–Well, now it's your turn to die."

Now, there comes a time in each and everyone's life when we all need a little help from those around us and Jonathon Fisher was no exception, big as he was; for as soon as Cabin had finally concluded his revealing dialogue, Bernard Yates began to stir and so Cabin, walking over to the recumbent Irishman bent over him to shake him into complete consciousness without relaxing his eyes or the gun from Jonathon Fisher for a single second. And it was at this precise moment that Felicity, gathering all her wits about her perceived the opportunity to help her son. It was but a brief moment from moving noiselessly to pick up the pistol that Sam Wingfield had dropped in his agony, to causing the terrifying explosion which filled the kitchen and reverberated throughout the whole of the house; temporarily deafening all its stunned occupants and causing much confusion. Joseph John Cabin clutched at his buttocks in torturous agony, expelling gas and air profusely while staining the trousers of his light grey suit with growing patches of red and brown at his rear end as he bent over the ever moaning prostrate figure of Bernard Yates.

"Oh no Jeremy, it's 'im ag'in," said a bewildered Sid, as the two police officers entered the now not so cosy kitchen of Akworth House.

Their deplorable deportment was much the same as on the other occasions that Jonathon had had the misfortune to witness it and to Jonathon, there appeared no appreciable way of altering it; not significantly anyhow.

"Sid, you are becoming so predictable," returned Jeremy, outwardly annoyed at his partner's risible remark.

"Am I Jeremy—thanks," said Sid.

The presence of the two policemen, yet again, was more than Jonathon could manage and so he wandered aimlessly through the broken back door and into the night seeking some fresh, clean air which always goes a long way in helping the stresses and strains brought about by moments such as these and the sweet scented air performed its miracle wonderfully. After going over the past events in his mind yet again and filling his lungs for the umpteenth time, Jonathon was delighted to hear, at last, the welcoming sound and see the lights of an ambulance approaching the house; for this indeed was what he had been waiting for; the opportunity to clear all of the rubbish out of the house and eventually get some much needed sleep.

All three injured men were loaded aboard the creamy white wagon and taken to the local hospital under the explicit supervision of two of the fiercest looking burly police officers imaginable. While an inspector, a sergeant and two police officers namely Jeremy and Sid were left behind to have a word with the remaining party.

Jonathon and family went into the lengthy explanation of the evening's events in great detail, painting the picture most lucidly, but insufficiently, or so it appeared, for they were all requested to accompany the police officers to the police station where each would be asked to provide individual statements formally and separately.

At precisely four forty-five in the morning they all returned to Akworth House and seated themselves in the drawing room enjoying a hot cup of Ada's special brew which was generously laced with brandy.

"You might have shot Cabin in a rather more appropriate place in his anatomy mother," said Jonathon smiling.

"Yes I too thought that at first darling, but then upon reflection I considered it to be the most appropriate place possible. But in any case, it was the only target I had available at the time that was large enough. Actually, between the four of us, I think I did rather well considering I had my eyes closed at the time," laughed Felicity.

"One thing bothers me about all this, what was Bernard Yates doing in Bergholt when he killed an innocent man?" asked Jonathon, looking bemused.

"I expect he was visiting his old friend Cabin in Colchester for whatever reason. And East Bergholt being only a short drive away he thought he would call in for a drink. Don't forget that we have it on good authority from Ada that Sir Nigel had relatives there and when he visited them he would obviously have been driven by his chauffeur. Perhaps they were in the habit of calling in at the White Horse on such excursions, who knows. Clearly the chauffeur would not have been invited to join the party at the Eld place so perhaps they were in the habit of enjoying a drink together on the way home. But I am sure that all of these questions will be answered in the fullness of time, probably at the trial," answered the very nice lady.

The whole of the Akworth household slept soundly that night. And Susan returned to Hampshire the following weekend when she and Jonathon skimmed flat pebbles over the surface of the small pond.

PART TWO

— CHAPTER ONE —

The arranged sale of Akworth House took somewhat longer to bring about than most people imagined. And it was not until after the trials of Messrs Cabin, O'Keefe and Wingfield had been brought about, and the judges found to be more than willing to mete out harsh punishments to those involved in murder, theft and other such crimes (the like of which would be too numerous and unnecessary to list at this point), that the Fishers and the Hutchins' were finally able to vacate the Hampshire village of Sutton Scotney and say farewell to Akworth forever.

True to her word, Lady B. had been instrumental in obtaining a charming cottage for Ada and her daughter; the picture collection being sold at auction for a goodly amount and part of the proceeds spent on the purchase of the cottage; this being far enough away from The Mansion so as not to bring about a situation of total dependency yet close enough to afford the odd pleasant social visit from time to time. In actual fact, the association between the two households became less and less involved as time progressed and the relationship with Jonathon that Susan had pined for hadn't developed; she eventually being content with a junior partnership in a small law firm in Lincoln immediately she had successfully finished university.

The months drifted passed to the summer of 76, the June of which was hot to the extreme. Many people fearing a touch of sunstroke might easily be forgiven for seeking a cooling cure to this severe thermal problem by total submergence in water. Any old water would have done the job adequately: salt water, water tainted with chlorine or just plain old fashioned fresh water, so long as it was cool and wet and deep enough.

In the Fisher's village of East Bergholt this meant only one thing; an invasion of Jonathon's beloved River Stour and in particular the pretty river crossing called Flatford where Jonathon and Joe Cabin had spent an interesting afternoon together; that being a short while before Jonathon had found the true colours of J. J. Cabin as being not quite up to par.

Visitors by the coach and car load were currently pouring into the village, which in itself was not totally unexpected; after all John Constable had seen the beauty there, captured it on canvas and claimed it for himself to share with the world. But because of the totally unpredicted suddenness of the unbearable heat wave, the quantities of milling people had escalated out of all proportion.

Be that as it may, Lady B., Felicity and Jonathon were of like mind. That is to say, because the month of June had turned quite mad, they too sought a panacea for the airless noonday heat. They too sought the stimulating and refreshing effect that only the wet stuff could provide. And so they, like the numerous other overheated horde that had converged upon the Stour's grassy banks, seeking its pure and calming waters, decided to do the same.

Of course the indivisible threesome might easily have stayed at The Mansion, after all, the small lake situated in its extensive gardens and which was about half the size of Akworth's smallest pond, could easily have satisfied their immediate needs; there being certainly more than enough shade to go round and more than enough cool water as well. But they had each decided, individually and without hesitation, that the river was the in place to be; something to do with ---

"---- The waters flowing all around one, affording a soothing yet energising relaxation with sparkling coolness." Lady B. had affected the remark in her opined speech to her children prior to the visit.

The Fishers hadn't exactly gone down to Flatford that day but had merely crossed the road, which led past their house, walked the meadow, which lay beyond the road, and gained the river half a mile or so further upstream at just the spot where Jonathon enters the water on most mornings of his life for his early swim.

The water here was low in part, comparatively speaking, and exceptionally clear with only the subtlest of sepia tints visible. Multicoloured pebbles adorned the riverbed at the shallow edges while leafy shadows, formed by the rivers willowy margin, mingled with the rays of light that danced lightly over its rippling surface and played upon the small round stones causing a kaleidoscopic array of colours with ever changing patterns. Jonathon had examined these remarkable effects before and on many other occasions he had marvelled with wonderment and immense fascination at the abundant skills of Mother Nature and was so thankful that it was he, among the many, which had too been equipped with the wherewithal to appreciate them.

Jonathon was swimming effortlessly up and down this stretch of the river that had been laughingly approved by his mother as being 'safe for small children' and was enjoying the serenity of a relaxed atmosphere; albeit, some pent-up emotion did linger in his mind rather, and were, at this very moment, proving aggravatingly impossible to erase.

The mothers by this time had exited the water and were now lazily drying themselves in the warmth of the sun; their opinion now being that enough water was enough and besides, the desired effect had been successfully achieved.

Over the past twelve months or so the family of three had unwittingly achieved a certain notoriety among the inhabitants of Bergholt, ever since the Cabin / Yates affair had hit the limelight, (by courtesy of the local press). As already stated, the Judges had dealt severely but justly with all three convicted men for their roles in the murder of Mr Watts; and for theft and for smuggling and for all the other associated acts of criminality; which was totally envisaged. But it wasn't until the aftermath of the whole affair had been established and the tongues had been set wagging and fingers pointing that a certain amount of irritating veneration was caused to the family for their part in bringing all of these appalling men to justice. Not that the family minded being minor celebrities that much, who would, but it did grow more than a little tiresome after the period of twelve months or so had elapsed. The situation brought about by continuous and unsolicited attention being heaped upon them became somewhat boring, no matter how well intended it was deemed to be.

After thirty minutes of tirelessly swimming back and forth, Jonathon came out of the water, towelled himself dry, partially dressed and seated himself beside the womenfolk to partake of some lunch and to admire the immediate scenery, his mind still gripped by a thoughtful presence that appeared to affect the young man in such a way that caused him much disconsolation.

"We are so fortunate to be living in the Stour Valley, don't you think?" he spoke the question rather than asked it after a longish pensive pause. Then taking his time to ponder some more he continued in rather an unusual sombre and subdued manner.

"There is, I am sure, many other pleasant areas in this England of ours but this gentle valley must be among the loveliest," he said quietly, almost to himself, as he lapsed into a state of semi-melancholia. And with a degree of disquiet spreading his face he cast his eyes to the ground immediately in front of him as beads of cold dampness rippled his forehead.

"Darling are you alright? Only you are not looking your usual chirpy self at the moment. You appear to have been rapt in thought ever since your cooling swim, a swim which should have had a more positive effect on you, I should have thought. Won't you tell us what it is that's bugging you Jonathon?" asked Felicity, concerned that her son should be enjoying the warmth of this most pleasant June day and not looking quite so woeful as he most certainly was.

Jonathon failed to respond to his mother's anxiety instantly and instead continued looking at the ground in front of him as before. Then all at once he made an effort to appear more composed and an orchestrated feint beam of repose darted across his gloomy face. And he affected a hesitant brief smile at last.

"I'm fine thank you mother, just a temporary bout of lugubriousness that's all, nothing to worry about I can assure you. It's just that I have been in the water for almost half an hour and for the whole of that time I have had Mr Watts on my mind continuously, bless the man. Where do you think he is now grandmama? The psalmist David wrote about 'the valley of the shadow of death.' Do you think it at all possible he might be there? What hindrance hindsight is," he continued with his comments without allowing his grandmother the opportunity to answer.

"When I look back over that terrible morning," he said, "the morning of Mr Watts's death, I think that maybe if I had stayed with him for just a little longer, before running off to report to the police, then maybe I might have been in a better position to have assisted him. If I had only stayed, then maybe he would still be alive today." As he spoke, the words seemed to stick and moistness glistened in his eyes causing the young Adonis a look of agitated and agonising anguish.

"Now you listen to me Jonathon Fisher," said Lady B., unsmiling. "Not only did the court completely exonerate you from Mr Watts's death but you were continuously praised throughout the whole of the hearing for the part you played in that sorry business. You did more for that poor man than any other could possibly have done. Who else in this world could have extricated him single handed from the weedy entanglement he was in. You know very well that it took two frogmen almost three quarters of an hour to locate him and free him the second time. And in any case the experts considered him to be dead when you brought him out of the river; they didn't give much credence to the theory of the man dying twice now did they." Lady Barbara's kindly words attempted to bring comfort to her grandson although a smile failed to settle upon his pensive face.

"Yes that is true grandmama, everything you have said is perfectly true and I am nonetheless appreciative in your saying it. But that is not really what I am concerned about. I suppose the thing that is uppermost on my mind is the waste of a life and the confusion I am feeling because of it. I mean, here is a perfectly ordinary, drinking sort of chap who found himself in a situation about which he had no control. OK, he used his mouth in a way that may have brought about an amount of retribution under normal circumstances, but to be killed for speaking out of turn? I don't think so. Had he died from more natural causes, then there would be no problem for me, but he didn't, and I *was* involved, no matter what any court may have said about it. And, well, I was wondering if because of the circumstances of his death and of his pitifully premature demise, whether the same religious technicalities would apply," said Jonathon dully, and speaking in a tone that engaged all three faces with worryingly serious expressions.

"Well if you mean that because Mr Watts died without the usual formalities of a man of the cloth being present to administer his blessing and to give him the last rites and that entire sort of ritual, would he actually qualify for the 'here after?' I suppose the painful alternative would be to spend all eternity wandering this earth in some sort of time capsule. Well the answer to that question my dear would be we do not know; but I shouldn't think that the way a man dies to be at all important. Surely it's how a person lives his life that counts and not how he dies. Anyway, all we can do is trust in the Lord's good grace and try not to hypothesise on the subject too much," said the very nice lady, herself now radiating the warmth of a smile.

"Do you ever get the feeling of being watched?" This was Felicity resolutely interrupting the general flow of the discussion and endeavouring to inject a less solemn mood into the conversation. "I experienced the sensation a while back and now I have it again. Must be suffering from a mild attack of schizophrenia I should think," she laughed.

The light hearted statement appeared to have the desired effect for both Jonathon and Lady B. looked promptly about them with much curiosity and with a smile apiece.

"There are your mysterious onlookers mother, see, over there in the meadow; cows." Jonathon chuckled loudly with his mother; the significant spell had now been broken.

It was the very nice lady's turn to be ruminative as they gazed out beneath the enormous elm's spreading limbs far across the meadow to where indifferent black and white cattle lay nonchalantly chewing their partially pre-digested grass. Above them a common kestrel intently hovered, as if suspended by the invisible strings of a puppeteer, waiting to swoop onto some unsuspecting rodent to eat for its midday meal. On the one hand complete tranquillity on the other a catastrophe waiting to happen. The two juxtaposed yet unconnected, separate yet often together; one of natures fascinating disparities in evidence. The very nice lady viewed the scene and smiled discretely to herself. *'Will the vulnerable lamb ever nestle against the king of the beasts?'* she wondered. *'Someday perhaps, someday.'*

— CHAPTER TWO —

The gentlest of breezes rustled benignly the leaves of the towering tree under which the Fishers sat taking great pleasure in the demolition of the tasteful picnic they had earlier prepared. One of the drowsy Friesian heifers, in the field beyond, raised itself onto the knees of its fore legs then stood fully erect, its eyes bulging at the effort employed in the undertaking and disturbed its family and friends into a state of alertness as two humans entered their meadow from the top road. Only the intrusiveness of man, it seems, have the faculty of upsetting these bovine beasts; his presence alone being enough to cause them harassment and confusion. The cattle turned their heads in unison, as if rehearsing for the current production, toward the pair of people as they paced leisurely across the mead, wilfully encroaching upon the heavy-eyed heifer's private preserves.

A tall, gaunt looking man approached the Fisher family closely followed by the diminutive figure of a flaxen haired boy who was in turn being pursued by four of the Friesian cattle. After a while the cattle stopped and stared, their protuberant eyes then followed closely the tall man and the small boy as if they had never seen humans before. The man and boy continued their leisurely pace until they reached the family group. Jonathon, rising to his feet as they approached, extended his hand in a welcoming greeting which was warmly taken by the tall gaunt looking man.

The tall gaunt looking man, with a fixed smile both wide and open, exposed a set of ill fitting, nauseous dentures which clearly displayed the remnant evidence of a recently eaten meal. And then as if aware of some embarrassment quickly closed his muzzle but continued his smile with one ragged grey eyebrow slightly raised.

"Hello ladies and Jonathon. How are you all?" said the tall man, as his smile widened even wider. "I guessed somehow that I might find you here enjoying this most beautiful weather we are all having at the moment."

Lord Gilson, Rob to his immediate friends, was elderly and a gentleman in every sense of the word. His speech was eloquent, if a little muted, and at this particular point in time he sounded slightly breathless. His neat apparel was decidedly casual, with a sporty cravat being tucked inside his pale beige, slightly stained, open-necked shirt and his baggy, leather belted trousers matched perfectly his shirt, complete with a slight stain here and there. (Obviously the tall man's laundering capabilities left much to be desired). A pair of open toed sandals, shiny and new, completed his ensemble.

"Hello Rob, how lovely to see you again, how are you? I must say you are looking very distinguished as usual." It was Lady B. who opened the favourable speech on behalf of the family a radiant beam perpetually upon her countenance.

"I'm very well Barbara, thank you for asking and all the fitter for this really beautiful weather we are having at the moment, even though the pollen does seem to have a hostile effect on my head and chest.

"I've left poor Walter beavering away in the vegetable garden hoeing laboriously at the carrot bed, the perspiration simply dripping off the man. Young Arthur here, came to work with his father this morning, I suspect to appease May, and as I felt he was being overly helpful to the hard working Walter, decided to bring him along with me," said Lord Gilson, still with a merry flush upon his sunken cheeks.

Arthur was quite a small child of twelve years, or thereabouts. His straight blonde hair, being unruly at the best of times, was being held in place today with dried water or grease of some description; it being difficult to decide precisely but whichever it was, it seemed to be having the desired effect. He was dressed in a home-made, short floral shirt below which could be seen a pair of maroon swimming trunks. His modest feet were shod with a pair of black plimsolls that appeared to be two sizes too large for the little boy but he didn't seem to be aware of the oversight in any way. One plimsoll was tied in a bow quite satisfactorily but with a brown shoelace. The other was held together by a piece of ragged binder twine. But for all of this the lad appeared happy enough; and he, completely unaware of the fashion statement he presented, seemed quite content with his lot, although he did colour up at the mention of his name and looking down at the ground immediately in front of him started to mark the soil with the toe of his plimsoll.

"I am quite surprised that Walter George has a young family, he never speaks of them to me and he certainly has never brought Arthur to The Mansion. I somehow thought that his children were much older and had quite flown the nest by this time. But as one likes to keep abreast of these things I shall certainly chat with him about his family," said the very nice lady with a charitable expression forming her beautiful face and a gemmed smile brushing her lustrous lips.

As already mentioned in the very first chapter of this saga, Walter George was employed as head gardener at Lord Gilson's extensive estate and was regularly made available to The Mansion without charge; although Lady Barbara did graciously help the noble lord with the organising of much of his charitable works without her being otherwise rewarded and so the reciprocal bond between the two had grown to a lasting friendship.

"Oh yes indeed, Walter and May had six kiddies in all, but in two batches as it were. The first batch, I believe, have all flown the nest by this time, as you so eloquently put it, leaving just the two youngest boys still at home. I believe there to have been some eight or nine years between the fourth and fifth child but Arthur here is the youngest and quite a handful at times by all accounts," said Lord Gilson, glancing down at young Arthur as if blaming him for his late arrival or perhaps for his behavioural patterns and causing the boy to colour up once more, obviously embarrassed at receiving such attention.

"Anyway that aside, I am calling on you today seeking an act of exceptional kindness about which I earnestly hope your benevolent help will be forthcoming. You see, my niece Jane is due to visit with me tomorrow and I was hoping that one of you good people would be extremely kind in fetching her up from Manningtree Railway Station for me. I suppose I really ought to learn to drive myself but I really don't seem to be able to muster enough enthusiasm for the task, not at my late age. Besides, being surrounded by such lovely people as you, I would consider it to be a sad disparagement on my social activities if I *were* able to drive; what I mean is, I wouldn't have the same excuse to spend quite as much pleasurable time in your charming company, now would I," said Lord Gilson, chuckling to himself as if he had told a momentous joke and immediately securing everyone's polite laughter; with the exception of Arthur that is, who simply stared into space, curious to know what the joke was about.

"I am fully aware that you all devote your Sunday mornings worshiping at the Methodist Chapel," resumed Lord Gilson, "but as the train isn't due until well after midday I was rather hoping that this little jaunt would fit in with your routine comparatively easily."

"No trouble at all sir. I shall be delighted to fetch your niece for you myself," offered Jonathon enthusiastically. Then turning his attentions to the small flaxen haired boy he grinned and placing his large hand upon the boy's head he ruffled his stiff greasy hair saying:

"So you are Mr George's son are you Blondie? I think I noticed you last Sunday morning peddling your cycle down the Rectory hill. Looked as if you were heading for The Street with flowers in your hand, am I right?"

The ruffling of his hair caused Arthur some irritation and even more embarrassment as his countenance reached an all time high in vivid colouration.

"Yes sir," he said, meeting his humiliation with total distaste. "I was visiting my sister Gladys sir; I do that most Sundays," he added, thinking and hoping that that was the end of the inquisition. But it wasn't, besides this, there was a humiliating continuous investigation to face as well.

"I see. So this sister of yours, she lives down The Street does she?" asked Jonathon inquisitively.

"No sir, she's in the cemetery; I was visiting her grave."

A deathly silence, temporary but immediate, fell upon the small group stunning them into a state of depletion as they looked from one to the other quite mortified at the information as it reached their ears. Even Lord Gilson appeared unaware of the situation regarding the George family history but it was Felicity who stepped hastily forward to comfort the young lad.

"Arthur darling, we are so sorry, we didn't know," she said, almost tearfully, placing a caring arm about him.

"Oh that's alright ma'am, you see I never knew Gladys, she died before I was born, and she was six when she died but my mum, she always insist my brother or me take down some flowers each Sunday morning after Sunday school so she's never forgotten." A gleam in his eyes lit up the small boy's face as if he had at last managed to score points on the grownups.

"Oh I see," rejoined Felicity sensitively. "What was the matter with your sister? Did she have a terrible accident or something?"

"I don't remember ma'am, some sort of fits I think but I really don't remember what me mum said it was," returned Arthur, who appeared not to be concerned about *this* sort of interrogation, not in the slightest; it allowed the young lad to occupy the centre of the stage without causing him the slightest embarrassment.

"Right, some sort of epilepsy I expect," replied Felicity.

"Yeah, that's what mum said it was elepisy, elpsticity," he gave up trying to pronounce the word and settled for, "what you said," instead.

"How awful, your poor mum and dad, well it must have been terrible for them, losing a child so young. It must have completely devastated the whole family I should have thought," said Felicity a tiny tear at last made its way down her cheek and was quickly mopped up with her dainty handkerchief.

"Yeah I think so, 'cause my big sister Eva, she told me that mum held Gladys close to her to try and keep her warm 'til it was time for her to go," said Arthur, rising to the grim story. In point of fact, the young lad wasn't averse to continuing the topic for yet a while longer, it was amusing to him to see soppy adults in a state unnecessary anguish and would have gladly played out the scene had Jonathon not decided that a changing of the macabre subject was indeed called for.

"Would you like a sandwich Blondie and a drink to help it down?" he asked, successfully washing the subject from Arthur's mind and replacing it with something more appropriate.

"Coo yes please sir," said Blondie, without having to give the matter too much thought and hungrily took the dainty sandwich from the plate that Jonathon was offering. After eating the sandwich and taking two more for good measure, he then proceeded to gulp down the cup filled with fizzy Corona with hardly taking a breath or waiting for the others to be served.

"Thank you sir, that was nice," he said politely and eying the cake tin with the same relish he grabbed a handful of cakes and biscuits that were being offered as well.

"Blondie, you don't have to call me sir you know. Lord Gilson is the only one here you must address as sir. All of my friends call me Jonathon and you may certainly do the same if you care to," said the big man, grinning.

"Oh right sir, thank you sir—I mean Jonathon," said Blondie, over elated at the prospect of such familiarity as the gleeful feature on his ever changing countenance returned to one of embarrassment once again.

Lord Gilson, who was standing beside his friend Lady B. for all of this time, shuffled his feet as if wishing to prepare himself for his departure.

"Well," he said, "if we have everything sorted out, then I must bid you all adieus and a pleasant remainder of the afternoon. I shall hasten my return to the village and to Orvis Croft with a settled mind and confident in the knowledge that you will meet Jane's train tomorrow at twelve thirty Jonathon. Thank you so very much for that, it is indeed very much appreciated I assure you."

"Oh must you leave so soon Rob? Won't you stay awhile and partake of something to eat with us? A slice of Dundee cake and a refreshing drink maybe, just to stem the hunger and thirst a little," pleaded Lady B.

"Very tempting Barbara, but thank you no. As you are fully aware, we have the gardens open to the public on tomorrow week and there is still an awful lot of work to be done. I must not leave it all to Walter and his team of three now must I? There are things to be organised for such an occasion, things that are important for me to organise and me alone. So please release and excuse me dear lady, it has been a pleasure seeing you all again. Come along Arthur, we must make a move."

"Sir, if you wish it, Arthur could stay with us for the remainder of the afternoon and I could take him back to Orvis Croft later," said Jonathon, thinking that it might be good for Blondie to have a little freedom.

"How very kind. Would you like that Arthur?" said Lord Gilson.

"Yes please sir, I should like that very much. But sir, will you be OK going back all that way on your own? It's a long way sir and I shouldn't like you to get lost," said Blondie, most concerned.

"I think I might manage that alright," said Lord Gilson, quite relieved and with his usual grin upon his face. "That's settled then, I shall tell your father to expect you around five thirty. Now remember young man, best behaviour at all times if you please and don't let these nice people down with any of your foolish pranks, do you hear me?" ordered the kindly gentleman.

"No I won't sir; I'll be as good as gold," said Blondie, at which everyone laughed affectionately, causing further awkwardness to the small boy.

— CHAPTER THREE —

Lord Gilson strolled slowly back across the droughty meadow casually followed by the small inquisitive herd of Friesian cattle. The picnickers on the other hand sat back in their chairs and lounged on the dried grass finishing up the remnants of tasteful food and iced drink they had brought; at least Blondie did, his being the larger of the appetites available. They all chatted freely endeavouring to make the small boy more at home in their society so that he might discard his unfortunate nervousness.

The big man's mind was clearer now and the troubling weight of the Watts' affair was lifted almost completely from him, only at the periphery of his mind was it still evident but this he ignored for now. So, with his head clearer he decided to occupy what was left of the afternoon giving his newly found friend some lessons in the activity of swimming. Anyway, this was the immediate plan, but of course, he had no way of knowing just how far Blondie's ability had progressed since the episode at Flatford, if it had at all. And so he suggested they entered the water together in order to settle the question once and for all.

"Well Blondie have you learned how to swim yet? Only a year or so ago I remember you diving into the river off Flatford Bridge and one of the bigger lads taking you to task because you were doing so without being able to swim properly," said Jonathon, producing a smile rather dubiously.

"Oh yes sir, I can swim like a fish now and without one foot on the bottom and all. But I think I swim better under the water than I do on top," said Blondie.

"Tell you what then, you show me just how good you are, come on," said Jonathon, stripping down to his bathing trunks once again. Blondie followed suit and they both ran to the river and dived into the cool clear water. They swam for awhile together; well, Jonathon swam while Blondie splashed about enjoying the moment. The big man watched as the youngster showed off his suspect swimming ability and wasn't at all impressed. The boy obviously wasn't as capable as he had boasted but instead of being overly critical Jonathon tried to give the lad some encouraging advice. Blondie was proving not to be the most cooperative of pupils he being more concerned about what he would like to do rather than what he was being instructed. And once again commenced to overstate his ability in underwater swimming.

"I tell you I am much better under the water than on top," he shouted, "watch!" And with that the young lad duck dived to the bottom of the river and swam to the surface once again to prove his point; all that was proven, however, was his ability to float naturally to the top when once he had gained three feet, or thereabouts, beneath the surface. But Jonathon not wishing to be overly disparaging considered it more appropriate to give encouragement at this juncture and praised the endeavour by giving the young lad some hearty applause.

"Very good Blondie," he said warmly. "Now let me see how good you are at doing the crawl," ever hopeful that this basic stroke would prove to be well within the young boy's capabilities; even at his tender age. Jonathon stood waist deep observing Blondie's futile efforts as he hopelessly floundered about thrashing his legs and flailing his arms aimlessly, twisting and turning his body with minimal coordination and not gaining advancement in distance either. Jonathon's sigh of despair was long and deep, the young lad had no idea at all about the rudiments of swimming and there seemed little hope of ever teaching the hopeless individual; not in the couple of hours left available this afternoon anyway.

'Perhaps he might prove to be more successful at the breast stroke,' thought Jonathon, despair all too evident and hope deserting him. And when Jonathon suggested Blondie should attempt this particular stroke the sorry story repeated its disappointing self. It was patently obvious that Blondie had not the remotest idea how to perform in the water, all the anticipated talent was completely missing and one thing was painfully obvious, Blondie would never be able to swim, not ever, never in a month of Sundays would he be proficient.

Then a brainwave swept into the big mans reasoning.

'Perhaps if I could give the lad more of an incentive, perhaps show him how exciting swimming could be for him, then maybe his tiny brain might click into the mode of determination and accept guidance as a way forward and not be so reluctant in obeying commands no matter how gently communicated. Perhaps to view swimming as a necessity to ones survival as walking or running and not just for the pleasure it provided—then again, perhaps not. Perhaps the pleasure aspect is quintessential to the sport. Perhaps if he could be shown exactly what it is really like to be able to experience the underwater aspect of swimming we might get somewhere; after all Blondie reckons he can swim better beneath the surface than on top then perhaps I ought to move in that direction. Perhaps he should be shown what life below the surface is really like and how exhilarating viewing it can be—in reality.'

The young Adonis ruminated awhile weighing up the pros and cons of the idea which had sprang into his mind. *'There would be no real hidden dangers'* he thought. *'I have performed these acts dozens of times in the pool at university with no problems, no problems at all.'*

Jonathon quickly exited the river and wandered over to his swimming bag and retrieved the spare pair of goggles that he always carried. He then returned to the river's edge and commenced to adjust the elasticated strap. Then calling the young boy over to him he fitted the glasses to Blondie's face. After a further slight modification the glasses fitted perfectly.

"Right young Blondie," said Jonathon, "we are going beneath the river's surface in tandem. That means you will be riding piggyback with me, with your hands and arms firmly holding on to my neck and your legs trailing behind."

Blondie appeared delighted at the prospect and showed he was being overly excitable which was not what Jonathon had in mind.

"Look Blondie this is serious business and I need you to apply yourself to it with resolution and concentration. This is no laughing matter Blondie so please use your intelligence and show some sense; as soon as you start fooling about the show is over—got it?" said Jonathon sternly, peering deeply into the young lad's eyes.

"OK, I understand," assured Blondie, adopting an air of sensibility at last and standing patiently waiting for the next procedural instruction as Jonathon swam up to the lad.

The sun still shone brightly and the day was still quietly calm and peaceful, only the sound of the waters disturbance slighted the setting as Blondie settled upon the burly back, his spindly arms clinging most tightly around the sturdy neck and his eyes focusing over the head of the big man.

"When I shout 'NOW' I want you to breathe in and out deeply, three times. The forth breath you must hold for as long as you can then I shall dive to the bottom of the river. As soon as you feel the need for more air just give me a gentle kick and I'll take you to the surface again." Jonathon was as explicit with his instructions as he could possibly be and was guaranteed that all was positively understood.

The first effort was a disaster. Blondie seemed to be still taking air onboard as they dived and ended up spitting and spluttering and gasping for air. The second attempt was better but no sooner were they beneath the water then Blondie kicked frantically. The third effort was very much improved and so they were able to stay down for fifteen seconds, or thereabouts. This was indeed encouraging and Blondie was finding the experience most exhilarating.

"That was wonderful Jonathon," the young boy cried, as they resurfaced. "I could see everything so clearly and a fish came up to me and I could see it real good."

The forth endeavour was perfect and so they were able to stay down even longer. After a while Jonathon felt a kick from Blondie and so began his assent slowly to the surface. As they did so, the water appeared to be getting strangely darker when the opposite would have been the norm. And the final six inches was almost impenetrably black, as if a ton of crude oil had been dumped into the river and left to putrefy its purity. As soon as they broke the surface, their heads and lungs were filled with the malodorous stench of rotting fish with not an ounce of clean air to be had anywhere. And the wide surface of the river was piled up with thousands of obscene dead and dieing fish, in both directions upstream and down as far as the eye could see. Fish, with gawping mouths and staring eyes, flattened gills continuously moving searching for their craving, and fins and tails constantly flapping; if indeed they were still adjoined. Their bodies rotting with decay beyond reason each one fused in or on the one next to it, all mangled and tangled up the one with the other while the nauseating stench unbearable and totally unimaginable, lingered.

In less than an instant and without hesitation, Jonathon grabbed hold of Blondie and dived headlong through the mire leaving the dire carcasses and skeletons of the dead and dying fish in his wake and using his long legs, his feet, his free arm, and his powerful body to propel them both out of the murky waters to clearer cleaner parts.

Soon they had gained the familiar scene of his beloved Stour's verdant banks, where the willows stood on parade at the south side and the rushes bent in the gentle breeze amid the white lilies in their finest, fullest bloom.

The youngster gasped, gulping in the fresh clean air without hesitancy or instruction when at last they surfaced. And Jonathon, diligently ensuring himself that the boy was safe and well, posed the undying question -

"What on earth happened back there Blondie? I've never seen anything like it in the whole of my life. So weird, so obnoxious."

After the young lad had fully regained his composure he answered without hesitation.

"Why? What happened?"

"Just then, when we surfaced back there you must have seen it!"

"We didn't surface did we?" queried the young boy.

At once, Jonathon perceived that young Blondie hadn't experienced the nightmare and that he, Jonathon, alone, had been aware and participated in the awful occurrence.

'But where have we been?' He searched the far reaches of his muddled mind to collect an answer, any answer. *'Surely some hideous and frightening place,'* he thought. *'But where? That is the essential question I must find the answer to.'*

They swam back along the familiar stretch of water to where the ladies still sat enjoying the mid afternoon sun when Jonathon realised that

Blondie was achieving a much better effort than he showed before. His arm strokes were strong and coordinated nicely with his leg movement. *'Well something good has come out of it,'* he thought, but said nothing to the lad.

They both quickly clambered out of the water and hastily towelled themselves dry. Jonathon urgently tried for an effort of normality and to appear composed when all along his head was being tortured by what he'd witnessed.

"We were beginning to think you had lost your way Jonathon, you've been gone so long. A few more minutes and we would have had to send a search party for you," said his mother, with an attempt at humour.

"Sorry about that mother, I somehow got carried away in showing Blondie the rudiments of underwater swimming; seems to be doing quite well and will no doubt improve as time passes and of course with concentrated practice. Don't you think Blondie?" answered Jonathon, a look of false cheer invading his features.

"Why do you insist on calling Arthur by that silly nickname Jonathon? I'm certain his parents would never approve." Lady B. had always been most particular about people not using foreshortened names as Susan had quickly discovered and certainly not nicknames of any description, much too common.

"Oh no ma'am," put in the young lad. "Blondie is just fine, really it is. My uncle Dick used to call me that, besides, it's much better than the name they call me at school," said Blondie sheepishly.

"Why, what do they call you at school Blondie," inquired Jonathon glad that a lighter topic of conversation had gained the fore.

Blondie looked at the ground in front of him nervously and commenced to mark it with his toe as he had done earlier while his face coloured up to a rosy hue.

"They all call me 'Little Arthur the donkey man with lovely legs,' that's what," he said at length.

A suppressed grin hidden by cupped hands passed over the faces of the ladies which appeared to add insult to the little boy's embarrassment.

"Oh that's not very nice now is it," said Felicity trying to hide her amusement. "What ever did you do to deserve that?"

"Well–I've always been called Little Arthur because of my size. Then because me mum couldn't afford to buy me long trousers like the other boys they started calling me 'Little Arthur with lovely legs. Then when Squire Eld opened his gardens last year I was asked to help the lady with two donkeys give rides to the toddlers and when the boys saw me doing it they called me 'Little Arthur the donkey man with lovely legs,' and so it has stuck ever since," said Blondie, his face by this time had turned a bright crimson.

"Well now," said Lady B. sternly. "I don't hold with bullying in any shape or form, so we must try to put a stop to this at once." She thought awhile." Perhaps if you were seen in the company of Jonathon once in a while you may be surprised to learn that those awful boys may have better regard for you. You must also visit with us at The Mansion occasionally that should do the trick I should think."

Remembering the promise made to Lord Gilson that Blondie would be safely returned to Orvis Croft before five thirty and the time now being four forty five the family set off across the meadow. Felicity was in front holding young Blondie's hand; both chatting merrily away as they ambled along. Jonathon brought up the rear, with his grandmother, he, carrying two folded chairs and a picnic basket with his swimming bag strapped to his broad back; the early frightful experience once more to the fore of his troubled mind.

The now standing black and white Friesian herd remained unconcerned and merely ogled the humans as they slowly passed; more content with chewing the boring cud and no matter how dry the grass was when it started its journey it was now most certainly wet and they salivated over their chins dribbling onto the ground below in a stringy mess to prove it.

At last Jonathon decided to develop the subject he had broached earlier to his grandmother, mindfully aware of a possible tie up with the subject of his ghastly experience down in the river.

"You didn't exactly answer the question I posed earlier," he said firmly, as though needing an instant reply to an unspoken question.

"What question was that Jonathon? Please jog my poor deteriorating memory," was the amusing reply.

"Well if you remember, I asked about the Twenty Third Psalm especially the piece about the 'valley of the shadow of death' with regards to Mr Watts. And I was speculating if you considered there to be such a place of that nature in existence," asked Jonathon tentatively.

"Well I'm sure that King David thought there was such a place otherwise he wouldn't have written about it?"answered Lady B. adroitly. "Personally I consider he was referring to a state of mind we all occasionally find ourselves in, you know, when we feel temporarily deserted by all our friends and everyone else, including God. But I'm sure you didn't have that in mind, did you? Far too obvious I expect. I suppose you were thinking it to be more of a place where the disbelievers of this world might go while they quietly ruminate about the credibility of God's existence. You know, in St John's gospel we are told that the dead shall live if they believe in the Christ; well maybe that's it, perhaps it's a place where some go to cogitate while they make up their own minds about His credibility. Is that more along the lines you had in mind dear?" said his grandmother, not feeling that interested after such a warm and sunny day.

Jonathon failed to rejoin with the answer Lady B. had given straight away. Instead his mind tarried awhile in the disgusting, murky depths of the Stour and the hideous scene it evoked. His grandmother noticing him in his perplexity, said:

"Are you alright Jonathon?" Only you appear totally preoccupied for some reason at the moment. I'm very sorry and I apologise if I am unable to supply you with all of the answers you're looking for darling but you must remember I am only human after all."

"Oh I'm sorry grandmama. Yes, I guess I'm OK." said Jonathon smiling reassuringly. "But I wonder, might the three of us have an in depth discussion later this evening. I think I might need mother's opinion as well and not just the two of us in debate, if that's alright."

The topic of conversation was dropped instantly and the four figures continued their way back across the meadow towards The Mansion.

Jonathon retrieved the big black Bentley from the garage and drove Blondie to the top of Orvis Lane where Lord Gilson was waiting in deep conversation with Walter George outside the extensive buildings of Orvis Croft, the ancient and picturesque home of the said gentleman. After receiving gratuitous remarks from both men and promising the boy further swimming lessons, Jonathon turned the large motor and headed back toward The Mansion.

— CHAPTER FOUR —

Dinner at The Mansion that evening was a solemn affair. Lady B. had prepared her daughter for the eventual discussion while Jonathon had journeyed to Orvis Croft with Blondie but nothing was mentioned about it until dinner was finished and the dishes had been washed and stacked neatly away.

When the threesome seemed more relaxed, or as relaxed as they could possibly be with the pending discourse, like the sword of Damocles, hanging over them, and after the brandy had been declined, first by Jonathon and then by both ladies following suit, the threesome sat down in the drawing room ready for the anticipated family debate to commence.

Jonathon decided to embark on the awaited discussion resolutely not wishing to promote any unnecessary alarm with hesitation or by dithering about carelessly.

"To put you both firmly in the picture I have for the past months been inadvertently reflecting upon the death of poor Mr Watts. Well, more than a little in actual fact and quite unconsciously at times. These thoughts seem often to be with me and more frequently than I would like and are far more habitual than I consider good for me; in fact he seems to have taken over my mind to some extent just recently, which I am finding extremely disturbing. When we were away, down in Hampshire, I was hardly bothered at all, except maybe when I was swimming alone in the big lake at Akworth House, and then only on the odd occasion. I suppose I had a good deal on my mind then, as indeed we all had, what with the problems continuously going on around us, and dear old Mr Watts was obliterated almost wholly from my mind. Immediately upon our return, however, the problem started in earnest and I have been troubled with these disquieting sensations ever since. More so lately, and also to a greater intensity until they culminated in the weirdest experience one could possibly imagine down in the river this afternoon.

"Let me explain. I believe I mentioned the fact that I had been troubled with thoughts of Mr Watts earlier this afternoon, before Lord Gilson arrived with young Blondie in fact. Well that wasn't the half of it. You see, after Lord Gilson left us, I assessed Blondie's ability in propelling himself through the water; this so called ability was none existent at the time I hasten to add, but which has since mysteriously improved; that however is another story.

"As you both know, it is important to me that everyone should attain a certain proficiency in swimming, if only for the sake of ones own safety;

after all we none of us know when we will need to use this ability. Anyhow, I toyed with the idea of showing the boy the interesting aspect of under water life, considering that if he was able to examine life in the river first hand, as it were, he would be more likely to obtain the obsession that I have for swimming. And so I fitted him up with a spare pair of swimming glasses I had handy and we searched the river together in tandem. He appeared to thoroughly enjoy the exhilarating experience and seemed to be getting much more out of it than I anticipated, and I have to say, behaved in a most orderly and responsible manner.

"We were now getting down to a depth approaching eight to ten feet, when the situation became more than a little topsy-turvy. You see, as we were surfacing during the final attempt, a few abortive efforts now firmly under our belts, I noticed the water to be getting somewhat cloudy when I considered the opposite to be more usual and the nearer we approached the surface the murkier the water seemed to become until the final six inches, or so, became very dark and appeared to be densely unnavigable. It looked incredibly as if tons of crude oil had been dumped into the river contaminating everything and as we broke the surface I discovered the air to be so foul as to be not fit to breathe. The surface of the water was completely strewn with dead and decaying fish, thousands of them, heaped up for as far as the eye could possibly see and in both directions. And the stench! Well, it was absolutely and completely unbearable.

"We had arrived alright but where had we arrived? In some God forsaken and mysterious place that's for sure. Everywhere around us appeared to be in monochrome just like one of those old black and white movies only much greyer and more sombre. I quickly grabbed Blondie, both of us having to take in a lungful of the foul air, and dived back into the disgusting river, back to where the water was clean and friendly, back to the civilization I knew. The amazing thing about the revolting incident, apart from the obvious horror, was that when we surfaced again young Blondie was completely oblivious to the event, he remembered nothing, nothing at all." As Jonathon finished the telling of the saga a look of shocked dismay focused the faces of the two mothers both aghast at the terrible plight their son had experienced.

"What a frightfully macabre incident darling," said Felicity, her pallid face betraying all the motherly concern of a beleaguered bereavement so distressed was her feelings for her son. And then she continued as her countenance turned to one of puzzlement. "Why ever didn't you say something just as soon as you returned to us?" she queried, weekly and slowly.

"Under more normal circumstances I would have done of course," answered Jonathon. "But remember Blondie was with us and I saw no reason to cause him any unnecessary anxiety, especially when he had retained no knowledge of the ordeal."

Lady B. appeared engaged in deep thought, although her beautiful eyes failed to leave those of her grandson's for a single second. And wearing a burdened look, she toyed briefly with a smile, endeavouring, in all probability, to diminish her own excessive unease as well as that of her grandson. Eventually, breaking with her pensiveness and with a fixed grim determined smile upon her countenance she rose from her seat and walking over to her grandson and placing a comforting arm around his wide shoulders she gently kissed his forehead.

"Jonathon darling," she said at last. "I'm so sorry, but I have to ask you the undeniably obvious and disagreeable question," here she paused briefly. "Are you telling us that this experience actually happened and could not possibly have been brought about by the creation of an over active imagination? I feel terrible in asking it Jonathon but it has to be answered at some point in time. Don't forget dear, the weather has been particularly warm today and the heat of the noonday sun, as everyone knows, can play all sorts of tricks to the unsuspecting mind." Lady B. spoke with an out of character tenderness but the look on the young Adonis' face did nothing to fall in line with this her caring demeanour. And his voice was raised a couple of octaves as vehemently he defended the statement he had made.

"Let's get one thing straight right now shall we? I'm not a child who has flights of fancy and continuous daydreams!" he remonstrated. "Nor was I hallucinating in any way. The event which I have just described to you both was as real as we three sitting here and talking together. I certainly hope that that is now perfectly clear," his head nodded a couple of times to emphasise his words before he carried on.

"It was just as if I experienced another dimension or something so weirdly supernatural as to be beyond all human comprehension. Of one thing I am more than certain, this place is not at all pleasant or fit for human habitation, on the contrary, I cannot imagine anywhere on earth more noxious, demoralizing or fearful."

Felicity's look of apprehension and unease became even more acute as she, ever fearful in knowing her son's determination, explained her anxiety clear and detailed, with no room for confusion or doubt.

"Jonathon!" She spoke his name firmly and worriedly. "One thing I hope, is very clear to you, you must surely never attempt recapturing your most terrible experience. If you do, then who knows what may befall you. Chances are that you will never be able to get yourself back to us again."

But the instruction was far too late and so Jonathon removing his eyes from his mother's countenance did not respond to her appeal. He was already determined in his own mind to investigate the experience further, no matter what, and if possible to re-enter the realm of the as yet unknown.

Felicity could easily see through her son's look of ambivalence. She knew full well that if Jonathon set himself to do something, then nothing on this earth was going to stop him. And so she decided to play along as if she had never appealed to his dubious common sense.

"Jonathon!" She said his name again with equal force then readjusted her tone. "You described the scenery as being 'in monochrome.' Are you saying that the landscape had no colour to it at all, or at least, only varying tints of the same one?" She asked the question desperately trying not to sound alarmed in any way but merely to show a profound interest in the continuing debate, ever hopeful and mindful that an obviously uncontroverted explanation might easily be discovered soon. Something true and simple that everyone could understand and ponder over.

Jonathon looked at his mother, sympathetic with her concerned thoughts, guessing what she was going through.

"Presumably there was a light source somewhere," he said, "but I can assure you that no sun was shining, no intense light prevailed at all, although there were shadows. But absolutely nothing stood out as being colourful only tinges of neutrality. Yes I am sure I'm correct in describing the place as being monochromic for there was no hint of colour, only varying tones of grey."

During the mother and son exchanges, Lady B. had considered other options; she was still not convinced that her grandson was not going through some sort of distressing disorder akin to that of shell shock commonly experienced after the first war. This would be a gut wrenching nervous stress, she thought, one that had disturbingly been brought about by the finding of the unfortunate body of Mr Watts and it was painfully clear to her that Jonathon had been having illusionary trances and concluded that he must have unwittingly imagined the whole sordid business.

"What about the geographical location Jonathon?" she asked, trying to ascertain the validity of her suspicions and not attempting to trick her grandson in any way. "Do you consider you found yourself on the banks of the River Stour or were you in some obscure place completely unknown to you?"

"Do you know I hadn't really considered that question before? But it must have been the Stour. Yes of course it was, I'm quite certain now, it couldn't possibly have been anywhere else? It was further down the north bank where no footpath exists and where I have never walked before; about a quarter of a mile from the Dead River where Mr Watts was drowned."

The following day Jonathon met the twelve thirty train from London as promised on which Lord Gilson's small niece had travelled un-chaperoned. She didn't get out of her carriage straight away and it wasn't until she had been prompted by a travelling inspector that she made her way onto the spotlessly clean platform of Manningtree Railway Station. And not being at all familiar with the person sent to meet her, the pretty ten-year-old looked inquisitively up and down the platform hoping that someone would take the initiative and speak to her.

A very tall man approached the small girl with a huge grin and an extended hand. The tall man, it seemed to her, was nice enough and not at all as daunting as his size might have portrayed. And so she took the hand, tentatively at first and then more fervently.

"I'm Jonathon Fisher," he said; his manner was gentle and kind. "You must be Jane Strawn, am I right?"

The small girl nodded and held on to his hand without hesitation and the big man and the small girl walked from the station to the waiting big black Bentley that was parked outside the entrance to the deserted ticket office.

Jane said that her journey had been 'OK' when she had been asked and hopped into the large front seat of the big motor car next to a flaxen haired young boy who was already ensconced therein.

"Jane this young man is called Blondie," said Jonathon casually almost as if it was an afterthought. Blondie detected Jonathon's lack of enthusiasm but he didn't mind too much as he much preferred the seclusion, security and the silence of the background in these situations.

"He has kindly volunteered to be your escort for the next few days or until the length of your stay with Uncle Rob has been decided."

Blondie failed to smile as he shook the dainty hand of the pretty young girl; although he wanted to of course but considered showing that he found the newcomer to be at all attractive would not be the best way forward. After all he didn't wish to appear bold or overly confident. But that tiny hand—it was so cool and soft—and he would so much liked to have held it a little longer.

"Are you a V.K.?" asked the newly arrived, tantalisingly and using an exaggerated la-di-da voice.

"V.K.? Whats a V.K.?" asked the young boy nervously but hoping against hope that the question may prove to be some strange compliment.

"Well if you don't know then you must be one. A 'village kid' of course silly," retorted Jane, employing unrestrained confidence.

Blondie's young face dropped a mile. He hadn't expected to have been blatantly insulted quite so soon after such a short acquaintance or quite so abruptly by such a stupid girl as this, no matter how pretty she appeared to be at first sight. He hadn't volunteered or even desired to be the companion to some silly girl in the first place no matter what Jonathon Fisher may have said. But now he had discovered that not only was the girl stupid but she was rude into the bargain.

Blondie was livid. A few well favoured expletives might have done his welling temper some good. He sifted through some bad words; words that he had been forbidden to use by both his parents long ago, then he filed them away again for future reference for some future date; *'who knows, they may still prove useful,'* he thought, *'if she annoys me again later on in the next few days as she will surely do. Jonathon's promise that Jane's visit to Orvis Croft would be fun days seem now to be completely out of reach,'* he said to himself continuing with his musings, *'she has made sure of that.'*

He glanced casually across at Jonathon; after all, it was Jonathon's idea that had brought about this dreary dilemma down on the young lad's head, surely a look of consolation or a cheery word of comfort might be forth coming. But his sideways glance gained no response from the giant. *'Maybe he hadn't heard the insulting remark that had been hurled at me,'* he thought. *'After all, he does prefer to concentrate on his driving, when he's in the car, rather than listening to silly girls prattling on being silly.'*

Jonathon had indeed heard the childish ribbing but had decided to stay out of it. *'Blondie must learn to handle these situations for himself,'* he thought.

The Bentley arrived at Orvis Croft just ten minutes after it had left the railway station. The two children exited the car almost before it had stopped; the one skipped merrily down the short drive to the big house without a care in the world. The other walked slowly along the White Horse Road to number eight where his tea would be waiting for him, if he was lucky, feeling very unhappy.

— CHAPTER FIVE —

The avidly awaited Sunday afternoon had arrived; this, being the afternoon of the opening of Lord Gilson's gardens to the eager viewing public and was proven to be more than a little farcical; it turning out to be like unto a demonstration of the noble gentleman's generosity rather than the horticultural display it was designed to be.

Some, but certainly not all, of the local inhabitants of the village who turned out in dribs and drabs drifted along the roads to be there; especially those, of course, who wished for the opportunity to be seen mixing with, and in the company of, the upper echelon of the community; those hoping to further their station in this parochial society, albeit in mind alone and restricted to the said afternoon at best when everyone was purporting to socialize as one class. All of the local dignitaries were most certainly in attendance: Colonel This and Colonel That and Captain The Other. And of course, the beauteous Fisher family the Lady Barbara Fisher-Jones and her nearest and dearest Felicity and Jonathon Fisher, who incidentally, where in favour to both sides of the social divide, they were most certainly there. Everyone who was present looked most well turned-out for such an auspicious occasion, having taken their finery out of mothballs specifically for the event, more than likely.

Small groups of people, individuals and couples as well, sauntered around the freshly mown, patterned lawns and the recently weeded paths around the borders, carrying and sipping from glasses of the finest sherry and holding cigarettes carefully between their fingers or placed adroitly between their lips; (in cigarette holders of course), and sounding awfully knowledgeable and frightfully authoritative on the countless varieties of plant life being exhibited. In fact the whole charade was exactly that, a charade, and not for the faint hearted either and certainly not for ardent lovers of superb horticulture.

Jonathon, idling around some flower bed or other, noticed young Blondie George tramping about the place close to the house giggling to himself and with a half filled glass of sherry in his hand. Feeling rather perturbed and let down by this sighting, the big man marched, with larger than usual strides, and with a disapproving look disfiguring his handsome face, over to where the small boy was standing.

"Just what do you think you are doing Blondie?" asked Jonathon sternly. "I'm certain that your parents wouldn't approve of you drinking sherry, especially at a function of this importance where you could easily make a fool of yourself in front of everyone. For goodness sake be sensible

Blondie. Who on earth was irresponsible enough to give you the drink in the first place?" asked the big man clearly infuriated with the lad but failed to confiscate the glass.

"Jane gave it to me," he answered frivolously. And taking another sip of the fortified ruby fluid commenced to giggle again defiantly. "Mum saw me and just laughed. She called me a young devil; nothing else. She didn't tell me off or anything,"

"Well she was probably too embarrassed to do that; not wishing to make a scene and hoped that no one else had noticed you, I expect. Anyway, please don't have any more; you'll make yourself ill if you do!" said Jonathon soberly.

Then turning away from the lad in disgust he observed the portly figure of the Reverend K.B. Renouf ambling slowly toward the large wild pond with its range of bamboos, reeds and wide variety of grasses their grey green and variegated hue blending nicely with the dark grey of its murky water.

The tall, red moustached, blush faced man was a little more than slightly obese but which didn't seem to pose a problem to him for he always moved about the establishment with agility and apart from his aforementioned blushed face, seemed in reasonable condition.

He was half of the way through his first five year stint as the presiding minister at the local Methodist Chapel where the Fishers were wont to worship each Sunday. The minister was an approachable man, a little apt to attire himself in overly official investiture at times when taking the service, but other than that, congenial and well respected by all the members of his modest congregation.

Jonathon called quietly to the devout gentleman and with a muted cough, walked over to him. The Reverend Renouf turned at the mention of his name and exercised an expression of delight as he recognised the tall figure of the young man following him.

"Hello Jonathon, it is good to see you." The minister's voice was precise; pronouncing the beginning and ending of each word with the uttermost emphasise and clarity and the heart of each word with a clear correctness. "I must say," he continued, "you are the first church member I have had the pleasure of meeting since I arrived here fifteen minutes ago."

"Oh really!" said Jonathon, in surprise. "Well the two mothers are here somewhere. I expect they will catch up with you later."

"Anyway, how are you Jonathon?" asked the minister. "I must say you are looking singularly well."

"Yes I am minister thank you, very well indeed," replied Jonathon. "And yourself I do hope you are the same, only I haven't seen you lately, not for well over a month in fact."

The minister made a tiny gurgling sound with his throat which he seemed often so to do and which, according to other well informed members of the church, was attributed to some nervous disorder of sorts, especially if he was on the defensive in any way.

"That's right Jonathon," he rejoined. "There are other churches in the Ipswich circuit that I tend as well as the East Bergholt chapel as you well know, and which are equally as important to me believe it or not; I have had to devote more of my attentions to those just recently as there is sadly a shortage of lay preaches at this point in time." His blushed face deepened all the way to the tips of his ears as he stood his full height.

"Minister, I didn't mean to imply you have been neglecting us only that I haven't seen you lately that's all.

"Anyway, I am so glad that I have bumped into you this afternoon as there is something that I have been meaning to ask you for some considerable time now but on each and every occasion I see you, you appear to be busily caught up in earnest conversation with other members or preoccupied in one way or another," said Jonathon hoping that the minister wouldn't take that particular observation the wrong way as well.

The minister didn't, but he did appear to be instantly thoughtful and being a man who proudly anticipated his flock's desires tried hopelessly to determine Jonathon's question prior to its being asked but sadly ended up by pronouncing:

"Well by the look on your face Jonathon it must be something exceedingly serious indeed, I am all agog, please ask away, whatever can it be?"

"I do hope this won't sound too ludicrous minister but I need your opinion and some information about the twenty third psalm and especially the part that relates to the valley of the shadow of death," asked Jonathon a little hesitantly.

"My goodness, what an unusual request I would never have guessed that one, not in a thousand years. I know you to be a religiously studious young man, Jonathon, but I surely wouldn't have thought of you as searching the hidden depths and antiquities of the psalms; more a New Testament man I should have thought.

"Well before I am able to impart my knowledge on the subject I shall need to know more specifically the context in which I am supposed to account my views to you. After all, the twenty third psalm like all the other psalms is first and foremost a religious poem or song which was and still is used in the public and private worship of God. So, from which particular view point does your interest come; from a religious or from a more poetic slant?" The kindly reverend gentleman's brown eyes showed a benevolent smile as his eyebrows arched questioningly above them.

Jonathon thought for awhile and then said:

"Well both really." He answered the question in a somewhat equivocal manner, preferring to remain as ambiguous as possible and not wishing to invite any further interrogation after receiving the valued information.

The reverend gentleman scratched and inclined his head debating the subject with himself for a few seconds and revealed a questioning look as though the theme was proving to be quite a problem.

"I see, well now,—perhaps I should start at the beginning. Being the youngest of Jesse's children it would have been David's duty to look after and tend the sheep. These would have been halcyon days for the young boy; days that he would undoubtedly look back on with great affection having all the time in the world for thoughtful meditation and prayer; little wonder that he was able to write such beautiful poetry. I'm sure, however, that if there was a worldwide census of opinion taken to establish the finest poet the world has ever produced, then I doubt that David would receive a mention at all, yet to my mind he is clearly the greatest writer of poetry the world has ever seen.

"Be that as it may, contrary to some schools of thought I do not personally consider that the twenty third psalm was written in David's younger days at all. I think it more likely to have been written when he was much older, and well after he was made the second king of the whole of Israel. Probably after he had been installed in Jerusalem when once the Jebusites had been ousted of course. I say this because, in the psalm, he clearly states that the Lord prepares for him a table in the presence of his enemies. Now, you may interpret that as you will, but to my mind it is saying that King David is settled in his job of work but has incurred many back stabbing people within his court. You see the whole of the psalm is written on a very personal level," said the reverend gentleman now feeling at ease with the subject.

Jonathon looked a little disappointed at the answer given thus far and wanted to move on to the more important and pivotal aspect of the question.

"Yes I fully understand that the history of David is largely open to conjecture and I can appreciate your thoughts regarding the chronological side of events but what interests me more is the geographical feature of the psalm. I mean, David talks about walking in the valley of the shadow of death, well walking to my way of thinking is a physical exercise whilst the psalm, which has been a favourite throughout the centuries, maintains a strong spiritual influence," said Jonathon, feeling a little out of depth in this discussion.

The reverend gentleman once again inclined his head in concentration applying his fingers to it vigorously.

"Jonathon, I'm wondering why your interest lay in the more morbid aspect of the psalm when David clearly states that the Lord is with him, even in the depths of misery. However, I am sure that he had a specific location in mind if as I say he was situated in Jerusalem at the time. Two possible candidates spring to mind and both of them are situated more or less south of the city. The Kidron Valley is south east of Jerusalem and was used as a common burial ground in ancient times. But it was also used as a dumping ground for the ashes of idolatrous symbols when the temple had to be cleansed. Kidron is also identified with the valley of Jehoshaphat as being the valley where all the nations are to be gathered for judgement. The other possible location lies south west of Jerusalem and is called Gehenna or the Valley of Hinnom, if my memory serves me correctly. This, I would consider to be the most likely candidate as it was the place where children were sacrificed to the god Molech at the high place of Topheth and offal was traditionally burned there. It eventually became known as 'the place of woe,' so you can tell from that that it must have been a distressing sort of place.

"So–you may take your pick young man. But I really fail to see the real importance of locating David's valley of the shadow of death; its poetry Jonathon and it doesn't matter at all what place David had in mind when he penned the verse; you might even consider it to be almost anywhere, it really doesn't matter," concluded the Reverend Renouf.

"Yes I do see and understand clearly that the valley could indeed be anywhere and possibly everywhere, depending on your train of thought I suppose. Thank you for your time Reverend you have been most helpful. I only hope I haven't disturbed your afternoon on this lovely day," said Jonathon, most happy with the answer to what he considered to be his now resolved question and feeling he was now able to apply the answer any way he wished.

"Not at all Jonathon, anytime one of my flocks feels the need of being enlightened then it is my duty, indeed my pleasure, to assist in any way I can.

"On a lighter note Jonathon, did you notice the beautiful display of climbing roses tenaciously clinging to the south wall of the big house? Truly magnificent I should say. Temporarily a little past their best perhaps but still very lovely," said the reverend gentleman beaming.

Jonathon happily agreed, shaking the minister's hand firmly as they parted.

The big man walked aimlessly down to the two acre apple orchard and past the pigsty where two black and white mud splattered animals grunted contentedly as they gluttonously gobbled the garbage over-spilling their iron trough.

He mused awhile; his active mind still captivated by the enthralling conversation with his pastoral friend and admired silently the almost ripe apples hanging in abundance on the carefully shaped trees.

Walter George, dressed in his Sunday best, sauntered by and the two men exchanged the time of day, with Jonathon congratulating the gardener upon the well groomed appearance of the gardens, hoping that one day The Mansion grounds would look half as appealing, when all at once a roar went up; a mixture of screams punctuated with the sound of laughter filled the air seemingly stemming from the house or very close to it. Jonathon hastily excused himself from the gardener and made his way quickly back to the pond that he had left little more than a minute ago.

The comic scene that greeted him caused the big man to pause, place his hands on his hips and to smile broadly. Lord Gilson's niece Jane was stuck fast half way along an old tree trunk which had fallen across the pond some years ago and had been left where it had fallen for ecological reasons. Her arms were clinging in desperation to the slippery trunk while one of her legs was dangling aimlessly in the muddy water. The other leg, which was continuously attempting to gain a suitable foothold, was not providing the little girl with any benefit whatsoever. And Jane's nice new candy pink dress was no longer nice, new, or candy pink; at least only in part was it so, but was embarrassingly hoisted up above her thighs and was decorated with copious spots and splashes of the thickest most viscous green sludge. The little girl had quite obviously been intent on reaching a deserted moorhen's nest, complete with two eggs, that was safely established at the end of the log where two pronged branches held it most firmly in their crutch; one didn't need wizardry gifts to be able to unravel the stratagem here, the evidence was plain enough to see.

However, although Jane Strawn was in no real danger, uncomfortable maybe, but not dangerously situated, Blondie considered the circumstances warranted quick and positive action and so was seen to be two thirds of the way across the pond wading in the murky water up to his waist desperate to make a do-or-die attempt to rescue the distressed damsel.

Daringly he moved forward, unsteady at times with his slim arms held high above his head and the muddy water now beyond the level of his slender waist and with the foul-smelling ooze and duckweed gathering immediately in front of him, the young boy battled on. Slowly and deliberately Blondie traversed the filthy pond until he reached his arch-enemy then stretching out his fledgling arm he encouraged the young girl over to a branch of the tree which was nearer to him then turning slowly round he also encouraged her onto his back.

Jonathon, still smiling and watching patiently, resisted the urge to enter the murky water himself in order to assist the young boy; deciding that as both rescued and rescuer were perfectly safe and unscathed he would allow the development of Blondie's undoubted bravery to take its course.

After a full ten-minute struggle and slipping badly on more than one occasion, almost depositing his all too precious cargo into the filthy water alongside him, Blondie, at last, clambered to the safety of the stodgy strand amid tumultuous applause. His mother took the muddy figure of her dear child into her arms, filthy though he was and making filthy, into the bargain, what was hitherto her very best dress. But this did not seem to matter in the slightest, for her son was safe and a hero to boot and she, along with the small crowd that had gathered, heaped praises onto the small boy who appeared to be outwardly enjoying every single part of the seemingly inexhaustible supply of fuss and adoration. Clean white towels were brought with which to wrap the two youngsters and a teaspoonful of sugared brandy was administered, (supposedly for shock).

Jonathon had quietly followed the small crowd of well wishers into the large oak beamed kitchen and had placed a congratulatory hand upon the hero's shoulder.

"Well done there young man, you did marvellously," he said, in a friendly lucid voice so there could be no denial of the intentions of his meaning. "But it beats me, why you didn't follow Jane across the tree trunk and tried to help her that way," he added.

"Because the trunk was covered with thick green slime that's why and I didn't want to join her in the helpless state she was in, now did I? What would have been the sense in that? There would have been two of us in trouble then," said Blondie, proudly.

Jonathon smiled.

The two children both enjoyed a deep, hot, soapy bath, especially Blondie, as this was the deepest bath he had ever had and he was going to make the most of it. A change of clean clothing had been prepared for them and they went happily down the stairs to meet their public.

— CHAPTER SIX —

That evening, again after dinner had been eaten and enjoyed, Jonathon pressed the two mothers for an extension to the discourse they had had just a few days earlier. He felt that the pertinent statement made by the Reverend K.B. Renouf should be shared, if the ladies were willing to listen. The two mothers were feeling more than a little disconsolate with Jonathon's overtures to their shared fine friend the minister but were instantly and hugely relieved to learn that the unfortunate approach was somewhat limited and that the reverend gentleman was not in possession of the full facts after all and that his edifying remarks, being confined to the twenty third psalm and to that portion of scripture alone, could be considered mildly satisfactory.

"I am not at all happy with your continued ponderings over this matter Jonathon. I quite hoped that you would have put this unfortunate matter well and truly behind you by this time and I consider the whole episode to be grossly unhealthy both physically and mentally as well." Felicity offered the remarks trying hard to dampen her son's enthusiasm for the subject but at the same time needing to give him her whole hearted moral support. These remarks, to Jonathon's way of thinking were completely unwarranted and unhelpful in the extreme.

The two most important women in Jonathon's life were both quietly concerned about this rash and foolhardy affair. Concerned, because they felt that this traumatic experience was having a detrimental effect upon his mental stability. They had discussed the matter with each other on several occasions and had jointly formed the opinion that the Stour incident was more fictitious than the actuality that Jonathon claimed it to be and that the whole episode was in his mind alone. But this is exactly where they didn't want it to be. They desired their son's mind to be completely free of the ghastly business, free of the worry, free of the turmoil, the unrest, the uncertainty and all the other barbaric encumbrances that accompany such an acute dilemma. All of this had been bottled up in their minds firmly, and with no escape, ever since Jonathon had sprung the matter onto them a few days earlier and now they felt that a more positive stance should be taken for all of their sakes.

Felicity's worried manner was apparent to both her mother and her son. She sighed with unmitigated emotion allowing her feelings upon the matter to flee her mind for a brief while only to hover above her head and finally return to the intellect that nurtured them.

"Jonathon I'm sure you have no idea what it is you are putting us through. We are both experiencing unnecessary sleepless nights with you harbouring thoughts of your determination to recapture that grotesque experience you claim to be your version of reality. Please darling, I implore you to give it up and seek some psychiatric help." A tear moved to the corner of her eye and rolled slowly down her lovely cheek as her desperation showed itself to be overwhelming.

Lady Barbara looked anxiously at her daughter but offered no consolation even though she knew what Felicity was going through. Indeed she did know because she was being tormented by the same tortuous feelings herself but this wasn't the time for emotions this was a moment to use her inner strength in the face of disproportionate bleak emptiness and it was Jonathon who needed her strength right now, not Felicity.

"I must say that I do agree with your mother Jonathon. I am finding the whole concern quite incomprehensible and I consider it about time you sought some professional advice for yourself. The last thing you need right now is for this situation to get out of hand, don't you agree? Otherwise you could easily end up with a nervous breakdown or something much worse," said Lady B., dispassionately.

Jonathon didn't feel or look at all pleased with the remarks he had just heard. Support was what he needed; he thought he had it. Clearly he was mistaken. He remained silent for awhile debating within himself about the matter and wondering what he must do to obtain the sympathetic reassurance he thought he needed. Quite suddenly beads of perspiration appeared on his forehead and a feeling of worthlessness and weakness overshadowed him and his concentration on the matter before him now seemed unsteady and the recollection of the dire event became intrusive. *'Mother talks of sleepless nights. Doesn't she realise the nightmares I have suffered when Watts visits me from the grave. Of the countless moments; moments when I have doubted even my own sanity; of the times when I feel as if I was finding him all over again, and still the list goes on, endlessly.'* He tried desperately to pull himself together, summoning sufficient strength to fake a smile and wipe his moistened forehead, then lastly to reach out for his mother's hand and offered her a faint smile.

"You have it all wrong, I do know what you are both going through; but don't you see, I need both your strengths and your support; I am beginning to feel useless and numb not being assured that you are both on my side," said Jonathon, as he felt the perspiration now running freely down his back compelling him to feel tarnished and soiled; the need to wash or take a shower, anything to cleanse this irrational germ phobia that had taken hold, which was at this moment, uppermost to his needs.

He quickly excused himself and ran to his bathroom. He disrobed and hosed himself of the rancid noisomeness and felt the better for it. He dressed once more then ambled down the stairs to the drawing room where his mothers were waiting with pent-up emotions wondering about their son's hasty departure. The departure, it should be expressed, had taken a full thirty minutes and more than enough time to convey to the ladies that something further amiss had filled their son's mind.

After reseating himself, Jonathon took up the reins from where he had left off without a word of reason about the unexpected withdrawal and without a word about the change of clothing he now wore; it was just as if he had not left the room at all. The two lovely ladies eyed each other with cast expressions on their faces and their eyebrows were raised with spontaneous questionings but they said not a thing. It seemed they must now adjust themselves to their beloved son's uncharacteristic and odd behaviour or somehow point him in the direction he must follow.

"You know I am beginning to think it was against my better judgement to have discussed this matter with the two of you in the first place," said Jonathon, taking up where he had left off over half an hour ago. "I really thought you to be the only people in the world who clearly understood me and who would have plied me with support without question come what may. Clearly, I was sadly mistaken. Look, I know I have said it before but at the risk of sounding a bore, I'll say it again; please be assured that I have not taken leave of my senses and no matter what you both may think, this experience actually happened to me! There, I'm sure I couldn't have been much clearer than that, now could I?"

Jonathon was feeling more than a little exasperated by this time and he found that his temper was beginning to get the better of him and he thought it must be showing at the very least; but he fought doggedly to keep it under control and once again forced a puerile smile.

"Darling you must know how we both care about you and love you and at the same time have every confidence in your heretofore good sense ---" Felicity was interrupted before she was able to continue.

"Heretofore good sense! What on earth do you mean by that? Are you saying that my good senses have now all suddenly up and left me? Is that it? Speak mother, please explain yourself," retorted an angry young man.

"Sorry dear, a bad choice of words, But—to my way of thinking you are not showing us very much of your good discernment at the moment are you? Anyway, please allow me to continue. Jonathon, there comes a time in everyone's life when we all need a helping hand in one way or another, and we, as your nearest and dearest, firmly believe that you may be in need of some counselling right now."

Jonathon toyed with the idea for a while, eventually holding the view that it was not possible to convince these scatterbrained women of his need for his kind of support; not theirs. And that the line of least resistance was probably the best way forward at this particular juncture anyway. So, he may just as well go along with their zany idea; that way he might slowly convince them of his suspicions once he had seen the whole episode through to the bitter end and at the same time keep all further notions and developments strictly to himself and keep all further communications on the now rejected subject to an absolute minimum.

"OK, maybe you are right." He tendered the resigned acceptance of the idea uneasily and with his fingers firmly crossed, (metaphorically speaking). "Maybe it might be a good idea to have a chat with someone more experienced in these matters," he said; "who would you suggest?"

He eyed the ladies apprehensively as a slight interlude wavered and calculated glances were exchanged.

"No, no, a thousand times no. Most certainly not that old witchdoctor Randolph Richard," said a more reasonable, unwound and relaxed Jonathon.

"No dear, Randy is not the man for this job. But maybe he might be able to put you in touch with someone more suited to the task," said Lady B. thoughtfully hoping against hope that a breakthrough was about to take place. "Would you like me to test the waters for you dear?"

Jonathon was stranded now; there was no turning back for him. *'Anyway the experience might be interesting and I have nothing to lose,'* he said to himself resignedly.

"OK, I'll leave it to you grandmama, whatever you think is best."

And with that, the matter was, for the moment, firmly closed.

— CHAPTER SEVEN —

The following morning dawned to find Jonathon Fisher up and about at his usual hour of five thirty. But on this cloudless morn, like most mornings recently, he was again feeling exceptionally tired and worn after yet another bout of anxiety generating yet another bout of sleeplessness. This time it followed close on the heels of the two mothers putting him through the wringer the previous evening, more or less determined to use their only son as a psychiatrist's fodder; which he detested most vehemently. But during the sleep-lost night he had gradually acclimatised himself to the idea of being used as a subject for experiment when deep down he positively knew that it was all for nothing and that sooner or later the two ladies would realise that he was not pushing around some 'get me in the limelight quick' fantasy.

As already stated, it was a cloudless morning, showing signs of becoming yet another scorching day. Jonathon closed his bedroom window a little, from which he had been gathering the information for his personal weather forecast, pulled on his favourite swimming trunks and shoes, gathered his swimming bag containing towel, goggles times two, a snorkel and flippers which he rarely used but carried with him on the off chance, and slung on his top as he silently left the room. He closed the heavy oaken front door quietly and made his way to the road which passed The Mansion on its way to Flatford Bridge. Crossing the narrow road, which was little more than a lane in reality, he leapt the low fence and traversed the meadow where his most favourite Friesian herd of cattle lie, contentedly munched away day in and day out.

He reached the riverside without much ado and sitting himself down on the dry grass he began to remove his shoe type sandals at once. Almost immediately extreme tiredness overshadowed the big man and so he lay back awhile falling into a bottomless sleep, a sleep that he felt was friendly and most desirous, a sleep he wanted never to be waken from.

Dreamily and in complete nebulousness he sat up once more; he removed the one remaining shoe from off his foot and stood awhile. He unzipped his jacket and threw it on top of his bag, instead of carefully folding it and placing it together with his shoes inside the bag as was the norm, and as he did so he simultaneously plunged headlong into the clear wet coolness of the river in a fuzzy misty haze.

He smiled sedately to himself as he dived beneath the calm surface then up he came again, rolling over and over in the water's disturbance he was causing, then down again appreciating, no loving, the refreshing and energising sparkle he always felt when first he crossed the threshold of the Stour.

After the foggy frivolity was over, he began his swim steadily upstream at a goodly pace now, until he reached the spot where before he had dived with Blondie as his passenger. He launched himself immediately to the bottom of the river then slowly rose to the surface once again. Nothing! He looked around him, carefully noting the position of the coppiced willow trees that lined the bank on the rivers edge. He was certain he had found the right place. And so he dived again. Still nothing! The third attempt, to achieve what he was seeking, proved fruitless as well and so the young Adonis plunged a forth time. This time the ill-defined situation altered, the water was cloudy, very cloudy; and as he reached the surface it became cloudier still. Then he remembered. It was not until the forth attempt that the phenomenon occurred before; was this indeed significant? Or merely happenstance! It didn't matter; he had found what he came for!

As before the final six inches, or so, of the murky water was black. He closed his eyes as he entered its darkness and broke the surface quickly as he had done before. And as on that awful, previous occasion he was greeted by the tens of thousands of dead and dying fish and the intense foulness of the acrid stench their decomposition was creating.

He dragged himself, as quickly as his tired body would allow, onto the slimy mud embankment and rolled over, in a state of fearful confusion, onto the dead reeds and grass that provided a deathly lining to that hideous river.

He looked back from whence he came and retched then vomited copiously as the vile, pungent repugnancy of the revolting air filled his lungs. He lifted his body for a moment and sat there, still, his eyes taking in the colourless scene around him and the parading view of intense grey ugliness before him. The trees, if indeed that was what they were, appeared misshapen, cruelly deformed; and from where he stood, to the horizon, was seen an incredible bleakness; and an intensely cold, dismal mistiness existed everywhere, engulfing everything.

He slowly glanced upstream, then downstream trying to establish the exact location of this hellhole. *'The bend in the river,'* He thought, *is vaguely familiar and the malformed willows across the way look as if they are positioned perfectly.'* Yes, he was right when he'd told his grandmother that it was the north side of the Stour; this indeed is where the big man was.

'*How could anything so beautiful in reality turn out to be so hideous in a faculty of improbability,*' he wondered. '*We all of us have our darker sides I suppose, but this—this is ludicrous.*'

He turned again and facing upstream noticed a large broken, decaying trunk of a willow tree some twenty yards away, and needing to mark the spot where he exited the river he went over to where the log lay partially buried in the grey grass and picked it up as though it was nothing. He returned to the location he needed to mark and placed the log upright so that he would be able to see it clearly from a distance. Then, without taking thought, he bent down to wash away some mud from his hands in the oily water, a slight dirtiness, nothing more, that the tree had left behind. Taking his hands from the water he noticed the droplets as they fell from his fingertips to be pure and clean, sparkling like unto diamonds in the greyness of the grassy bank. Instantly he examined his hands and arms. They appeared tanned and strong as they always did; not at all in black, grey and white as he would have assumed but in vivid colour and glowing with a luminosity of phosphorescent richness. He glanced down to his feet and legs; these also were shining with the same incandescent brightness.

Words from the immortal psalmist's pen filled his mind, *'For Thou Art With Me --- Thy Rod And Staff They Comfort Me --- Art With Me --- Art With Me --- They Comfort Me.'* The coldness he had felt immediately on leaving the water now was gone and in its place was a warmth he could never again lose. Gone too was the foul, acrid smell of rotting fish that he had found so nauseous and in it's place was air so pure and clean that his nostrils dilated and quivered with it's freshness as he filled his lungs over and over enthralling his body with rejuvenated newness. He was now charged with inner warmth; a comforting inner warmth that seemed to radiate throughout the whole of his body to the depths of his very soul. He wasn't afraid, why should he be? He would never be afraid of anything evil again. There was nothing the world could throw at him or lay before him that would make him ever fearful. He paced back and forth for a while, smiling a smile of confidence knowing that it was not of his own making but Another's and hoping that this confidence and warmth would stay with him always even for the rest of his days.

His dreamy, questioning reflections and the weighing up of the present situation in which he now found himself was abruptly interrupted by the disturbing, rasping, gravelled noise of someone chanting a slow recitative incantation, followed by a hideous and most disturbing high pitched chuckle. Then suddenly, from out of the bleak grey sky, as if from nowhere, the large black form of a crow like bird dived deliberately at the young Adonis but the evasive action he employed caused the assailant to miscarry its objective at first and so it soared once again into the sour air flapping its wings vigorously as it quickly ascended to attempt a second offensive. This time, Jonathon was prepared for the assault and dealt the wretched bird a hefty blow with his clenched fist as a black feathery down floated haphazardly to the ground. The crow like bird, not feeling at all persuaded that yet another debacle would be in its best interest, decided against trying the third swoop and flew off in the direction of the sound of the chanting babble instead.

"God made Satan; Satan made sin so God dug a deep hole to put the devil in." The olden age childish rhyme was repeated ever continuously in an incantatory but discordant manner over and over again, interspersed only with the airy high pitched cackling sound of a hideously distorted laugh.

Slowly and cautiously Jonathon approached the huge arrangement of bramble bushes in the distance with their thorns as big as the leaves they bore and behind which he could clearly see a narrow pillar of white smoke rising in the noxious air until it mixed with the darkened mysterious mists above.

An old bedraggled crone was seated on a large rotting log behind the malformed bushes continuously reciting the countless canticle repartitions in the same obnoxious drone; her white gnarled hands hopelessly reaching out for the warmth of the flameless fire with its billowing smoke spiralling intensely. The huge, raving raven with its shaggy beard was now perched agitatedly upon her repulsively bent, bowed back attempting to straighten out the broken feathers that Jonathon's heavy blow had ruffled and its hollow pruk-pruk squawking voice proclaimed a painful uneasiness with its dilemma and added a certain drama to the already dismal scene.

The old haggish woman wore a shabby black shawl about her head that fell down over her misshapen shoulders and finally merged with the long black tattered dress which encased the rest of her bony body. The only parts of her anatomy to be discernable were her scrawny filthy face with its extremely wrinkled and pockmarked appearance; and that only in part, it being mostly shadowed by her black shabby shawl, and of her equally scrawny hands with their long tapering fingers, ending with unevenly curved, soil encrusted fingernails of some considerable length. Her large hooked nose could easily be discerned however, protruding as it did, beneath her darkened eye sockets with its warty appendages almost totally covering its facade and a slimy wetness hanging from its pointed tip.

The ugly, old, woebegone woman ceased her incessant chanting immediately upon Jonathon's arrival and looked up to seemingly recognise the big man, for she displayed no outwardly indicative surprise at his presence. But instead she radiated a wide cavernous smile displaying but one single tooth in her otherwise toothless mouth.

"Well if it ain' Saint Jonathon Fisher 'is self," she uttered sarcastically, "what you be doin' 'ere exactly? Not gone an' murdered yerself 'ave yer?" she chuckled at the thought before quickly adding- "Nah course not—you wouldn't do a blame stupid thing like that, now would yer! Not the 'igh an' mighty Jonathon Fisher, far too la-di-da I'm sure o' that!"

"Madam, you seem to have me at a disadvantage, to whom do I have the pleasure of addressing?" asked Jonathon, in an overly polite manner.

"To whom do I have the pleasure of addressing?" she repeated the question, almost singing it in her own fashion, word for word. "Core, posh t'day aint we Jonathon Fisher?" cackled the old crone. "Well if yer mus' know, the 'andle's Betsy; Betsy Yarrall. Tha's with two rs an' two ls." The old crone maintained her wide grin as she spoke but didn't move her head in any direction whatsoever.

"May I ask what you are doing here?" asked Jonathon, maintaining his proper politeness and courteous manner.

"What am I doin' 'ere I 'ear you ask? Well where else would I be yer great pumpkin 'ead? I'm a witch ain't I? An' a black'un at that, so where else would I be but in this God forsaken 'ole!" she retorted vehemently. And taking up a forked stick she poked around in the ashes of the fire for awhile, although not a single flame was produced by her action, which didn't seem to bother the old crone in the slightest. Soon she replaced the stick where she had picked it up, while the raven shuffled itself about on her deformed back to find a more comfortable deportment. She turned her ugly head to look at Jonathon.

"Now you give ol' Betsy a nice little kiss just like a good Christian man ought too an' then we shall talk some more," she said, lifting one of her oversized eyebrows and with a grin that stretched her sunken face.

Jonathon inwardly cringed at the idea but bent down to touch the repulsive mouth being offered to him but his aura prevented the big man from making contact which the old hag failed to notice.

"There tha's more like it," she responded, "thank you kindly my dear. Now we can talk together as ol' friends talk, can't we! Now where were we, are yes, what am I a doin' of in these parts you ask?"

The old woman cackled awhile dryly and wriggled herself about restlessly to a more comfortable position as the bird had done before.

"Yes me dear, me ol' lady, she was a witch, an' 'ers afore 'er, so you sees I come from a long line of witches that I does, datin' right back t' the dark ages I shouldn't wonder," she added proudly.

"How did you know my name Betsy? I hope you don't mind mine asking but I am rather curious," questioned the big man, with an intrigued look upon his countenance.

"Oh I know everythin' an' everyone in these parts that I do. Make it me business t' know, I do. I go over t' your side sometimes; aint that a surprise?" Here she paused for yet another chuckle. "I seen yer many a time an' talked t'you too, that I 'ave. But you wouldn't 'ave known ol' Betsy, oh dear me no; takes on disguises yer see, oh yes,"

Just then a huge black cat appeared on the scene and leapt onto the old witches lap, its mouth closed tightly upon five rodent tails left hanging, all wriggling and squirming in desperation to free themselves from their unhappy trap.

The hag let out a croaking laugh at the newcomer saying:

"Dolly, my dear little Dolly, what yer got there fer yer mummy eh? A nice little present is it? There's a good boy t'think o' yer mummy like that; what a dear little Dolly you are you are, what a cleaver Dolly you are." She aped the timeless stanza of the owl and the pussycat rhyme and commenced to stroke the cat behind its mangy ears. The cat raised its head, opened its mouth slightly and gulped. Swallowing hard and fast, three of the mice escaped their fate while the remaining two ended up in the cat's stomach.

"There's a clever boy," announced the old hag as she attempted to swipe the escaping rodents without success. Look you here Dolly," she continued, "this nice gentl'man is Mr Fisher, an' 'e's come t' pay 'is respec's, now ain't 'e a nice kind Mr Fisher t'do that?"

Although she was looking into the cats eyes as she spoke, the intention of her sentiment was clearly for the ears of the big man as she continued with a sternness of voice that pierced the air like unto a poisoned arrow flying to the heart of its prey.

"Is that right Jonathon Fisher?" she yelled. "Is that what you come 'ere for? T'pay yer respec's t'me?"

Jonathon instantly was taken aback by the verbal thrust but maintaining a composed demeanour, decided to humour the witch.

"Err, yes, yes of course Betsy," he said meekly.

"LIAR," she screamed with harsh intensity. "LIAR," she repeated angrily. "Yer never knew I existed, so 'ow could yer 'ave done. No, you come t' find that good fer nothin' seedless pumpkin Watts didn't yer? DIDN'T YER?" she repeated piercingly.

As before mentioned, Jonathon was unafraid even though the dauntless voice of the crone would have unnerved even the most resolute of men.

"Yes I confess it Betsy, you are perfectly correct, that is my paramount objective. Are you telling me you know where he is to be found?" he asked, determined to force his way to Mr Watts if he had to. "It has recently become imperative for me to find him as you probably already know; you, appearing to know all else about me. He was cruelly murdered you see and it was I who found his body in the depths of the Dead River a while ago. And now I seem to be in the deepness of despair with speculation and am finding that the whole episode has taken over my mind to a much greater extent."

"Ahh 'as it now? Dear me, poor Jonathon, what *are* you goin' to do?" A long pause followed as if the crone intended to torment the big man. "--- 'Course I knows where 'e is yer great idiot—Betsy knows; ol' Betsy, she knows everything, didn't she tell yer so, not two minutes ago? But it ain't no use yer speakin' to 'im, oh dear me no, 'e don't answer no questioning's, I knows I tried, that I did. Yer see, 'e don't speak no sense, no sense at all 'e don't, 'cause 'e's all remorseful—tha's what 'e is—remorseful; the great seedless pumpkin. Aah ha-ha-ha, bit late fer that now I reckon—no use 'im bein' sorry now," laughed Betsy, lapsing into a state of delirious derangement for a short period which soon was gone.

Jonathon, absorbed in his own ruminations, all but totally ignored the witch's spell of lively amusement and considered the scene where he was certain the Dead River was located. He looked back at the witch Betsy hoping for an answer to a question he deemed would be appropriate if he used the right tactic.

"Betsy," he said interrupting the old crone's mirth, "what makes you so sure that he is remorseful when you haven't even been able to converse with the man. Surely one has to make conversation in order to establish a fact of this nature." He wasn't at all happy with the way he had posed his concern; he was soon to learn he clearly hadn't.

"So yer think me daft do yer Jonathon Fisher?" she asked, her mood instantly reverted back to one of piqued displeasure and annoyance. Well I may not 'ave 'ad all the fancy worldly edification and schoolin' like what you 'ave but I'M NOT DAFT," she said, raising her voice again.

"No of course not, I didn't mean to imply that for one moment Betsy," said Jonathon, exasperated, "but you have to realise how anxious I am about Mr Watts and how important it is for me to find him."

"Well there is no need for yer t'worry, 'es alright jus' sittin' there talkin' to his self; yeah 'es alright, as right as nine pence as they say," she said, calming herself once more.

"But sitting where Betsy," said Jonathon, shifting about with impatience and now all but pleading with the witch. "Would you kindly tell me where it is that he is sitting so that I might go to him?" he added.

"I'd a thought you might 'ave guessed that one Jonathon Fisher. Why, 'es a sittin' down by the bridge where 'e copped 'is lot. Keep on a sayin' as 'ow it was 'is own stupid fault 'e was done in that night. Keep sayin' as how if 'e 'adn't a bin so boozed up it would never 'ave 'appened. Keep sayin' as 'ow 'e 'ad bin a wrong'un all 'is life, as 'ow 'e should've bin better to 'is poor ol' mother an' to 'is lovely children—bit late now t' think on such thin's don't yer think?" said Betsy, resisting the temptations of merriment. Then continued as before-

"Anyhow, I seen it all 'appen yer know, oh yeah, I seen it 'appen all right. 'E staggers down the lane half ridin' half pushin' 'is push bike like what 'e do most nights, only this time 'e was followed by the ginger Irish bloke. He says the pumpkin would feel better if 'e 'ad a bath in the river, the Irish bloke did. So the seedless pumpkin, 'e go an' slung 'is bike on the ground 'an 'e do jus' that—lay 'iself down in the river jus' like a babby 'e did, he-he-he-he," the old crone squawked, fidgeted and gesticulated with her hands in a frenzy as she allowed the excitement to almost control her reason until she continued -

"Then the Irish bloke, 'e 'eld 'im down till the bubbles stopped, aah ha-ha-ha-ha-! Didn't take a couple o' minutes that didn't, then when it was all over, 'e goes an' pushes 'im out into the middle of the river an' 'e waited awhile till 'e sank. Then you come along, yer great pumpkin jus' like a knight in shinin' armour yer did, so the Irish bloke 'e took off up the lane afore yer could see 'im. Well now, after you done yer heroic bit—an' failed—an' you went up the lane t'fetch that nice copper Sergeant Pedley, I crossed over the bridge an' rolled the pumpkin back into the river agin, ohh aah ha-ha-ha-ha-!" The old hag laughed until tears filled her ugly eyes and rolled down her cratered sunken face. When at last she had gained some semblance of control she carried on as before.

"Then jus' t'muddle thin's up a bit I went an' wrote me letters in the mud, he-he- he-he" she tittered, uncontrollably.

— CHAPTER EIGHT —

Jonathon Fisher was stunned. He just stood there quietly for a moment in complete and utter shock immersed in his own veritable meditations and standing next to the old, still seated, crone, who had at last declared the final piece of the puzzle which had played so fiercely upon the young man's mind. His entire faculty of reasoning and power of body had now suddenly escaped their fetters and were now once again joined together to form the man.

Again he searched for the distant, haze hidden horizon of this hideous place seeking the region where his tormentor had dwelt for the past twelve months or so, ever hopeful that his soul might at last find the restful peace it sought and the forgiveness it needed for others and, most of all, for himself. His active mind dwelt for quite awhile upon these grave reservations before it returned abruptly to the here and now.

Betsy Yarrall, who was still intent upon the ebulliently comical aspect of her saga, sat tittering away with her forked stick in hand. She poked ardently at the white, smoke-filled fire with no effect whatsoever at about the same time that Jonathon abandoned his meditations.

"Betsy," he said, with a cheerfulness that had eluded him of late, "I would like to thank you for your confessional part in this whole exceptional chronicle. And, for the explanation of what took place here, all those months ago; you have certainly put my mind at rest on a number of issues which were plaguing me and I appreciate your enlightening me. The thing is what to do next? I haven't quite fulfilled my mission in meeting up with Mr Watts as you know, and, to a greater extent, the matter doesn't really rest here, now does it? So the pertinent question remains: where do I go from here and what do I do next?"

The old witch looked most puzzled as she continued her exercises with the forked stick.

"Do next?" she said, as a look of bewilderment crossed her distorted countenance. "Nothin' *to* do. 'E'll be back 'ere ag'in soon, if I'm not very much mistaken," she added, as she raised her shabby head to focus her eyes on Jonathon, then noticing his perplexity added with impunity, "The ginger Irish bloke, stupid! You wait an' see, 'ell be back. Strung 'iself up in 'is cell last night, couldn't live with all the guilt, or so 'e say, so 'ell be back 'ere, jus' like you, to find that pumpkin. 'E wants t'make 'is peace with 'im, tha's what 'e wants," said the old crone, with a ghoulish smirk upon her sunken, pocked face.

Jonathon didn't wish to make reply or enquire further upon the subject, he automatically assumed the hag knew what she was talking about and so he waited with patience, his eyes searching the mist swirling distance for a sign of what was to come.

He didn't have long to wait however, soon a sorely broken, ruined figure of a man approached. His back, not unlike that of the witches, was bent down and his head was bowed in sorrow. He came suddenly out of the twisting murky mist, presenting himself in a livery belonging that of a prisoner, a convict of yesteryear, a grey apparel which seem to match the greyness of the aspect here and was at home in this goddamned awful place. His step was slow and faltering, and his hands were steeped in the shallow pockets of his baggy slacks and his head was bare and cold and wet as the endless mist encased him in its mournfulness. It was the other B.Y.

He didn't cease his faltering step as he passed by. And he failed to look in Jonathon's direction, for, had he done so he would, no doubt, have recognised the man who captured him and brought about his painful downfall and exposed the man for what he was. But he didn't stop, he didn't look; with head held low he simply trudged relentlessly on.

"So yer made it then yer stupid, great Irish pumpkin! Yer made it then!" It was Betsy Yarrall who screeched out after the sunken man. She knew who it was alright, Betsy Yarrall knew everything.

"Couldn't take yer bird couldn't yer?" she shouted again, in a mockingly derisive tone as though she enjoyed seeing a broken man sink further into the mire.

"Nasty to yer was they, the other jailbirds? Couldn't sleep at nights neither I 'spect! An' that 'orrible grub, it got yer down did it? Still, what d'yer expect yer great lummox." She said the final few words in a lower tone.

The old witch wouldn't, or couldn't, let up with her barrage of abuse and so she continued to exploit her vulgar offensiveness to the maximum, heaping insult upon insult, hurt upon hurt and humiliation upon humiliation. Either the bent man couldn't hear or wasn't in the mind to hear for he trudged warily on unheeding the coarseness of the verbal onslaught.

"So yer want t'see 'im do yer, yer great pumpkin? Want t'make yer peace with 'im, do yer? Want t'kiss an' make up I 'spect! Well 'es down by the river, nex' t'the bridge where y'left 'im—no need t'hurry, 'e ain't goin' nowhere," she screamed out, as he put a distance between them and ending her barrage of insults she finished her discourse with a bout of raucous laughter.

It had taken quite a while for the Irishman to pass the gauntlet of intimidation in order to reach his goal, but he did it employing no inappropriate retaliation on his part and was gradually swallowed up by the cold, foggy mistiness.

Jonathon followed the downcast wretched man through the dank grey haze, as the old crone returned to poking the flameless fire. Twice he thought he had lost him and twice he was able to regain pursuit, and not wanting to lose sight of him altogether the big man increased his step now keeping a discreet distance but close enough not to be intrusive; the big man being intent only on witnessing events from a respectable distance without personal intervention.

Jonathon saw Mr Watts at last, sitting on the side of the grassy embankment where Betsy had inscribed her initials and where he had placed the drowned man after pulling him out of the river. He looked dejected, with his head held firmly in his hands. Jonathon watched the Irishman go to the pitiful figure hunched up in complete despair. He saw Watts look up and the two men talking for a short while. He saw Watts jump to his feet. He saw the two men embrace one another like two long lost brothers. He saw the two men completely surrounded in a most beautiful aura. He saw them both walk up the stony lane together, their arms entwined. With a swelling in his throat and tears welling in his eyes, Jonathon Fisher stood and gazed for a spell, while a pertinent line from a Fanny Crosby hymn flooded his mind; '--- *the vilest offender who truly believes that moment from Jesus a pardon receives.*'

Jonathon was happy, he had achieved all he'd set out to do and his faith had been stretched to a size that would never be diminished. Slowly he turned himself about and made his way back to where the old crone Betsy Yarrall lounged.

The air was ever damp and the mistiness, being heavier in places, and the impossibility to discern a visage beyond ten yards with any degree of certainty was plainly evident, and so the young Adonis walked slowly, entranced by that which he had seen and ever thankful that all was now well.

Jonathon was almost on top of the fire before he noticed the light grey column of smoke, straight and unmoving from its perpendicular drift into the disturbed and seething air. He knew he would find the witch still sitting in its smokiness, reciting the boring and meaningless words to pass the time away, (if indeed such a thing as time is a reality in this awful place), or with the forked stick as when he left her, poking away without incentive.

She didn't stir herself when Jonathon approached, or look into his face as she, in her bitterness, listened for the words she'd already anticipated.

"Well, seen everythin' 'ave yer? Seen 'em kiss an' make up 'ave yer? Well there's nothin' left t'keep yer 'ere Jonathon Fisher so yer best be on yer way t'see mummy he-he-he-he. Lovely girl that Felicity not another one t'match 'er, I should know, I seen em all. Pity yer didn't bring 'er along with yer, I could certainly teach 'er a thin' or two–he-he-he-he-," only a suppressed laugh escaped the old crone's mouth as her mind dwelt briefly upon the young mans mother.

Jonathon ignored the old woman's remarks knowing full well they were designed to antagonise him and he wasn't in the mood for rising to any witches taunts. But Betsy was right, he did need to go and rid himself of this place of desolation to wander again the landscape he loved and missed.

"Yes you are quite right Betsy; it is time I took my leave of you. I have accomplished all I set out to do with complete satisfaction," he said, as he slowly walked away. Then he stopped awhile and turned to the old crone but rejected the idea of going back.

"But what about you Betsy? Come with me! It's never too late to make reparations you know. Never to late to see the light," said Jonathon with a meaningful smile on his face.

Betsy laughed again as she made her reply but this time it was tainted with a certain amount of impenitency although uncertainty seemed to linger on her lipless mouth.

"Me? I be alright—the master, 'e said 'e would save me that 'e did, no need t'worry 'bout ol' Betsy—she'll be alright—tha's fer sure," said Betsy, with difficulty as she struggled with her words.

Jonathon wasn't at all happy with the way the witch had made the specious reply knowing that she was relying upon implausibility.

"Save you Betsy? Why, that one won't even be able to save himself so how do you suppose he'll be able to save you? Better to take my advise and come over with me," returned Jonathon, anxiously and with purpose.

"Don't need t'worry 'bout ol' Betsy," she repeated, still not stirring or wanting to see her guest from off her domain. Then after a moments hesitation she stood and looked in the direction of the river close to where Jonathon stood and shouted so her voice might carry and be clearly heard at the distance -

"Why don't yer come an' see ol' Betsy ag'in some time? You know there's always a welcome 'ere for yer, Mr Fisher."

Jonathon smiled inwardly to himself although he was fully aware of the hopeless plight of the old crone so that his feelings were plainly disturbed.

"No Betsy," he said loudly, "I shall never be coming back." his voice was free yet sorrowful as he said the words. "Now don't forget what I said, it's never too late," he added, and left.

As he took the last few, slow steps toward the river, the final voice of the old crone reverberated through the mist-

"Never say never Mr Fisher, you hear me? Never say never --- jus' say yer don't know."

Jonathon found his marker tree trunk still standing on the riverbank where he had left it and holding his breath he dived into the oily water then resurfaced to a bright and sunny morn.

Once again, as it had when he entered the river not long before, an inexplicable tiredness overcame the young Adonis as he sat down to dry and dress himself and to which he succumbed most willingly. The hypnotic trance lasted but for a short moment, no more than the blinking of an eye it seemed but which was both restful and reinvigorating. When he eventually came too, he found himself to be already dry and was clothed in his shoe type sandals and top. He ran his fingers through his blond, wavy hair; it was as dry as if he had never entered the water in the first place. He examined his hands, arms, feet and legs closely; everything was back to normal except for the feeling of inner warmth.

He raced across the meadow, disturbing the lazy cattle in his wake, and leapt the fence. He crossed the road in a stride and entered the wrought iron gateway to The Mansion; so very thankful to be home once again.

His beautiful mother was in the garden and about to enter the kitchen doorway when she turned round smiling sweetly to acknowledge her son's greeting.

"Hello darling, you are looking good --- did you have a refreshing swim? Jonathon, you will never believe what I heard on the news just a moment ago. That ---" Her sweet voice was promptly interrupted by that of her son's.

"--- That Bernard Yates hanged himself in his cell last night? I already know mother," said the big man, his countenance still full of the joys.

"But Jonathon," replied Felicity, her face aghast at Jonathon's declaration as she looked at her son completely mystified. "How could you possibly have known that? The news has only just been released, well only a few moments ago anyway."

The big man took hold of his mother and clasping her tenderly in his strong arms he lifting her off the ground to give her a most loving embrace. Then placing her firmly onto the ground once more he said:

"It's alright mother, don't worry, I haven't flipped my lid or anything like it, but you can tell grandmama to cancel all thoughts of any psychiatric arrangements she may have in mind for me, I no longer need them.

"Come on, let's go into breakfast, I'm starving and besides I have something to tell you both regarding a matter of great importance."

ISBN 1425157722-6
9 781425 157722